The Strawberry Garden

By

Michael William Molden

Published by

Cauliay Publishing & Distribution
PO Box 12076
Aberdeen
AB16 9AL
www.cauliaybooks.com

First Edition
ISBN 978-0-9564624-2-8
Copyright © Michael William Molden 2010
Cover design by Jason McKnight © Cauliay Publishing
Cover Photograph by David Young

A CIP catalogue record for this book is available from the British Library.

For
My beautiful wife
Elaine
And our son
Findlay

Chapter One

It was a warm, dry summer's day when the man in the upstairs study looked out through the French windows and ran his eyes thoughtfully over the beautifully manicured velvet lawn below. He was the owner of the scene before him but he wasn't the artist who had laboured so lovingly to produce it. Part of him wished that it had been his creation, but it was the same part of him that wished he had been the creator of everything that was good and beautiful in his life. Indirectly of course he was, but only in the sense that it was his money that allowed for such surroundings. He let his eyes drift naturally to the neatly shaped flowerbeds and beyond to the woods that separated his kingdom from the outside world. He was indeed a lucky man to have been blessed with such good fortune, a secluded mansion house set in acres of rolling countryside, sleek, fast cars, a yacht moored in the marina, all the trappings of success, but at that moment he couldn't help but envy the life of the man whose duty it was to keep the garden pristine. *He doesn't suffer the frustration of my kind of creation, the false starts, the agony of the writer's curse, the utter disillusion of the story going nowhere fast. He plants the seed and the bulb and waits for the sun to bake, then, break the earth with all its springtime colour and raging glory.*

A wood pigeon broke from its afternoon roost and with it went the brooding thoughts of Richard Deacon. He watched as it fluttered down to the lawn and began to peck mechanically for insects in amongst the grass. He turned to the half written page on the computer screen before him then looked at his wristwatch. He deleted everything he had written that day and shut down the computer. His mind wasn't on the job. He didn't know exactly where his mind was—but he knew he wasn't going to focus anymore on writing one more word. Neither the garden nor the pigeon nor his envy was going to give him the slightest spark of inspiration and at times like that, he knew, it was best to take a step back.

He walked away from the rosewood desk and lifted the receiver of the internal telephone. "Yes Mr Richard?" answered the sweet, charmingly accented voice of the young Spanish housemaid.

"Coffee,"

"Shall I serve it in your study Sir?"

"No, I'll take it in the games room, Maria."

He put the receiver down and made his way through the marble entrance hall of the house and into the games room. He wasn't really in the mood for games but he thought it would ease the tension in him to knock a few snooker balls around the table. Maria brought in the coffee and laid it on the coffee table by the fireplace at the far end of the room. "Will that be all Mr Richard Sir?" Maria asked.

"Could you bring my diary through from the morning room Maria? Then that will be all for today."

Maria returned moments later with the dark green, leather-bound dairy and put it down by the tray of coffee on the table. "I will see you tomorrow Sir. Is there anything you need me to bring in with me in the morning?"

"Yes, I'd like you to bring me about a handful of inspiration. Do you think you could manage that?"

"Sir?"

"I'm just kidding Maria. I'll see you in the morning."

Maria went to the door and hesitated. "Is there something else Maria?" Deacon asked.

"I was just wondering when Mrs Deacon will return from London Mr Richard, so that I can prepare her room?"

"Ah—a very good question my dear, and one which I do not have the answer to just now. But you can rest assured that when Mrs Deacon confides in me, I shall duly pass that information on to you."

"Thank you Mr Richard. Good Night Sir."

"Goodnight Maria."

With that Maria left and Deacon carried on blasting the cue ball against any ball that he thought he could easily pot. The snooker therapy worked for no more than a few minutes, he was having as much luck with his potting as he was with his search for inspiration. He laid the cue along the side cushion and took the cue ball in his hand. *If you were a crystal ball, what would I ask? How does my story end? What happens to the bad guy? Would I be happy pruning roses instead of living in this constant vortex where my whole future depends on the next word that appears on the page before me?* He sighed deeply and rolled the cue ball slowly up the full length of the table. *Coffee. Why on earth did I ask for coffee? How common, who ever heard of coffee in the afternoon? Coffee in the afternoon, wishing I was the gardener, my God, I'm becoming uncivilised, I'm one step away from becoming a savage! If I pour this coffee now then all is lost!* No—it was no use. He couldn't even find inspiration in farcical drama. He poured a coffee and picked up his diary to check his appointments for the rest of the week.

Richard Deacon had a strict routine—and like most writers his strict routine was flexible when it suited him. His routine was to rise early, eat a light breakfast; then lock himself away in his study to write until one in the afternoon. His orders for the day very rarely changed. No phone calls, no appointments, absolutely no visitors—especially family, and no noise. If he wanted anything he would call for it using the internal phone. And if the staff ever suspected that something terrible had happened to him on the far side of that locked oak door. They were to wait until the unmistakable stench of a rotting corpse emitted from the room and permeated the whole house before they were allowed to even knock on the door.

His afternoons were usually kept free to conduct his writing-related business. Interviews, book-signings, meetings with his agent, meetings with his publisher, and the meetings he detested most of all, meetings with Daniels his financial advisor. Deacon was a very rich man. Besides being a successful writer he had also inherited his father's shrewd business brain and he had invested his royalty income wisely. Strangely though for such a wealthy man, he had no desire for money for money's sake. He saw money as an unavoidable aspect of the life he had chosen. His writing paid him well—very well. And as any wealthy man will tell you, not being interested in money does not mean that it goes away if you ignore it. You buy what you want with it and any residue has to be managed. So rather than relinquish financial control of his residue wealth to some city whiz-kid, Deacon had decided very early in his career that he would use his investment opportunities as a form of recreation. And he was exceptionally good at playing money games.

He ran his eye down the list of the week's engagements and stopped at the double asterisk. Friday. Lunch with Sebastian. *How delightful; Lunch with my only son and heir. I wonder as to the theme of that encounter? What unforeseen rocks has his unstable clipper run aground upon now?* Deacon was checking his diary to see which commitments he could shelve, or better still, get out of completely. He had to put more time in on his latest novel to meet the deadline and he was beginning to feel the warm breath of his publisher on his neck. *Sorry Sebastian, you'll have to go. I'll send you a cheque to put you back in the fast lane for a while.* Deacon took out the gold pen from the spine of his diary and scored out his son's name. Cancelling that lunch date would give him a few more precious hours and hopefully a good run up to a productive weekend. *Sebastian would understand.*

Deacon went through into the drawing room and opened his writing desk. He wrote a cheque for two thousand pounds to Sebastian and scribbled a half-hearted apology. He slipped the cheque and the note into an envelope and tossed it into his *out* tray for Maria to post in the morning.

With the most important part of his coming week safely re-arranged, and finding himself at a loose end, he did what he usually did when his personal creative muse was AWOL. He marched stealthily over to the drinks cabinet and poured himself a large whisky. As the amber aesthetic splashed into the Japanese crystal Glass—a gift from his agent when his debut novel sold half a million copies—he smiled inwardly. *How easily we fickle humans change allegiance from one spirit to another in times of stress.* Thinking of stress, he had another thought. Before he got himself completely inebriated he thought it would be a good idea to call his better half in London. He picked up the phone and dialled his wife's office. The answer phone said that she was out. He dialled her mobile number only to be told that she was not available, but would he like to leave a message. He took a sip from his glass and spoke to the machine: "Sorry to disturb you darling, I just rang your office and I was told by your other machine that you were out. From that information I gather that you are either, shopping in Bond Street, dining in Basil Street or having another consultation in Harley Street. Maria was asking recently when we could expect your ladyship home in order for her to prepare your boudoir. Would you indulge me with a return call when things become apparent so that I can inform the girl? And where is my black tie? I have to show my face at a funeral on Wednesday. So if you could call before then, it would be greatly appreciated."

He put the ornate mother-of-pearl inlaid antique receiver back in its cradle and walked over to his quadraphonic HI-FI sound system. He ran his finger along the rows of neatly stacked Cd's and he selected The Great Mass in C Minor by Wolfgang Amadeus Mozart. Savouring the sombre awakenings of Kyrie and the subtle peaty caramel of his twenty one year old single malt, he settled into a white leather Italian armchair and closed his eyes. By Benedictus he was halfway down the Japanese decanter and halfway to oblivion. His last semi-conscious thought of the day was to raise an index finger to the world that had laid Mozart down into a pauper's grave. *Here's to a man who shares his terrestrial headstone with Jesus Christ.*

Chapter Two

Deacon woke early the following morning to the sweet sound of birdsong. Although his room was still darkened by the heavy drapes he could tell from the optimistic, high-pitched tones of song thrush and blackbird that it would be another fine day. He walked from the bed to the drapes and opened them just wide enough to step into the floor-space of the bay window beyond them. The early morning sun was already burning off the dewfall from the lawn and thin wisps of steam rose skyward like a Mohawk offering to the God of the new day. The warmth of the sun on the bare floor-boards beneath his feet began to rise through his ankles and into his lower calf muscles. Something told him that it was going to be a good day for writing.

It would be another two hours before Maria arrived for work and that would give Deacon what he needed most—sober solitude.

He dressed quickly and stepped out into the garden in front of the house. A cool breeze blew gently into his face and ruffled his unkempt, thinning, blond hair. "Nature," he whispered as he breathed in deeply and filled his lungs. "She is exactly what I need. Here, nestling somewhere in her abundance is where I'll find my elusive final chapter."

Deacon's latest novel had been like a troublesome pregnancy. He had had to nurse it with the exquisite touch of a master puppeteer and the urgency of a bomb-disposal expert right from its conception, all through every heart-stopping pause in the blip on the foetal monitor. And now, he was a hair's-breadth away from triumph or disaster. From the very beginning he had known that his latest novel, above all others, was going to be the best... or the worst he had ever written. The final chapter would be the pivotal factor. That would be the snipping of the life or death wire at the centre of the bomb. That would be the decisive moment when the doctor orders the caesarean section.

He walked slowly over the lawn towards the clump of rhododendron bushes that lined the last length of driveway approaching the house. He took note of every deliberate step, like a highland crofter jealously measuring out his share of acreage. His eyes scanned the view before him as he searched the face of nature for a clue to her hidden treasure. The mixture of scent from the various plants teased his memory as they battled for supremacy in the air. Brightly coloured Roses, Pansies, African Marigolds and a choir of other siren singers let loose their voices of survival. Somewhere amongst those silent, irresistible lures was his own destiny, his own survival. Well, his literary survival anyway, because without that, he might as well just dry up and wither away. Writing was all he knew, all that he was capable of being a true master of, and every determined step he took was a reminder of the lonely, but potentially glorious path that every true master must walk no matter what their calling.

He reached the rhododendron bushes and stepped onto the gravel driveway crunching the loose gravel beneath his heavy shoes. He looked down the driveway to the ornate wrought-iron gates that kept intruders out and hopefully had kept his runaway muse in. The woods on the far side of the driveway were fresh and cool, birds fluttered in the branches overhead and their calls seemed to interact with the rising hum of the awakening insect population. He walked deeper into the wood towards the small headstone on the animal grave that he had found two years after he had bought the house. At the grave he dropped to his haunches and brushed aside the overgrown weeds so that he could read the inscription once again. *Tina. A true friend and a lady to the end.* He let the weeds fall gently back into place before he stood up. *Can a dog really be a friend? Can a dumb animal really invoke such feelings of loss in a grown man? How can a human being love an animal more than another human being?* He shook his head slightly as he briefly pondered one of those questions that have baffled the greatest thinkers of the world since time began—the relationship between man and beast. Or, to be more precise, the relationship between some men and their beloved beasts. *Nature, she has all the answers, but she's not quite ready to give away all her secrets just yet.* Perhaps he would return to ponder that question when he had less pressing matters on his mind.

He walked on through the bracken leaving the grave undisturbed again to slumber on into eternity. He reached the old wooden fence that bordered the field which ran the full length of the mansion house and gardens. It was his field and he collected rent from it every year from the farmer who worked it. Soon the rich smell of the harvested barley would hang in the air and remind the birds that it was time to fly south for the winter and the hedgehog that it was time to make his bed for that long night ahead. *Mother Nature, you tell the animals so many things, you guide them with your gentle ways. So tell me, tell me how to end my story.* He listened for her response. He felt that if she could find a way, she would whisper the answer like a school friend would mouth the answer when the teacher's back was turned.

He was about to turn away and head back through the wood when he caught sight of a fine old shire horse prancing in the distance. It was black like a moonless night and its tail and mane where a thick creamy white. It looked mighty and proud as it tossed its main and stamped its great hairy boots like a fearless Zulu warrior dancing defiantly in full battle dress before Chelmsford's cold-hearted murderous cannons. Deacon could picture the horse's ancestors with their noble, armour clad riders charging in spectacular formation into the shuddering ranks of their unfortunate foe. He wondered if the horse before him could have somehow inherited its ancestor's memory and like the Zulu warrior was re-enacting the glories of former bloody encounters. As he watched every graceful stamp and followed the majestic ripple of its enormous thigh muscles he could feel the sharpness of his imagination returning like a long lost friend. The scenes were vivid and memorable, he could pause and rewind every frame and suddenly he knew... The path to his final chapter was opening up like a shimmering river that leads to the ocean. His study was calling him like the pull of the moon on the tide and he knew that if he closed the study door behind him, he would emerge with the manuscript of a lifetime.

11

This time the trees flew by in a blur of distortion as he ran towards the house, the muse had returned and she was stabbing his brain with great bolts of possibilities, any one would be just as good as the next, but time was of the essence. *Oh God, not yet! My kingdom for a pen!*

As he neared the driveway he could see Maria's car trundling up through the wrought iron gates. He slowed then stopped to wait for her to pull up alongside him. She wound down her window and looked at him with an expression of surprise and confusion on her face. "Are you all right Mr Richard?" she asked, "is anything wrong?"

Breathing heavily he leaned his arm on the driver's door. "I'm fine Maria," he smiled, "you have arrived like the cavalry, just in the nick time. I have to work all day today and you have to make sure that no one gets within a thousand yards of my study. I want no calls, no interruptions and I don't care who it is."

"What if it's your wife sir, and she insists on seeing you?" Maria asked.

"Even if the creator of the universe calls and says he wants to make me an equal partner and it's a one time only offer, I want you to tell him 'Not today.'"

"I guess it's serious," Maria said solemnly.

"It's everything," he said.

Deacon walked quickly round to the passenger door and got in. "Forward," he said dramatically as he pointed his outstretched arm in the direction of the house.

"Can I get you anything before you lock yourself in Mr Richard?" Maria asked as the car rolled to a halt outside the front door.

"Yes, this walk in the fresh air this morning has given me quite an appetite. Could you make me one of your famous *Fruit of the sea salads* before you start on your other duties? Oh, and a generous helping of raspberries. Leave it on my tray outside the door and knock once only."

He was in the house and heading for his study before she had time to turn off the ignition. "Fish food salad and a bowl of raspberries for breakfast Mr Richard, are you sure?" Maria shouted after him.

"Not fish food Maria, that salubrious concoction is brain food and brain food is what I need to supplement and sustain my new-found zest for life."

"Fine," Maria said under her breath as she turned away with a wry smile and a shrug of her shoulders, "And a very good morning to you Mr Richard."

Maria had been the Deacons' daily help for the past four years. She had come to England to work as an au pair seven years before when she was eighteen. She left her first employer when she was just turned twenty one and she had been with the Deacon's ever since. Besides her native Spanish she was also fluent in English and French. She had learned as a teenager at school that the key to success in languages is to master the natural native accent of the language. Her French teacher had told her that it was better to make a fool of herself in front of her giggling classmates than to make a fool of herself when trying to converse with a Frenchman speaking French in a Spanish accent. As a direct result of that teacher's wisdom, if a Frenchman heard her speak French he would say that she was Parisian, and if an Englishman heard her speak English, he would say that she was from any one of the Home Counties.

Over the years she had become accustomed to Deacon's brusque ways regarding certain issues and she put his abruptness down to his general eccentricity. She suspected that underneath his cold exterior there was a warm hearted, generous, thoughtful individual, but so far suspicion was all she had to go on, because she had seen no real evidence of it. She often wondered what he really thought of her. Deacon knew that she was far too intelligent and too experienced to be doing that kind of work, but he was too fond of having her around to ever contemplate sitting her down and seriously advising her to put her intelligence to better use. He also paid her well above the national average wage for a domestic help. In short, their working relationship was one of unwritten compromise—she liked working for him and he liked to have her around—so until she felt the need to put her intelligence to better use for the good of the common man, she would remain in her 'Extortionately well paid post' as Deacon liked to put it.

Maria prepared his breakfast and duly delivered it as per Deacon's meticulous instructions. She went about her duties for the rest of the day and Deacon's study door remained firmly closed to the outside world. At 5pm Maria finished what she was doing before she went to do her final task of the day which was to collect the breakfast tray. She listened outside the study door as she stood with the empty tray at her feet. She could hear the tell-tale tapping of the computer keyboard that told her that Deacon was still in full swing. As she bent to pick up the tray she noticed a scribbled note. It was brief and customarily to the point. *Coffee…one knock.*

Anyone else may have taken offence but Maria was used to his remarkable economy. She made his coffee, knocked once on his study door then headed home for the evening. She gathered up the out-going post on her way out and dropped it into the letter box at the end of the lane.

The following morning Maria arrived for work and set about her duties. It wasn't long before she realised that Deacon had been working in his study all night. There were no pots in the sink and his bed was still made. Outside his study door was the tray and on another hastily written note were her ultra succinct orders for the day, *Brain food!*

Maria gazed out of the kitchen window as she prepared his breakfast. The sun was streaming in through the kitchen and reflecting off the highly polished white wall tiles. The thought of Deacon crouched over his keyboard like a miser counting his gold on such a beautiful day made her want to dash into his study, rip open the drapes and fling open the windows to let the goodness in and the staleness out. She knew that when he did finally emerge from one of his marathon writing stints that he would smell like a goat and look like a shipwrecked sailor with a shabby growth of grey/black whiskers. When he was at his best Maria thought he was handsome and suave but when he was at his worst he looked like a ragged hobo.

She placed the tray outside the door and still the tapping of the keys echoed from beyond the door. She knocked once and turned to leave. Before she could take a step Deacon stopped writing and spoke quickly and quietly. The sentence needed no lengthy reply: "Maria, I am out of the country until late Monday."

"Yes Mr Richard."

Maria knew exactly what he meant. He meant that she was now on official guard duty until her shift finished on Monday evening. Messages were to be taken and callers—expected or not—were to be turned away. She was to put aside any weekend plans she may have had and remain in the house at all times. Despite the short notice, she didn't really mind. He would not have asked her if he didn't think her staying over was vital. It wasn't that often that he imposed on her time so categorically and she would be well compensated financially.

Back in the kitchen Maria rang the local grocer for all her groceries, the local fish monger for fresh supplies of Deacon's *Brain food* and the wine merchant for new stocks of whisky and a bottle of Champagne. She put in her orders to be delivered later that day and as usual the delivery vans were not to use the driveway. She would meet them at the end of the drive at 4.30pm. Maria had ordered the Champagne because she knew that Deacon would mark the end of his novel in his usual manner. With a cigar by El Rey Del Mundo and a bottle of the legendary cuvee by Louis Roederer *Cristal* created in 1876 especially for Tsar Alexander II.

At 4.25pm Maria set off in her car to intercept the delivery vans and ten minutes later she was back in the house with the weekend supplies neatly packed away. With any luck her weekend would be quiet and Deacon would emerge from his study on Monday stinking like a goat and high on Champagne and cigar smoke with his finished manuscript. With any luck...

Chapter Three

Saturday went by following virtually the same pattern as Friday. Maria popped up to Deacon's study door at regular intervals and responded to his notes whenever he had left any. The brain food seemed to have been working overtime because it had been a while since she had seen him work so furiously for so long. Towards the end of the day she sensed that his work would soon be complete and that she could get back to some semblance of normality. Yet, despite her intuition, he was still locked in is study—writing like a demon—when she eventually retired to her bed at fifteen minutes past midnight.

Maria was awake and up early for guard duty on Sunday morning. Her first job was to check the tray for orders...*nothing*. Now that was a very promising portent. She cooked herself some breakfast and cast her eye over the morning papers as she sat down to eat. No sooner had she put the first forkful in her mouth when the internal phone rang.

"Is my Champagne suitably chilled Maria?" Deacon asked in a surprisingly fresh and cheerful voice.

"Eight degrees Celsius for optimum epervescence Mr Richard, as always," Maria answered tongue-in-cheek.

"Ah, how refreshing it is to learn that someone in this house actually listens and what is more, clearly benefits from a little cultural guidance now and then. It is now nine thirty, I shall have it in my study at precisely seven minutes past ten."

With that he put the receiver down and leaned back triumphantly in his sleek leather chair. The manuscript on the screen before him was satisfactorily complete. He reached into his box of cigars and ran one of them under his nose as he inhaled to savour the rich elegance of its fragrance. He reached for his silver table lighter which had been cast in the shape of Aladdin's lamp and he put his cigar into the flame and puffed out his cheeks until the cigar was fully ignited. He could feel the pent up tension of the creative energy that had driven him for the past two days slowly beginning to ease. He associated the mental winding down process with the physical actions of an army striking a well established camp and moving deeper into new uncharted terrain. With every luxurious inhalation a tent was folded and thrown onto a waiting wagon for transportation to some future war zone, but for now, peace, glorious peace. The manuscript was finished and the muse was already on her way through the swirls of blue cigar clouds to ease the torment of some other lonesome soldier of creation.

It was ten minutes to ten so Maria had precisely seventeen minutes before his lordship's serving of Champagne. She took some washing from the machine and dropped it into a bright yellow washing basket. The day was warm and blustery so the clothes would get a good airing if she hung them out to dry in the morning sun. She would have just enough time—if she hurried—to peg the washing out and deliver the Champagne on time.

Ever since she had worked for Deacon she suspected that he had some weird, perhaps compulsive ideas about numbers, odd numbers to be exact. Everything had to be odd, even the digits in his telephone numbers and his bank accounts. They could have even numbers in them, but the sum total of all the numbers added together had to be odd or he would have to change them. You and I would be laughed out of the bank if we tried to get them to change our allocated bank account details, but I suppose certain concessions can be made when the customer is Richard Deacon and each account he held would be enough to write off the third world debt. Working for someone with eccentric tendencies can sometimes be difficult, but when the eccentric employer has an added fixation with numbers, the difficulties are magnified enormously.

Maria reached up to the washing line and began transferring the contents of the basket to the line. She was in the garden known as the *west* garden and the sun would shine there until around noon when it moved to the front of the house. She reached up with the very last item of clothing before she hoisted the empty basket onto her hip, as she turned back to the house she heard the unmistakable crunching sound of motorcar wheels on the gravel driveway. She dropped the basket and moved smartly and diagonally across the lawn towards the front of the house. Whoever it was would have to be intercepted and detained even though she knew that Deacon had finished his manuscript. The hour of solitude after completion was absolutely crucial to Deacon and Maria knew that only too well. She hoped to see the postman at the door as she moved to the front of the house. They would exchange polite greetings and he would be on his way. *It can't be the postman this is Sunday.* She began to worry. Her hopes were dashed completely and her heart dropped when she arrived just in time to see Sebastian fling open the door of his gleaming red sports car and emerge with a face like thunder.

"Where is he?" Sebastian demanded as he headed for Maria. She had quickly taken up her sentinel position at the front door.

"You're angry Sebastian," Maria said, "Why don't you take a moment to calm down?"

"Oh I'm not angry Maria," Sebastian said in a strained act of composure. "I am only going to kill him once!" he erupted with the emphasis on the word 'once'. "Now where is the slimy weasel?"

Maria put her hands out to contain him if he should get any closer. Thankfully he stopped short of bursting past her and he stood on the step just below her. "Sebastian please, please wait…just for one hour. By that time my job here will be done and I can go home and you can do whatever you want with him." She stole a furtive glance at her wristwatch and saw that it was dangerously close to five minutes past ten.

"I want to see him now, this minute so that so that I can give him the full benefit of a lifetime of pent-up rage compounded by utter frustration. Now step aside Maria this really isn't any of your business."

"I have explicit instructions not to let anyone near him until he says so in person. Just give me one hour and I will tell him you are here, please Sebastian, do this for me."

Sebastian softened and let his shoulders sag as he considered her request. He knew that she had her work cut out

18

working for his father and he also knew that she would feel his wrath long after he had left.

"I'll give you one hour," he said finally.

Maria let out a sigh of relief, her watch said six minutes past ten and she could feel the tension rising through her whole body. If that Champagne wasn't outside Deacon's door in one minute all would be lost.

"Come with me through to the kitchen Sebastian, I have one quick thing to attend to and then I will make you a coffee and we can talk for a while. You can tell me what you have been doing with yourself."

Sebastian followed Maria as she hurried through the entrance hall and into the kitchen. He looked up the grand staircase as he walked by it and the thought crossed his mind to seize the opportunity to take his father by surprise. He dismissed the thought and continued instead after Maria. *Perhaps it will be better if I calm down a few degrees first.*

He pulled out a wooden kitchen chair and sat at right angles to the table. His eyes followed Maria as she took out a silver tray and laid it on the table. The pent-up rage that moments earlier had been tempered by Maria's skilful reasoning suddenly erupted again as he watched her take the Champagne from the wine cooler and place it on the tray. He left Maria speechless as he jumped to his feet and bounded up the servants stairway at the rear of the kitchen leading to the upstairs landing. *If he thinks I'm going to sit and wait like Buddha whilst he sips Champagne he has got another think coming!*

Maria's mind was so set on delivering the Champagne on time that she didn't even consider the effect that seeing it would have on Sebastian. She charged after him but she was hopelessly lost in his slipstream. Sebastian reached his father's study and banged hard on the door. "Open this door now!" he demanded.

Deacon sat upright and looked at the clock in dismay; it was seven minutes past ten.

Damn it, this isn't supposed to happen, where is my Champagne?

Sebastian banged again. "I know you're in there and I know you have finished writing. I can smell that cigar all through the house. So get this door open!"

That boy is getting too damn smart, "What do you want?" Deacon shouted.

"Have it your way father. I am going to count to ten and then I am going to rip the door down."

"I'm not going to be terrorised by my own son in my own house, so do your worst," Deacon replied. He thought that his bluff would make Sebastian think again and try a more civilised approach. He listened as Sebastian began to count and he suddenly had visions of his son battering the beautiful oak door with the bottom of a fire extinguisher. The bluff clearly wasn't going to work.

"Alright, alright, I'll open the door but I warn you, this had better be good."

Deacon unlocked the door and quickly stepped back into the study leaving Sebastian to open the door for himself. A moment later father and son were facing each other in awkward silence like duellists on an eerie misty morning just a few feet apart. Deacon turned and walked back behind his desk as Sebastian glared at him coldly as if he were waiting for him to speak first. Maria appeared at the open door and began to apologise: "I'm sorry Mr Richard. I tried to tell him…" Deacon cut her short, "Leave us Maria."

Maria dropped her eyes to the floor and quietly closed the door behind her as she made her way dejectedly back to the kitchen. She felt as though she had failed in her duties even though Sebastian had every right to be in the house and even more right to have access to his father.

"Well?" Deacon said simply.

Sebastian looked at his father and only really saw him for the first time. His face was covered in three days of patchy facial hair growth and his weary red eyes were surrounded by dark bruise-like circles. Despite the strong smell of tobacco Sebastian could smell stale perspiration emanating from the direction of his father. He looked frail and gaunt, almost haunted. "Two minutes ago I wanted to punch your face to make you feel the pain that I feel. But now, looking at you, I don't think you deserve such a kindness. You haven't got a clue why I am here have you?"

"No. So why don't you enlighten me, then return to whichever woman's bed you left this morning before she realises that her income is missing?"

Sebastian reached into his pocket and took out Deacon's cheque for two thousand pounds. "This income?" he said as he began to tear it into little pieces. "I have my own practice now father and my very own income. When are you going to emerge from the fog you have been in for the last twenty years?"

"So to what do I owe the pleasure?" Deacon asked, "You didn't come here just to point out that you have finally worked out how to wipe your own backside."

Sebastian looked around the room until his eyes settled on what he knew would not be too far away—his father's diary. It was lying closed on a small table beneath a reading lamp on the left hand side of the study. He picked it up and opened it at the previous Friday's date then handed it to his father. "Does this ring any bells father?"

Deacon looked at the date and the scored out appointment with his son. "Yes, we had a lunch booked, but I had to cancel, so what?"

"Do you remember why and how we made that appointment in this very room?"

"No," Deacon said, "I don't."

"Does the double asterisk help in any way?"

"What about it?"

"Friday was my birthday father and we put those asterisks there as a bond between father and son over nine months ago. We even joked that it had to be a double asterisk, one for each of us so that you couldn't possibly forget. Is one lunch in the year with my father on my birthday really too much to ask?"

"I've been busy! You don't know what its like to have people breathing down your neck to meet deadlines. You haven't got a clue how it feels to be a month behind with a week left to deliver. How do you think I have kept you in the lap of luxury all your life? How do you think I sent you to boarding school and gave you the best education that money could buy? It wasn't by breaking for lunch when I should have been working. Where the hell do you think I have been for the past three days and nights?"

"I guess you have been in the same place you have been all my life, on the end of a scribbled note and a hastily written cheque. Did it ever cross your mind that I just wanted you? Where were you when I rode my first bicycle? Where were you when I scored my first run? Yes I know that when I said I wanted to play cricket you bought me all the kit and packed me off to the local club for professional instruction. But all I wanted was a ball and a stick and a game with you on the lawn for Christ's sake. And on Friday all I wanted was to sit and share a sandwich with my father. I can't believe that I stayed in that restaurant waiting like a little lost boy for four hours for you to arrive. Even after that length of time I convinced myself that you wouldn't let me down; not this time. But I was as far away from your thoughts as I have always been."

"That's not true Sebastian I have always been proud of you and I always took an interest in what you were doing."

"Did we ever catch a fish?"

"No."

"Did we ever have a pretend fight?"

"No we didn't do that either."

"Then I rest my case father."

"Did you ever go hungry? Did you ever need clothes? Did you ever miss out on trips abroad? Were you not educated in the finest schools in England?"

"I lost count of the nights when I cried myself to sleep because I couldn't climb onto your knee and hear you say that you loved me. That's all I ever wanted. But did you ever ask what I really wanted? No you never did until nine months ago when we set that date for lunch and I waited like a fool, embarrassed and humiliated, making excuses for your absence like I did with my school friends all those years ago when all their father's came to support them and mine didn't." Sebastian opened his hand and let the torn pieces of paper fall slowly from his hand like confetti. "You keep your fortune father, who knows, one day it might even love you back. I don't suppose we'll see each other again. Good luck with your book, I'll see myself out."

Sebastian turned and left his father in stunned silence. Somewhere between being born and that Sunday morning Sebastian had become a man and Deacon saw it for the very first time. He heard the sports car fire up and lurch noisily over the gravel, his son was gone and Deacon slouched back into his chair.

Maria walked slowly towards the study when she knew that Sebastian was gone. She peeked sheepishly round the open door to find Deacon with his back to the door looking thoughtfully out of the window and up into the sky.

"May I go home now Mr Richard?" she asked quietly.

Deacon didn't say anything or turn from the window, he simply grunted and Maria left.

Chapter Four

Knowing that his manuscript was complete Deacon spent the remainder of Sunday alone in the house and proceeded to drink himself into a stupor on a mixture of whisky and wine. The Champagne would keep until another suitable occasion warranted its airing.

He went to bed late on Sunday evening and did not rise for two days. The sleep he had missed returned and demanded interest, but it was far from restful. A concoction of thoughts and dreams fused with momentary glimpses of consciousness created a bizarre screenplay in his troubled mind. His dead father appeared in the form of a grotesque zombie and followed him down a corridor of dull yellow light. He ran until his lungs burned but he could not escape the outstretched arms of his lumbering pursuant. He woke drenched in perspiration as his father's fingers lunged towards his throat. His eyes darted round the room and he searched frantically for his father until reality dawned and he realised that it had all been a dream. *My God, what was all that about? And what was he doing here?* He sat up on his bed and gathered his thoughts before he got shakily to his feet and headed clumsily in the direction of the bathroom. He leaned into the sink and splashed his face with cold water. Then dabbing his face with a hand towel he went back to the bed and lifted the internal telephone.

"Yes Mr Richard?" Maria answered.

The sound of her sweet voice was like golden honey to his ears. *Thank God she's still here.* "Are you still there Mr Richard?" Maria asked in the pause that followed.

"What time is it Maria?" he asked.

"It's ten forty five," Mr Richard.

"Am or pm?

Maria shook her head as she answered casually.

"It's morning Mr Richard."

"Ah, and which morning might that be Maria?"

"It's Tuesday Mr Richard."

"Could you bring me a cup of hot, sweet coffee Maria?"

"Yes sir."

"By the way, have you any idea what happened to Monday?"

"Just like any other day Mr Richard, it came and it went."

"Any urgent calls?" he asked.

"Mrs Deacon called and asked if you were able to come to the phone," Maria said, "But she didn't say it was urgent."

"What did she say exactly?"

"She said that she would be in touch."

Be in touch? How very odd, he thought.

"Is that all she said?" he asked.

"Yes Mr Richard, I told her you couldn't come to the phone and she said she would be in touch."

"Very well, I'll take my coffee now and my bath at seven minutes past eleven."

"Yes Mr Richard."

Deacon walked across the landing to his study as Maria prepared his coffee. He looked at his computer and debated whether to print off the finished manuscript ready for posting off to his publisher or wait until after his bath when his thoughts had had the chance to organise themselves into some kind of logical order. Maria came in with his coffee and laid his coffee gently on the desk in front of him. "Your bath is almost ready Mr Richard," she said.

He instinctively looked at his watch as he leaned back in his chair, then with a thoughtful expression on his face he asked: "Have you ever thought about raising a family Maria?" The unexpected question took her by surprise.

"When I was a little girl I thought about having children as most girls do, but I haven't given it any thought since I came to England. I believe that things will happen when they are supposed to happen," she said.

"And what would you do with them once you had them?" he asked.

Maria looked at him questioningly, "What do you mean?" she asked.

"The question is plain enough," he said, "What would you do with them, your children?"

A plain question deserves a plain answer, she thought.

"I would love them and bring them up," she said.

"And is that all we need to do?" he asked. "Is that the sum total of our commitment to them, our parental obligations fulfilled?"

Maria could see where his line of questioning was heading and she didn't want to be caught in the middle or be coaxed or hoodwinked into taking sides. "If you are asking me to sit in judgement on what went on between you and Sebastian on Sunday then I won't answer any more questions. All I will say is that you both have issues and you are both as right and as wrong as those issues allow you to be. You are both single minded and stubborn and somewhere amongst all this is the cause of your argument."

Deacon looked at his watch again conscious that the minutes were ticking towards seven minutes past eleven. Maria had caught him out in his surreptitious trawl for sympathy and support so he tried a slightly different tack to try to cover his tracks.

"You should have studied law Maria," he said, "Or better still, diplomacy. Also known as sitting on the fence; so I'll put the question another way, do you think it is acceptable for my son— any son—to come barging into a father's home and start dishing out family ethics as though I am some kind of heartless stoic?"

"It doesn't matter what I think Mr Richard because the first thing I learned about domestic work is the golden rule, never to allow yourself to be involved. If I did that then when you two have found your common ground and you are friends again, it leaves me out in the cold. I have to sit on the fence. Now, it's five minutes past eleven Mr Richard and your bath is waiting."

She should have been a bloody politician, he thought as he quickly drank his coffee and placed his cup on the tray. Maria followed him out of the room and as he headed for the bathroom she went back to the kitchen to prepare his lunch.

Deacon submerged his whole body in the great, deep, reproduction Edwardian bath which dominated the centre of the bathroom. He lay there like a Roman consul as the hot steam rose from the sweet scented water that Maria had prepared with such devotion to duty. His thoughts drifted off in no fixed direction as the warmth relaxed his body and the scent filled his nostrils. He thought about his manuscript and tried to regenerate the feeling of satisfaction that was so rudely interrupted by Sebastian's unpredicted outburst, but that train of thought only lead him back to Sebastian and all the things he had said. *All that fuss over a missed birthday lunch? I thought I had brought him up to be tougher than that. I've always told him never to rely on anyone and never ever to let anyone see that you're hurt.*

He had been in the bath for several minutes when Maria tapped lightly on the door.

"Mr Richard," she called.

"Maria, whatever it is, not now," he said lazily without opening his eyes.

"Your solicitor just rang to ask if you were in and he wants to know if he can come out to see you today. He says it's very urgent," she said.

"Maria, everything to do with solicitors is very urgent. It's an age old ruse they employ which allows them to plunder the pockets of unsuspecting clients as soon as possible. For instance, that phone call you have just had with him has cost me in the region of £500," he said.

"Well it could actually be more than that Mr Richard because he is still on the phone. He has insisted on waiting for your reply."

Deacon sat up quickly splashing water onto the floor around the bath. *The damned cheek of the man, is nothing sacred anymore? Anyone would think he's paying my bills.* "Tell him that I will call him back in fifteen minutes and make it quite clear to him that I am not happy at being badgered like a…Oh to hell with it, my bath is ruined now anyway, tell him I'll be there in two minutes."

Maria went back to the telephone as Deacon stepped from the bath and began to towel himself off. *The bloody man, his excuse for this intrusion had better be life and death.*

Maria held the receiver out to Deacon as he stomped into his study with nothing but a bath towel wrapped around his waist. He covered the mouthpiece with his hand to speak to Maria as she was leaving: "Maria, the bathroom floor is drenched; could you see to it before it soaks through the whole damned house?" he growled.

"Would you like me to bring you a bathrobe first, Mr Richard?" Maria asked calmly.

Deacon looked down at the towel and paused for a moment like a rabbit caught in the headlights of a speeding car. The cool composure of Maria's question seemed to hit him like bucket of cold water. His momentary reflection on the absurdity of the situation tempered his rage and instead of exploding down the phone to his solicitor he let the towel drop and stood there stark naked. "Yes Maria, I would like a bathrobe," he said.

Unfazed by the flamboyant display of his eccentric schoolboy humour Maria tsked as she smiled and left the room.

"What is it Redfearn?" was Deacon's gruff opening gambit.

"Ah, hello Richard; Warren Redfearn here."

"Yes I know who you are, so what is it that is so deathly important?"

"Are you sitting down Richard?"

"Well actually I'm standing here as naked as the day I was born and I am getting progressively more frustrated with each passing moment. So, could you get to the point before hypothermia sets in and besides my morning attire I lose my faculties altogether."

Redfearn completely misread Deacon's mood as he began to introduce the reason for his call. "I'm glad to find you in a playful frame of mind Richard but I'm afraid that what I have to say is not so humorous at all," he said. Once again Maria's timing played an important part in the events that followed. She knocked lightly on the study door and walked in with Deacon's bathrobe without waiting to be asked. She walked directly round behind Deacon and held it open for him to slip his arms into. Her actions had saved Redfearn from the ear-bashing that Deacon was about to deliver.

"It's Eleanor," Redfearn continued.

"Hold on a second Redfearn," Deacon said as he covered the receiver with his hand again. "Coffee," he said to Maria as she walked towards the door. He waited until Maria had closed the door behind her before he spoke to Redfearn again.

"Eleanor, what about her?" he asked.

"Well, in a nutshell old boy, she wants a divorce."

"A divorce? Eleanor? That's ludicrous, are you sure?"

"That's why I asked if you were sitting down Richard. I hate to be the bearer of bad news but that's one of the unsavoury elements that go with this job."

"This isn't April the first is it Redfearn?"

"I wish I could say that it was Richard—but no it isn't— and she's adamant that she wants a divorce."

"On what grounds?"

"According to the papers on my desk the grounds are two years separation."

"So, let me get this straight, are you are saying she wants a separation?"

"No Richard, I'm saying you have had your separation, she now wants to go through with the divorce."

"This is preposterous Redfearn, there must be some mistake; she only called me on Monday."

"When was the last time you actually saw Eleanor Richard?" Redfearn asked calmly.

Deacon stood and thought for a moment before he answered: "I was only speaking to Maria the other day about preparing her room for when she comes home."

"Yes, but when was the last time she actually was at home?"

"How the hell should I know? I've been busy earning the money that allows her to live like a queen bee, whist she flits around spending it like water all over God's creation!" Deacon snapped.

"Calm down Richard, getting angry with me won't help matters at all."

"Don't patronise me Redfearn, I am not getting angry, I am completely calm, I'm merely stating a fact in a forceful manner."

"Please Richard, I know this has come as a bolt from the blue and I contacted you first and foremost this morning as your friend. So now you know that there is a nasty storm brewing which we have to deal with I will put my solicitor's hat on. From here on in we have to be straight with each other. Any bullshit is my department so leave that to me along with any mud-slinging. Now have you and Eleanor slept under the same roof at any time during the past two years?"

Deacon sighed heavily, "Probably not," he said quietly. "But I had no idea we were separated, we have always had a unique relationship, doesn't that count for something?" he added.

"Yes Richard, it counts as grounds for divorce."

There was a long silence. "So what happens now?" Deacon asked finally.

"Well for starters, might I suggest that I drive over to see you this afternoon so that we can plan our course of action? The sooner we respond to this letter from Eleanor's legal team the better."

Deacon paused to think for a moment before he agreed: "Yes I suppose we had better do something today, but I'm not one for long drawn out theatricals, I will expect some sound legal guidance which will resolve the issue quickly, I don't want legal wrangling and all the associated hassle hanging around like a bad smell for the next five years."

"But Richard, this is your marriage we are talking about, not some business deal," Redfearn protested.

"Correction Redfearn, this is my *divorce* we are talking about and that makes it business. If you have papers on your desk from Eleanor and she says she wants a divorce, then I know her well enough to know that nothing I say or do will change her mind, so let's approach this from that angle. And what's more if she has already gathered a legal team around her that means she has a head start and she is thinking money." *In plain language Redfearn that means I don't want you and her legal team getting fatter still, feasting on my misery by prolonging things one moment longer than is necessary.*

"Yes Richard, if that is the case then I agree; I will be with you at two this afternoon if that will suit you," Redfearn said.

"I will have to make it suit me won't I?"

Deacon put the receiver down and stood for a moment to gather his thoughts. He walked slowly round to his writing chair as the conversation he had just had began to sink in.

Divorce? Legal team, Christ Eleanor that's a bit strong isn't it? The media will have a field day, there will be reporters camping out all over the lawn and hiding in the bushes like cowardly snipers. I won't be able to take a pee without one of them emerging from the bowl to take a front page snapshot of my uglies! Oh Eleanor what are you thinking of?

He slumped dejectedly into his chair before he reached across the desk to take up the half smoked cigar that had burned itself out after Sebastian's interruption. He re-ignited it and spun his chair to face the window. *Waste not, want not; this could be my last extravagance for a while,* he thought as he blew a cloud of smoke into the air.

He turned back to his desk and lifted the receiver of the internal telephone to speak to Maria.

"Could you organise some sandwiches for two people for around three o'clock this afternoon Maria please. Serve them in the conservatory with afternoon tea."

"Yes Mr Richard. At what time will your guest arrive?" she asked.

"You can expect Mr Redfearn at two o'clock, hold all my other calls and turn away any other visitors. By the way, alert me if you see anyone—anyone at all—sneaking about in the grounds especially if they have cameras and if anyone at all should ask you anything your answer is to be succinct, 'No comment' is that clear Maria?"

"Yes Mr Richard."

Maria put the receiver down knowing that something was very wrong in the Deacon household. She also had the niggling thought that her vows to stay neutral in any and all situations were about to be broken by powers beyond her control.

Chapter Five

Deacon stubbed out the last of his cigar and started up his computer; he checked the printer for paper and began to print off his novel for dispatching to his publisher. Despite all the advances in modern technology his publisher still insisted on having finished manuscripts delivered in hard copy, probably something to do with the proof-reading and editing process. Anyway, that was no concern of his; the novel was complete and his end of the bargain was done and dusted, another blockbuster on the bookstore bookshelves and another fortune in the bank. The publisher was suitably appeased because the production deadlines could now be met with a degree of certainty, Deacon was relieved because he had managed to create such a fine novel under intense pressure and ultimately the book reading public's thirst for more of Deacon's work would be thoroughly satisfied—at least for the next few months.

Deacon sat and thought as the printer churned out page after page. He thought about the strange complexities of life and he began to juxtapose the process of the production of a novel from it's concept to the mind of the reader with the process of life itself. How life—like a novel—begins with a consummation, the joining of male and female sperm and ovaries like the joining of reality and fiction as the author—like God—devises a way of suspending disbelief to create a new and independent life. And just like the suspense and drama of a well written novel, life spins and lurches from triumph to disaster and back again. *Life is a succession of cruelties punctuated by hope and so made bearable.*

As the printer laid the final leaf on top of the neatly piled novel Deacon gathered it up and placed it on his writing desk before him. He thought about the imminent arrival of Redfearn and what tedious and odious plans they would have to concoct in order to defend their precariously exposed position; and as he straightened the pages so that they were perfectly aligned, he began to speak to his novel as though he were speaking to one of the characters within. "Two days ago when I wrote your final line

I finished my masterpiece. As I breathed life into you along the way I gave you the key to my soul, you were the pinnacle of my life's labours, my dreams, my visions, even my epitaph. You were my investment for my future and now, one phone call later, it seems as though my sacrifice for your creation will ultimately cost me everything, my son, my wife, my home, everything." *Life is a succession of cruelties punctuated by hope and so made bearable.*

Deacon picked up the telephone and called his publisher, he told him that the manuscript would be sent by special courier and he could expect to receive it over the next couple of days. He also asked him to let him know when it arrived safely. With that phone call out of the way all he had left to do was await the arrival of Redfearn. He walked over to the rosewood drinks cabinet on the left hand wall and lifted the heavy crystal bauble top from the whisky decanter, he paused with it in his hand before he let it fall noisily back into the neck of the decanter to seal it again, the dull sound of it dropping back into place reminded him of an arrow thudding into a live target and the thought of betrayal suddenly had a sound as well as a mental image. As far as he was concerned Eleanor had stabbed him in the back and made a mockery of everything he had tried to build. *No, no drink until this business with Eleanor and her legal team is out of the way. Drink numbs the senses and I want to feel every single blow she delivers so that I can begin to hate her with the same passion that drives me to create.*

Instead of pouring himself a drink he went back to the desk and picked up the internal telephone.

"Yes Mr Richard?" Maria answered.

"Maria, what are you doing just now?"

"I'm preparing sandwiches for you and your guest this afternoon."

"Ah yes, well when you have a minute call the courier company and have them collect a parcel for immediate overnight delivery to London," he said, "and bring me some freshly squeezed orange juice."

Maria hated life with Deacon when he was at a loose end. He behaved like a bored teenager. He was unpredictable and challenging at the best of times but those elements coupled with his eccentric disposition made life with him as appealing as po-going through a mine field. She hoped that his next project would spring into his mind before his boredom did any permanent damage.

When Maria served his orange juice she found him leaning with his backside against his desk facing out into the centre of the room. He was running his open hand through the flame of his Aladdin's lamp cigar lighter.

"You'll do yourself an injury Mr Richard," Maria calmly observed as she walked by him to lay his orange juice down on his desk.

"An acceptable risk in the name of scientific research, my dear," he sniffed.

"And how will the dying embers of your former hand enrich the minds of the next generation of scientific researchers? It won't, so stop it!" she said.

"I appreciate your concern for my wellbeing Maria but have no fear. This is what is known as a controlled experiment," he smiled as he passed his palm through the flame once again.

"No Mr Richard; that is what is known as playing with fire and if you carry on you will get burned just like every other curious little boy showing off."

"Maria, let me ask you a question, how did the Fakir's of ancient India discover that they could walk through fire unharmed?" he said, still moving his hand provocatively above the flame.

"Let me ask you a question Mr Richard, what good did it do them to find out that they could?"

Deacon closed the lighter and conceded. "A very good question Maria, and one that I shall ponder as I await the arrival of my guest this afternoon."

"Will there be anything else Mr Richard, a fire blanket perhaps?" Maria asked.

"Just give me a call at seven minutes to two so that I can be settled into the conservatory for when Redfearn arrives. I want him to feel the discomfort of imposition for the duration of his stay and the best way to do that is to establish my domain."

"Yes Mr Richard." *And whilst you're at it why don't you urinate in every corner?*

The telephone in Deacon's study rang at the specified time and he made his way through the house to the conservatory. He sat in an armchair by the fire with his back purposefully to the door and he opened a newspaper to give the impression that he had been there a while. Maria tapped gently on the door and announced the arrival of Redfearn.

"Show him in Maria," Deacon said as he began to fold the newspaper—he would complete the operation once Redfearn was in full view.

As Redfearn approached Deacon with his hand outstretched Maria asked if that would be all. Deacon took hold of Redfearn's hand and looked past him to answer Maria.

"Yes that will be all for now Maria," he said as he motioned for Redfearn to sit in the opposite armchair.

"May I begin by saying how sorry I am to be here on this dreadful business?" Redfearn said.

"Yes, and may I begin by saying that your outpouring of heartfelt sympathy will only add to my distress in this dreadful business from a financial perspective. So with that in mind will you spare me any sentimentality and cut to the chase?"

"I know all this has come as a complete shock Richard and I don't blame you for being upset but you must remember that I am on your side."

"He who pays the piper calls the tune Redfearn, would you agree?" Deacon said.

"Yes I would agree but I am not only your legal representative I also consider myself to be your friend," Redfearn smiled as he moved uneasily in his chair.

"Then as my legal representative and as my friend I am asking you to resolve this issue as a matter of the utmost urgency."

"Richard, please excuse me if I am being a little too frank, but I asked you earlier to leave the bullshit to me. I cannot bring myself to believe that a man of your wealth could have any reservations at all regarding payment for my services. Whatever my final invoice amounted to it would be a drop in the ocean to you. We could agree right now on a fixed amount, where time spent on the case would not involve additional costs, but I think we both know that money is not the real issue here. So what exactly is on your mind Richard? Let me know now and we can start this conversation afresh."

Deacon sighed heavily: "You know Redfearn you are not as obtuse as you look. In fact your little speech just reminded me why I choose to retain your extortionate services," he smiled. "Forgive my appalling manners, would you like a drink?"

"I'll have a small whisky Richard and over our drink you can tell me what is really on your mind."

Deacon poured a glass of whisky and handed it to Redfearn; he filled his own glass with soda water and sat down as he began to speak: "You are right, it's not a question of money—although your offer of a fixed fee does sound rather tempting," he joked. "It's just that I can't function properly as a writer, as a businessman, in fact as a human being, with something like a lengthy divorce hanging over me. It would sap all my creative energy. In my world within a world Maria is my protection, although she doesn't fully know to what extent—and I would rather she didn't know—she understands my needs without ever questioning them, as if it is instinctive to her. Do you understand what I'm trying to say?"

Redfearn didn't say anything at first he just did a curious thing with his head, almost a wobble; it looked like a circular motion somewhere between a nod and a shake.

"I understand some of what you are trying to say; I understand why you want to resolve things quickly anyway and that's all I really need to understand for now. Shall we make a start?"

From his reply Deacon had the feeling that Redfearn had read more into his explanation of his relationship with Maria than was intended, but rather than protest too much and add fuel to the flame he thought it best to take Redfearn up on his offer to make a start. Deacon looked at his watch and it was seven minutes past two. *A perfect time to start.*

Redfearn opened up his leather briefcase and took out a neat bundle of official looking papers. "These documents represent the bulk of your wife's claims and conditions or to put it another way they represent what she regards as a fair divorce settlement."

Deacon took a sip from his glass and mentally steadied himself for the first stinging body blow. "Go on, I can't wait to learn what financial value she has placed on the dissolution of our life of wedded bliss."

"She wants twenty five million pounds Richard."

"And?" Deacon asked nonchalantly.

"That's it Richard, did you not hear what I said? She wants a twenty five million pounds divorce settlement."

"Right, so can I leave you to see to it?" Deacon asked calmly.

"Now hold on a second Richard, this isn't quite how it works. They suggest a figure and we haggle by suggesting an alternative figure, then we meet halfway."

Deacon leaned forward in his chair. "Now you are getting into the realms of prolonging the issue. Not two minutes ago I said that is exactly what I don't want to do. She wants twenty five million pounds; that works out roughly at one million pounds for every year we have been married. Knowing me as I do, I think that is a reasonable compensation for her. And in addition to that she obviously has no idea of how much I am actually worth, otherwise she would have asked for ten times that amount. She has arrived at that figure after consultation with her retinue at the beauty salon rather than with her legal team so why should I ruin a perfectly good gross miscalculation by contesting the amount?"

Redfearn leaned forward and struck a similar simian pose to Deacon's: "But Richard, what about my prepared courtroom spiel? Don't you want to hear it?"

"There is absolutely no need for courtroom drama, no need for complications. You draw up the papers and I will advise my financial people to release the money. Put your bill in at the same time and everyone will be satisfied with the outcome. Now if you want to give me your prepared spiel to give your drama at least one performance, be my guest."

At that point Maria knocked on the door and backed into the room pulling a trolley with tea and sandwiches.

"Ah our refreshments," Deacon said, "Didn't I tell you that Maria had impeccable powers of intuition?"

Maria poured the tea and uncovered the sandwiches.

"We will help ourselves Maria," Deacon smiled as Redfearn instinctively rose to his feet in the presence of a lady. Maria smiled back at the two men and left.

"So what happens now exactly?" Deacon asked as he filled his plate.

"Once Eleanor's legal team are aware of your acceptance of her settlement, the actual divorce will be a simple formality. There will be a period of several months between the issue of a Decree Nisi and a Decree Absolute—a sort of cooling off period—and after that you will be a single man again."

"Is it really that repulsively simple?" Deacon asked.

"It's the reaching of agreements that makes things simple and contrary to popular conceptions, it is not in the interests of legal advisers to prolong these proceedings. It is up to people like me to advise our clients on a suitable course of legal action which will hopefully ensure the most favourable outcome. And we swear a solemn oath to uphold that principle."

"Thank you for that Redfearn, and if I were you I would consider that speech adequate recompense for being denied the opportunity to deliver your well rehearsed spiel in the courtroom," Deacon smiled.

"I'll drink to that," Redfearn smiled and raised his teacup.

The two men shook hands and Deacon took the unusual step of walking a guest to the door. Despite their initial guardedness towards each other Redfearn had earned Deacon's respect and whatever his faults and eccentricities he was always prepared to recognise a man who openly showed the courage of his convictions. As Redfearn was about to leave he turned to Deacon. "I believe your son Sebastian is making quite a name for himself in the city as a very capable lawyer."

Deacon shrugged his shoulders, "It's been a while since he and I have had time to catch up."

"That's one of the drawbacks of the lives we lead," Redfearn nodded. "Just one more thing Richard," he added, "Can I ask you a question."

"As long as you don't bill me for it later," he smiled.

"How could you not know that Eleanor was missing from your home for two years?"

Deacon sniffed the air: "I guess that's another one of the drawbacks of the lives we lead."

Deacon stood and watched as Redfearn drove slowly down the drive and out of sight. Without turning he sensed that Maria had joined him at the door.

"Is my Champagne suitably chilled Maria?" he asked.

"Eight degrees Celsius for optimum epervescence Mr Richard, as always."

Chapter Six

Deacon stood at the door for a while looking out over the grounds. The afternoon was warm with a clear blue sky and the peaceful silence was broken only by the excited, melodious calls of newly fledged birds as they played and tumbled frantically amongst their new and as yet undiscovered world. A feeling of emptiness descended on him as he thought where he fitted into those surroundings. They were suddenly surreal; everything seemed foreign to him, cold and distant. Years ago when he had first found his paradise there it was the culmination of a life of hard graft. It was his gift to himself for the hours of solitude and dedication that were the necessary evils of the path that he was on. Now it was slowly becoming clearer to him as he stood and tried to recapture that initial feeling of belonging that things were changing. *I'm fifty years old, on the verge of divorce, estranged from my son, I'm about to lose twenty five million pounds and I'm ordering Champagne to drink alone. Something is missing from this plot; this can't be how the story ends.*

He turned his back on the scene and left his thoughts to mingle with the chattering of the birds as he went inside. Maria found him in the drawing room as she brought in his Champagne. He was standing with his hands in his pockets looking up at a portrait of his father hanging over the old fireplace and she could see that he was troubled. She laid the tray on the coffee table between two elegant sofas and waited for his response.

"Do you know what Redfearn wanted?" he asked.

"Not exactly Mr Richard, a few minutes ago when you asked for this Champagne I thought it was good news, but looking at you now I have the feeling I was wrong," she said.

"Not entirely my dear, there is good and bad in every hand that fate deals us. I won't beat about the bush, the thing is Maria, Eleanor has asked for a divorce and I have agreed. Now that does not affect you immediately but I have no doubt that it will affect you at some point in the near future."

"In what way will it affect me Mr Richard?"

41

"I am not really sure, I haven't given it a great deal of thought just yet, this is all new to me and the way forward I suppose is to handle things as and when they arise so as to cause minimal disruption. But having said that, there will obviously be some disruption and what I am saying is that you don't deserve to have your life disrupted in any way at all. Yet if you stay here it is unavoidable. Eleanor and I are your joint employers in a technical sense but I am speaking now from a loyalty perspective, do you understand what I'm driving at?"

"In a word Mr Richard; no."

"Well, let me put it like this, the Champagne I am about to consume is symbolic rather than celebratory, rather like the launching of a magnificent new ocean going liner. I have just completed my finest novel and almost at the same moment my wife of twenty five years says—through a third party I might add—that our lives together are over. So you see my fate has been decided, I have no other choice than to launch myself towards a new horizon, you however do have a choice. Now do you see what I mean?"

"Am I being fired Mr Richard?"

"My dear of course you're not being fired, quite the opposite, I'm putting my bid in for your services before Eleanor realised that she values them every bit as much as I do."

"I can't even remember the last time I saw Mrs Deacon so why should she suddenly decide that she wants me to work for her?" she asked.

"Because Maria, for the past two years Mrs Deacon has been living the high life down in the city; it's been a case of out of sight out of mind. When she does finally settle down somewhere it will simply be a matter of time before she realises how much she needs you to run things for her like you have done here for the past few years. Now you know Eleanor just as well as I do and inside that granite exterior of hers there beats a heart of wrought iron. Whatever she wants, she gets and very soon she will want you and the carrot she will dangle to get you will be difficult to refuse."

Maria hung her head and tears began to roll down her cheeks.

"What's the matter?" Deacon asked.

Maria shook her head, "Nothing," she said, "I just need a while to pull myself together that's all, may I be excused Mr Richard."

For a moment Deacon didn't know how to react to Maria's tears or to her request. He could easily have given one of his characters the right words to say or given them a suitable dramatic response, but in reality things are always bigger than the imagination and he was stuck for words. Maria provided the drama when she simply turned and left the room in silence.

In the silence of the drawing room Deacon turned to his father's portrait and spoke to it: "What did I say?" *Perhaps she is overcome with emotion at the thought of my marriage breaking up? It could be that she is happy because I want to keep her here with me?* "What do you think father?"

Deacon opened his Champagne and filled his glass. He raised his glass to his father, "Good health old boy, and here's to a fresh start, to new horizons, new beginnings and future prosperity."

He was half way down the bottle when he heard Maria's car engine turn over. He listened as the tyres crunched out onto the driveway and melted away into the evening. He was alone in his world, a wealthy man without a friend, a husband without a wife, a father without a son, an emperor alone in his vast empty empire.

Chapter Seven

Maria tapped lightly on Deacon's bedroom door just before nine o'clock. Deacon poked his head from the blankets like a drowsy old badger emerging from hibernation.

"Come in," he called sleepily.

Maria went into the bedroom and placed a cup of coffee on the bedside table.

"Mr Daniels called first thing this morning, he asked if you would call him back at some point today," she said as she moved towards the curtains.

"Could you leave the drapes for now Maria, my eyes are a little tender this morning, I'm afraid I may have drawn rather too much water from the well last night. After the Champagne I started on the Claret and finished with a wee dram or two of the old Highland malts; not the best idea I've ever had, but good fun at the time nonetheless."

"Shall I run a bath for you?" Maria asked.

"As long as you put a silencer on the taps Maria, I really am in a poor condition."

"Shall I prepare it for seven minutes past nine or seven minutes to ten?"

"I'll take the latter option Maria," he said as he tucked his head back down into the blankets.

Maria made a start on the housework in the downstairs rooms; she began by clearing away the debris of Deacon's one man party. *How can a human being drink so much in one night and live?* Deacon's ability to consume so much alcohol and still retain enough mental stability to produce such great literary works had long since been a source of miraculous wonder for Maria; it should not have been physically possible. *Perhaps it's just another symptom of his eccentricity?*

Maria had not had an easy night herself, since she left the house the previous evening she had done nothing but turn over in her mind the curious conversation she had had with Deacon about retaining her services. She had found the whole thing disturbing.

44

His ability to accept that his marriage was over in a matter of minutes without the slightest hint of compassion or sense of loss was troubling her. And the cold-hearted way he treated Sebastian *his own son* with such indifference, even when he knew he may never see him again was also preying heavily on her mind. Something in her mind was telling her to do something but she didn't know what. Despite Deacon's eccentricities she had grown to like him, perhaps more than she should like an employer. Was that because she knew how much he depended on her? Somehow she allowed all those thoughts and emotions to cross over and become entangled. Yes Deacon had said that he wanted to retain her services but there was no warmth towards her in his deliberations, it was so cold and businesslike. The way he had put it was as if she was a bone for two dogs to fight over and whichever dog won would slink away and bury it. The victory in the contest would not be in winning the bone but in preventing the other dog from having it. Deacon was right about one thing however and that was in his implication that no matter how much she tried to remain neutral, she would have to take sides sooner or later simply by choosing one of them as her sole future employer. Mrs Deacon had been away for two years, but in the time before that she was always kind to Maria and generous. They often took trips out shopping together and talked about things as friends over lunch. Maria had even been away on trips abroad with Mrs Deacon and she was always treated as one of the family.

On that morning she went about her duties on auto-pilot, her thoughts were focused on doing the right thing. She knew that her energy would be better spent on her own soul searching. Whatever decision she made she knew that ultimately she would be the only loser. If she stayed with Mr Deacon it would alienate her from Mrs Deacon and vice versa. The more she thought about the whole sorry situation the more she realised that she would rather hurt herself than hurt any of them beyond repair. By the time she had finished cleaning the downstairs rooms she had reached a very difficult decision and one that would change the direction of her life in equal proportion to that of the warring

Deacons. She would tell Mr Deacon before the morning was out that she would like to work one month's notice.

As she began to run his bath she ran the scenario through her head of how she would drop the bombshell of her imminent departure on him. She imagined herself facing him in his study and him pleading with her to stay. She suddenly stopped that train of thought when she realised that the subject of her scenario was Richard Deacon. *Come on girl get back to reality, this is Richard Deacon we are talking about. The man who allowed his son to walk out of his life with as much grief as a man swatting troublesome flies; this is the same man who ended a quarter of a century of marriage with a bottle of Champagne. I will wait until he is bathed and dressed and then I will tell him that I am leaving next month and any struggles with emotional composure will be entirely mine.*

At ten minutes to ten she knocked on Deacon's bedroom door to announce the time and to let him know that his bath was ready. He responded with a gruff groaning noise which started when his head left the pillow and steadily rose in volume abating only when he was upright on the floor. Maria stood back from the door as he emerged from the room in his dressing gown and headed for the bathroom. She immediately went into the room to draw back the curtains, make the bed and lay out his clothes for the day. On her way back downstairs she stopped at the bathroom door to ask if he would like breakfast. He answered with another growl which Maria had learned to recognise over the years as a negative.

Maria busied herself in the kitchen taking stock of food items and making up a shopping list. She heard the faint drone of the postman's delivery van on the driveway and she went through to the front door to meet him. The postman smiled his usual cheery smile as he handed her a bundle of letters, "Good morning Maria, how are you on this fine day?" he said.

"I'm fine thank you and how are you."

"All the better for seeing your beautiful face," he smiled. "Shall we go somewhere exotic this afternoon, Mauritius, perhaps or Tamil Nadhu?"

"I'd love to but I have a pie to bake," she laughed, "maybe tomorrow."

"Just my luck, I'm going fishing tomorrow," he said as he climbed back into his van and blew Maria a kiss. She couldn't help but compare the greetings she had received that morning from two very different men and she transposed those greetings into a mirror image of their lives. One man had everything and yet had nothing. The other man had nothing and yet had everything. *What a strange and complicated world we live in.*

Maria was back in the kitchen when the internal telephone rang. Deacon was in the drawing room asking for coffee and toast. That was a good sign. The bath must have gone some way to clearing his head and his request for toast told her that his appetite would probably be back to normal around five o'clock that evening. More importantly though it presented her with the perfect opportunity to do what she had to do and get it over and done with.

Deacon was going through his mail when Maria brought in his tray of coffee and toast. "Ah Maria was I dreaming this morning or did you inform me that Daniels had phoned earlier?" he asked without looking up from his mail.

"He called first thing and asked if you would be so kind as to ring him back at some point today," she said, "Will that be all Mr Richard?" she asked.

Again without looking up he simply said: "Yes."

Maria hesitated subconsciously just long enough for Deacon to notice. "Was there something else Maria?" he asked, this time looking up from the letter in his hand.

"Well, yes Mr Richard, there is something else, but it can wait until you have a spare few minutes," she said. Inside she was berating herself for being such a coward at the crucial moment. She was about to turn and leave when Deacon surprised her by indirectly inviting her to stay. "There is no time like the present Maria," he said, "so fire away, right now anything would be a welcome distraction from the drivel I am confronted with every damn morning and expected to respond to," he added referring to the content of his mail.

Don't blow it this time Maria, let him have it.

"Well, it's kind of in relation to what we spoke about yesterday, about my future employment to be precise," she said.

"Ah good girl, you have decided to stay on here with me I take it?" he said confidently.

Hit him with it now Maria before he makes it impossible.

"Actually Mr Richard I would like to give you one month's notice from today sir," she said.

"What! Are you serious Maria?" he asked incredulously, "What's the matter? I mean, you can't do this, where would you go? What would you do?"

It was the first time she had ever seen Deacon agitated like that and she had seen him in some pretty heated situations. She would have to think fast because he wanted immediate answers and she had to be convincing—that wasn't in her scenario.

"This isn't something I have rushed into Mr Richard, you have paid me very well over the years and I have been saving hard to pay for myself to go to university to study for a degree in languages. Now I have enough money and the opportunity so I want to take it."

If ever the right words were spoken at the right time it was then. Those few lines delivered like that were exactly the right response in terms of what would satisfy Deacon's disbelief at her wanting to leave his employment. In the same moment he was crushed and elated.

"If it had been a matter of money Maria I would have doubled, no, trebled your salary and still thought of myself as fortunate to have your services. But having said that, I have secretly longed for this day; I have often thought how looking after me and this place have been a waste of your promising young life. I suppose I have been selfish in not pointing this out before. The truth is Maria I will be lost without you, but you will be lost with me. You must go to university and you must get your degree; that will be your passport to the very stars."

Maria looked at the smile on Deacon's face like that of a proud father and it took every ounce of self control to hold back her tears. She managed to smile even though she was breaking up inside. "Will that be all Mr Richard?"

"Yes Maria, and thank you," he said.

"Thank you for what?" she asked.

"Thank you for the last four years, and thank you for making me happy this morning," he smiled.

Maria contained herself just long enough to dash through the house and back into the kitchen. She hated herself for lying to him like that but what else could she do? He may have appeared to be cold-hearted and without emotional feelings to the outside world, but she had always suspected that he was one of those people who suffer in silence—who absorb heartache and keep it locked away. The things he had said to her that morning gave her more than a fleeting glimpse that her suspicions just could be well founded, but now it was all too late. She had in effect burned her boats, she had seen the joy on his face when he thought that she was going to university—there was no way back. *God forgive me, I hope I have done the right thing.* She put her hands to her face and opened the floodgates of her pent-up tears.

Chapter Eight

Deacon went up to his study; he lifted the telephone receiver and dialled Daniels's office. His secretary answered and put him through immediately.

"Hello Richard, Daniels here," Daniels said.

"I know it is Daniels I just called you, what's on your mind?"

"Yes, sorry Richard, I wasn't thinking. I had Redfearn on the phone last night asking me to release twenty five million pounds, it's no wonder my mind is in a bit of a state this morning. Do you know what it's all about?"

"Why didn't you ask Redfearn what it's all about when he was on the phone last night?" Deacon asked casually.

"Well of course I discussed the matter with him Richard..."

Deacon cut him off mid sentence: "So what are you playing silly games with me for? Release the money."

"Steady on old boy, might I advise a little caution here; after all I am your financial advisor. We are not talking of a few hundred thousand here we are talking of twenty five million pounds."

"Before we carry on with this conversation let's put one or two things straight," Deacon said coldly. "First of all, Redfearn may have jumped the gun a little; I would have preferred to tell you to release the settlement myself, but in Redfearn's defence I did tell him to settle the matter post-haste. Secondly, you are my financial advisor and it is your job to give me advice as and when I ask for it. And I don't recall asking you for it."

"Richard please, I'll consider myself well and truly corrected but surly you don't expect me to sit by and do nothing when this amount of money is about to be lost? It is my duty to question it," Daniels argued.

"Again Daniels we seem to have a difference of opinion in terms of understanding our position and our strategy. I commend your devotion to your perception of duty whilst at the same time I must challenge your wisdom and agenda in challenging *my* financial acumen. I do not consider that settlement as 'lost' quite the contrary—I see it as a sound investment. My estranged wife has asked for that amount and that amount she shall have."

"But Richard you seem to be a little naive as to how these things work," Daniels said.

"My name and naivety don't belong in the same sentence, especially where money is concerned, so please, enlighten me," Deacon said.

"We could get away with paying half that amount."

"Yes and I—not we—could end up paying double that amount. Allow me to enlighten you. If I contest the amount, Eleanor will employ the most expensive legal team ever assembled and at the end of the five years of wrangling with affidavits, claims and counter claims the judge will announce that I must pay her what she has asked for and in addition I must pay her legal costs which will inevitably amount to a further twenty five million pounds. So you see Daniels I am not as naive as you seem to imagine. Now, be so kind as to work very closely with Redfearn to close this issue."

Daniels conceded to Deacon's argument even though—like most financial advisors—he was deeply hurt when he had to part with money even if it wasn't his. It was in his care and that was enough to elevate it to revered status.

"Is there anything else?" Deacon asked.

"Yes there is Richard, Ingrid and I would like to have you over for dinner on Saturday evening. Would you do us the honour?"

Deacon would normally have turned down the invitation on the suspicion that it was a ruse by Daniels to use the occasion to re-open the monetary issue. But after a brief mental check he remembered the last occasion he dined there. Ingrid—Daniels's wife—was an excellent hostess and an extremely good looking woman. Another big plus in the equation was that Daniels's wine cellar was second only to his own. "Seven thirty for eight?" Daniels suggested during the pause.

"Thank you Daniels; that would be lovely," Deacon said as he replaced the receiver.

He sat in the silence of his study and thought for a while. *Perhaps I was a little too hard on old Daniels; after all he is only doing his job. I would have thought it damned bad policy if he hadn't made contact with me over that amount of money. He's not a bad sort; maybe I should make more of an effort to like him. It's not that I don't like him it's just that his conversation is so one dimensional, if it's not money then he is speechless. Ah but Ingrid, she was jolly good company the last time we met. And after the events of the past few days I could certainly do with a bit of old fashioned hospitality.*

Deacon had several cars at his disposal and each one was kept in immaculate condition with its own special place in an extended garage at the rear of the house. He wasn't an avid collector with a penchant for the latest models exhibited at exclusive motor shows for the world's rich and famous. His cars were the top of the range of course but they were purchased for their practical use rather than their prestige. Each car had its own personalised registration plate and as you can imagine they all added up to odd numbers, even the letters included in the registration had been carefully chosen for their numerical position in the alphabet. On an occasion such as attending a quiet formal function he would inevitably use the Bentley. He never drove it himself but neither did he employ a full time chauffeur; he retained the services of a local farmer to act as his driver as and when he needed one. The arrangement suited Deacon and the farmer and it seemed to work surprisingly well. The farmer was a good looking chap and always well turned out by his young wife. As a businessman Deacon had empathy with the plight of modern day farmers and especially hard working young men who were trying to hack out an honest living. Deacon's father had told him years before that the British Empire was built as much on its agricultural prowess as on its industrial strength, and it was something he never forgot. Whilst Britain had the best farmers in the world it could never be starved into submission. Paying a young farmer to drive his car now and then was his gesture, his *tipping of the hat* to his father's wisdom. The farmer for his part liked to drive fancy cars and be very well paid for it.

On Saturday Maria played her part in making sure Deacon was at his best. She laid out his evening attire and saw to his other whims with her usual meticulous timing. Maria had made all the arrangements with the farmer during the week and his wife dropped him off for inspection at six o'clock on Saturday as arranged. He stood to attention in the hallway like a soldier on parade and smiled as Maria walked around him and nodded approvingly.

"You look very smart James, ten out of ten," she smiled.

"I always do my best for Mr Deacon Miss Maria," he said.

"Have you taken him to the Daniels's place before?" she asked.

"Yes, it was a while ago but I remember it."

"Good, as long as you remember to bring the car round to the front of the house at..."

James finished off her sentence: "Seven minutes to seven. Don't you worry about a thing Miss Maria I have everything covered. I will make sure he arrives safely and on time and I will do the same with his return. And if his night out is as successful as the last time he was there I will also put him to bed," he smiled.

"Yes, well, if that does occur, do me a favour and hang his suit up nicely before you leave."

James went out to the garage to check the car over and make sure everything was in order. He switched on the light and looked around at all the gleaming vehicles. The silence of the garage was broken only by the gentle hum of the humidifier and temperature regulator. The inside of the garage was kept at a constant temperature to ensure maximum airflow and minimal condensation. *These cars are better looked after than my animals. Still, if you are going to have something worth having then it is worth going to any lengths to maintain it. I have to hand it to you Mr Deacon you have certainly got style.*

James drove the car out into the courtyard after checking the oil and water. He looked over the gleaming sleek bodywork and nodded in admiration. *What a thing of beauty you are.* The evening sun shining on the polished black paintwork made it look like a gigantic black pearl. That certainly was something for every young businessman to aspire to. *Eighteen hour days for thirty years would be worth every minute if you were the prize at the end of it my beauty.*

Back at the house Maria was lovingly brushing Deacon's suit as he lounged in a hot bath filled with jasmine and crushed marigold leaves. She laid his white shirt and black tie on the bed and put out his shoes. She put a pair of his gold cufflinks in the centre of the dressing table on top of a neatly folded handkerchief before she looked around the room at her preparations to make certain that nothing had been overlooked. She walked over to the bed and began to point at the items as she spoke under her breath, 'Suit, shirt, shoes, cufflinks, handkerchief,' she then began to count them, first forwards, then backwards; one, two, three, three, two, one. *Oh my God! I'm even beginning to act like him!* She suddenly thought. *His eccentricities are rubbing off on me. Perhaps I made the right decision to leave here after all.*

She forced herself to stop her ridiculous counting ritual and she turned to leave the room. She paused by the door and looked back into the room at his suit on the bed. Once again she was overcome with a feeling of sadness. She realised that it would probably be the very last time that she would have to help Deacon to prepare for an evening out.

Maria looked at the clock on the kitchen wall when she heard the car draw round to the front of the house. It was twenty minutes to seven. She knew that Deacon would be coming down the main staircase within the next few minutes so she went through into the hallway to meet him and see him off. He appeared at the top of the staircase right on cue. Maria couldn't help but notice her stomach flip as she breathed an inward sigh at the sight of the tall, handsome man as he descended the stairs with an air of refined poise and gentlemanly elegance. He paused at the foot of the staircase and held his hands out to the side. "How do I look Maria, will I do, as they say?" he asked with a smile.

"You look…resplendent Mr Richard," Maria said thoughtfully.

"Resplendent? What a marvellous choice of words Maria. Resplendent, yes I like that, it is rather fitting even though I say it myself. And it's all down to you as usual. I shall miss you terribly you know Maria."

His final unexpected comment cut into Maria's heart like a knife but she managed to absorb it and find a suitable reply: "And I shall miss you Mr Richard, but life goes on," she said.

"How true, an unfortunate truth, but true all the same. Right Maria, I am away to get very drunk so you might as well take the morning off tomorrow my dear. If anyone calls I shall be dead to the world anyway so you will have no need to fend them off. Will you be around in the afternoon?" he added.

"I will tap on your door just before one o'clock, will that be alright?"

"That's a date then," he smiled, "Tally ho."

Maria stood at the top of the front steps and watched as James held open the door of the Bentley. Deacon ducked inside and sat back out of sight. The car drove off and as Maria followed the car with her eyes she hoped—albeit half-heartedly—that Deacon would perhaps turn and wave but she was disappointed. In a strange way she was comforted by that, it brought home two stark realities. Firstly, that she was out of sight out of mind, and secondly—and despite her devotion—she was, after all, just the hired help.

Chapter Nine

James drove the car in a stately manner down the tree-lined exit driveway and out onto the quiet country lane which cut through the lush, undulating countryside. After two miles or so they joined a busy dual carriageway. The drive along the main road took about ten minutes to reach the outskirts of the city. Once in the city it was perhaps a further ten minutes to the Daniels's place. James felt like a celebrity as heads turned to look at the car as it purred gracefully through the city streets. Daniels lived in a fine old Edwardian townhouse set back perhaps two hundred metres from the main road in a leafy stock-market suburb. James turned the car into the driveway and slowed down to a walking pace as the car ghosted past immaculately sculptured hedges and billowing purple hydrangeas. He dipped the clutch and rolled up to the front of the house in absolute silence. He paused—almost as if to milk the drama of the entrance—before he got out and opened the rear door of the Bentley. The moment was almost ruined when he found Deacon sitting in the back seat with a glass of whisky in his hand, totally unprepared to alight.

"Are we here already James?" he asked.

"Yes we are Mr Richard, the roads were surprisingly quiet this evening."

"What time is it?" Deacon asked.

"It's almost twenty past seven," James said.

"Climb on in James," Deacon said, "We have a few minutes yet, tell me, how is business down on the farm and how is that young wife of yours?"

James knew that under normal circumstances it was highly inappropriate for him to join Deacon in the back seat but he was also aware of Deacon's own special brand of social correctness. He did as he was asked and joined Deacon in the back of the car and the pair began to chat like old friends. "The farm is doing fine and my wife is the same as always, I don't think I could manage things without her," James smiled.

Deacon nodded. "A young man like you needs a good strong minded woman behind him," he said, then after a pause he added, "I hope you don't mind me using you like this."

"I like driving, especially a car like this, and the extra money always comes in handy," James said.

Deacon laughed, "No I don't mean using you to drive me about; I mean using you to talk to before I go inside to be bored to death by Daniels's sparkling conversation, not to mention that irksome laugh of his. I am cramming as much stimulating conversation as I can so that I can feed off it as I pretend to give ear to Daniels during dinner. And this whisky I hope will help take the edge off my senses and so lessen the burden of his tedious financial verbosity."

"Glad to be of help Mr Richard," James smiled, then, looking at his watch he said, "It's time to go Mr Richard. You're on your own from here on in, good luck."

"Thank you James," Deacon said, "If I am not out by midnight, come in and rescue me, there's a good chap, and don't take no for an answer."

With that Deacon tilted his head and drained the last drops of whisky from his glass. James held the car door open and Deacon stepped out and climbed the few stone steps up to the front door and rang the doorbell.

Daniels opened the door and shook Deacon warmly by the hand. "Come on in Richard it's good to see you," he said.

As they stood in the hall Daniels took Deacon's coat as his wife came from the drawing room to greet her illustrious guest, "Oh Richard thank you so much for coming, you look so good."

Deacon took hold of Ingrid's elbows and eased her towards him before he kissed her gently on the cheek, "And you look sensational my dear, absolutely ravishing." Then turning to Daniels he said: "I hope you realise how lucky you are Daniels." Daniels just smiled as Ingrid answered, "It's been a struggle at times, but he is finally beginning to realise it. Shall we go through to the drawing room for aperitifs?"

"An excellent idea Ingrid," Deacon said, "Lead on."

Ingrid was in a word 'beautiful', she had all the right credentials. She had been through the private—all girls—school system and onto finishing school to learn those all-important refinements which distinguish a real lady. She was tall, blonde and willowy with classic high cheekbones, full lips and porcelain skin. She was in her early thirties—a time when most men believe that a woman reaches her full potential—in short she was the complete package, well educated, witty, delightfully charming, and she had film star looks. On that evening she was wearing a white evening dress and her hair was swept back away from her face which made her elegant neck look even longer. She was a picture of perfection.

Ingrid and Deacon sat together on a cream coloured Chesterfield-style two-seater Italian sofa as Daniels sat opposite in a single paisley patterned armchair. They were attended to immediately by one of the temporary staff who had been hired for the evening. As far as Deacon was concerned the evening couldn't have got off to a better start. Ingrid had made it quite plain that she was keen to let Deacon know that—conversation wise—she was *his* for the evening. Deacon knew that Ingrid was an excellent chef, but she had gone to the trouble and expense to hire staff simply so that she could devote her entire evening to her guest and he was suitably impressed. It also meant that his earlier fears of being cornered by Daniels were pleasantly dispelled.

"What would you like to drink Richard?" Daniels asked. "I have a fine selection of old malts at your disposal."

"Sounds good," Deacon said, "music to my ears." *This evening is getting infinitely better by the minute.*

"You decide Daniels; think of something light, not too smoky with perhaps a subtle hint of aniseed, nothing like a smooth, light whisky to waken the appetite."
Daniels ordered a thirty seven year old Glengoyne single cask whisky for the men and a sweet sherry for Ingrid, Deacon was impressed yet again.

"I see you have picked up a little refinement since the last time I was here Daniels."
Daniels raised his glass, "To your very good health sir."

"We were so sorry to hear about your break up with Eleanor," Ingrid said as she reached out to touch Deacon's hand as an expression of sympathy. Deacon put his glass down and gathered up her hand into his and covered it lightly with his other hand.

"Thank you Ingrid, it's sad I know but these things happen. I suppose it was inevitable really with our constantly developing and differing lifestyles, perhaps I should have seen it coming but I didn't. One must 'move on' as they say these days, to 'move on' is the current buzz word Daniels, probably our latest import from America," he said turning briefly to Daniels.

"You seem to be taking it rather well Richard," Ingrid said.

"Is there any other way to take something that one can do nothing about?"

"I suppose not," Ingrid said, "I would never dream of trying to interfere but I feel it is important to let you know that we are here for you if ever you should need friends. Is there nothing at all that any of us can do?"

"What could I possibly offer Eleanor that I haven't already given her? What could I promise her that would make her want to reconsider divorcing me?" Deacon asked without requiring an answer.

"Perhaps she just wants more time with you," Ingrid said.

"I know I spend long hours locked away writing and when I am not writing I have my business dealings to attend to, but a major part of what I do is also who I am. Therefore if I change what I do, I change who I am and nobody has the right to ask another human being to be anything more or indeed less than who they are. I took Eleanor for who she is, warts an' all, as they say."

Deacon patted her hand and looked over to Daniels again. "It's very kind and thoughtful of you both to be concerned and it is much appreciated. But, it's done and dealt with so let's hear no more about it."

From that point on Ingrid very tactfully steered the conversation onto brighter issues and the conversation developed accordingly. Canapés of field mushroom and hollandaise tartlets, king prawn and mange tout skewers with lemon mayonnaise and parmesan and black olive shortbreads with parsley pesto and goats cheese were served on solid silver platters in the drawing room before they were formally invited through to the dining room for the main meal. Deacon couldn't help but smile at the fake boars head—complete with apple—which dominated the dining table. On either side of it were two silver candelabras each with seven candles. Three young waitresses stood smiling behind the three Queen Anne reproduction dining chairs and they bowed politely as the trio entered. Deacon was treated to a sumptuous meal of Lobster bisque followed by steak au poivre and finished off with a dessert of apple and blackberry crumble with brandy butter sauce. The table wine was a nineteen sixties vintage of red Bordeaux Cruaud Larose. There was no doubt that Daniels had pushed the boat out and Ingrid's expert range of sparkling chat made the evening most enjoyable. The only blot on the conversational landscape was the intermittent crackle of Daniels's seemingly manufactured laughter which Deacon hated. Every time he or Ingrid said something remotely amusing Daniels would erupt into his irritating laugh; it rose in the back of his throat and came out as a curious clucking noise as if he were about to lay an egg.

During dinner Ingrid asked about Deacon's latest novel and enquired genuinely about its release date, she would be one of the first to buy a copy as she had devoured with relish every one of his novels to date. Daniels too had improved and extended his range of conversational topics—probably due to Ingrid's tutoring or her private admonishing, but he had done nothing to dilute his clucking.

As the evening progressed the effects of the meal and the wonderful array of fine wines seemed to have taken their toll on Daniels and his heavy eyes soon became noticeable. Deacon on the other hand was just getting into the party mood. Ingrid looked over at her nodding husband and spoke to Richard: "I do apologise for this Richard, it's so embarrassing, but he has been working very hard lately. Would you mind terribly if I packed him off to bed?"

Deacon looked at his watch, "What a shame, I was just beginning to loosen up; still it is time I was on my way I suppose."

Ingrid laughed, "Oh no Richard, I'm not suggesting you should leave, quite the opposite, I haven't had a night like this in months, you are not going anywhere. I will put him to bed and we will resume where we left off."

Ingrid roused Daniels and he woke just long enough to clumsily shake Deacon's hand and mumble a drunken good night before Ingrid escorted him up to bed. She returned minutes later looking as radiant as ever. She refreshed Deacon's glass just as a member of the temporary staff knocked lightly on the door to announce that they were done and ready to leave. Ingrid thanked them and saw them out. It was just turned eleven o'clock when she and Deacon found themselves virtually alone in the house. "Thank you Ingrid for a first class evening," Deacon said as he raised his glass. "It has been a pleasure Richard," she smiled, "What are your plans for the immediate future?" she added.

He shrugged his shoulders. "Do you know, I haven't really thought about it," he said.

"Why don't you take a break, go on holiday somewhere?"

"Where would I go?"

"That would depend on what you want, wouldn't it?" Ingrid said.

"At this moment, I don't know what I want," he said, "I am just enjoying your company and your husband's whisky," he added with a smile.

"In that case, why don't you go somewhere quiet, somewhere different, until you decide what you want? It seems to me that you have reached a certain crossroads and you don't know which road to take; am I right?" she asked.

"Your powers of persuasion are almost as keen as your powers of perception Ingrid. Let's pretend for a moment that I am going to take your advice, where—in your opinion—would be suitably quiet and suitably different to stimulate a thought pattern conducive to long term planning?"

Ingrid thought for a moment: "I think I have the perfect place. A few years ago Malcolm and I rented a beautiful secluded villa in the heart of the French countryside; it was down near a place called Angouleme. It was perfect in every way, I would live there tomorrow if I had my way Richard; it really was Heaven on Earth."

"What was it about the place that makes you talk of it in such poetic prose?" he asked.

"It had peace, tranquillity and above all it had an indescribable air of medieval romance," she said as her eyes misted over with whimsical longing at the thought.

"It sounds quite special," Deacon whispered not wanting to dispel the magic of the moment.

Then—like a scene from Cinderella—the front doorbell rang and as Deacon instinctively looked at his watch Ingrid was brought out of her reverie. It was exactly seven minutes to midnight. "That will be my man," Deacon said, "it's time for me to leave."

"You are more than welcome to stay the night Richard," Ingrid said.

"Thank you Ingrid but I must be getting along, I have had a most wonderful evening and like all good things it has come to an end," he said.

Ingrid put her arms around him and gave him a kiss, "You look after yourself Richard Deacon and consider what we talked about."

"I will," he said as he turned and made his way to the front door. James was there holding the door of the Bentley open. Deacon looked up at the dark night sky and realised that it was raining quite heavily, he walked quickly down the steps and into the car. As James pulled slowly away Deacon leaned forward to take a last look at Ingrid. She stood alone like the statue of liberty as her evening gown fluttered in the breeze. The rain on the car window made her look distorted but that only added to the seductive beauty of her mystique. *Daniels, you lucky dog.*

62

Chapter Ten

Deacon arrived home safely—and relatively sober—at half past midnight. James had no need to put him to bed, he put the car away instead and called a taxi on his mobile phone to take him home. Inside the house Deacon went through to the drawing room and poured himself a large whisky. He kicked his shoes off and sat by the open fire that Maria had thoughtfully lit for his return. It had been a while since Maria had left but she had put plenty of coal on to last well into the early hours and Deacon was grateful. There was no finer feeling as far as he was concerned than the heat of a real fire on his face and the glowing warmth of a real whisky in his chest.

As he looked abstractedly into the dancing, swirling, brightly coloured flames his mind drifted back to his conversation with Ingrid about her suggestion of a break. Perhaps a trip abroad wasn't such a bad idea. The fire threw shadows all around the room in the subdued light and the only sound was that of the low crackling as the burning coal released its gasses trapped there a million years before. Suddenly the ringing of the telephone on the table at his side reverberated through the room and Deacon let it ring several times before he answered. He was pleasantly surprised to hear Ingrid's voice at the other end of the line.

"Hello Richard, I hope I haven't disturbed you."

"Not at all Ingrid," he said, "As a matter of fact I was just thinking about you."

"I just called to make sure you made it home safely, but now I am intrigued as to why I was on your mind," she said playfully.

"I was thinking of what you said about me getting away for a break, somewhere quiet and reflective where I could think about my next move. The more I think about it the more I think you could be absolutely right."

"Well at the risk of repeating myself Richard, I think it's the best thing you could possibly do right now," Ingrid said.

Deacon took a sip from his glass. "That place you mentioned, how big is it?"

"Angouleme, it's perhaps the same size as York. Why do you ask?"

"I didn't mean the city, I meant the villa you and Daniels rented."

"Oh the villa, it was massive. It was a kind of cross between a chateau and a small stately home."

"Hhmm, that sounds a little too much like this place, I would want something that I wouldn't rattle around in, perhaps a three bedroom farmhouse, something of that nature anyway. Do you know of any places like that in that region?" he asked.

"We really must be on the same wavelength tonight Richard, as the words left your mouth a picture of my friend's house just popped into my mind. We met a lovely old couple who are originally from Bristol whilst we were there and they invited us over for dinner one evening. Their place was the quaintest little house I have ever seen, straight out of a storybook. It was a delightful little farmhouse set in about two acres of garden and surrounded by open fields. The fields were in-turn surrounded by woodland, it was beautiful."

"Are you still in touch with them?" Deacon asked.

"Yes we write every now and then, Christmas and birthdays," Ingrid said, "you know how it is."

Deacon took another sip of whisky and mentally slipped his business hat on.

"Are you doing anything special tomorrow Ingrid?" Deacon asked.

"Nothing that can't wait; why?" Ingrid asked, a little bemused at the apparent change in the direction of the conversation.

"Because I want you to contact your friend and buy her cottage for me," Deacon said in the same matter-of-fact manner as one might order a take-away meal.

Ingrid forgot momentarily who she was talking to and she laughed impulsively. "I can't do that Richard."

Deacon was genuinely puzzled by her reaction. "Why not?" he asked.

It was then that Ingrid remembered who she was talking to and she quickly got hold of herself. "I don't think my friends would ever consider selling their home for any price. It's their retirement home, the culmination of their life's labours. They would perhaps rent it to you for a month or so," she said.

"Ingrid, if there is one thing I have learned in all my years in business, it is that everyone and everything has a price. Some people ask for more than others, but at the end of the day everything is for sale. You must have an idea of the value of your friend's property; you have my permission to offer her three times its current market value. If that doesn't work then get back to me and I will make the offer even sweeter. Will you do that for me?"

The final sentence was said in such a way that it meant, 'you *will* do it for me'. Suddenly she felt a chill through her whole body; firstly at the prospect of even approaching her friends with Deacon's offer—even though it was vastly inflated—and secondly, because of the cynicism with which Deacon broached the whole subject. He wasn't offering to buy apples from a market stall he was offering to buy someone's dreams for Christ's sake! She began to regret having mentioned her friend's cottage at all, or even the whole idea of a holiday. Yet she knew that if she didn't approach them with Deacon's offer then he would do it through her husband and he would stop at nothing to please his main benefactor.

"Are you still there Ingrid?" Deacon asked after a long pause in the conversation.

"Er, yes Richard, I'm still here," Ingrid stammered, still reeling from suddenly finding herself in the terrible position of go-between that she had inadvertently talked herself into.

"Good, get some rest then Ingrid and let me have the verdict tomorrow evening. And thank you again for a most wonderful dinner tonight," Deacon said cheerfully.

"Bye then," was the most Ingrid could muster as she put the receiver down and began to reflect on what had just taken place. *My God, what have I done to those poor people? Why couldn't I have kept my big mouth shut?* Ingrid could hardly take in the fact that one minute she was making a final phone call that would round off a perfect evening—knowing that her guest was safely home—and the next minute Deacon had thrown her life into such guilt-ridden turmoil. *What a cold, distorted view of the world he must have; I'm beginning to understand now why Eleanor is divorcing him.*

With that thought in mind she poured herself a large brandy and swallowed it in one gulp. *Goodnight Richard, I hope you sleep better than I will tonight.*

Deacon went back to watching the flames in the fire blissfully oblivious to the consternation he had just caused. He reached over the table for a remote control handset and from his seated position he pointed it in the direction of the quadraphonic sound system. He closed his eyes and mentally conducted the London Philharmonic Orchestra playing Dvorak's 'Going Home'.

Chapter Eleven

Deacon woke surprisingly early on Sunday morning; he looked at the clock and it was just leaving seven o'clock. *A perfect start to what I hope will be a perfect day.* He lay in bed until the clock turned to seven minutes past seven and he jumped out of bed feeling on top of the world. He sensed that things were beginning to look up, even the birds' songs sounded more optimistic than they had on previous mornings. His head was clear and as he drew back the drapes as the sunlight streamed into the room illuminating it with a brilliant golden glow. He went through to the bathroom and began to run a bath. No sooner had he turned on the taps than he changed his mind. *A drive in the country is what I need right now. I'll take the Morgan for a spin.*

He dressed quickly in a heavy check shirt and thick corduroy trousers; he finished his attire off with his favourite Harris Tweed jacket. He tied an old fashioned pilot's scarf around his neck and put on a white 1920's golfing cap. He looked in the mirror and smiled at the reflection smiling back at him; he looked like The Great Gatsby.

Ignoring breakfast he went out to the garage and fired up the Morgan, it had been a birthday gift from his father twenty five years earlier and it was in the same pristine condition as the day he acquired it. During those twenty five years it has clocked up a mere three thousand miles and neither its flawless bodywork or its luxurious upholstery had endured one single drop of rain. At the rear of the house he looked up at the clear cloudless sky to make sure that there was absolutely no chance of it happening on that day either. He revved the engine just to listen to the sound of engineering perfection. Where he might go had not even been thought of, all a Morgan needs is a few miles of open road and the driver will be in Paradise. All his other vehicles had been bought for their practicality but his father's gift of the Morgan was his one and only motoring indulgence—it was his *baby.*

The conditions for a run in the country could not have been better, the bright sun rising so early had burned off the morning dew, the sky was crystal clear and the air over the sprawling countryside was fresh and still. He drove the Morgan out onto the driveway and where it met the lane at the end he turned left and headed east away from civilisation. Between his house and the sea thirty miles along the road there was nothing but idyllic farmsteads that seemed to have been trapped in a time warp since the Great War and mile upon mile of open countryside. His scarf fluttered in the slipstream as he went up through the gearbox until he was at cruising speed and anyone fortunate enough to have experienced what Deacon was feeling would realise that it was right up there with the ultimate thrill.

The road before him turned first one way then the other, down into dips and up around hairpin bends; a car like that needs to be driven and Deacon was putting it through its paces. On straight stretches of open road he gunned the accelerator to the floor and the Morgan responded like a thoroughbred racehorse; two strides and it was in full flight, a glorious, pulsating example of what can be produced when man and God work in harmony.

It seemed as though only minutes had gone by before the unmistakable waft of fresh sea air filled his lungs; over the next rise in the road was the vast expanse of the old, cold North Sea. Once over the brow of the rise Deacon pulled over into a rough dirt lay-by and cut the engine. Silence immediately descended on the scene. In the distance he could see the ripples on the water made golden by the sunlight on its surface, its whole mass was like a shimmering blanket pulled tight from the shoreline to the horizon. *What would Van Gogh give to be here with me and to be able to capture this?*

The water was calling him with the same heavenly song of the sirens that drove Ulysses to temporary insanity. Unable to resist he fired up the Morgan and drove down the hill to the secluded, deserted beach. He leapt from the car and threw his jacket along with his cap and scarf onto the seat behind him, then, as if mesmerised by the song of the sea about his ears he walked slowly to the water's edge shedding his clothes as he went. Naked he waded in until the water reached halfway up his thigh, then he allowed his whole body to relax and he plunged into the next wave head first. Even though he was fully submerged his mind was surprisingly clear, he suddenly had a vision of John the Baptist standing over him at the river Jordan, chanting some ancient Aramaic words over him as his soul was symbolically purged of its original sin. The shock of the ice-cold water against his warm skin was exhilarating but the sensation was most definitely not unpleasant. A few moments later he rose like Neptune from the waves and opened his mouth wide to gulp in a great lung full of air. The water cascaded off his muscular upper body and he raised his arms above his head like a triumphant pugilist. Invigorated, almost euphoric he made his way majestically back to the sandy beach. Without bothering to dry his body he began to replace his clothing until he was back at the car and fully dressed except for his socks and shoes. Over to his right the ground rose to a grassy mound that was perhaps fifteen feet higher than the ground he was on. He slung his jacket over his shoulder and walked to the top of the mound. From there he had a panoramic view of three hundred and sixty degrees, the countryside he had just driven through seemed to billow away like a ground hugging patchy green mist and the sea before him—his baptismal font—was a carpet of cerulean blue. He sat on the grass to take in and savour the unspoilt beauty of his surroundings. As he closed his eyes to brand the image onto his mind for future reference his Utopia was shattered by the sudden beeping of his mobile phone. Deacon turned reluctantly and visibly deflated to the sound emitting from his jacket pocket. *Did whomever invented you have any idea of the possible extent of your bloody intrusiveness? Did they not foresee that you were imbued with the potential to make even the most fertile moment so miserably impotent?*

Despite his mental protests he reached into his pocket and looked at the screen of the mobile phone. Considering the day was Sunday he was surprised to see the name 'Meeks' in bold black letters, it was his publisher.

Deacon pushed the answer button and put the phone to his ear. "Hello Deacon here."

"Hello Richard, I apologise for calling you like this, I tried you at home but you were obviously out. It's totally inappropriate I know but I just had to talk to you immediately," Meeks said without pausing for breath.

Deacon's initial surprise was compounded into a fleeting feeling of anxiety. He knew that Meeks would not even dream of calling him unless it was most urgent and he did seem rather flustered.

"What is it that can't wait until Monday?" he asked bluntly.

"It's not that it can't wait until Monday Richard it's just that I don't want this to wait until Monday. I have just finished reading your manuscript, I have been up all night to get it finished and it has been a very long time since I was compelled to do such a thing. This manuscript Richard is simply the finest novel I have ever read bar none and I couldn't wait to tell you. Now if you are busy the rest of this conversation can be finished off at a more agreeable time, I just had to say that this is a stroke of pure literary genius, a masterpiece."

Deacon could hardly take in what he was hearing, he knew alright that his manuscript was good but he never imagined that it would warrant such a response, not from a chap with Meeks's experience anyway, he had worked with the best in the business for the most part of twenty years. "That's very kind of you to say so Meeks and thank you so much for calling to let me know." Then with an uncharacteristic stab at impromptu humour he added rather clumsily, "And I'm sorry to have kept you up all night."

"Don't mention it Richard it was my pleasure. Just one question before I let you go Richard if I might?" Meeks said.

"Of course, go ahead."

"How on earth did you come up with all this? I mean usually a story has peaks and troughs but this one never lets up, I could hardly catch my breath," Meeks said obviously deeply impressed.

Deacon's reply wasn't exactly the stuff of novels that Meeks was hoping he would be treated to. "I wrote it just like all the others, I sat in front of a blank screen and wrote down whatever tumbled from my brain and hoped that at the end it would all make sense."

Deacon's reply was a little white lie; in fact I would go as far as to say that it was an outrageous untruth and one worthy of perjury in any courtroom. But it was in keeping with the way he worked. If he could keep the secret of his work to himself then it would be up to others to speculate and so add the element of mystery to any future hype...the kind of hype that sells books by the million.

Before Deacon wrote the first word of his latest novel he had promised himself that it was going to be something special, something extraordinary. All his novels that had gone before were to act as his training ground for it and he was determined to bring his experience and accumulated literary maturity to bear on every syllable. Whatever *tumbled* from his brain was scrutinised from every angle before it was committed to the page. He was known as a man who liked to consume more alcohol than was good for him but during his time writing his latest novel he had often worked well into the night and often after ten hours of hard sober graft he only had one sentence that he was satisfied with and on more than one occasion he was left with just one word at the end of a marathon writing session. His love for writing and his obsessive behaviour had possibly become entangled and if that was the case then the world of literature was all the wealthier for it, because his obsessive determination to produce the perfect novel had—in the eyes of Meeks—come to wonderful fruition. Deacon had contrived to make every sentence flow with the rhythm and music of a well constructed poem and every chapter would tell its own story. Charged and driven by his unique imagination and infused with all the esoteric literary devices known only to a handful of writers across the globe and used to lure the hearts and minds of readers like insects to a Venus flytrap. Once intoxicated they are captives forever, helpless, yet demanding to be teased and tortured at the whim of the master.

"Well Richard," Meeks said, "Wherever this novel tumbled from I'm glad that it landed in my lap. This not only has all the hallmarks of a best–seller Richard, this is going to break records all over the world, well done."

Meeks's childlike enthusiasm and his breathless machinegun rat-a-tat delivery during the conversation and of course its content had an immediate affect on Deacon. He was lifted once again to the heights of emotional satisfaction that he had reached before the telephone rang with the help of his natural surroundings. For the first time in his life he felt complete, he had aimed for the moon and he had reached the stars. Despite his highly charged emotional state he did not let his guard down for one moment, that would have been a luxury too far and one not in keeping with the situation. Instead of metaphorically leaping down the phone to hug Meeks, Deacon simply said: "Thank you Meeks, no doubt we will be in touch over the coming months." With that he ended the conversation by pressing the end-call button.

Under any other circumstances Meeks might have felt that his conversation was somewhat of an anti-climax but he had known well before he picked up the phone to call Deacon that what followed was likely to be unpredictable. The fact that Deacon had thanked him for his trouble made his efforts well worthwhile. He also had the added satisfaction of knowing that he was clutching the manuscript of the best novel ever written to his chest and it was going to make him wealthy beyond his wildest dreams.

Deacon let the phone drop from his hand and onto his jacket. He walked the few steps to the edge of the mound and looked out to sea. A warm gentle breeze began to blow into his face and he breathed in deeply. He watched a seagull in flight as it skimmed several feet above the surface of the sea. As he followed its course he saw it veer upwards and off to its right as if it had suddenly remembered that it had somewhere else to be. The full implications of Meeks's conversation began to sink in and Deacon opened his arms as if to embrace the scene before him as a long lost friend. "Wherever you are now you gorgeous creature of creation," he called to the sea, "Thank you for bringing me the light and shining it from the first word to the last. Together we have secured immortality my beautiful queen."

He hoped that the elusive muse that had rescued him and nursed him on those dark sterile nights could hear his heartfelt thanks, for she was as deserving of the laurel leaves as he was.

Deacon took one last look at the panorama and headed back to the car. He brushed the sand from his feet and put on his socks and shoes and the rest of his driving paraphernalia. Within the hour he was gliding gracefully back up the driveway of the house to let the Morgan slumber in pampered, air-conditioned luxury until the following summer.

Chapter Twelve

Deacon was in the bath washing the sand and saltwater from his body when Maria knocked lightly on the door in the early afternoon to let him know that she was in the house.

"It's Maria Mr Richard. Can I get you anything?" she asked.

"No thank you Maria, I will be in my study most of the afternoon and I will take a light snack at seven minutes to three," he said.

Maria carried on with her duties as Deacon lounged in the bath for a further half hour. Just after one o'clock he dressed and went through into his study. He took down a large atlas from one of the oak bookshelves and opened it up on his desk. *Let's see now, Angouleme, where are you?* He found the pages for France and began to run his eyes over the contours of the map. He had never really had a close look at France before—he had had no reason to until then. The first place that caught his eye was inevitably Paris, that great shining jewel of culture, of romance and of course haut cuisine. But soon his eyes were drawn westwards to the curious outcrop of land at the northern end of the Bay of Biscay. It looked like a giant dragon's head spitting fire out into the Atlantic Ocean. Brest was its flared nostril and Chateaulin was at the base of its tongue of fire. He followed the coastline down to Lorient and further down still to St Nazaire. There didn't seem to be much but open countryside below that until he reached La Rochelle. From there it was just a short hop to the place he was looking for…Angouleme. His eyes widened when he saw something familiar and exciting…Cognac! *Ah yes, I might have known that you would not be very far from the belly of France.*

Angouleme seemed to be—at a rough guess—about one hundred and fifty kilometres from the coast. Like most medieval cities it was built on the banks of a river, in this case the river Charente which rose in the mountains of Limousin to the east and heaved its way majestically to the ocean in the west.

Deacon sat back in his chair and tried to picture the region around Angouleme, he could tell from the map that it was an agricultural area, and the fact that it was neighbouring the brandy capital of the world was another giveaway that mile after mile of countryside would be dedicated to the growing of grapes and the production of France's answer to the highland malt. He could almost taste the angels share as its evaporating nectar left the maturing cellars and drifted tantalizingly upwards to Heaven.

He was about to explore the region beyond the Massif Central when the internal telephone burst into life. He lifted the receiver without taking his eyes from the map, "Hello Maria, what is it?"

"I have Mrs Daniels on the other line and she is asking to speak to you. Shall I put her through?"

"I'll take it in the drawing room Maria, just give me a minute and put her through. I'll take some tea whilst I'm there too Maria, there's a good girl," he said.

He went down to the drawing room and lifted the receiver. "Ingrid how nice of you to call, and thanks again for last night, I've been in fine form ever since."

"That's very kind of you to say so Richard," Ingrid said, "And I'm glad that you are in such fine form because what I have to say is likely to put you in even finer form if that's possible."

"The way the cards have been falling for me lately Ingrid anything is possible. I take it your friend has agreed to sell?" he said confidently.

"It's even better news than that. I must admit Richard I was reluctant to put your offer—generous though it was—to my friend because I know how much the place means to her. I had spent the morning running over in my head how to put it to her and not two minutes into the conversation—and without me mentioning a word—she told me that she had put the house on the market only last week. Isn't that amazing?"

"That's an incredible coincidence," Deacon said, "Why is she selling?"

"Her husband has not been keeping too well lately and they have reluctantly decided that they would be better off with a smaller place closer to the sea. To maintain a house and garden like that, one has to be fully fit and active."

"It would seem that their loss is my gain. Will you tell them that I will cover the cost of their removals?" he said.

"You just leave everything to me," Ingrid said cheerfully, "I will be in touch soon when everything has been finalised and settled."

"Thank you for everything Ingrid. You have made a perfect day even better, and the next time we meet, you and Daniels will be my dinner guests and you are in for a treat you will remember for a very long time."

Deacon and Ingrid said their goodbyes just as Maria entered the drawing room with his afternoon tea.

"When are you thinking of leaving Maria? Deacon asked as she laid the tray of tea on the coffee table.

"Around five o'clock Mr Richard," Maria answered.

"No, what I meant was, when are you leaving my employment to go to university?" he said.

Maria's stomach did a somersault, she had given him one months notice the week before but she had put all thoughts about it out of her head ever since so that she could cope with it emotionally. His casual question put like that was like a hammer blow but she had to stay cool and collected. "I suppose it will be on the last day of June," Maria said trying and succeeding to sound as casual as Deacon. "Will that be suitable for you?" she added.

"Well if everything else goes to plan then your leaving should coincide nicely with my leaving," he smiled.

Maria was surprised for a second time. "I thought you would live here forever Mr Richard, why are you leaving and where are you going?" she asked.

Deacon could see that besides being surprised, she was genuinely concerned. "Nothing is forever Maria. The unexpected termination of your employment here substantiates that fact. But don't worry about my leaving here; it's only a temporary arrangement. I'm taking a long overdue vacation for a short while in a cottage I have acquired in France. Don't you wish you could come along with me?"

Maria suddenly had the opportunity to quickly reconsider her decision to leave. *No, I made my mind up to leave for all the right reasons and those reasons haven't changed despite his allusion to the fact that nothing is forever. Friendship and loyalty are forever Mr Richard, at least they are to some of us.*

"I think you deserve a good long break Mr Richard, but as for me wishing I was coming with you, I have had my own plans and my heart set on university for a long time now. Nothing could tempt me away from that," she said convincingly.

"Well, you can't blame me for trying one last time Maria. What sort of a dependant would I be if I didn't try?" he laughed.

Maria determinedly forced her mind onto more practical things to keep herself focused. "Who will look after this place whilst you are away?" she asked.

"See, now that is a perfect example of why I am dependent on you Maria. I haven't given that point any brain room at all," he said.

"Why don't you ask James to keep his eye on the place when he comes over to check on the cars?" she said.

"This is exactly why you are worth your weight in whisky Maria. Will you see to it for me? You could also ask his wife if she would like to call in here once a week and flick round with a duster whilst James is working on the cars. Tell her I will make it worth her while."

Maria saw that as an ideal opportunity to dismiss herself. "I'll see to it right away Mr Richard, will that be all?" she asked.

Deacon nodded, "Yes that's all Maria, I'll finish my tea in here and then I'm going back to my study. There shouldn't be any other calls but if there are, put them off until Monday, I've had enough contact with the outside world for one day."

Maria saw Deacon very briefly once more that weekend; that was when she took him his light snack at seven minutes to three. He hardly looked up from his desk as she placed the tray on the table on the right hand side of the room. She said goodbye and told him that she had made the arrangements with James and his wife and that everything was in order. He nodded as if he was lost in thought as he wrote something on a notepad on his desk. She added that she would see him in the morning; she left the house just after five o'clock.

As she drove home she began to think how quickly the week had flown by and how quickly her remaining time there would pass. She thought about all the things she would miss about the place, but no matter how hard she tried the only thought that kept coming back to her and filling her mind so completely was how much she was going to miss that *crazy old devil* Deacon.

Chapter Thirteen

A week had past since Ingrid had been in touch with Deacon about the cottage and although nothing appeared to have been happening she had been very busy securing the transaction with quiet efficiency. She had no need to contact Deacon about the financial aspects of the purchase because her husband had the authority to release the money once the papers had been signed and a figure had been agreed. In those high-powered business circles deals are concluded fairly quickly by ordinary standards. Buying a cottage to Deacon and his associates would be similar to a housewife popping to the local store to buy a loaf of bread.

The contracts were duly signed and within the week Ingrid's friends had vacated the property and were heading for temporary accommodation on the west coast. With £200.000 of Deacon's money in their bank they were in no rush to buy something just for the sake of it. They could afford to relax and shop around; the rush for them had been to make it to the ocean, so with the main objective achieved it appeared that everyone had done well out of the deal.

Two days after the cottage was vacated, the keys arrived by courier at the Daniel's house and Ingrid began planning a nice surprise for Deacon. She thought she would have some fun by putting the keys on a red velvet cushion and delivering them to him personally. She knew Deacon well enough to know that in order for the joke to work she would have to go through Maria and let her in on her little ruse. The timing of such a thing would have to be precise. She would have to catch him off guard, in a receptive mood and relaxed and he was very rarely in any one of those conditions let alone all three. Maria's help in the matter would be vital.

Ingrid called Maria the following day and explained her clandestine plan. She wanted to catch Deacon in his study totally unawares and present him with the keys rather like one might surprise a work colleague with a birthday cake or a leaving gift. In order to do that Ingrid would have to make sure that Deacon would be where she wanted him and when. He being a creature of habit most of the time predicting his movements would not present too much of a problem. Maria said that the best time to catch him would be mid afternoon when he was most likely to be in his study. Sometimes he could be unpredictable but that was likely to be in the mornings. Ingrid saw the irony of Maria being able to predict when Deacon was most likely to be unpredictable.

It was arranged for Ingrid to drive over on the following day and park up in the lane at the end of the drive just out of sight; then she would call Maria from her mobile phone to check that the coast was clear and the deed would be done.

Maria put the receiver down and when she fully realised what she had agreed to she began to reflect on it. Under any other circumstances she would have accepted the prank at face value but in that situation and considering the people involved she couldn't help but try to analyse the whole thing in more detail. The thought itself was a lovely gesture and it would have been in keeping with a close knit office community, but somehow it didn't seem fitting to do something like that on this occasion, it would be wasted on Deacon, a man like him would find it highly embarrassing, perhaps even infantile. He would not appreciate the sense of fun intended, surely Ingrid knew him well enough to know that her intended actions were more likely to make him squirm than shriek with glee? *Perhaps she has another motive to get him alone in his study and in a playful mood?*

Maria's train of thought suddenly changed direction. What if her intentions were of an amorous nature? She began to visualise Ingrid entering Deacon's study with the keys on a velvet cushion in one hand and a bottle of Champagne in the other. She could see her wearing a full-length trench coat and very little else underneath. *Of course that's it! She is coming over to seduce him!* A pang of intense jealousy suddenly gripped her heart as in her mind's eye Deacon succumbed to Ingrid's advances. Deacon looked up from his desk in a state of semi-shock then smiled submissively as Ingrid slowly moved towards him. She put the cushion on the desk before him and walked seductively round to Deacon. She draped herself across his lap and allowed the trench coat to fall open just wide enough for him to see the ampleness of what was on offer besides the Champagne. The more the scene unfolded in her mind the more intense her jealousy became. Ingrid was by now peppering his neck with butterfly kisses as he ran his eager fingers through her tousled blonde hair. Maria's mind suddenly took off on a morality tangent. *How could she cheat on her husband like that? And how could he have such contempt for the wife of one of his most trusting associates? Hardly one week ago you dined at his house for Christ's sake!* Maria had worked her mind into such a state of frenzy that she didn't notice the ringing of the internal telephone until it was on its fourth ring. She quickly pulled herself together before she virtually sprinted the few steps to the wall where the phone was hanging.

"Hello," she said in as calm a voice as possible.

"Who was that on the phone just now Maria?" Deacon asked. "I heard it ring as I was on the landing, was it anything important?"

Blast! The one time ever in his life he wants to know who was on the phone and I can't tell him. Think fast girl or you are going to blow it!

"It was the grocer," she said again in a calm voice that belied her inner turmoil.

"What on earth would the grocer want?"

Any other time you irritating man you would have been happy with that answer, now you want an inquest!

Again Maria had to come up with a feasible answer to avoid any suspicion. "He just rang to say that he has noticed that he left the potatoes I asked for off the order and he wants to know if he can drop them off later."

"And what did you tell him?" Deacon asked, again totally out of character. He never took any interest in the running of the house so why all the questions? Maria suddenly saw a window of opportunity open that she could put to good use later if she played her cards right.

"I told him that I didn't need them desperately and he could drop them off when he was passing." Then to avoid further questioning she added: "He said he will be out this way just after lunch time tomorrow so he will deliver them then."

"Oh I see," Deacon said finally, "Could you bring some coffee up to my study?"

"Yes Mr Richard," Maria said before she put down the receiver and breathed out a huge sigh of relief. She had no idea that Deacon's interest in the phone call was because he was expecting a call from Meeks about production deadlines and he wanted to pencil them into his diary. The production deadlines would involve radio and television appearances as well as the usual attention from newspapers and the numerous editors of magazine features hoping for an exclusive scoop, but settling for what was offered anyway. His hope was that he could enjoy his break in France before the carousel of promotional events took over his life yet again for the foreseeable future.

Maria congratulated herself on having the presence of mind to tell Deacon that the grocer would deliver the potatoes tomorrow after lunch. That spark of inspiration would allow Ingrid to drive up to the house without Deacon wondering who it was if he should hear the engine approaching. That feeling of self-satisfaction was short lived however when she was struck by another thought which re-ignited her earlier chagrin—how easily she had lied to Deacon. *Oh my Lord! This deceitfulness, is it so virulent a virus that it can travel down the telephone line from a wanton mistress and infect the mind of an innocent housemaid?*

It was then that reality raised its head—a seemingly rare event in the Deacon household lately—and Maria forced her feet back firmly onto the ground. *Why should I care what Deacon and his friends get up to? Stop being so foolish Maria, Ingrid's motives are probably innocent anyway.*

What was really bothering Maria was that she did care; and perhaps even more telling was that the seduction scenes in her imagination between Deacon and Ingrid could well be rooted in one of her own private fantasies. For the rest of the day Maria went about her duties in silence and with an added efficiency wilfully designed to stifle at birth any extraneous thoughts.

Chapter Fourteen

Maria drove to work through a driving rainstorm on the morning of Ingrid's proposed surprise visit and she thanked her stars for that timely heavenly intervention. The windscreen wipers flapped furiously across the screen at full speed but Maria still had difficulty making out the road ahead. Despite the awful conditions it was better than sunshine because the heavy rain would almost certainly ensure that Deacon was snugly holed up for the day. He detested bad weather for walking in yet on the other hand he loved it because it often gave him inspiration for his writing. He loved nothing better than to watch bad weather from the warmth and comfort of his study—especially when he had the added comfort of a wee dram in his hand—the sight and sound of it never failed to fuel some part of his imagination. Maria tuned in the car radio to listen to the shipping forecast and what was bad news for the fishermen was music to her ears. *I hope those poor boys haven't left port just yet.*

Deacon was fast asleep when Maria looked in on him and from the sound of his stertorous breathing coupled with the sickly-sweet smell lingering in the bedroom she deduced that he had been no stranger to the malt whisky decanter on the previous night. To find him in that condition was potentially another good sign—whilst he was sleeping he couldn't cause trouble. She went about her duties with more care than she normally exacted so as not to make even the slightest noise. The longer she could keep him in bed—until lunch time at any rate—the better.

She looked in on him again just before eleven o'clock and he was still dead to the world. If he hadn't moved within the next half hour she would wake him so that at least he had a fighting chance of looking presentable for his surprise guest. He would hate to be roused from his drunken slumber, but Maria also knew that he would not be too pleased about her leaving him to rot once the surprise visit was out of the way. She was in on the plot—albeit reluctantly—so if it all went horribly wrong then inevitably she would bear the brunt of the blame. And if Maria had allowed Ingrid to find him bleary eyed and unshaven when she surprised him, that would mean things had gone horribly wrong from Deacon's post mortem perspective. With that thought in mind she went back to the kitchen and went about her work with one eye almost permanently fixed to the clock on the wall and one ear homed in on the internal telephone.

The clock moved painfully quickly round to half past eleven and still there was no sign of life stirring in the master bedroom. This meant that Maria was now presented with another major problem—on what pretext to wake him? She had to think of something that would not only wake him but also make it necessary for him to get out of bed. She drummed her fingers on the kitchen tabletop as she set her mind to work. *I'll tell him that I want to change the bed sheets. No, he would only tell me to come back later. I'll tell him that he has had an important telephone call. No, that will have to be followed through and substantiated and it could back-fire rather cruelly spoiling everything.* No matter what she thought of, it was quite evident that nothing was in the least bit feasible. *What an awkward man you are!* Eventually she reached the cold conclusion that she would have to take the bull by the horns and perhaps sacrifice herself for the greater glory of the prank. She decided to use the tried and trusted housewife's favourite, the one that has been *innocently* employed by women the world over ever since the dawn of the household appliance revolution to exhort a little devilish payback on the hung-over husband, the old vacuum cleaner on the landing technique! Once she realised that she had found the only possible solution she wasted no time at all in putting it into practice.

Once Maria got to work Deacon's first thoughts were that the Russians had invaded and that a T34 tank was about to smash its way into his bedroom at any moment with all guns blazing. "What the hell is going on out there?" he demanded when the real source of the din occurred to him through the dust and confusion of battle. Maria—mindful of the fact that if she stopped after the initial assault that he would try to re-settle—continued as if she couldn't hear him. "Shut that infernal racket up!" he shouted.

That's it lazy bones, get angry and get out of bed. Maria thought as she rammed the machine from hell against the foot of his bedroom door. Deacon could stand it no longer, the pain in his head was as though a pneumatic drill was about to enter his head through the crown of his skull. He flung the duvet back and staggered to his feet, swaying momentarily like a stunned boxer who hadn't seen the vicious right cross that had floored him seconds earlier. He blinked his puffy eyes several times and when he found his bearings he made for the door like a scalded rhino. He almost tore the door off its hinges in his eagerness to silence the beast. He looked out onto the landing and the first thing he saw was the manufactured—and well rehearsed—look of shock and horror on *poor* Maria's face. Before he had chance to vent his anger Maria flicked off the noise and began her sincerest apologies. "Oh Mr Richard you gave me such a fright! The place was so quiet this morning I thought you had gone out early. Oh Mr Richard my hands are shaking, will you look at yourself, you look like a ghost, are you alright Sir?"

Maria's *attack is the best form of defence* tactics paid off spectacularly as Deacon stood speechless in the doorway of his bedroom like a ticked off schoolboy. She had managed to convince him with those well delivered lines that she was in fact the wounded party. "I do apologise Maria," Deacon stammered as he hung his head in a combination of acute head pain, sorrow and shame. "I didn't mean to give you such a start, I just didn't know what all the racket was about. Heavy night, you know how it is?"

Maria managed to *pull herself together* surprisingly quickly. "You don't look too well Mr Richard; shall I run you a nice hot bath?"

"You are a life-saver Maria; that would be most excellent."

"I'll do it this minute," she smiled.

Then before he could protest at what she was about to do she brushed past him in the doorway and opened the drapes. Deacon stumbled to the bed and sat on the end of it facing his dressing table mirror. He rubbed the top of his sore head and clicked his tongue against the roof of his mouth in an attempt to generate some saliva to moisten his parched mouth. He looked up and saw the sorry reflection staring back at him. *No wonder you nearly gave the poor girl a heart attack.*

Maria went though to the bathroom as he sat on the bed and reflected on what a wonderful personal assistant Maria was. If he had known the truth behind his rude awakening he would have cheerfully strangled her. Since the beginning of time men have deluded themselves into thinking that they are the smarter sex, but on certain issues—namely who's fooling who—women were sending rockets to the moon whilst men were still chasing Woolley Mammoths across the frozen tundra.

Maria breezed back into the bedroom. "Your bath will be ready in two minutes Mr Richard," she smiled sweetly.

Deacon half turned to her from his position on the bed, his head was still too tender to turn fully to face her. "You are an angel Maria, an absolute angel," he whispered.

"Will there be anything else sir?" she asked.

"What time is it?" he asked.

"It's eleven fifty."

"Give me one hour, then bring some coffee and an assortment of biscuits through to my study and hold any calls until further notice," he said. "Oh and bring me a large glass of ice cold water immediately."

Perfect! Maria thought. *If Ingrid rings whilst he is in the bath she can be the one to deliver his coffee and biscuits and the keys to his new house. What a surprise that will be.*

Things were indeed perfect. At twelve twenty five the telephone rang and Maria pounced on it after the first ring. Ingrid was out in the lane waiting for the right moment to drive in un-noticed. Maria told her to wait for ten more minutes then make her way in; Maria would meet her at the front of the house. Then, just to be on the safe side Maria went upstairs and tapped lightly on the bathroom door. Deacon was laying in the bath which was filled to the brim; he had a wet flannel covering his face. "Yes Maria," he muffled through the cloth.

"That was the grocer just now on the phone, he will be here in ten minutes, I will see to him then I will bring your coffee through," she said.

"Yes that's fine Maria," he muffled again.

She went to the front door and looked down the driveway. She saw the bonnet of Ingrid's car appearing round the stone gate posts precisely as planned. As the car drew closer Maria craned her neck to try to steal a preview of what Ingrid was wearing. *Any sign of a designer trench coat?*

Ingrid's usually gleaming white Mercedes convertible had been tarnished by the bad weather and the spray from the mud splattered country lane, but Ingrid still looked every inch the elegant lady as she opened the door and gracefully emerged preceded by a Gianfranco Ferre umbrella. Maria couldn't take her eyes off Ingrid's slender legs…which were tastefully covered by a pair of the latest Gucci trousers. "Thank you so much for helping me to pull this off Maria," Ingrid smiled as she made her way to the rear of the car to collect the cushion from the boot, "I can't wait to see his face."

Maria was immediately taken by a warm rush of what she initially perceived as a kind of scented breeze. She quickly realised that it was in fact a combination of Ingrid's natural aura and her own instincts picking up on the genuine sweet disposition of the beautiful woman before her. Her previous fears of there being an ulterior motive for Ingrid's visit were fully dispelled with Ingrid's unexpected request. "I have booked a table for the three of us as a kind of celebration luncheon for later this afternoon, please will you join us Maria? I really can't thank you enough for this and you are as much a part of the surprise as I am."

"Let's get inside out of this dreadful rain first," Maria said as she led Ingrid up the steps.

The two of them went silently through to the kitchen and immediately put their heads together to plan the final approach to his study like two mischievous schoolgirls. Ingrid took the keys from her handbag and placed them on the cushion. Then she produced a pink ribbon which she lovingly tied around the keys in a bow. "There, that's perfect," she said as she looked admiringly at her creation. Maria looked at the clock as it moved closer to ten minutes to one. "His study is the third door on the right off the middle landing, but mind you wait until seven minutes to, he has a thing about that," Maria whispered.

"We're doing this together Maria," Ingrid smiled, "You're not getting out of it that easily. His face will be an absolute picture of childlike confusion and it will be far too funny for you to miss," she added. "You knock on the door and ask to go in then allow me to go first. It will be such a hoot; he won't know what to do," she giggled.

The two women crept up the main stairway and stood silently outside his study door. Maria knocked and they both took a deep breath. "Come in Maria," Deacon said. The bath had obviously helped to revitalise his powers of speech so that was a promising first sign. Maria opened the door and Ingrid stepped in moving towards him like a regal pageboy bearing gifts to a royal personage. Maria quickly stepped in behind and to her right to catch a glimpse of Deacon's all important initial reaction. He looked up and his jaw dropped like an anvil before his face cracked into the biggest smile Maria had ever seen him produce. "What's all this?" he laughed as Ingrid bowed before his desk and laid the cushion in front of him.

"The keys to your new kingdom m' lord," Ingrid smiled, "and a crash course in French thrown in as part of the service."

"Did you know about this?" Deacon asked turning to Maria.

"Of course I did," she smiled shyly, "Did you really believe that I didn't know that you were in the house this morning?"

"You mean all that business with the vacuum cleaner this morning was part of the set up?"

"I felt really bad about having to resort to that Mr Richard but I couldn't let you spoil Mrs Daniel's painstaking plans could I?"

"Well I did wonder," he said, then turning back to Ingrid he asked: "And what's all this about a crash course in French?"

"Just a few basics Richard, nothing to fret over; when in France you will need to be able to indicate food to avoid starvation for instance. And that is quite simple, you point to the item on the menu that looks most appetising and you say *d'accord,* it works remarkably well. Then you point to the wine list, move your finger down the page and exclaim *La!* Whilst pointing to your chosen vintage. And should you require a drop of the hard stuff you simply say *Scotch* that is the only word in the English language that is universally understood. That my dear just about sums it up; now find yourself a smart tie because the three of us are going out for an obscenely expensive lunch."

Deacon rose to his feet smiling like a dolphin and he held out his arms to embrace Ingrid. As he wrapped his arms around the smiling Ingrid, Maria stood and watched in amazement, it was the first time she had ever seen him have any kind of physical contact with another human being other than the briefest of handshakes. After a moment or two he let go of Ingrid with one arm and beckoned for Maria to join their embrace. Unsure at first she waited for an inward turn of his wrist which indicated a second invitation. Still uncertain but conscious of the fact that she could ruin the moment if she didn't accept she moved towards him and he clasped his open arm around her. The three of them stood for a moment in that unlikely huddle. Maria could smell the freshness of his recently bathed skin through the fabric of his shirt and the sweetness of it contrasted sharply with the feel of his surprisingly hard muscular body.

"If I need a crash course in French my dear Ingrid I only have to ask Maria, she speaks it like a native," Deacon said as he relaxed his playful hold on the women.

"Yes Richard but the French can sometimes react very curiously to someone speaking their language badly. They don't seem to have the same tolerance or respect as we do for people who try to *have a go* as it were and get it wrong. Some of them seem to be of the opinion that if you can't speak it fluently you shouldn't bother at all."

"And what do you think Maria?" Deacon asked.

"Some French people in the channel ports can be quite amusing—some might say ignorant—when they hear English people struggling with their beautiful language. They immediately start to speak in equally bad English believing that they will be perfectly understood. The air of sanctimonious satisfaction about them has to be seen to be appreciated. But don't worry, once you travel beyond the coastal regions where people speak only French you can get by on the universal language of hand signals and smiles." Then—and with an unperceivable sideswipe aimed at Deacon—she added, "Some of my most interesting conversations have been conducted with little more than a grunt."

"Precisely," Deacon agreed, "A determined man can make himself understood anywhere on the planet." Then with a deft arm movement with the finesse of a Flamenco Dancer he slipped his hands from their shoulders and planted them firmly into the small of their backs and gave a discreet guiding push towards the door. "Right, enough of this idle chatter, if you ladies retire to the drawing room and give me half an hour to get ready I shall join you for lunch."

Maria escorted Ingrid to the drawing room and made sure that she was comfortable before she went back upstairs to lay out Deacon's tie. As she was trawling through his tie collection hanging neatly in the built-in wardrobe for one that would suit the occasion Deacon appeared and asked Maria to run him a bath. She was just about to remind him that he had only just taken a bath when she turned and saw him begin to delicately unbutton his clean shirt. Unaware that he was being watched he was clearly being careful not to touch the shirt on the sides where the ladies had been. Once the shirt was fully unbuttoned he turned with his back to the bed and let it drop from his shoulders. Then he gathered it up into a ball making sure that he didn't touch the outside of the shirt. She almost recoiled in horror when she realised that in his mind it was his contact with her and Ingrid had made it unclean, it was they who had contaminated him!

Maria suddenly felt trapped—violated even—she was frozen to the spot with a feeling of nausea, unable to move and afraid to speak. She wanted to march over to him and slap his face to bring him to his senses. *Have you any idea how offensive this crazy behaviour is? No, of course you don't because no one has ever told you! How can one person have so many sides to his personality? One minute he is a charming gentleman and the next he is such a vile, irrational, self-centred creep.*

Instead of allowing her sudden anger and disgust to erupt with any discernable body language or expressive action she focussed her thoughts on Ingrid's wonderful display of thoughtfulness and kindness and the sad futility of its intended purpose. She didn't think that it was right or fair that someone like Deacon—who had the very best of everything that life had to offer—should accept such gifts of affection as if they were his God given right and then blatantly wash the dirt of the people who gave them off without giving it a moment's thought. Her feelings of happiness which had moments earlier surged through her being like a sweet Arabian simoom evaporated into feelings of emptiness and frustration. *How can I sit down to a meal with him after what he is about to do?* Then in the next instant she thought about poor Ingrid. *I will do it for her! Even if Deacon doesn't have the emotional capabilities to appreciate what that sweet lady has done for him, I do. And I will make sure that her gesture has the recognition it deserves.*

Maria lifted a light blue tie from the rail and holding it to her open mouth she breathed along its entire length before she calmly closed the wardrobe doors. She laid the tie gently on his bed. Deacon—who by this time and deposited the offending shirt into his washing basket—looked at Maria and smiled. "Thank you Maria," he said. Maria smiled back and nodded. *I hope my germs on that tie gather round your neck and choke you.* She walked through to the bathroom and began running his bath for the second time and as it filled she went defiantly to the mirror to make herself presentable for Ingrid's lunchtime treat.

Maria left the bathroom and went downstairs determined to put on a front for Ingrid's sake. She and Ingrid chatted like old friends as they waited for Deacon to appear. Maria was impressed by Ingrid's natural easy manner and Ingrid was equally impressed by Maria's obvious intelligence and her youthful beauty. During the conversation Ingrid asked Maria about her future plans. Maria mentioned university and Ingrid began to impress on her the virtues and value of pursuing such an admirable goal. Maria's keen interest in listening to the advice of such an obviously well-educated, articulate woman was bolstered even further when Ingrid said that she had studied psychology before she married Daniels. Maria wondered if Ingrid had any idea at all how erratic Deacon could be. It was such a shame that the circumstances would never allow Maria to explain what she had just witnessed in the bedroom and other of Deacon's peculiarities to see under what category Ingrid would place his psychological profile. *Is he a flawed genius or an extremely lucky nutcase?*

It was just over half and hour before Deacon entered the room wearing a smart suit and—to Maria's devilish delight—the sullied by her breath, germ infested blue tie. He remained by the open door. "Shall we go ladies?" he announced.

The trio went to the front of the house and stood for a moment under the shelter of the portico. "You Ladies wait here," Deacon said as he turned and went back into the house. Moments later he emerged smiling from the rear of the house at the wheel of his beloved Bentley. He got out and opened the rear door for them, "Today you shall travel in style my dears," he said. They ducked quickly out through the rain and slid into the car; Ingrid had put on the expensive lunch so Deacon thought it fitting that he should provide the luxurious carriage.

The car wound its way down the driveway and headed for the most exclusive French restaurant in town. At the restaurant the manager greeted them at the door and showed them personally to their table. The place was surprisingly busy and the air was filled with a mixture of humming chatter and soft background music. Maria looked around the room at the opulent surroundings and gave an inward sigh, she had an idea how the other half lived but she never thought for one moment that she would find herself right there amongst them—albeit by abstract chance—but she was there just the same. She smiled politely at the well dressed young couple at the table immediately to her right as they looked up to see who was about to occupy the reserved table beside them. The walls were covered in expensive pastel patterned wallpaper and the alcoves were painted in El Greco style murals. Great black marble columns formed Roman arches at two ends of the room and appeared to be topped with solid gold. The chairs were in the elegant style of exquisite rosewood Queen Anne and the carpets appeared to be designed by Carmen Stallbaumer and specially imported from Germany. Each table was decorated with fresh flower arrangements and the value of the cutlery on that one table alone would have been enough to pay off her mortgage for the following three years. If she thought that was expensive she had yet to see the menu and the wine list. The exclusion of any prices at all was a clear indicator that if one had to know the price one couldn't afford to dine there in the first place. Prices in a restaurant like that would be viewed as common verging on downright offensive to the people in the higher echelons of society. Maria looked furtively round at the other diners and thanked her lucky stars that she always dressed well for work for the rare occasions that she was called upon to act as hostess to any of Deacon's business associates. All the other guests were dressed in the latest designer clothes. One could easily have believed that—the female diners anyway—had just stepped off the catwalk of the Milan Fashion Show.

When the trio were comfortably seated the smiling manager deftly signalled to a waitress to bring over the menus. She handed them out and returned to her standing position beneath one of the Roman arches to await her next signalled instruction. Ingrid smiled at Deacon and asked, "What does your heart desire?"

"It's your treat, you decide for the three of us," he said.

"That's fine with me too," Maria said as she looked at the mouth-watering dishes on offer.

"No," Ingrid said, "The menu is in English and French, I would like to hear Maria's command of the French language. Will you order for us Maria and show Richard how it should be done in France?"

"Of course I will," Maria smiled, "You decide on the meal and I will order." Ingrid suggested the chef's soup of the day for starters followed by venison medallion flamed in mampoer and served with an herbed polenta cake. Deacon smiled at the thought of Maria's task. It was a French restaurant but that meal was of a more cosmopolitan blend. To order it was difficult enough in English but to translate that into French she would really have to know her stuff. He tapped lightly on the table to attract their attention and when they turned to him he laid down a challenge.

"Let's have a little wager," he said.

"Oh I do love a flutter," Ingrid giggled. "What's the wager?"

"If Maria doesn't manage to convince the waitress that she's French then you pay for the meal, if she does then I'll pay for this meal and everyone else's meal in the restaurant."

Ingrid turned to Maria, "Will my bet be safe?" she smiled.

Maria saw it not as a light-hearted bet between two friends but as a perfect opportunity to get some payback for the way he had treated her germs earlier.

"Let's put it this way, if I don't convince her then I will pay for everyone's meal," Maria smiled confidently.

Deacon's smile visibly faltered slightly when he realised that the girls had joined forces and he may be about to be landed with the biggest bill in the history of the restaurant.

"Now hold on a second Ingrid," he said, "How will we decide if the wager has been won fair and square if you and I don't speak the language properly?"

"We will ask the waitress at some point during the meal to guess where Maria is from, how's that?" Ingrid said.

"That's fair enough," Deacon agreed, "providing none of us leave the table before we ask her."

Maria looked at the menu one last time and thought for a brief moment before she nodded almost imperceptibly to the manager who appeared instantly at the table like a ghostly apparition and asked if they were ready to order. Maria answered in the affirmative and he in turn hailed the watching waitress. She came smartly over to their table and took out her pencil ready to write. Without hesitation Maria rattled off their order with that wonderful flowing French lyricism that one usually associates with nineteenth century European romance. The waitress jotted down the order, smiled politely and turned for the kitchen without saying a word. The waitress had given nothing away at all by her expression or her body language and in such a high class place that was all they had to go on for the moment. The staff would never dream of speaking to the customers out of turn so they had no way of knowing which way the bet was going. Ingrid was just about to introduce another conversational topic when the manager signalled to the wine waiter who promptly arrived at the table with a bottle of the house's finest Champagne. The manager smiled at Deacon and said it was compliments of the young couple at the table opposite. Deacon looked over to the young couple who smiled and raised their glasses. He had never set eyes on them before but that sort of thing often happened. *They are probably readers wanting their photographs taken with me.* He smiled back and nodded in appreciation of the gesture. The young lady rose from her table and walked over apparently to introduce herself and formally request the photograph. Deacon had made up his mind that he would oblige them seeing as they had had the good manners to ask before his meal had begun. He was halfway to his feet when the young lady arrived at his table but instead of speaking to Deacon she ignored him completely in favour of speaking to Maria. As Maria rose to her feet the young lady took her by the arms and they embraced each other with the traditional French greeting of a kiss on each cheek. The young lady spoke entirely in French and she and Maria commenced to go at it like two washerwomen. After the first exchange Maria politely introduced the young lady to her dining companions. By then it was fairly obvious that the young lady spoke no English at all. Maria turned to Ingrid and said: "It looks like you won't be paying after all."

95

"Who is she?" Ingrid asked, "And where does she know you from?"

Maria began to laugh, "Let me call the manager over to explain."

Deacon sat back in his chair with a look of bewilderment on his face. The manager arrived and Maria asked him if he would be so kind as to translate why the young lady had sent over the Champagne. "Certainly madam," he smiled. He spoke to the young lady for a few moments and then spoke to Ingrid and Deacon. "This lady sent over the Champagne so that she could make the acquaintance of this lady...a fellow Parisian."

Maria looked at Deacon and smiled, "She has been in this country for just over two weeks, she works for a French holiday company and she is here checking out hotels and restaurants. She woke up this morning feeling terribly homesick and hearing a fellow Parisian like me has just made her day. Deacon dropped his shoulders pretending to be devastated at losing his bet, but he was sporting in defeat. He did find one thing rather uncomfortable though and that was when the young lady asked him to take a photograph of herself and Maria.

Deacon told the manager that he would pick up the bill for everyone's meal that had been fortunate enough to be in the restaurant at that time and Deacon was given a rousing round of applause when the manager made a general announcement to the other diners. The diners had no idea why they were being treated and the young French lady went back to her table without the slightest notion that she had been introduced to one of the richest men in the country and one who was about to be one of the most widely read authors on the planet.

At the end of the meal Deacon thanked Ingrid for making his day so special and he thanked her again for doing all she had done to buy his property in France. He also reminded her that he would pay for the old couple's removal costs and furniture storage costs until they found their new house by the sea. Ingrid leaned over and patted Deacon's hand. "I have already taken care of that Richard," she smiled, "that is my going away gift to you, so you go away, don't worry about anything and above all try to relax and enjoy yourself."

With that, Deacon settled the bill and they made their way back out through the rain and into the car. As they drove back along the duel carriageway Maria couldn't help but think about Ingrid's wonderful kindness to everyone around her and especially to Deacon and in particular the parting gift she had just given him. *Would Ingrid be so kind and generous to him if she knew the full extent of his selfish eccentricities? Why do all the good things in life always seem to gravitate to the people who have everything in the first place? I suppose in the final analysis we are all who we are and no outside elements or influences will change any of us or the natural course of our lives. Wouldn't life be grand if we could change the things we don't like about people as we would change the decoration of our homes?*

Maria's thoughts on the mysteries of life and its inequality and unfairness were brought to an abrupt end when the Bentley came to a halt outside the front door of Deacon's house. Ingrid looked at her watch and announced that she would have to dash. By then the rain had eased off and Maria and Deacon walked her to her car. Deacon held out his hand to Ingrid who took it gently in her's as she smiled and asked him to send her a postcard. Maria sensed that Ingrid was disappointed with the cool formality of Deacon's goodbye and she felt like saying: "Don't be offended Ingrid, it's not you he doesn't want to touch it's your filthy germs." Then, perhaps as much as an act of defiance as a show of affection Maria hugged Ingrid as if they would never meet again. As Ingrid slid her elegant legs into the car she smiled and asked her to keep in touch. Deacon and Maria stood and watched Ingrid drive out towards the lane, her practical joke and her kindness had made Deacon's day so good and memorable and at the same time it had shown Maria yet another side to her boss that she would rather not have seen.

Chapter Fifteen

The weeks leading up to the end of July flew by so quickly and before Maria knew it her final day in the employment of Richard Deacon had arrived. She drove towards the house on that morning with her emotions almost as if they were separate from her and in a subdued, desensitised world of their own. She neither felt elated, sad, relieved, or any of the feelings that she had imagined might manifest themselves when her last day arrived. It was a feeling of flatness, a flat-line blip on the monitor of couldn't-care-less.

In those same few weeks Deacon had been busy planning his holiday and he had gone about it in the same way as he went about writing one of his novels. He started with an idea and played around with its feasibility until he worked it up into something he could experiment with and develop. So what had started off as the organising of a trip to France had been worked up in his mind to be the beginning of an adventure that was as mouth-wateringly attractive and exciting as one of his well thought out scenarios. He had been on to his local French car dealer and ordered a left hand drive four door saloon which was due to be delivered at the end of the month. He had worked out his route down to the ferry port and he had booked the overnight ferry from Portsmouth to St-Malo which would land him nicely on the dragon's neck to the east of Brest and to the north of Rennes. That stroke of genius was decided upon partly to put him closer to his final destination but mainly to avoid having to travel through the more northern French ports which by now—in his mind anyway—were populated entirely with sanctimonious French linguistic perfectionists.

He had also been in touch with Meeks—his publisher—to finalise a production schedule. That involved proof-reading, editing, spell-checking, cover designing and pre-publication promotion. All of which would need only minimal input from Deacon until perhaps mid October when the final proofs would have to be read and signed off. The promotion would begin in earnest in November and the book would be available in the stores just in time for Christmas. With all those things in place all that remained was for Maria to work out her final day and for Deacon to load up his new car and head south.

Whilst Deacon was away in France it had been arranged that Ingrid would take over Maria's role as go-between—or guard dog as Maria mentally referred to herself—between Deacon and his numerous associates. She would be his only point of contact with the outside world for the duration of his stay in France and Ingrid had been well briefed that he was not to be disturbed unless it was a life-or-death situation.

Maria was surprised to find Deacon sitting at the breakfast table drinking coffee when she let herself in at the back door.

"Morning Maria," he smiled, "Would you like a coffee?"
Maria looked at him with an expression of bemused uncertainty.

"Are you alright Mr Richard?" she asked light heartedly.

"I can fully understand why you think I may have flipped Maria, but I can assure you that I am fully compos mentis. You have waited on me for the past four years so I thought it was time I let you put your feet up. Besides I have to practise foraging for myself because there will be no one but me out there on the wild frontier."

"You're going to France Mr Richard, not outer Mongolia. They do have shops there you know."

"Have a seat Maria whist I pour your coffee, I want you to tell me if there is anything else I need to know about France before I leave."

Maria sat at the table and watched as Deacon fumbled his way around the kitchen opening cupboards and closing them again as he searched for a second mug.

"Third cupboard along," Maria said as she shook her head.

"No Maria, don't give me any clues, I must do this thing on my own. You can tell me where I went wrong over coffee."

Maria sat and watched as he finally located the mugs and proceeded to make the coffee. He went about it rather like a scientist would, carefully adding the different compounds to a test-tube in order to conduct some delicate, detailed experiment.

"There!" he said with a boyish smile on his face as he placed the results of the experiment on the table before her, "taste that young lady and give me the verdict."

Maria blew across the surface of the coffee to cool it before she took a sip.

"Hhhmmm, I'm impressed," she smiled, "well done."

"I've been practising," he beamed like a son explaining the acquisition of his new-found skill to a proud parent, "So, getting back to my question, what else do I need to know about the French?" he asked.

"The French are a wonderful people, they are friendly and hospitable. You have to take them as you find them because that is how they will take you. In the country, where you will be living, they take life at their own pace, they lead a simple life really, they buy their bread in the morning and they sit down to a family meal at night. In between those two essential and non-negotiable activities they do what they have done for centuries…they make wine and drink it in copious amounts."

"Is that it?" Deacon asked incredulously.

"What else do they need to do?" Maria smiled.

"Well how do they amuse themselves? What do they do with their leisure time? What are their local politics?" he asked.

"Unlike our politics theirs are quite simple. Where as we have managed to maintain a kind of three tier class system which operates everywhere in the United Kingdom, they seem to have developed a rather quaint two pronged system. You could say that it is separated into the city dwellers and the country folk. The city dwellers take care of the industrial side of things and the country folk take care of the agriculture. In our system we have city dwellers interfering in country life and vice versa, which in the cold light of day means that influential people can become involved and make policy on things they know nothing about and before you know it we all end up in a mess. The French don't allow that to happen. The farmers decide what crops to grow and the tailors decide what clothes to make. Quite revolutionary isn't it?"

"It all sounds so wonderfully simple," he said.

"Yes, but the best bit is that the French see their politics as a mirror image of their family unity and co-operation. If the family is stable, then the community is stable and the country is stable. As for amusing themselves and leisure time, isn't France supposed to be the birthplace of love and romance?" she smiled playfully as she took another sip of her coffee.

"You know Maria, I think I'm going to like France," he said.

Then rising from the table he announced that he was going through to his study to make some last minute phone calls. As he was leaving the kitchen he turned to Maria as he remembered something. He asked her to drive over to Daniels's house at noon to pick up a parcel from Ingrid and drop it off in the dining room at seven minutes past one. Maria nodded as she took the dirty cups over to the sink. "Washing things after you is an important part of food preparation and presentation Mr Richard," she smiled, "shall I show you how it's done?"

"One culinary secret at a time is quite enough for one's brain to assimilate," he called as he disappeared into the shadows of the back staircase.

Maria carried on with her household chores until it was time to leave for Daniels's house. As she drove down the driveway she wondered what the parcel could contain. *Was it some vital piece of equipment that he would need on the wild frontier and if so, what could it be?*

Deacon watched her car turn into the lane from behind the curtain of the window in the upstairs landing which looked out over the front garden. When she was out of sight he made one last phone call.

Maria arrived at Daniels's house and Ingrid answered the door smiling.

"How nice to see you again Maria, do come in."

Maria was led through to the living room and she was asked to make herself comfortable whilst Ingrid went to fetch the parcel. Moments later Ingrid appeared with a rather heavy looking, bulky, flat cardboard box. Ingrid put it on the table and offered Maria a coffee. Conscious of the time restraints placed on her by Deacon and at the same time not wishing to seem impolite Maria glanced over to the oak encased clock which dominated the fireplace, if she hurried she would just have enough time to have a coffee with Ingrid and still be back in time. "I would love a coffee thank you," she smiled.

Ingrid smiled after noticing Maria glance at the clock: "I knew you might be pressed for time, Richard being the way he is, so I ordered the coffee in advance so that we could sit and have a relaxing chat without unnecessary pressure."

Maria felt immediately relieved and she inwardly smiled at Ingrid's cool understanding of her situation. Her comment about *Richard being the way he is* also gave her the impression that perhaps she knew more about his eccentricities than she was letting on. Moments later a maid entered with a tray of coffee and laid it gently and silently on the table. Ingrid thanked her and began to serve the coffee. "So this is your last day as an employee of Richard, how does that make you feel?" she asked.

Maria thought for a moment, the question seemed to act as a kind of catalyst which suddenly agitated her dormant emotions and she felt momentarily overwhelmed by the surge. The powerful impulses made her answer more ambiguous than she would have liked. She answered without first identifying the sudden awareness of emotional sensation that the question had invoked. If she would have been unaffected by the question she would have simply given a polite stock answer like, *I haven't really thought about it*, the kind of thing we all rely on from time to time when we really mean, *I should feel different than this and I can't for the life of me work out why.*

"I feel as if there is something wrong," Maria said at last. The words seemed to grow into grotesque shapes and reverberate round the room like voices booming in an echo chamber and she immediately wished that she could haul them back into her traitor mouth. She knew that Ingrid would require a full and thorough explanation and she simply didn't have one.

"Wrong! In what way is there something wrong?" Ingrid asked.

Maria why did you have to open this can of worms that was screaming to be left alone? What are you going to do now girl? A nervous, uncertain smile appeared on Maria's lips, luckily the cuteness of it belied the inferno of frantic thought which was desperately trying to back-peddle out of the bizarre situation. *Now that I have triggered this line of inquest which has the potential to develop into a debate of parliamentary proportions, how do I stop it?*

"Perhaps the word wrong is in fact the wrong word to describe how I feel. I think what I should have said was that it will feel strange not going into work tomorrow as I have done for the past four years."

Ingrid nodded sympathetically. "Change can sometimes be very upsetting; it can distance us from our spiritual touchstone, our in-built centre of gravity. The thing to do in this situation is to stand back and re-group, re-evaluate your situation and re-align your bows in accordance with your newly identified celestial body. Follow the new star until it too begins to fade. You feel the way you do because your star is fading and you haven't yet found your new direction."

Maria sat like a stunned audience, mesmerised by the drama of Ingrid's eloquent soliloquy. Once again she had been surprised to find yet another profound side to Ingrid's understanding of human nature. Could her apparent complete grasp of the irrational complexities of human emotions be the result of her psychology studies? This thought was uppermost in her mind as she thankfully allowed Ingrid's sympathy to dilute her pent-up anxiety. Ingrid had not only given Maria a hand out of the hole she had moments earlier been effortlessly digging herself into, she had planted the seed in her mind that there was a possible correlation between the heavens and the individual.

"Can we really choose our own destiny by wishing on a star?" Maria asked. This time it was Ingrid who glanced at the clock. "I'm afraid we don't have the time for me to even begin to answer that question satisfactorily. But what I will say is this, we all have the ability to change—and I don't mean adapt to change like a Chameleon—I mean change fundamentally from the inside out, and yes, you could liken the will to change as wishing on a star."

The clock chimed and Maria saw that it was time to go. She could have cheerfully given anything for just one more hour in the presence of Ingrid. Maria was convinced that she could learn everything she needed to know about herself with just sixty minutes more. But it was not to be; Ingrid lifted the parcel from the table and carried it for Maria out to her car. Maria opened her door and took the parcel passing it carefully onto the passenger seat. As she lowered the parcel she noticed how light it was in relation to its bulk. She turned to offer her hand to Ingrid but she had other ideas. Ingrid folded her arms about Maria and hugged her like an affectionate sister. "You take good care Maria, and make sure you find a safe pad to land on," she smiled.

Their brief meeting had been such a surreal experience for Maria, disjointed and dreamlike, but it ended there in Ingrid's arms as though it had been the most natural, wonderful thing ever to have happened to her. As she drove away her emotions returned from their neutral settings and her eyes filled with tears of happiness. Yes, she was leaving the influence of the star of Richard Deacon, but she was heading for the star of a whole new beginning, of that she was now certain.

Chapter Sixteen

The drive back gave Maria just enough time to reflect on what had just happened; she was able—with the help of her new-found emotional awareness—to put all the parts of the jig-saw into place and view the picture as a whole. Her last day of her old life was to be the first day of her new life and when viewed like that it was a very useful emotional by-pass.

She pulled into the driveway at two minutes past one—just enough time to be in the dining room at the designated time. She parked her car at the rear of the house and entered through the kitchen. The faint smell of cooking wafted over her as she laid the parcel on the table and took off her light summer jacket. *Smells like he has been foraging again, I wonder what he has concocted for himself this time?* She glanced at the clock and saw that she had two minutes to spare so she went over to the sink and quickly dried the mugs that she had washed earlier. As she looked through the window out onto the side garden she saw a tiny bird hanging from a round food cage which was fixed to the underside of the bird table. "I'm going to miss you little fellow," she whispered as she watched his workmanlike approach to his own foraging. The tiny bird seemed to know that he was being spoken to and he stopped his frantic pecking to look at Maria. She smiled as he did the most curious thing; he dipped his head several times in quick succession in a kind of bowing motion rather like an over enthusiastic Chinese servant. It was as if to say: "And I am going to miss you too."

She put the mugs away and gathered up the parcel, her stealthy walk to the dining room meant that she didn't notice the smell of cooking becoming stronger. If she would have done she would have perhaps been better prepared for the sight that met her eyes as she entered. In her absence Deacon had called the catering company and told them that it was safe to approach the house. He had pre-ordered Maria's leaving meal the previous day and his sending Maria over to Ingrid to collect the parcel had been a ruse to get her out of the way to complete the surprise. Maria opened the dining room door to find Deacon standing smiling at the head of a beautifully laid out table for two. The centre of the table was furnished with an amazing collection of exotic summer blooms. Deacon walked over to Maria as she stood motionless and speechless in the doorway. He gently took the parcel from her and guided her to her seat at the table. "Your employment with me is now at an end Maria. For the rest of the day you are my honoured guest." Maria's poor heart was racing with shock and excitement. "You have done all this for me Mr Richard, I don't know what to say," she smiled.

"Maria, don't say another word, you just sit back and enjoy it. This is my way of showing you how much I have appreciated having you here looking after me. I feel as though I have been treated like this everyday just by having you around, so I wanted you to know how you have made me feel for the past four years."

"I was only doing my job Mr Richard and I was very well paid for doing it," she protested.

"Nonsense, you have approached your work here in exactly the same manner in which I approach my work. Besides dedication and vitality, you have brought style and perfectionism and if ever I am asked to provide a reference for you it will reflect those qualities. Now, enough of this talk, we will sever our working relationship in a way that will be as memorable to us at the end of our days as it is here and now."

Maria gave a playful shudder, "To sever our relationship sounds awfully harsh Mr Richard. Couldn't a man with your vocabulary make it sound more poetic?"

"I would never use poetic at the expense of dynamic. The word was well considered to portray the brutal devastation of its consequences. The implication is one of the reality of loss rather than the sugary romance of passing."

Maria lowered her eyes as it dawned on her for the first time just how much she had really meant to him. She was determined however to follow Deacon's lead and not give way to sentiment. He wanted to celebrate their *loss* as only a man as unique as Deacon could and she was not about to rain on his parade. If his actions were sincere—as she hoped with all her heart

106

they were—then she was indeed truly honoured. If however, they were an elaborate enactment of a scene from his next novel, then her last day in his employment would not only have been served with her enjoying the best of haut cuisine, it would also be immortalised in the pages of an international best seller. She was in a win, win situation and she was going to sit back and enjoy every last minute of it...after all she had earned it.

Deacon picked up a small hand bell and shook it once. A heated food trolley was wheeled in from the secret hideaway of the drawing room and Maria gasped with delight as the food was expertly served by two of the staff from the French restaurant. Deacon filled their glasses with Champagne and toasted Maria.

"To your future Maria," he said.

"To the success of your holiday and to the success of your latest novel," Maria smiled.

"Sante!" Deacon laughed, "I have been practising that too."

"Yes, good health to you too Mr Richard, that's really all we need."

At the end of the meal the table was cleared and the staff from the restaurant left. Maria and Deacon sat facing each other for a moment in silence. Then, pointing to the parcel that Maria had brought from Ingrid's house Deacon said: "That parcel Maria, bring it to the table and open it, it's for you, it's my leaving gift to you, but don't get too excited, I chose it for it's practical use rather than for it's beauty and I want you to keep that in mind."

Maria had felt the lightness of the parcel and she wondered what could be so practical and weigh so little. Her curiosity was soon satisfied. She broke open the outer cardboard packaging to reveal a white oblong box tied up with a delicate pink lace bow. She carefully untied the bow and lifted the lid. Inside she found the most exquisite evening gown imaginable, it had been commissioned from the top fashion designer in France and it took her breath away. "Oh Mr Richard it's beautiful," she whispered as she ran the back of her fingers over the material. She was almost afraid to touch it let alone take it out.

"Let me see it against you then," Deacon smiled.

Maria gently lifted out the dress and held it against her. "Do you like it Maria?" Deacon asked.

"Oh Mr Richard I love it, but how is it more practical than beautiful?" she asked.

"Because it is specifically for your graduation dinner my dear—three years from now," he smiled.

Maria suddenly felt as though she had been kicked in the stomach. Once again, in an instant she had plummeted from the heights of ecstasy to the depths of despondency. But this time it had nothing to do with Deacon's stoicism or his germ paranoia or his infuriating eccentricities. Her pain was self-inflicted, brought on by a sudden bout of intense guilt. She had no intentions of going to university; she had used that as an excuse for not having to get involved in a potentially messy divorce. But if the dress wasn't bad enough, worse was still to come.

Deacon mistakenly perceived Maria's silence as being overwhelmed by his gift and unknowingly he carried on with his torture. "There is something else of a practical nature still in the box Maria," he said.

Maria let the top half of the dress fall away from her body and walked slowly back towards the box. From a distance she peered in and saw the edge of a white envelope. *Oh God please don't let that be what I think it is.* She tentatively reached out her hand and lifted it out, as she began to open the envelope she prayed that the floor would open up and swallow her. She took out the contents of the envelope and her worst fears were realised, it was a cheque for £30.000 to help towards the costs of her university degree. She knew that Deacon deserved a suitable reaction and once again she asked God to give her the strength to see it through despite the inherent dishonesty of it. Almost as if God answered her prayers a thought flashed into her head that she could destroy the cheque any time she liked so the only thing she would have really obtained by deception was the designer dress and in Deacon's own words she had earned it.

"Mr Richard, I'm just so…so happy, I don't know what to say," she said finally.

"Then in that case Maria it is best to say nothing. The thanks is all mine, this is my way of recognising and supporting your potential and helping you to lay the foundations of your future. Now, there is nothing else for you to do here and I have a lot of loading up to do so we will just say goodbye now." With that he thrust out his hand at a diagonal angle. Maria—still dazed by the twisting of events like a stupefying bombardment—held out her hand limply, but instead of Deacon shaking it as she had anticipated he took up her hand and bowed as he swept it up to his mouth to kiss it. "Goodbye Maria and good luck, I shall miss you."

Maria wanted to let her hand linger under the warmth of his breath and the softness of his lips against the back of her hand but she realised that the moment she was gone he would be under the shower to wash away her germs. She pulled her hand away abruptly but made light of it when she saw the faint trace of hurt in his expression. "That tickles," she managed to smile, "Goodbye Mr Richard, I shall miss you too."

She folded up the dress and packed it back onto the white oblong box before she turned and left Deacon alone in the Dining room. Feeling self-satisfied and without the faintest idea of the turmoil he had inflicted on Maria, he walked over to the coffee table and opened the rosewood cigar box. He lifted one out and ran its length under his nose. *Today has been like the ending to a novel so I feel it fitting to break my rule and smoke one for good luck.* He lit the cigar and walked thoughtfully over to the window. He was just in time to watch Maria drive slowly down the driveway and out of his life for the very last time.

Chapter Seventeen

The smoke from his cigar filled the air around him and through the blue, grey mist he let his mind wander across the channel to his destination, to his home for the next month or so. He wondered what discoveries he would make and if he would be inspired to re-kindle his sleeping creativity in the beauty and serenity of his new surroundings. He listened to the silence all around him as he looked over the garden. *I hope Maria finds what she deserves.*

Maria drove home along the dual carriageway and pulled up outside her house. She sat for a moment without thinking and without moving. She felt as though someone had pushed the pause button on her life and she could neither press play nor rewind. In a word she was deflated; a message in a bottle at the mercy of the current and the tide waiting to be collected and delivered. Finally she forced herself to look up at her house, it looked cold and uninviting and the sight of the front door made her realise that she had nowhere else to go. She turned to her parcel on the seat beside her but she couldn't bring herself to touch it. In a way it represented everything in her life that she wanted to get rid of. She fumbled with the handle of the door and stepped out into the road. *Perhaps if I leave you there long enough, some kind thief will take you from me.* She left the dress in the car and walked up the steps to the front door. It was then that she remembered about the cheque in the dress box. She went back to the car and pushed her hand into the dress box as though she were thrusting her hand into a barrel of slime. She took out the envelope and immediately tore it into pieces before she stuffed it into the empty ash tray in the console of the car. She turned and looked around at her neighbours' windows for any give away twitches of the curtains, satisfied that her curious antics had not been observed she went back to the house. The afternoon was warm and the sun shone brightly through the loosely fragmented clouds, but she felt none of its bounty, she had no connection with anything but her inner desolation.

She put the key in the door and as she pushed it open she saw the usual array of letters behind the door. She gathered them up and took them through to the kitchen, she put them on the breakfast bar and put the kettle on; perhaps a coffee and some good cheer in the mail would bring her back to some semblance of normality. As the kettle boiled she quickly browsed through the jumble of take-away flyers and other assorted junk mail until she found something which could be construed as interesting. There it was—sandwiched between a credit card balance and a gas bill reminder—a plain white envelope with a hand-written address on it. She filed the official letters to be dealt with later, put the junk mail for re-cycling and left the personal letter on the side until the coffee was made. She didn't recognise the handwriting at first but on closer inspection she thought that it looked like Deacon's. *Why should he write to me, we have only just seen each other?*

She sat at the breakfast bar and opened the letter…it was from Deacon.

My dear Maria

I know what you are thinking; why is he writing to me when we have only just parted company, am I right? No need to answer that I know I am. *Arrogant bastard!* Well I am writing for several reasons. Firstly to say thank you once again for devoting the last four years of your working life to me, and secondly to say that I know the cheque I gave you is now in pieces. *How the hell could he know that?* Don't be surprised Maria, I know you better than you might think. I also know that being the person you are that you could never continue in my employment with things being the way they are between Eleanor and I. The only possible excuse you could have given me that you were confident I would accept would be that you were leaving to go to university or to better yourself in some other similar way. I am not disappointed in you for not being honest with me, quite the contrary. I admire you

111

for your loyalty to Eleanor and I thank you for not wanting to hurt my feelings. However, your dilemma left me with a dilemma which was, how do I let you know that we are still friends and you do not have to let your conscience become an obstacle if our paths should ever have the chance to cross again? Yes, you were dishonest, but your intentions were honourable and respectful so that makes it acceptable in my eyes.

Right, now that that matter is cleared up I will tell you why I still bought you your graduation dress. That is because I believe it is your destiny to go to university to study hard and eventually to join the ranks of critical thinkers that apparently only such establishments are qualified to produce. Now, because the production of critical thinkers has certain—obscene—costs involved these days and because I knew you would destroy the cheque, I have arranged for £10.000 per annum to be deposited into your bank account for the next five years. It is yours to do with as you wish but I would sincerely hope that my actions and this letter will serve as evidence that intelligence can be acquired just like any other commodity. My father paid for my education and I would like to help to pay for yours, should you choose to follow that path. If you could ignore the pinch of cynicism—which I couldn't resist—aimed at academics and religious scholars whom throughout the ages have managed to convince all but the few that success is worthless unless its course can be chartered back to a source of planning, philosophical reasoning and mathematical deduction, you will understand that intelligence is perceived in this world only through the name on a certificate beneath the name of a recognised seat of learning. Without it the gateway to the stars is infinitely—and shamefully—narrowed.

Now go and take the dress from the car and keep it safe until you win the opportunity to wear it.

Take care

R

Maria read the lines over and over again and her feelings fluctuated between giddy relief and acute embarrassment. She wondered at what point he knew that she was lying to him. For some reason—probably due to her knowledge of his eccentricity—she understood why he had chosen to write to her instead of speaking to her face to face. She could read the letter a thousand times without showing her vulnerability or her awkwardness of being caught lying. If they had spoken, the essence and true value of what he had to say would have been lost amongst the flying debris of it all.

Maria went out to the car and retrieved the dress. She had resolved to think long and hard over the next few days; if working with Deacon had taught her anything it was that only fools rush in.

Deacon stubbed out his cigar confident that Maria had encountered her second surprise of the day and would act on it in due course. All that remained for him was to load up the car with his essentials and get an early night for the long drive south in the early hours of the following morning.

Chapter Eighteen

Deacon was up at first light, he fixed himself a meagre breakfast of coffee and toast; he didn't want to eat too much in case it made him drowsy at the wheel before he was fully awake. The night before he had put his bags at the front door ready for departure and he had left his new car parked at the front of the house. In the vestibule he tucked his soap bag into the end compartment of one of his canvass bags and did a final mental check. *Money, credit cards, wallet, watch, reading glasses, keys…ah yes the keys.* He looked at the keys as he took them from his trouser pocket and he smiled at the memory of how he had acquired them. The smile on Ingrid's face as she walked towards him with the keys on the cushion was a picture that he would never forget.

When he was confident that he had everything covered and accounted for he loaded up the car. The sun was steadily rising in the eastern sky as he fired up the engine and slipped quietly down the driveway. His route to Portsmouth had been meticulously planned and—allowing for any hold-ups—it would take four hours if he took it easy. It was a brand new car and although there was no need to let the new engine bed-in—as one had to do in the old days—he wanted to let everything warm up gradually. The ferry was due to sail at eleven o'clock so by the time he rolled into Portsmouth he was well in time for check-in.

He pulled onto the ferry terminal harbour and joined on the end of one of the waiting lines of assorted cars, motor homes and motorbikes, the coaches and heavy goods wagons queued on another part of the terminal. He looked up at the electronic notice board suspended above a steel gantry which periodically flashed messages in English, French and German and he saw that loading would commence in fifteen minutes. He and several other drivers and their passengers took the opportunity to leave their vehicles and stretch their legs. His drive down had been uneventful and he had arrived at nine thirty. He stretched the stiffness from his neck and shoulders and looked admiringly at the vessel that he was about to join.

Just before ten o'clock the electronic notice board flashed that boarding was about to commence and that people should follow their respective instructions. One after the other—and very efficiently—the lines of cars drove past the passport control kiosks and disappeared into the belly of the ferry. Deacon followed the car in front and once on board ship he was directed by stewards clad in luminous overalls to his final parking spot. Although the crossing was during the day he had taken the precaution of reserving a private cabin in case he wanted to sleep during any part of the estimated nine hour crossing.

He collected his cabin key from the reception desk and dropped off his coat and hand luggage before going up on deck. There was one sight that he particularly wanted to see and that was of his boyhood hero Admiral Lord Nelson the hero of the historic Napoleonic sea battle of Trafalgar whose flagship HMS Victory stands in number two dry dock in Portsmouth and still retains a captain, officers and crew. It is the oldest surviving ship of the line to be found anywhere in the world. Besides it being the scene of Nelson's greatest victory—of which there were many—and the place where he met his death, it was a great monument to British craftsmen and marine engineering. HMS Victory can bee seen clearly from the decks of any passing vessel as it slips from harbour out into the channel or indeed on its return. Deacon watched in awe and took in every detail of that magnificent fighting ship as the ferry heaved from its moorings and sailed majestically by. He remained on deck as the ferry swept out into the Channel at the head of the Solent—the narrow strip of sea that separates the mainland from the Isle of Wight. He had even planned the route the ferry would take even though its course had nothing at all to do with him. Being a writer he was curious of all things and over the years he had thoughtfully developed the invaluable ability to absorb details that would be unimportant to others. Every detail he had ever collected had resurfaced in some form or another in one of his novels. After leaving port the ferry would pass the Isle of Wight on its right and its path across the channel would resemble the gradual curve of a banana. After crossing the main body of the channel the ferry would slip between the Channel Isles and the French mainland passing the islands of Alderney, Guernsey, Sark and Jersey on its right before heading straight into St-Malo. As the ferry moved further out into the sea leaving the mainland to shrink at its stern Deacon looked at his watch and decided it was time to find his first meal as a lone adventurer.

After a brief tour of the ship's lifeboat locations—*just in case*—he went in search of a suitable place to eat. He was surprised—and slightly bemused—to find that there were several signs indicating various places to dine. There was a snack bar, a bistro, a restaurant and a grill bar. He then had to decide which one was most appropriate to service his immediate needs. After a moment's thought he plumped for the bistro, he concluded that a bistro would be a hybrid of a common café and a restaurant. In his earlier pre-trip planning he had decided that he would try to *mingle* as much as possible with the great unwashed without actually making physical contact with them. If he was to derive any meaningful satisfaction at all from his adventure he had to learn to deal with other people in a vastly different way than he had been accustomed to. The everyday people in the street were not his employees, nor his fawning associates; they were people who would more than likely have their own opinion of things and not be shy of voicing them. Therefore, until he reached the relative safety of his final destination he would treat the journey as a kind of covert undercover operation.

The first thing to strike him as he walked into the bistro was the combined smell of well used cooking oil and cigarette smoke. *What a delightful combination!* The place was already quite busy and the sound of incoherent chatter filled the air. He stood just inside the doorway and looked around for a free table, he didn't see one free but he noticed one table for four people only had one lady sitting at it. He strutted over to the table and addressed the lady: "Do you mind if I join you?" he asked. The lady looked up and smiled before she answered in a broad Lancashire accent, "Aye, sit thee down lad, I'm on mi own." The sound of her voice made him immediately regret asking the question but it was too late to back out. The lady continued to eat as he shuffled his feet before reluctantly sitting down opposite her. She was tucking—with great gusto—into what looked like a kind of braised steak with a mountain of chips and a sparsely disproportionate amount of vegetables. She looked at him for a moment or two and said: "Are yer not well lad, feelin' a bit seasick like?" At first he couldn't make out exactly what she was saying but his brain quickly fathomed out that she was running all her words together and occasionally missing the first or last letter off seemingly randomly selected words. When he ran the sentence through his mind again he understood roughly that she was asking if he felt unwell. "No I feel fine," he sort of half smiled, more at his own clever deciphering than out of politeness. "Yer no' tungry then?" she said.

Tungry? Ah she means hungry! "Well I am rather peckish actually," he said. He was beginning to enjoy this guessing game; *what an excellent way to pass the time.*

"Well if yer tha' tungry lad, yerd best get t'ert counter an' tell yon chap what tha wants before it gets packed out. In five minutes yer'll not be able ter sling a cat roun' in 'ere."
Deacon looked at her with a mixed facial expression of horror and disillusion. "You mean there is no waitress service?"

"Aye, 'at's wot I'm sayin' lad," she nodded, "it's serve thasel."

"So I have to go to the counter and tell them what I would like to eat and they prepare it for me?"

The lady looked at him strangely: "'Ast tha bin away fer a while lad, onny yer don't seem to know the drill like?"

"It's just that I'm not used to this sort of thing," he said.
The lady could tell by his public schoolboy accent that he was out of his usual environment and the *little boy lost* look on his face made her take pity on him.

"They don't 'af ter prepare it lad, it's already done. Thi keep it 'ot in them metal containers behin't glass. Point ter wot yer wont an' eel slosh it up fer yer," she said, "it's gettin' a bit full now

117

in 'ere, so why don't yer go an' order, an' I'll tell folk as this seat is taken, 'ow's that fer yer like?"

Oh my God! Metal containers! Slosh it up? Sounds disgusting, is this food we are talking about or pig swill? He was immediately torn between a myriad of equally obnoxious options. Did he risk letting people believe that he and the lady were remotely associated and thereafter have to dine with her? Or did he decline her offer at the risk of losing his place? Did he even want to dine there at all? In the end his *tunger* got the better of him and he chose a combination of the first option and the last. She was clearly in her mid sixties, she was quite plump and her ruddy complexion—which was not too skilfully concealed by powder and paint—suggested to Deacon that she was no stranger to the odd G and T. He consoled himself by telling himself that no one in their right mind would even consider that there might be some kind of romantic relationship between them.

"That's very kind of you madam," he said as he rose to his feet and went to the counter. The old lady smiled at his charming manner, if she had known what he was thinking moments earlier she would have crowned him with her braised steak and chips and thought nothing of it. At the counter things were not half as bad as the imagery that the lady's description of things had invoked. The food was indeed in metal containers, but they were all neatly laid out side by side in a surprisingly appetizing manner. The gentleman serving the food was dressed in an immaculate chef's costume complete with hat and apron. As Deacon stood at the counter perusing the delights on offer he could feel himself being involuntarily nudged along by the line of people backing up behind him. The pressure was eased slightly when the rotund, jovial-looking chef smiled and asked him what he would like. Deacon pointed to the tray of gravy soaked meat and asked what it was. "That's my speciality sir, braised shin beef, melts in mouth sir. Would you like to try it?" It didn't resemble any beef he had eaten before and he was in two minds to accept or decline. The pressure at his back resumed and that prompted a swift decision. "Yes," he said.

"Would you like boiled potatoes or French fries with it sir?"

Another nudge and he plumped for the fries. The chef held up the plate and asked Deacon to put up his tray because the plate was mad hot. "I don't have a tray," Deacon said.

"Did you not collect one at the beginning of the queue sir?" the chef asked still holding out the plate. Just then the gentleman who had been exerting most of the pressure at Deacon's back came to the rescue. "Here take mine," he said tsking impatiently as he handed his tray to Deacon. Then he turned and shouted to the woman at the far end of the queue. "Pass us a tray along here will you love? Otherwise we'll be here all bloody day."

Deacon held up his tray and the chef expertly slid the hot plate onto it. Realising that he was holding people up he passed on the offer of picking up a dessert of Swiss roll and custard and he moved to the drinks dispenser. The operation of acquiring a coffee was straight forward enough; he put the cup under the spout and pushed the coffee button. He paid for his *slosh* at the cashier desk at the end of the counter and went back to join the old lady.

"A see yer managed ter fathom it out then lad," she smiled. Deacon looked around sheepishly at the rapidly swelling numbers of diners as if to make sure he wasn't being watched before he half smiled and nodded. The lady started on her dessert as Deacon took his first ever mouthful of shin beef…and it wasn't as bad as he thought it might be. In fact it was surprisingly tasty, the French fries—which were dubiously titled because of their thickness, they were more like potato wedges—also tasted fine. The lady finished her dessert and began to watch Deacon as he ate; she appeared to be scrutinizing his features. When he happened to glance up at her she took the opportunity to say what was on her mind. "A know you frum somewhere," she said, "ast ever bin ter Bowton?"

"Bowton?" Deacon said with a forced facial expression designed to imply that he was actually trying to recall if he had been there or not, knowing full well that he hadn't.

"Aye Bowton, 'at's wer am frum Bowton. Course you might know it as Bowton," she said, then she proceeded to spell it out. "B_O_L_T_O_N, Bowton."

"Ah Bolton!" Deacon smiled, "no I have never had the pleasure."

"Beautiful awld town is Bowton, a yer sure yerve never bin there lad?"

"I think I would have remembered," Deacon said.

"Well I ne're forget a face; my Willy, Gawd bless 'im, used to say as a wer a genius wen it came ter faces. 'an am tellin' thee I know you frum somewhere."

Deacon almost choked on his next mouthful of shin beef when she suddenly exclaimed, "Yer off telly. Av seen thee ont telly."

Deacon leaned forward in panic, "Shhuussshhh!" he said, again looking round, "Please don't talk so loud; I don't want to draw attention to myself." The lady gave a big self-satisfied grin as she leaned back and clapped her hands. "A telt yer, my Willy wasn't wrong was 'e when 'e said I wer a genius, a knew a was reet. A've seen thee ont telly talkin' about them books yer write 'aven't a? On one o' them arfternoon talk shows wot discusses books. Wot yer doin' on a boat like this any'ow? Ow come yer not ont Concorde or sumat?"

Deacon was desperate to shut her up even though no one else seemed to be paying the old lady the slightest bit of attention. The room was far too full of background chatter for anyone to hear anything that wasn't said directly to them, but his panic made him oblivious to that fact. "I'll tell you what I'll do if you'll just be kind enough to change the subject," he said, "there must be a bookshop on board, I'll go and buy one of my own books and I'll sign it especially for you. Would you like that?" The lady looked at him with indignation. "A would not like that! Yer books are rubbish! A tried ter read one once but a gave up 'arf way down t'first page. They're full o' big werds that onny swell 'ed professors can understan'. No lad, gimme a proper book anytime, yer can't beat a good romance!"

120

For the first time in his life Deacon was speechless. His books had been reviewed by the cream of the world's literary critics and classed as brilliant from every quarter. Yet here was an old girl from Bolton saying they were rubbish, so rubbish in fact that she didn't even want a free copy, and a signed one at that! That one piece of criticism had more of a profound effect on him than all the other raving critics put together. He had always thought of himself as a writer of the people, but evidently he was not a writer of all the people and the chagrin inflicted was instant and painful. Perhaps it was something he would need to redress in future. It was one of those priceless moments in a man's life known as a reality check, otherwise known as a rude awakening; he didn't know whether to laugh or cry.

"Well how would you like me to treat you to a nice romantic novel and a box of chocolates?" he said as he recovered sufficiently from her—unintended—thunderous body blow to finally speak.

"E, now yer talkin' lad. Fer a Mills and Boon an' a box o' Roses I'll swear 'av ne'er set eyes on thee afore."

"What number cabin are you in? I'll have them sent to you," Deacon said.

"I 'aven't got a cabin lad, am on't pension. I'll be ont top deck in about arf an hour, am goin' up ter throw some bread t' seagulls."

With that she scooped up the handful of unopened sugar sachets that were lying on her tray and she dropped them into her open handbag. "Yer ne'er know when these might come in 'andy," she smiled as she waddled from the bistro and disappeared into the crowd.

Deacon finished his meal and made his way to his cabin where he stayed for the remainder of his voyage. He did stop off on the way however, to buy a *proper book* and a box of chocolates. He found a steward and gave him a description of the old lady and where he would find her asking him to deliver the goods. On the inside cover of the *good romance* he wrote this message: My dear lady, I have never been to Bolton, but if I ever do, I trust that I will find the rest of its citizens are as lovely and as honest as you. Bon voyage and all my very best wishes. Richard Deacon.

Chapter Nineteen

Deacon was snoozing on his bed in his cabin when the ship's public address system made the announcement that the ship would be docking in St-Malo in half an hour's time. It said other announcements would be made for foot passengers to disembark and for drivers to return to their vehicles. It also reminded passengers to put their watches forward by one hour. Deacon looked at his watch and it was seven thirty British time. He adjusted the time and worked out that he would be leaving the ship at nine o'clock French time. He gathered a few things together and put them neatly into his bag before he swilled his face and brushed his teeth. Just as he packed away the last of his things a steward knocked on his cabin door. Deacon opened it to find a young man smiling at him.

"Did you enjoy your stay with us sir?" he asked.

"It was most pleasant," he said, "Thank you."

"We will be docking in about ten minutes sir; the ship's senior steward will make an announcement any time now," the young man said as he quickly moved along the passage to knock on the door of the next cabin along. Deacon left the door open behind him and made his way onto the upper deck. He walked past people who were milling about and engaging in excited chatter as the passageway he had walked along opened out into a wide carpeted walkway. He walked past the closed cage-like shutters of the previously bustling brightly-lit duty-free shops. He opened one of the outer deck doors and stepped out into the fresh air. He wanted to see St-Malo looming into full view in the same manner that he had watched Portsmouth disappear behind him. The sound of the ship's great engines changed audibly as it slowed to make its harbour entrance. The evening was warm with only the slightest breeze and the sun shone on the brightly coloured town houses that he could see rising in the distance beyond the terminal despite the relatively flat landscape. As he stood and leaned against the safety rails a young man who looked to be in his late twenties appeared at his side with a young boy holding his hand. The young

123

man crouched down on his haunches so that he was the same size as the boy—obviously his son—and began pointing out different things of interest around the port. The little boy listened intently as his father pointed to an ancient building and told him that St Malo was once a walled city. Deacon looked at the man and boy and thought of Sebastian for the first time since they had fallen out over his son's missed birthday lunch. All the things Sebastian had said on that Sunday when he had called for an explanation also came flooding back and he felt a sudden pang of sadness. *Sebastian was right, when did I ever crouch down on the deck of a ship, or anywhere else for that matter and take the time to explain things to him? I'm sure I could have done if I had only bothered to try.*

The ship's chief steward interrupted his thoughts as he made the announcement for drivers to make their way to their vehicles. *No point in letting regrets hurt me now, I had my chance and I let it pass. Sebastian is all grown up now and doing rather well by all accounts, so I must have done something right.* The father and son walked off hand in hand and Deacon made his way below decks as the ferry glided safely and silently onto its dock. Minutes later he was being guided from the ferry by the same luminous clad stewards who had guided him on. He drove up the slipway ramp and onto the terminal area heading for one of the passport kiosks. For some reason Deacon expected every vehicle to be stopped and meticulously searched but he found exactly the opposite. He even found the French customs official's attitude to the potential of smuggled contraband quite amusing. A chap dressed in a blue/grey uniform complete with black beret was leaning with one elbow on his knee with his foot resting on a raised concrete kerbstone and one hand covering what looked like a semi-automatic rifle. He was casually watching the vehicles disembark as the girl in the kiosk behind him seemed to be waving people through without stopping to scrutinise any of the passports that were being held out of their owners' car windows. Anyone could see that the man with the gun and the girl in the kiosk had had their conversation interrupted and were eager to resume it. It didn't take a genius either to figure out what the topic of that conversation might have been. When Deacon saw what was happening up ahead, he followed suit and held out his passport. As he past the kiosk he heard the man with the gun and the girl in the kiosk shouting to each other and laughing over the din of the passing cars. *The language of courtship is in a world of its own; the words don't matter, the flirtation and the ambience of a conversation like that are understandable anywhere on the planet…providing the parties are in love.*

Before Deacon and the other tourists joined the main highway they were reminded—by a similar overhead electronic notice board to the one in Portsmouth—to drive on the right hand side of the road. Out on the highway he soon found his bearings—the street signs being so wonderfully clear—and he found himself heading out along the road to Rennes which he had worked out was about an hour's drive away. As he motored along down through the country roads he noticed every now and then how the trees on either side of the road touched overhead. He began to think how the sight was so typically French, that is until he realised how absurd that idea actually was. *How can trees overhanging a country road be typically French?* He knew that trees seen anywhere in Britain overhanging the road look exactly the same as they do in France. It was only when he thought about it further that he stumbled onto a remarkable truth. If we look at trees overhanging the road in France they appear to be hugging each other, whereas in Britain they appear to be shaking hands in a far more formal greeting. After recalling scenes from memory of his native England and comparing them with the scenes before his eyes, Deacon came to the conclusion that if he were ever asked to identify the French photograph of the same scene hidden amongst ten others from anywhere else in the world, he could identify the French one ten times out of ten. French trees must be imbued with the same affectionate openness as the French people and British trees must have the unique reserve of the British people. The other thing he noticed—which he thought was terribly odd— was how quiet the roads were, he had been driving for half an hour without seeing any traffic heading in the opposite direction.

He pulled into a lay-by and stopped the engine so that he could get out and stretch his legs.

It was only when he stepped from the car that he realised how tired he was, he had managed to lay down in his cabin but he didn't sleep in the true sense of the word. His rest had been ruined by his over-active mind and the strangeness of his temporary environment. He looked at his watch and it was nine thirty, he worked out—after subtracting the hour—that he had been on the go for almost seventeen hours and during that time all he had eaten was a *slosh* of stewed shin beef and chips. He thought about trying to bed down in the car for a couple of hours but the fact that he was in a foreign country made him think again, he didn't know the law in France and there was always the danger of bandits no matter where you are in the world. He walked the few steps back to the roadway and looked up and down its length, still there was no sign of any other vehicle in either direction, it was beginning to get darker and it was eerily quiet. He walked back to his car and went around to the far side of it but before he opened the door he peered into the dense woods beside him and shouted, "Hello!" His voice was immediately absorbed by the wall of wood, but the sudden sound startled a couple of early roosting birds and the sound of their flapping wings carried through the wood's high canopy before it faded once again to silence. It was then that a curious thought struck him and spawned an ambiguity of apprehensive fear and excitement that could only occur in the mind of Richard Deacon. He was alone in the world, lost in the wilderness, a tiny raft on the ocean of tribulation, if he were to survive this ordeal it would be by the sharpness of his own wit and guile and the strength of his will to live. Lost in his exaggerated thoughts, the faint rumbling sound in the distance became the rising of the thundering hooves of the Talisman of Set—the personification of sterility and evil—as he roared from the gates of the underworld to wreak havoc on the unsuspecting world. As the noise erupted into a heart-stopping crescendo Deacon ducked down behind the feeble safety of his car. The howling beast climaxed in a gust of dust-filled wind that not only shook Deacon and his car, it swayed the trees behind him in its evil wake. Unhurt and thankful that the Talisman had missed him this time, he emerged from the dust and blinked his eyes just in time to see a juggernaut speeding towards Rennes with its load of frozen goods for the local supermarket. *Get a hold of yourself Richard you are supposed to be on holiday not scaring yourself to death with a scene from one of your own novels!*

He climbed wearily back into the car and continued on in the wake of the Talisman towards Rennes—his plan was to find a place to eat and sleep for the night and resume his adventure in the morning—the thought of a warm bath and a bowl of soup at that moment was a vision of paradise.

A few miles along the road he came to a long straight stretch of highway and despite the growing gloom of the fading daylight he could see a fair way into the distance. He hoped that the clearing and the low building he could see up ahead would be a roadside café. As he neared the clearing he could see that it was; he pulled into the car park and it was obvious that he had found a truck stop. A mixture of dust covered cars and heavy goods wagons were parked up in no great orderly fashion at the far side of the rough dirt car park. He drove alongside one of the cars and cut the engine; he looked over to the rather tatty looking café and momentarily thought about moving on to somewhere a little more up-market. Luckily a timely combination of hunger, fatigue and common sense got the better of him and he decided that it would be foolish to press on. After all, there was no telling that the next oasis would be any better than the one he was at.

He got out of the car and walked tentatively towards the building, his earlier fears that he had stumbled onto a flop-house rather than a café were further compounded by the flaking paintwork of an ancient sign above the window at the side of the front entrance. The windows facing the road were caked in dust and grime; the only saving grace was the welcome sight of two beautiful arrangements of flowers in big pots at either side of the doorway—a clear indication of a woman's touch—always a promising sign. He opened the small door and ducked inside to find himself standing in a tiny wood-panelled reception area. He was relieved to see that the inside in no way resembled the neglected exterior of the building. The counter in front of him was of a highly polished walnut wood finish and to one side there was a gleaming brass bell with a word beneath it on a small card which indicated that he should ring it for attention. As he held out his hand above the bell a lady appeared through the door behind the counter and smiled at him. She spoke to him in French and it was obviously a warm welcome. Deacon smiled and began playing charades in the air in front of him. He pretended to be using a knife and fork and the lady soon had the message. With a graceful sweep of her hand she indicated that the dining room was through the door on his right. He opened the door and immediately he heard the sound of good natured chatter from the patrons already inside. The lady from the reception had come through to meet him and show him to a table. The room appeared to be divided into three sections; in his section there were several neatly laid out dining tables dotted around in no discernable order, the second section had the bar area complete with bar stools and to the side of this there was a games area with a game of table football dominating the centre of the linoleum covered floor. Two of the dining tables were in use, several men were propping up the bar and four men were playing doubles at the football table. The company—apart from the reception lady—was made up entirely of men, it was an out and out truck stop and despite the flowers at the door and the neatly laid out tables it was clearly a man's place.

Without making eye contact with anyone Deacon sat quietly at the table indicated by the lady, she smiled again as she handed him a menu. He looked at it as she said something before walking away at the behest of one of the men at the bar wanting his glass refuelled. Deacon ran his eyes over the menu but it might as well have been written in Braille, he simply had no idea what anything was. He remembered Ingrid's advice about pointing to something and saying a word, but for the life in him he couldn't remember what the word was, he knew it began with a D but that was all. *Come on Deacon, you are a writer for heaven's sake and here you are*

128

about to starve to death for the want of one tiny word. Oh what the hell is it? His desperation only made matters worse, his mind—probably due to hunger and fatigue—just would not think properly. It was then that he noticed a word on the menu that he vaguely recognised; cochon! *That's definitely pork...Bingo!* Moments later the lady returned to take his order and triumphantly he pointed to the dish excitedly and said repeatedly: "This, I want this,"

The lady looked at him with a kind of playful frown before she said something that sounded like, "Wait a moment." She then went over to the bar and spoke to a gentleman sitting on a bar stool eating a bowl of soup. The man began to laugh and turned to look at Deacon who wasn't at all impressed at obviously being talked about. The man let his spoon fall onto the side of the bowl and he walked directly over to Deacon's table. "Good evening my friend," he said, "Brigette—our hostess—seems to think that you may need help, seeing as you have just offered to buy the whole establishment. Apparently you have just ordered the Blue Pig, that's the name of the place. Would you like me to help you choose something smaller and more appetising?"

Deacon saw the funny side of it and he was relieved to find help.

"I've only just arrived here and I'm afraid I'm making a terrible mess of things."

"Don't worry, there's nothing lost, we all need help from time to time. Let's see now, she has chops, either lamb or pork, she has a lovely stew on the go, she can do you fish and chips if you like. Just tell me what you fancy and I'll order it for you, it will save Brigette a lot of time and you a lot of money."

"I'll have the fish and chips please," Deacon said, "Will you join me for a drink when you have finished your soup? I would like to thank you properly. I had just about resigned myself to the fact that I was going to starve to death right here."

"Thanks, maybe next time, I have to press on. I'm driving one of those rigs out there and I want to make Rennes by tonight. Would you like me to tell Brigette that you would like a room for the night, I presume you are staying?"

129

"That's an excellent idea it could save a lot of confusion and potential embarrassment later," Deacon smiled.

The driver gave Deacon a wry smile, "You couldn't embarrass Brigette if you strolled in here stark naked and demanded to be spanked. She spends her life waiting on amorous French truckers day in and day out, believe me, she has seen it all and heard it all, and between me and you and her bedroom walls, she will have done it all too." With that the driver called Brigette over and ordered the meal and reserved his room, then, turning back to Deacon he asked if there was anything else he could do.

"No," Deacon said, "but I do have a question."

"Fire away," the driver smiled.

"I'm curious to know why the outside of the building appears to be so run-down when the inside is so inviting."

The driver nodded his head and laughed: "To an Englishman they don't seem to do much to entice the undecided peckish motorist who might be influenced by outward appearances. I think that reflects one small part of their wonderful philosophy. The French put all of their efforts and their resources into the things that matter to them, cuisine being a perfect example. It's not how the restaurant looks that matters, its how it tastes. It's that aspect that brings all these people—myself included—back time and time again."

Deacon smiled in acknowledgement as the driver went back to the bar to finish his soup.

Deacon's meal arrived a few minutes before the driver prepared to resume his journey to Rennes. The driver touched his forehead with his finger in a friendly salute to Deacon as he walked by. "Enjoy your stay, it's a beautiful old country with some fine people," he said.

"Thanks again," Deacon smiled, "and yes, the food is delicious." The driver kissed Brigette on both cheeks as though they were old friends and Brigette walked to the doorway to wave him off. *Now that's what I call being a good hostess,* Deacon thought as he took another mouth-watering bite of his first meal on French soil. *If all the other meals taste as good as this then I am in for the time of my life.*

At the end of his meal Brigette showed him to his room and once the door was opened she held out the key. Deacon thanked her for the meal and thought how he might indicate just how good it was. His first thought was to smile and rub his stomach whist licking his lips but he dismissed that idea when he imagined how ridiculous that would look, he also recalled what the driver had said about being naked and asking to be spanked. Instead he formed a circle with his forefinger and thumb and kissed it…she got the message and smiled politely. He noticed then for the first time what an exceptionally good looking woman she was; besides her lovely face she was narrow through the hips and well-blessed up front…a perfect combination. She went back to the bar oblivious to his wistful—some might say lecherous—thought scenario of 'if only,' and he went out to fetch his overnight bag from the car.

The bathroom was down the hallway but his dreams of a relaxing hot bath evaporated when he noticed the faint discolouration of a tide mark on the enamel. The very thought of submerging his body in the collective secretions of several thousand sweaty truck drivers over the decades filled his head with all manner of monstrous germs waiting to devour him. Instead he plumped for the shower and he stood under the relative safety of its luxurious fountain for a full twenty minutes before he turned in for the night. The moment his head touched the pillow he was away in the land of dreams and he didn't return until Brigette tapped lightly on his door just after eight o'clock on the following morning to wake him for breakfast. He thanked her and rolled over onto his back and with his hands underneath his head he looked up at the ceiling and stretched. He had worked out briefly the night before that he was perhaps one hundred and seventy miles from his final destination and he wanted to make an early start. He felt good after his restful night's sleep and he was in the mood to do some serious driving.

131

Chapter Twenty

He packed his things together in his overnight bag after washing in the shared bathroom—sharing a bathroom had been another first for him and one he disliked immensely—and he carried it out to the car. The trucks from the night before had disappeared and apart from his car and one other the car park was deserted. The warm morning air was still fresh but he knew the day was going to be hot and the freshness would disappear with each passing minute. He could hear birds singing and calling in the woods all around the café and he could see them flitting from branch to branch in the trees on the far side of the Autoroute. They reminded him momentarily of the home he had left behind. It was going to be a good day for driving. He looked at his newly acquired car and he wished for all the world that it was his beloved Morgan; that beautiful little car incarcerated in the air-conditioned garage—cum—prison back home was built for days like those.

Shaking the hopeless thought from his mind he walked stealthily back to the café to settle his bill and say goodbye to his buxom hostess. Brigette smiled and held out her hand. A brief stab of horror flashed into Deacon's brain when he realised that being out amongst the common people he would be required to have infinitely more bodily contact with them than he was comfortable with. But despite his momentary horror the pause was not long enough for Brigette to notice anything peculiar as his hand moved slowly forward. As their hands touched Deacon became aware of a startling contrast which aroused all his senses simultaneously. The glorious smell emitting from Brigette—almost as if she had bathed in the finest French perfume—was an indication of absolute femininity, yet the roughness of her hands were how one might imagine those of a farm labourer to be. *How very odd?* Deacon thought as he slid his hand from hers and backed out of the tiny reception area that he had found so unappealing the night before. *This whole country seems to be one of contrast, tatty buildings serving such wonderful food and the most feminine of women with the most masculine of hands. Is this a good thing or a bad thing to find that nothing is inwardly how it appears to be on the outside? Such a beautiful woman in one of my novels would never have rough hands. I wonder what the old girl from Bowton would make of a romantic heroine like that in one of her 'proper books'?*

Deacon eased the car into first gear as he motored through the deserted car park, he could see clearly down the empty road in both directions so he was already in third gear when the car turned smartly onto the Autoroute heading south. By his calculations he would be at his destination near the village of Petit Saint Jean in just over three hours.

Despite the glorious warmth of the early July day the roads were surprisingly quiet. Deacon drove on for mile after mile and pondered on the surrealism of the conditions. Back home on a day like that the traffic would be nose-to-tail with any combination of truckers, holiday makers, workers, cyclists, delivery vans and parents doing the school runs, even in the country at times the roads could be as congested as the city, but here as he ghosted along he didn't see another motorist for fifteen minutes at a time. South he drove along wonderfully straight roads lined with guard-of-honour style trees and beyond those, endless fields stretching from the roadside to the horizon. One peculiar thing he noticed every now and then were tiny wooden cabins in clearings at the side of the road with the word 'dégustation' written above in brightly coloured letters. All he could think of was the nearest English word which was 'disgusting'. In his mind he quickly deduced that there was some kind of French farmers' protest going on. They were disgusted at the price they were being paid for their produce. He submitted the question to memory for clarification when he was next in touch with Ingrid.

The miles rolled on and soon he was seeing signs for Angouleme, he knew that his turn off for Petit Saint Jean was not much further along the road. Sure enough, right where Ingrid had said it would be, he came to the turning for his new home. It had taken just under two hours to reach the tiny market village which was going to be his only source of contact with the outside world for the foreseeable future and his heart soared like a rising falcon...there was not a living soul in sight.

He drove on into the town and turned into the main square, still not the slightest sign of any life, just the white painted houses which had no obvious signs of uniformity. Each house was of a different shape and size, but they all had one thing in common, they had shutters on the windows, but best of all as far as Deacon was concerned...they were all shut. *My god, this is Paradise on earth, I have discovered a ghost town.*

Deacon didn't even bother to stop the car and stretch his legs, if this was the town and it was so serenely beautiful, then he couldn't wait to see his new house.

He followed the directions to his cottage along a road which took him out through the opposite end of town. The road wound out of town for a couple of kilometres before he found the turning he was looking for. It led him down a narrow road and up over a small rise. He stopped briefly to look at the scene before his eyes, there below him where the road levelled out he saw his cottage for the first time and it took his breath away. It was even more beautiful than Ingrid had described. Despite the stiffness in his aching limbs from the hours of travel from England he could hardly wait to park the car in the driveway and explore.

The car rolled to a halt in front of the closed gates and as he stepped from the car he could see that the gates barred the opening to what looked like a partially covered courtyard. He pushed open the gates and they automatically swung back under their own weight and were secured against two small stone posts. He drove the car in through the gates and closed them to lock out the outside world. The exploration of his new home would be done in exactly the same way he penned his best selling novels, in absolute privacy, with every inch being mentally logged.

Chapter Twenty One

He stood in the courtyard and breathed in deeply; the sudden intake of fresh air after the stale air of the car made his head swim momentarily but it wasn't an unpleasant experience, if anything it added to the feeling of being drunk on nothing but the splendour of his surroundings. The car too seemed to be taking in the wonder of the moment as the engine made a gentle wheezing noise as it cooled in the shade of the lattice covered part of the courtyard. His eye was drawn to a brightly painted sign above and to the right of the old front door, the sign read: 'Le jardin du fraise', it was obviously the name of the cottage and he made a second mental note to add to Ingrid's list of translations. He didn't know it at the time but the answers to his questions were about to be answered by quite an unexpected oracle.

He walked to the door and gently put the key into the lock, the cottage had only been vacated a few days earlier but the spiders had wasted no time in spinning an intricate network of cobwebs over the door. Rather than brush them away he let them break as he pushed the door open. Before he stepped over the threshold he paused and wished himself good fortune in his new home.

The kitchen was bigger than he expected but a French kitchen is one of the most important rooms in any home so he should have had an idea that things were likely to be a little different than the way things are set out in an English kitchen. In England a kitchen is used to prepare food, in France a kitchen is regarded as a sacred place with the subject of complete devotion being second only to God Almighty and a very close second at that. It is also a place for family and social gatherings; in short, it is the hub of French life in the town or in the country.

Great pans and other odd looking, some even rather dangerous looking kitchen implements hung from ancient pegs driven into the old wooden beams holding up the ceiling, many of the things were unrecognisable to Deacon but all had the same thing in common, they had been well used and discoloured over

135

the decades. *I wonder how many families have tasted the delights of your culinary produce?*

On the long wooden kitchen table placed neatly in the centre were a bowl of fruit and a vase of sunflowers, leaned against the base of the vase was an envelope addressed to *Mr Richard Deacon.* Intrigued as to its contents he picked it up and turned it over to check for an indication of its author before he opened it. The back of the envelope was blank but from the delicately ornate handwriting on the front Deacon deduced that it had been written by a feminine hand and a very refined one at that. He took out the letter and began to read:

Dear Mr Deacon

My husband and I cannot thank you enough for coming to our rescue when we needed to find a buyer for our cottage; your offer was most generous. We both wish that you will be as happy here as we have been. It is with a heavy heart that we leave our Paradise behind, but it is gratifying to know that it has been passed into caring hands.

There are a few things which you may find helpful in your first few days here. The local folk will fall over themselves to help but they do not speak one word of English, so even the best intentions are likely to be misunderstood. Firstly we have left you a list of commonly used local words, you will not find them quite so easily in the English/French dictionary that you have no doubt brought along. They are written out on a sheet of paper behind the clock on the mantelpiece. Market day is every other Thursday and it is one of the few times that the village really comes to life, the market starts early in the morning and closes from 1-3 in the afternoon before it opens again until around 7pm. It sells everything from soap powder to sheep and from pans to piglets; so be warned. Haggle by all means for the more unusual, expensive things but the food prices are well marked and reasonable, so haggling is not commonly practised. For the past few months we have been approached by the local 'scugnizzi' offering to carry our shopping but a simple 'shoo' or a wave of the walking stick sees them off, we think they are the children of travellers so, hopefully, they will have moved on in a week or so. You may have noticed the name of the cottage 'Le jardin du fraise' it simply means 'The Strawberry Garden', it is not the postal address so feel free to change it if it doesn't suit you. Finally, and as a token of our debt to you we have left you a bottle of your favourite champagne in the 'cave' which is opposite the front door. The 'cave' is a part subterranean wine cellar and it will keep the champagne at more or less the exact temperature for drinking. You will also find that the cave is well stocked with various fine wines; my husband's illness means that he can no longer enjoy wine as much as he did. The cave and its contents are now yours along with our best wishes. Enjoy your stay here and may you find the peace and happiness to create your next best-selling novel; we do so love and enjoy your books.

Yours sincerely

Anna & Graham Bennett

Deacon smiled as he looked up at the clock on the mantelpiece and saw that there was indeed a page sticking out from behind it. His eyes went back to the letter and he picked out two phrases, 'The Strawberry Garden' and 'scugnizzi'. He liked the idea of the name of the cottage so that one was soon put to rest; the other phrase however needed perhaps a little more thought. He read the word again slowly and out loud "S c u g n i z z i." *I am sure that I have heard this word before,* he thought, *I think it is an Italian name for the gypsy street children of Naples.* He shrugged his shoulders as he put the letter back and breathed in heavily. The air in his nostrils was a mixture of freshly baked bread and the smell of lovely old sherry barrels.

Off the kitchen were three identical doors, he paused to decide which door to open first. The nearest one was at the side of the door leading from the courtyard and the furthest away was at the far end of the kitchen, but the door that intrigued him most was almost in the centre of the kitchen wall opposite the fireplace, *Yes, I think I will start with you.* He opened the door and found to his delight that it was what used to be known in England as a larder. That was in the days before fridges and chest freezers and was used to keep produce fresh because it was windowless and cool. He was even more delighted to see that the larder was still in apparent full usage. On the lower shelves were tins of food that the Bennetts' had very kindly left behind and lower still were the red wine shelves which were also handsomely well stocked.

Next he tried the door near the front door and found himself standing in a delightfully wood panelled study that still had enough bookshelves to suggest that it was once used as a library and could be again without too many alterations. He ran his fingers along the surface of the fine oak desk and rubbed them together; he always believed that he could tell both the quality of the wood and the quality of the craftsmanship of a piece of furniture simply by touching it. It was of course nonsense but it was something he believed and nothing would ever convince him otherwise. He perceived that the wood was of the finest quality and as such would be a perfect launching pad for his next literary masterpiece.

He backed out of the room whilst still mentally placing his personal belongings here and there around the room. He walked over to the third door and turned the well worn, shiny brass handle, he pushed the door open to reveal the full splendour of the living room. His eye was immediately drawn across the room to the French window which opened on to a garden. The exploration of the garden would have to wait until the inside of the house had been thoroughly absorbed into his senses. On the floor was an ornate carpet of ancient Persian design, if he wasn't mistaken, for it to fit so perfectly into the given floor area it would have had to have been specially made. To his right there was a magnificent old fireplace with everything as intact as the day it was first installed, which in his estimation was at the turn of the twentieth century. At either side of the fireplace were two plush leather armchairs and beneath the living room window was a great canvass covered sofa, one big enough, Deacon noted, for a man to comfortably collapse onto after a night of heavy drinking. At the far end of the room was the door which Deacon presumed would be the doorway to the bed chambers.

The upstairs he found to be more or less equally divided into four rooms, three spacious bedrooms and an ornately opulent bathroom, the door to each room was off the landing area at the top of the stairs. The exquisite, tastefully decorated bathroom was obviously renovated for luxury and not just a place to make the body clean and after his exploration and the rigours of his travel Deacon was eagerly looking forward to putting its promising delights to full use. The first bedroom he explored looked out over the front courtyard where the car was still faintly sighing. He looked out through the window over what was the front garden and he saw what had been described in the Bennett's letter as 'the cave'. This made him add another scene to his planned luxurious bath night, that of downing a couple of bottles of whatever delights he discovered in the cool shade of its interior. The two back bedrooms were almost identical mirror-images in terms of furniture and lay-out, each had a great king-sized bed which dominated the floor space yet left plenty of room to access the modernised walk-in wardrobes. Both rooms had his and her dressing tables which suggested that the Bennett's would have entertained many overnight guests in days gone by.

The view from the back bedroom windows made Deacon realize that there was far more land attached to the cottage than he had imagined. The garden was completely enclosed by a high gray-stone wall which was obviously designed for privacy rather than security; he could deduce that by the fact that to the left of the wall was a flower covered archway which led to a postern which in turn led to the wooded area which surrounded the cottage on three sides.

With the house more or less explored he went back through the house and into the courtyard. The scent in the air around him was sweet and dry as he savoured the slow, deep intake of breath *I have found the Paradise that I have searched for in every word I have ever written.* His eyes closed as he let the fine bouquet of the early afternoon excite his flared nostrils and when he finally opened them he was looking directly at the entrance to the cave. *Hmm, the exploration of the grounds may have to wait, depending on what treasures lie within.* The heavy padlock on the outer door of the cave was a good indication of the value of its contents but, where was the key? *Now if I was old Bennett, where would I keep the key?* Deacon thought for a moment before he had the idea that the key might be kept in the vicinity of the old larder in the kitchen. He walked back to the house and opened the larder door. Sure enough hanging on a nail at the side of the door was the key to a padlock. Two minutes later Deacon was in the cave surrounded by four walls decked out floor to ceiling with wine racks and although the racks were not fully adorned there were still visibly over fifty dust-covered bottles of different vintage and of course the bottle of his favourite champagne left as a moving in gift from the Bennetts. He closed his eyes like a child in a candy store and pointed his finger after rotating his arm. "I will have…you," he said as his outstretched finger came to rest pointing at a fine Burgundy Pinot Noir. He slid the bottle carefully from its dusty resting place and carried it like a new-born infant to the table in the kitchen. He uncorked the bottle and went back to the cave to put it back under lock and key as the wine had chance to breathe. His first full day in France was one of the most memorable days of his life. It had started with him touching the rough hand of an otherwise beautiful woman, a touch that momentarily made him recoil in horror and yet excited his wonder at the juxtaposition of arguably God's greatest creation, woman. And at the end of the same day he was savouring the fruit of the vine which gains unfathomable beauty with age and gives the world yet another mystifying enigma.

Chapter Twenty Two

Deacon awoke on his second full day in France in exactly the same position that he had crashed intoxicated on the previous night. The combination of travel fatigue and the fine Burgundy had taken an early toll on his aging constitution and he had fallen asleep on the comfort of the canvass sofa. He opened his eyes and smacked his dry tongue against the roof of his mouth. The day was bright but the room was cool, in that instant Deacon knew that the house had been purposely built to face south giving the courtyard the full benefit of the afternoon and evening sunshine. He made his way through to the kitchen and turned on the cold tap. He let it run through his fingers before he splashed his face. He cupped his hands and took a mouthful of water which he immediately spat out in disgust. It tasted like a mixture of drained vegetable water and cold coffee. *My God! No wonder they drink so much wine, this is raw sewage!* He turned from the tap and went to the fridge to find alternative light refreshment. His heart sank at the sight of the empty interior. There was nothing in the house to drink but wine and for the very first time in his life he was horrified at the thought. It was then he remembered that Mrs Bennett had mentioned a market in her note. He picked up the note and saw that he was in luck; it was market day. The exploration of the gardens would have to wait until his more immediate tasks had been accomplished, he needed drinking water and he needed it fast.

He fired up the car and backed it out onto the empty road; the sun was already blisteringly hot and adding to his discomfort. He pointed the car towards the village of Petit Saint Jean and he gunned the gas. Minutes later he found himself on the outskirts of town and to his chagrin he found that the road into the village had been blocked off to traffic for the duration of the market day. He found a place to park on the road further back along the road he had come and he began the long, thirsty, walk back to the village for his liquid supplies.

As he neared the market the steady hum of activity filled the air and grew in volume with every step. He was suddenly gripped by fear at the thought of having to rub shoulders with hordes of smelly French peasants who were busy buying and selling honking piglets and scrawny looking, semi-bald poultry. If it wasn't for his burning thirst he would have turned on his heels and driven to the next town for his water. He did what he could to bolster his courage by convincing himself that he would simply grab the first water bottle he found, throw more than enough francs on the stall of the lucky retailer to cover the cost and sprint back to the relatively germ-free refuge of his car to guzzle it down his parched throat. That is what he envisaged would happen, but his first tentative steps into the foray of a rural French market soon put paid to that idea. The first thing that took him stunningly off-guard was the wonderful attire of the shoppers, they all seemed to have dressed in their Sunday finery; an observer like Deacon could easily have mistaken the scene before him for a congregation off to church for a Sunday morning service. There was no sign at all of the cut-throat rogues that his mind had conjured up form his distant recollections of the French peasants in Victor Hugo's classic *The Hunchback of Notre Dame*. People smiled and nodded in his direction and the stall-holders called out to him and the other shoppers obviously inviting them to taste a small sample of whatever food they were selling. The other thing that immediately struck him was the wonderful smell of perfume lingering in the slipstream of every female that walked within nosing distance. *What a cacophony of delightful bouquets!*

Suddenly remembering his thirst and his mission, he moved quickly by the cheesemonger and the rotund, red-faced fellow selling cured sausage meat and headed towards the centre of the market. Sure enough, as Mrs Bennett had said in her note, there were people selling piglets and poultry on either side of him and as he stopped momentarily to assess his bearings he saw for the very first time the other curious thing she had mentioned…a scugnizzi! Of course he could not be entirely certain that the poor waif with the enormous brown eyes which were staring back at him as if *he* were the curiosity was a scugnizzi, but his powers of deduction soon led him to the unquestionable conclusion that he was right. Everyone else at the market was dressed in their finery and this ragged urchin was dressed in little more that the rags of a gypsy boy. The sight of the scugnizzi made Deacon forget about his thirst for a moment as he narrowed his eyes to look the boy up and down. He could see that the boy was no more than about nine years old and his dark complexion gave him more of a Spanish appearance than that of the local French folk. Sticking out from the boy's short trousers were the skinniest pair of legs he had ever seen, they would have looked more fitting attached to a sparrow than to a growing boy and Deacon wondered how on earth such rickety little things could hold the rest of his body upright. Gazing down to his feet he saw that the boy was barefoot. Suddenly Deacon became aware of a presence which came almost swaggering up to the side of him. He turned to come face-to-face with what was obviously the village bobby. The policeman nodded to Deacon who returned the gesture before turning once again to look at the boy. To his amazement the boy who moments earlier had been standing not ten feet away had disappeared seemingly into thin air. Deacon quickly deduced that the sudden arrival of the local constabulary could be the reason why the scugnizzi made such a smart exit and he turned once again to face the bobby.

The policeman spoke to Deacon in French and Deacon replied by splaying his hands and saying: "English." His voice cracked under the strain of the dryness in his throat and he coughed slightly to summon any dregs of moisture so that he could repeat himself. The policeman put up his hand to indicate his understanding and saved Deacon the trouble. The policeman then tilted his head and said in broken English: "Holiday." He said it in such a comical way that it sounded like, "Chollyday." Deacon nodded knowing full-well that he could never even begin to explain what he was doing there, instead he put his fingers to his throat and said: "Water." Miraculously the policeman immediately understood what Deacon was looking for and he turned and beckoned Deacon to follow him. The policeman swaggered on

143

through the market at what Deacon found to be an uncomfortably slow pace. It was as though the policeman was parading a dangerous exotic animal captured in the deepest African jungle before an awestruck public, rather than leading a thirsty tourist to a stall that sold water. Every now and then the officer stopped to exchange pleasantries with one of the locals and Deacon felt compelled to stop and wait until the officer was ready to move on again. Eventually the officer came to a stop at the end of a row of market stalls and pointed to a shop across the street. "Viola monsieur," he said in triumph as he used his other hand to urge Deacon forward. Deacon smiled at the officer and almost sprinted into the shop.

Bottled water is easily recognisable in any country and within a minute he was standing at the counter with a bottle in one hand and his wallet in the other. The bell on the door had clearly sounded to alert the shopkeeper that he had a potential customer so *where the hell is he?* Deacon thought. By then his thirst was making him feel decidedly faint and it took all of his composure to remain upright. It was then that he saw the scugnizzi for the second time that morning. The bell chimed behind him and the ragged boy marched straight up to the counter, he didn't even break his stride as he scooped up a bottle of the same water that Deacon was holding. The boy pointed at the price on the label and indicated to Deacon that he should leave that amount on the wooden tray at the side of the counter and take his water. *Ah, an honesty box, I have seen these before in remote rural areas back home but never in a shop.* Deacon duly put his money down and almost ripped off the plastic top before he drank the first quarter of the 3 litre bottle. He wiped his mouth with the back of his hand and turned to thank the scugnizzi…only to find that he had disappeared again.

Back out on the street Deacon knew that the only way back to his car was to walk back through the market, so he decided to take full advantage, take a deep breath and purchase a few supplies. He needed bread and cheese and potatoes and fruit, in fact he found something that he thought he would need on almost every stall. He followed the same ritual of pointing to whatever he wanted and offering a banknote, the stall-holders took their payment, gave him his change and off he went to the next stall to repeat the ritual. Soon he had quite a bundle of heavily laden shopping bags. It was as he struggled under the strain of their weight and the sweltering sun that he saw the scugnizzi for the third time. Once again he seemed to appear out of thin air. Silently he pointed to the shopping bags and indicated that he was strong enough to help carry them. Under normal circumstances Deacon would have done as Mrs Bennett had suggested and shooed him away but the boy had practically saved his life not half an hour earlier so he could hardly do that. He held out one of the bags and the boy eagerly took it. Together they walked back to Deacon's car and loaded up the boot. Deacon took out a 10 franc note and offered it to the boy. To his surprise the boy refused to accept it. Deacon looked at him and narrowed his eyes. The boy must have sensed the look of bewilderment on his face. He made a sign with his hands that meant the payment was too much for the service. When the penny dropped Deacon could hardly believe his eyes. The boy was haggling with him for less money than he was being offered! *What a strange country this is.* Deacon delved into his pocket and pulled out two one franc coins which the boy accepted. Deacon climbed into his car and pulled out onto the street, he looked in his rear-view mirror to take one last look at the boy, but once again he had disappeared, instead Deacon saw the massive frame of the policeman standing on the edge of town watching as the tourist drove out of sight.

Chapter Twenty Three

Deacon drove back to the cottage with a strange inner struggle going on. His flaming thirst had been satisfied, yet his mind had been inflamed to the same degree by thoughts of the boy who had helped him in the shop and appeared again later, apparently out of thin air to help carry his heavy shopping bags. *What a curious little character he was, what sort of gypsy boy turns down ten Francs and haggles down to only two?*

As he neared the cottage the sparkling fields on either side of the road and the fresh, clean air helped put the matter from his mind, besides, he had other business to attend to, namely, the exploration of the estate he had recently added to the Deacon Empire. He parked the car and began to unload the shopping bags, as he walked to the door thoughts of the young lad re-emerged as he felt the weight of the bag the young lad had carried. *How could those spindly legs bear such a heavy load?* The lad's knees resembled two knots in a length of string and yet he managed to walk alongside Deacon without a hint of physical strain. The boy's face re-appeared in Deacon's mind as he thought how he had negotiated the going rate for his services. His dark brown eyes had gleamed in the sunlight of the late morning and Deacon suddenly recognised retrospectively that the look in his eyes was one he had rarely seen in all of his business dealings…it was one of honesty. *I should have insisted that he take the ten Francs; in terms of relative effort that boy did far more to earn his meagre wages than Redfearn and Daniels have ever done.*

With the shopping put away Deacon decided to make a bite to eat before he set out on his exploration. An omelette seemed like the most appropriate and less troublesome dish, so he set to work. The first major stumbling block he encountered was in locating the buttons to ignite the cooker. After much deliberation he discovered that it was in fact a solid fuel contraption. His eyes moved dejectedly between the eggs and the means of cooking them in its stone cold, obstinate condition. He had never made a fire in his life, come to think of it, he had never made an omelette, suddenly he found himself in an impossible predicament, how to combine the two tasks and create something edible on the same day? He solved the culinary problem by hacking the end off a loaf, slicing it down the middle and making something that loosely resembled a cheese sandwich. He washed it down with half a bottle of red wine from the larder and his immediate hunger was satisfied; the conundrum of fire-making could be postponed until the extent of his out-lying property had been mapped out and identified. He pushed the cork back into the bottle of red wine and tucked it into a rucksack along with a glass and a napkin, if his exploration proved to be disappointing, then at least he could salvage some enjoyment from the fine old claret.

Once out in the courtyard he slung the rucksack over his shoulder and headed off towards the far end of the building. His plan was to explore the outside of the cottage and the outer buildings before he ventured out across the big open grassed area that was surrounded by the high garden wall. At the back of the cottage he found a delightful little herb garden, he paused just long enough to fill his lungs with the various smells wafting up in the air above them all vying for supremacy to entice the busy insects. To the side of the cottage he found himself standing in what appeared to be a former stable, there were two empty stalls where the horses would have been housed and an open space behind them where he presumed the carriage would have been kept. Up above the stalls and just below the high rafters was a mezzanine type hayloft. He thought about the old girl he had met on the ferry from Bolton and how she may have read about secret romantic encounters between the master of the house and the buxom scullery maid up in a hayloft just like that in one of her *proper novels*. He smiled and shook his head before he went out through the door at the far end of the stable and saw that it led to the patio that the French windows of the living room opened out onto. The patio was surrounded by a flower garden and beyond that was a large recently cultivated area that he quickly realised was a vegetable patch. *The Bennetts' certainly had green fingers.*

The immediate vicinity of the cottage had been fully explored and his exertions warranted a seat on the garden bench with a glass of wine. He sat in the sunshine and as he savoured the red nectar he planned his next move. He drained his glass and carefully wiped it with the napkin before tucking everything away ready for the next leg of his epic voyage of discovery. He would walk through the vegetable patch and begin his tour of the field at the rear of the cottage by sticking to the wall and following it around its full perimeter. At the far end of the vegetable patch he was pleasantly surprised to find a small orchard behind the stable, it was positioned in such a way that it could not be seen from the French windows in the living room, so until that moment he had no idea that it existed. *This exploration lark is far more exciting than I had imagined. Why a man could be self sufficient here indefinitely, wine and food in abundance, all I need to do is work out how to grapple with that ancient cooker.*

It soon became obvious after the first fifty metres of walking along the wall that there was very little else to see but a wide open grassed area, there was of course the postern that he had noted the day before. He had planned to make a start on writing ideas down for a possible scenario of his next book for later in the afternoon, but the postern had aroused his curiosity. He looked at his watch and decided there was still time enough to perhaps take a brief look at what was beyond the limits of his empire. He pushed the iron gate open and stepped out onto a well-worn footpath. It veered away from the wall and up through a small coppice that looked as though it spread up and over a low ridge. He walked along the path up on to the ridge and he saw that the coppice ended by the banks of a river. He listened to the babbling flow of the water and his heart leapt in sheer delight, he really was in paradise, he had found the most beautiful place on earth. *The poor Bennetts must have been devastated to have to leave this place behind. I would not have sold it for any amount of money.*

Just then as he pondered his good fortune the strangest thing happened, he saw in the distance on the far side of the river the gypsy boy from the market place. It was *him* of that he had no doubt, but what was he doing there and how had he made it there so soon? As Deacon stared at him in a trancelike fixation the boy raised his skinny arm in the air and waved an obvious hello. Remembering what Mrs Bennett had said about not encouraging the scugnizzi he refrained from returning the gesture and instead turned smartly round and headed back in the direction of the postern. Once back on his own land he wondered again what the gypsy boy was doing out there. He didn't know it then, but before the close of the following day he would know the answer...

Chapter Twenty Four

Back at the cottage Deacon hung his rucksack behind the door of the larder and made himself a coffee before he went into the wood-panelled study to set up his lap-top. If ever there was a day to work on new ideas then that was it. The sun was beating down on a glorious early afternoon and the study was cool and inviting. The window looked out onto the courtyard and an array of tiny, industrious birds flitted frantically from the ground to the wooden lattice work which was entwined with beautiful fresh clematis.

The lap-top was set up and ready in a matter of minutes, he pushed the 'on' button and lovingly stroked the oak desk beneath it as he waited for the screen to spring into life. Soon the study was filled with the familiar tap, tap, tapping of the keys that had dominated so much of his life. He didn't notice it though, because from the moment the first word was born onto the page he was lost in the impregnable world of his wonderful imagination…a world that everyone and everything came second best to.

He had been working for twenty minutes or so when he thought he heard a sound in the kitchen, he stopped writing and listened. No, there was only the sound of silence broken momentarily by the call of a bird and the hum of an insect in flight. He carried on with his writing until he heard the sound again, this time it was more distinct than the other sounds of the day. He listened and there it was again, the noise was a kind of slapping sound. He opened the study door and looked about the empty kitchen, there it was again. He turned his head to try to focus his ear on the direction it was coming from and realised that it was coming from the front door. Rather than open the door straight away he crept over to the window and peered round the curtain to see if he could indentify the mystery caller. He could see the area around the doorstep was clear upwards from what would have been his own waist height so whoever it was must have been less than a metre tall. *If I am about to be burgled I think I can manage to fend off someone half my size.* He opened the door with a manly tug to give himself an air of derring-do but found himself face-to-face with nothing more dangerous than a fish. He looked down at the doorstep and there at his feet was a lovely plump trout. It was so fresh that it was still flapping its tail against the stone step and opening its mouth to breathe. *Oh my word…brainfood! Where on earth has this little beauty come from?* He quickly gathered up the fish and carried it to the sink, he filled the sink with cold water and plopped it in. He waited until it regained its senses fully and began to swim before he went out into the courtyard to see how it had made its way to his doorstep. He opened the gates to the property and looked both ways down the lane; there was no sigh of anyone in either direction. *How very strange.* He walked around the cottage taking the same route he had taken earlier in the day but still he found no sign of a living soul. *What did it all mean? Was it some quaint old French tradition for welcoming new neighbours?* His first instinct was to give Ingrid a call back in England to see if she could offer a feasible explanation, but rather than risk making a fool of himself through his obvious ignorance he decided to wait until they next spoke and perhaps he would casually slip it into the conversation.

He went back into the kitchen and checked in on the trout, he didn't know how to kill it, so that put eating it out of the question. He wanted to give it some careful consideration before he disposed of it out of hand, just in case it was a gift of food from his neighbours. He didn't want it in the sink though so he ran a bath upstairs and transferred it from the sink to the bath via a five litre saucepan.

It was late in the afternoon when the tap, tap, tapping in the study finally subsided and Deacon emerged satisfied that he had done a hard day's work. An evening of wine and relaxation was calling him and he was just about ready for it. It was still far too warm for him to even contemplate having another go at fire making so he rummaged round in the larder until he found a tin of smoked sardines which he ate with the remainder of his French loaf. After his meal he went out onto the patio to enjoy another bottle of Mr Bennett's red wine. On his way through the living room to the patio he noticed several leaflets of local places of interest in a newspaper rack that Mrs Bennett had kindly left for him to browse through. There were several medieval castles, several distilleries and a Disney-like theme park. The theme park and the thought of heaving crowds was a definite no-go but the distilleries were a very tempting option for the day when he planned his first holiday excursion.

He spent the remainder of the day sitting on the patio bench, listening to the sounds of nature winding down as he wound down with his wine. He thought a little more about the gypsy boy and he pondered—without solution—the riddle of the trout which was currently making itself at home in his bath. Even if he couldn't eat it at least it had provided him with some humourous distraction and one day the event might even re-surface in one of his novels.

Chapter Twenty Five

Deacon's second night in the cottage was nowhere near as restful as the first night had been. Images of the day kept repeating over in his mind and he couldn't sleep. The night was hot and clammy and no combination of well used sleep inducing tactics could settle him long enough to doze off. Finally he threw the thin bed sheet off and made his way over to the window, perhaps letting in some cool night air would do the trick. The bedroom window looked out towards the river and as he pushed the window open he looked over to the trees in the coppice. At first he wasn't sure if he was seeing things or if the tiredness of his mind was playing tricks on him, but he could swear he saw a strange orange glow emanating from the far side of the ridge and eerily lighting up the immediate sky above it. His first impulse was to get dressed and go over to investigate but that impulse was soon discounted and flung from his mind when it dawned on him that it could possibly be the glow from a gypsy camp fire. *Oh my Lord, I could be living next door to a band of cutthroat gypsy bandits! If I go over there and they catch me, how do I explain that I could pay any amount of money for my freedom? What if they sell me into the white slave trade?* He had visions of himself being tied to a wagon and dragged barefoot out of France before being drugged and smuggled into Africa where he would be marched across the blistering dessert to be sold to the highest Bedouin bidder. *I know what to do… I'll ring Ingrid.*

He closed the window and dashed downstairs to the phone; frantically he picked up the receiver and paused to steady himself ready to dial. His fingers trembled as they hovered above the numbers: *What the hell am I doing frightening myself to death over a camp fire in the distance? What if it's just a bunch of local kids innocently camping out? Besides, what could Ingrid do about it anyway?* Slowly he lowered the receiver until it clicked onto its cradle and he poured himself a stiff drink. *I need to get a grip and stop behaving like a stir-crazy lunatic, I have only been here for a day and I know nothing about this place or its people and their customs, so why should I think the worst?* As he sipped his drink and let the familiar warm glow emanate through his torso he resolved to take a trip back to the village in the morning and see if he could find someone who spoke English, he knew there would be no market so he would not have to mix with the heaving masses. His plan was to find out more about the place so that he could estimate the safety of living alone in a cottage that was easily accessible to anyone who wanted to plonk a live fish on his doorstep and then melt back into the surrounding countryside without a trace.

Chapter Twenty Six

The remainder of the night passed without incident and he awoke to find that he was still alive and his property had not been invaded by all manner of thieves and vagabonds. After he had dressed and taken nothing more than a morning coffee it was time to drive over to the village to see if he could glean any information that would perhaps put his overactive mind at rest as to his immediate safety. He was not prepared for what was about to happen next. He opened the front door to find another surprise on the doorstep, this time it was a rabbit, but unlike the fish of yesterday, he could see that it was dead. *This is it, I've had enough! I am going to find out once and for all who is responsible for depositing all this unwanted wildlife on my doorstep. Perhaps there is a local witches' coven and I am the target of some kind of spell?*

Picking up a live fish the previous day was just about bordering on the limit of his contact with a beast with such potential for being ridden with germs, but a dead rabbit would be positively teeming with all manner of life-threatening disease. He closed the door quickly and retreated into the kitchen. Over by the sink he remembered seeing a pair of bright yellow rubber cleaning gloves so he donned them ready for the removal of the rabbit operation. He opened the door again and hoisted the rabbit up by its feet; he carried it over to the dustbin in the courtyard and unceremoniously threw it in slamming the heavy lid down behind it. *All I have to do now is hatch a plan to snare the culprit. My trip to town will have to wait, spell or no spell I will put an end to this or I'll be damned.*

After a brief reconnoitring of the immediate area he worked out that he would be able to observe the front door if he stood inside the cave, which was perhaps thirty metres from the cottage. His plan was to leave the cave door open with just enough of a gap to be able to spy out and survey the whole of the front of the cottage without being noticed. He took the key from the larder and unlocked the cave before he crept inside and began his vigil.

Three hours passed without anything other than the same familiar sounds of the garden wildlife. He was just about to desert his post when his plan paid off in spectacular fashion. To his right he heard the unmistakable sound of footsteps rustling through the grass heading towards the cottage. He was dying to open the cave door wider so that he could see who or what it was. He knew that if he sprung his trap too early all could be lost, so he held his nerve and he held his breath as the swishing sound of the footsteps grew louder. The tension and excitement in his stomach turned instantly to one of bewilderment and anti-climax when the tiny frame of the little gypsy boy breezed by the open door without a care in the world. In the boy's left hand Deacon could see that he was carrying another live fish. He waited until the boy was almost halfway between the cottage and the cave before he emerged and called to the boy, "I say young man. What are you up to?" Instead of turning round in shock as Deacon fully expected him to, the boy ignored him completely and carried on striding confidently towards the cottage door. "You there!" Deacon called again. The boy by this time had reached the front door and stood before it. He raised his hand and knocked just as if Deacon wasn't there. It was only when Deacon's shadow fell over the boy that he turned and saw Deacon for the first time. "What do you want?" Deacon asked. The boy simply smiled and held out the wriggling fish. From the very first time that Deacon had seen the boy on the market he suspected that there was more to him than met the eye. And now he was face-to-face with him in that bizarre situation he realised that his suspicion was well founded. The riddle of the fish and the rabbit should have been solved but now it was even more difficult to understand. Instead of pursuing his confrontational approach Deacon's demeanour softened when he could see that the boy was offering him a gift, "Is this for me?" he asked. The boy touched his ear with his free hand and shrugged his shoulders indicating to Deacon that he was deaf. *That's why he didn't stop when I called him.* Deacon pointed to the fish and then to himself. The boy nodded and his smile widened into a warm, instantly infectious grin. Deacon smiled back at the boy, perhaps just as much in relief than in gratitude, he now knew where the fish and the rabbit had come from but what he didn't know was why.

Deacon pointed to the fish again and again to himself before he opened his palms. The boy instantly read the question and replied in a way that Deacon understood, it was because the boy had caught two fish and he only needed one. *What a lovely gesture.* Deacon shook his head and made out that he was holding a frying pan to hopefully indicate that he didn't know how to cook it. The boy stood for a brief moment with his brow furrowed, then, with an obvious burst of mental inspiration, he pointed to the cottage door. *He wants to take it in the kitchen, oh well, this could be interesting.* Deacon opened the door and invited the boy to go first. Without hesitation the boy walked over to the sink and dropped the fish in, turning the tap onto it as it flapped furiously against the enamel. He then pointed to the stove. Deacon shook his head and held his elbows as if to say that it was cold. He then stood in amazement as the boy disappeared out into the courtyard and returned moments later with kindling and three small wooden logs. Deacon's instincts by this time were screaming at him to 'shoo' the boy away as Mrs Bennett had suggested, but the calmer, curious side of him was telling him equally forcefully that he should perhaps see how the scenario played itself out. *Besides, I need to know how to light that fire if I am going to be self-sufficient for any length of time.*

With the kindling in place and expertly stacked in the firebox the boy produced two small stones from his pocket and knocked them together sharply to create a spark. To Deacon's astonishment within moments the logs were on fire and the firebox was closed to do its job.

It was clear that the boy was about to cook the fish, so Deacon felt obliged to bring the other fish from the bathtub upstairs and invite his originally unwelcome guest to stay for dinner. When he returned with the fish he saw that the boy had already killed the first fish and was busy gutting it on the kitchen table. He clumsily offered the boy the second fish, but instead of taking it the boy nodded his head in the direction of the sink implying that Deacon should do as he had done with the first fish and wash it thoroughly. Deacon couldn't help but smile at the audacity of the boy. *Here I am in my own house taking orders off a gypsy boy! If old Daniels and Redfern could see this they would have a heart attack.* Deacon put the fish in the sink and let the tap water wash over it. Seconds later the boy took the fish by the tail and banged its head on the table, within two seconds its head was off and it was cut from end to end ready for gutting. The boy then pointed to an empty wine bottle and made a pouring movement above the fish. *He wants to cook it in wine, my word, I think this little gypsy boy knows what he is doing.* By the time Deacon had returned from the cave with two bottles of red and white wine, the boy had found a suitable cooking dish and covered the trout with onions, garlic and a sprinkling of dried herbs from the larder. He pointed to the white wine and Deacon duly set to work with the bottle opener. The boy poured the wine over the fish, popped on the lid and put it in the hot oven. *A full bottle of white wine, this had better be worth it.* Deacon then watched fascinated as the boy cleaned up the mess of fish heads and guts and began to set the table for two.

Soon the delicious aroma drifting from the oven was wafting through the air and it was enough to convince Deacon that judging by the glorious smell, the use of the wine was definitely worth it. Twenty minutes later the unlikely pairing of dinner guests were sitting tête-à-tête with a dish of perfectly poached trout before them. Deacon was impressed further still as the boy showed impeccable manners by waiting for Deacon to try the dish first. Deacon delicately lifted his fork and showed the boy a trick of his own as he expertly twirled the fork through his fingers before he broke away a small piece of meat and raised it to his lips. He paused tantalizingly as if he was the special guest at the annual Gastronomic Society dinner and he carefully placed the meat onto his tongue. He closed his eyes in complete satisfaction as it melted in his mouth. The boy smiled broadly as Deacon made an exaggerated face of supreme pleasure. Deacon then nodded and the pair tucked in with gusto.

After dinner Deacon went through to his study and emerged moments later with a pencil and a blank sheet of paper. There were questions that he needed answers to and that was the best way he could think of to communicate quickly and effectively.

He drew a stick boy standing in between a stick man and woman. He wanted to know about the boy's parents. Deacon turned his drawing to the boy and immediately he knew what he was being asked. The boy took the pencil and set to work on his reply. Deacon was equally quick on the up-take when he saw that the boy had crossed out the two figures and replaced them with trees. *He lives alone and he lives in the woods. That explains the strange camp fire glow in the woods the other night.* Next Deacon drew the parents again and put a simple question mark beside them. The boy answered succinctly with a simple shrug of his shoulders. The boy then pointed to his wrist indicating that it was time for him to leave. Before Deacon had the chance to decide whether or not he wanted to invite him to stay a little longer, the boy was out of the door and with a wave of his hand he was back across the open grassed area and out of the postern leaving Deacon with a feeling that had been a stranger to him for as long as he could remember…he was filled with pangs of sadness. For the first time in his life he was not in complete control of his emotions. He couldn't understand his sadness until it dawned on him that he would have given anything for just five more minutes of the boy's company. He sat at the empty table as the range of his mixed up feelings moved from sadness to shame. *Why on earth didn't I ask the poor lad to stay?* He looked over at the bottle of red wine and reached for the corkscrew; perhaps he would find comfort and a little understanding in the fine Merlot. He put the tip of the corkscrew to the cork but he didn't puncture it, instead he dropped it onto the table. *No! I need to feel this pain, I'll be damned if I am going to numb these feelings with liquid analgesia.* The feelings suddenly gnawing at his insides were very simple to understand to an ordinary man, but Deacon was no ordinary man. He had met someone who had immediately touched him deep down in a place that he thought was impregnable, in short, he had found warmth in the form of a little gypsy boy and the turmoil in his whole being was the tug-of-war with the side of him that has lived a life of cold distance with the burgeoning feelings of simple human friendship.

159

That night, he went to bed stone cold sober and for the first time in his life, he thought of someone else above himself.

Chapter Twenty Seven

Deacon awoke to the clattering sound of an electrical storm raging overhead. The room lit up with each crack of lightening and the windows shook with the vibration of the roaring thunder. He ducked back beneath the warm blankets as the torrential rain pelted noisily against the glass. His mind drifted back to his childhood school days and how in his dormitory on stormy nights like this he would listen to the rain and imagine that he was an explorer out beneath the canvass on some undiscovered foreign plain. All the wild beasts that he would encounter as a child in his reverie came flooding back and he captured each one all over again to parade before a welcoming public on his triumphant return to old England. Those boyhood dreams were the cultivation of his remarkable imagination and start of the adventures that would bring his later novels to such exhilarating life for a world of insatiable readers. Suddenly, as if a streak of lightning had flashed into his brain, he was struck with the mental image of the gypsy boy out there all alone in the storm. He bolted upright and flung the blankets from his warm body. *Oh my Lord! The poor mite will be washed away if I don't find him and bring him in.* He leapt from the bed and hastily threw on his clothes from the night before. It had not occurred to him to bring along any bad weather clothing over to France so he put on his heaviest jacket and ventured out into the howling eye of the storm. The wind almost blew him off his feet and all he could imagine was the waif of a gypsy boy hurtling through the air amongst the bending trees, which he surely would unless he had tied himself to the ground. Deacon took his life in his hands as he headed for the postern across the open lawn as the blinding lightening crackled and fizzled in the air all around him. Out in the woods he realised that the storm was far worse than he first thought, the driving rain made it impossible for him to see his own hand in front of his face and it would have been foolish for him to continue. As the thunder rolled on into the distance he could hear the gushing roar of the swollen river beyond the wood and he reluctantly decided that enough was enough. He was drenched through to the skin and for every step forward he took the wind was blowing him two steps back. It would make more sense to go back to the cottage and ride out the storm before trying to find the boy again. Hopefully the boy's obvious survival skills included coping with such freakish weather and he would know what to do. It was a faint hope but it was all he could do as he forlornly turned and allowed the wind to blow him towards the cottage.

Back at the cottage Deacon stuffed his saturated clothes into the washing machine and towelled himself down. He looked out again at the storm through the window and he cursed it. After putting on dry clothing he went wearily through into his study and slumped dejectedly into the chair facing the computer. He typed in the words, 'If there is a God, then look after the young lad out there alone in the woods.' He looked at the cold words on the screen and he banged his clenched fists onto the desk because he knew the words were as futile as his rescue attempt. He jumped to his feet making the chair crash onto the floor as he began to pace the room cursing the storm again at every shuddering thunder clap.

The minutes waiting for the storm to break seemed like hours but eventually the wind dropped and the thunder tailed off into the distant sky. Deacon set off once more across the lawn and was soon picking his way carefully along the treacherously wet banks of the river; he had no idea which direction he should take, therefore he reasoned that to head north was as good a direction as any. He cut a lonely windswept figure against the darkness of the unforgiving sky as he scanned the landscape for signs that the boy was safe. It was no use, he saw nothing except endless miles of river winding and stretching out for as far as his eye could see. Finally, he stopped and headed back the way he had trudged, if the boy had tried to shelter there then he could see by the flattened grass where the river had burst its banks that he would not have stood a chance. For the next three hours Deacon searched for miles in either direction until he reached the awful conclusion that the boy was gone.

As he made his way to the cottage a second time he toyed with the idea of driving into the village to alert the local police. He soon put that thought from his mind when he remembered how the boy had avoided being seen by the policeman on that first market day and if the letter from Mrs Bennett was anything to go by the police would view his disappearance as good riddance. Besides the feeling of nausea that swept over him he also felt hopeless for the first time in his life. Neither his money nor his influence could do anything to help the little chap and at that moment he would have used all of it just to know where he was.

Deacon stopped to check the door of the cave as he passed it, he had hoped, in forlorn desperation, that maybe he had left it open and the boy had somehow found shelter there. Like his other hopes it was groundless and fruitless, the cave was locked. With all the possibilities exhausted his mind was a blank as he opened the cottage door and made his way to his study. Picking up the fallen chair, he lowered his aching body onto it. He blinked the moisture from his eyes as the sleeping computer came back to life and he looked at the screen at his impromptu prayer still stark and cold in the subdued light. *Well Lord, it looks like my loss will be your gain.* He sat at the computer and tapped the space bar until the only words left were, 'If there is a God'. He read them over and over to himself until the words began to form on his lips and the sounds coming from his mouth merged with the words on the screen. *I wonder how many times those words have been uttered by countless thousands of troubled souls?*

Time slipped by unnoticed as his mind drifted in and out of conscious thought. *Is it worth another search?* He looked up from the screen and said out loud: "Of course it's worth another search! The heroes in my books would never allow such things as mere physical exhaustion to stand in the way of their noble objectives." *Put your coat on Deacon and go back out, if you can't find him alive then the least you could do is find his poor body.* Once again the chair was unceremoniously flung backwards to the floor but this time with a very different emotion…determination. Deacon marched to the door with renewed vigour and a sense of purpose in his stride. *I will find that boy if it's the last thing I ever do!* Inspired by the words and actions of one of his fictional characters he strode out once again across the lawn towards the woods. He almost tore the postern gate from its hinges in his eagerness to open it. Yet, before he took another step his computerised prayer was answered, there in front of him stood the bedraggled gypsy boy swaying with obvious exhaustion. Deacon's heart leapt so high it almost burst through the top of his head as he bounded towards the boy, but the overwhelming joy rising through his body instantly evaporated as he watched him slump awkwardly to the ground. Deacon gathered him up in his powerful arms and raced back to the cottage, he could feel that the boy was burning with a fever.

The first thing Deacon did was take off the boy's saturated clothing; he wrapped him in a towel and carried him upstairs to his bedroom. Looking at his emaciated body it didn't take a genius to work out that the fish they had shared the other day was probably the first proper meal the boy had eaten for a while. He put the boy in his bed and covered him with just the sheet. Luckily for Deacon he had researched the treatment for a fever for one of his storylines so he had a fair idea that getting fluids into the patient was the first priority. He also knew that it would be wise to try to bring the boy round to assess his level of consciousness. Getting the boy out of his wet clothes had ensured that the fever was at least checked and if it hadn't already infected his kidneys or chest then straightforward rest and re-hydration could beat it within 24 hours. Deacon filled a glass with bottled water and dampened a cloth to mop the boy's brow to try to wake him gently just long enough for him to take a drink. His research years earlier, which was stored in the files of his immense brain was recalled to serve him well. Within minutes the boy opened his eyes and smiled weakly. Deacon gently lifted his head and offered the glass to his lips and the boy took several good sips before he closed his eyes again. Deacon pulled up a chair to the side of the bed and there he remained watching over his tiny patient for the following 24 hours, moving only to make sure that the boy took on more water and to make sure that the fever was subsiding.

On the second day the boy was strong enough to sit up and eat a few mouthfuls of soup and Deacon was satisfied that the fever was gone, another day of rest and his patient would be as good as new.

Chapter Twenty Eight

For the first time in two days Deacon left his bedside vigil and as the boy slept he went quietly downstairs. The ragged pile of sodden clothes was still on the kitchen floor where they had fallen. Deacon looked at them and wondered whether to wash them or throw them straight into the bin. He picked up the tee shirt and inspected it, the only conclusion was the obvious one, it had to go into the bin, the worn fabric would never stand up to a rigorous washing. He wondered how such an item of clothing could possibly have held together for so long. It certainly did not have the capacity to offer any warmth at all, *No wonder the poor lad had a fever*. Deacon then picked up the short trousers which were in little better condition than the tee shirt and destined for the same fate. He put his hand into the pocket and took out the stones with which the boy had made a fire and he put them on the table. *A new set of clothes are coming your way young man before I do another thing.*

Deacon bundled up the boy's old rags and dropped them into the bin alongside the dead rabbit on his way to the car. He knew that his patient would not wake for another hour or so and when he did he would be in for a lovely surprise.

Within a few minutes Deacon was on his way to town with a firm mental image of the boy's size of clothing in his mind. He pulled into the village square and marched stealthily to the first shop that looked remotely like it sold children's clothes. He was in luck; no sooner had he entered the shop than a frumpy looking, middle aged lady approached him. Obviously she spoke to him in French but any language spoken would have had no effect on him because he was in his familiar no-nonsense approach to life mood, especially when he was on a mission. He brushed past her as though she were invisible and began picking items of clothing from the shelves that he thought would fit the boy. With three pairs of everything a boy would need under his arm he plonked them on the counter and produced his credit card. The bemused shop assistant had long since retreated to the safety and comfort of the sales counter, not so much so that she was in place to process his shopping, more so that she could observe him. With his shopping bagged up and paid for she watched him like a hawk all the way from the shop until he was out of sight, the expression on her face was: *I will be keeping an eye on you.* She wasn't the first person to think that and she certainly would not be the last, but what made her different from so many other people was that she was the village busy-body and locally she was very well connected. She made it her business to know everything about everyone, in short, if she didn't like someone she made trouble for them, and she had taken an instant dislike to Deacon.

Blissfully unaware of the suspicious eyes upon him as he walked back to the car his attention was suddenly caught by a shop window full of brightly painted colours. He veered towards it hoping to find that it was what he hoped it would be and he was not disappointed…it was indeed a toy shop. He went about his business in the toy shop in exactly the same way he had in the clothes shop and moments later he emerged with a junior cricket set and a football; all he needed to complete his shopping trip was a few tins of various soups and a giant box of matches. Back home in the cottage the boy was sleeping soundly, even in his wildest dreams he could never have thought that he would soon awake to the surprise of his life, laid on by the most unlikely person on the planet.

Deacon drove back to the cottage with a feeling of excitement inside that surpassed any of his greatest business successes, he was so focussed on seeing the reaction on the boy's face when he woke up that he didn't analyse the strangeness of it all, as far as he was concerned, he felt good and that was all there was to it. The only tinge of sadness was that he had the presence of mind to remember to park the car back in the courtyard as quietly as possible so as not to disturb him. He had forgotten of course that the boy was deaf and it hurt for him to suddenly remember. Nevertheless, he was determined to give the boy a treat like he had never had before and he went about his plan like a parent tip-toeing around with a sack full of gifts on Christmas Eve.

With the car unloaded he lit the cooker and put on a pan of soup, he knew that with the fever on the retreat his little patient would be ravenous. As the soup was coming to the boil he crept up the stairs with the clothes and toys and put them in the landing just outside the door. He popped his head into the room to make certain that the boy was still fast asleep before he went down to bring up the soup. He gently shook the boy's shoulder and when he woke up he propped him up into the sitting position. He was right about the boy being ravenous because although he was still visibly weak his mouth opened for more after every swallow like a young chick waiting for a worm. When the bowl was empty Deacon began his explanation as though he were playing charades. He indicated to the boy to close his eyes and to wait. Considering he had never had to do anything like it before he was very good at it and the boy had no trouble understanding what he had to do. When Deacon was certain that he wasn't peeping he went out into the landing and brought everything in laying it carefully on the bed. When he was ready he gave his patient a playful poke in the shoulder. He opened his eyes and almost fell off the bed! It was as though the frailness in his body had been suddenly replaced by the energy of ten excited children. Like most children his age, he by-passed the clothes and instead hoisted the football above his head as if he was lifting the World Cup itself. His reaction totally outshone even that of Deacon's most vivid imagination. That wonderful smile that had lit up the boy's face when he and Deacon first met lit up the whole room and it filled Deacon's heart with absolute joy. He stood back from the bed and encouraged the boy to throw him the ball; he didn't need a second invitation. Before they knew it the ball was whizzing through the air back and fourth and their laughter echoed through the cottage from the floor to the rafters. A passer-by would have thought there was a party in full swing. Deacon was aware that it was not wise to tire the boy out so he caught the ball one final time and rolled it along the floor to rest beneath the window. He picked up the cricket set and held it close for the boy to see and indicated that they would play with it outside when he was feeling stronger. Next it was time

168

to show the boy his new clothes and what followed was totally unexpected. Deacon gave the boy a shirt fully expecting him to try it on but instead he held it to his face and began to stroke it as if it were a puppy. Deacon realised that it was the boy's way of saying 'Thank you' whilst indicating at the same time just how much it meant to him. For the first time in his life Deacon felt inadequate: *My God, that one simple action is saying more than a thousand of my written words ever could.*

Deacon took the clothes from the boy and pointed to the wardrobe, he took them over and cleared a space to put them low down so the boy could reach them, he then took the pillows from behind him and laid him down to rest again. He figured that one more day of rest would see the boy up and about, that's what he figured...

Chapter Twenty Nine

As the evening wore on Deacon made himself a bite to eat and after he had finished he realised that the exertions of the past two days keeping vigil over the boy was taking its toll. He slumped into an armchair at 7 o'clock and he didn't wake until almost midnight. The last thing he did before he went to bed was look in on the boy and he smiled when he saw by the light of the rising moon that the boy had put the cricket set onto the bed beside him. As he watched him sleeping he suddenly thought of Sebastian and the last time they had met. He looked at the cricket set and remembered how they had argued in his office and the words Sebastian said came flooding back. Years earlier Deacon had bought Sebastian all the best cricket paraphernalia that money could buy, the bat, the pads and the padded gloves and he had packed him off for professional lessons; during that argument Sebastian had shouted: "But all I wanted was a ball and a stick and a game with you on the lawn for Christ's sake." As Deacon closed the bedroom door he thought, *Well tomorrow Sebastian, if the sun is shining and if this little fellow is strong enough, I may be able to go some way to putting that mistake right...*

Deacon went into the spare room and settled down for the night and as he lay on the bed looking up at the ceiling he began to think about the strangeness of the situation. His life had been far from ordinary since the day he was born, but even he could never have foreseen the events of the last few days. Here he was in a remote part of France looking after an abandoned street urchin; he had fame and wealth enough to rub shoulders with the cream of the world's society and yet, all he could think of was playing a game of cricket with the poorest boy in the world and the excitement welling up in his stomach was as though he had been invited to a royal garden party.

He hadn't been asleep very long when he heard the creaking of his bedroom door opening across the hall; there was no mistake about it because the lifting of the old metal latch had a quite distinctive sound. Deacon thought at first that the boy was going to the bathroom but he was surprised as he heard him passing the bathroom door to go down the stairs. His first thought was to get up and see what he was up to; perhaps he needed help or maybe he was sleep-walking? He knew that if that was the latter then it was best to leave him unless he was in danger of hurting himself. Instead he strained his ear to the faint sounds of the boy moving about in the kitchen. Suddenly the sounds took a more sinister turn as he heard the cottage door quickly open and close, he jumped out of bed and dashed over to the window, he was just in time to see the boy hurrying across the moonlit courtyard towards the postern with a bundle of something under his arm. Deacon's heart sank when he realised that the boy was not sleepwalking but leaving. He was hurt that the boy felt as though he had to leave by sneaking off in the dead of night like an escaping prisoner, he didn't have to do that, he could have left anytime. A moment or two later, after a brief reflection, Deacon gave a wry smile when he realised that he was also suffering the disappointment of a let down child because the chance of a game of cricket with him had been dashed; he had been so looking forward to it. He was however, curious to know what the boy had under his arm as he left, whatever he had taken could have had no real value and Deacon had no intention of spending any time at all that night in bothering to find out what it was, the dawn would come soon enough and he would find out then what, if anything was missing. He walked sleepily back to his bed and within minutes he was in an exhaustion induced sleep.

Deacon awoke the following morning feeling refreshed after a deep sleep but also feeling saddened because the boy had left the way he did. He put on his dressing gown and went out onto the landing, without realising it, probably through the force of habit and a lapse of concentration he pushed open his bedroom door to look in on the hastily vacated room. He fully expected to see an empty bed, but to his amazement, there he was…still sound asleep! *I don't understand it, what is going on? I distinctly saw him out on the courtyard last night appearing to leave, I know I was dog-tired but I*

171

wasn't hallucinating. So how is it that he is back in bed? His curiosity and confusion was suddenly replaced by an overwhelming relief that his unusual lodger was still around and with him the excitement of the cricket match which was now firmly back on the fixture list.

As he prepared a breakfast of cereal for himself and the boy he took a brief look round to see if there was indeed something missing, his reasoning was that if he could identify what was missing he could piece together where the lad had gone the night before and why. It was another mystery like the fish on the doorstep and one that he was determined more than ever to solve. *My, this holiday to France is proving to be quite an adventure; but not in the least way that Ingrid might have imagined it.* He smiled at the thought as he loaded up a breakfast tray and took it up to his patient; it was going to be an interesting day in more ways than one.

Chapter Thirty

Deacon put the tray on the bedside table and gently shook the boy, it was obvious by his immediate smile and the colour returning to his face that he was now well on the way to recovery. Deacon handed him his bowl of cereal and as he gleefully munched into it Deacon picked up the cricket set and took out the bat. He indicated in such a way that he asked the boy if he would like a game outside later, the boy's nodding head and wide smiling eyes told Deacon that it was an emphatic 'yes!'

Half an hour later the boy was out on the lawn dressed in his new clothes looking on bemused as Deacon meticulously paced out exactly half the length of a professional wicket and drove in the stumps. It didn't take Deacon long to explain what was required of both the bowler and the batsman, after showing him a few rudimentary batting strokes it was decided that he would put the boy in to bat and he would bowl. The first few balls were wildly swung at and miserable missed...as were the wickets by Deacon's rusty bowling technique, but the fifth ball of the innings whizzed back past Deacon's ear like a cruise missile. Deacon turned on his heels to stop it going for a boundary and as he gathered up the ball he looked back to see the boy jumping up and down triumphantly. In his eagerness to explain the bat and ball side of things Deacon had forgotten to mention that a chap had to run between the stumps to score a point after whacking the ball. Once the scoring system was established it didn't take long for the boy to knock up his first few runs. By this time the sun was high in the sky and it was time to take on some much needed fluid, after a long cool drink the boy decided that he would like to try his hand at bowling. Once again he took to it like a duck to water and before long Deacon had shown him how to spin the ball to make it curl in behind the bat. Time and again the young lad hurled the ball down the wicket and Deacon gave a display of supreme batting mastery. The boy was just as happy chasing the ball as he had been hitting it. No doubt from that moment on, he was hooked for life on the 'game of gentlemen.'

With the time approaching lunch Deacon declared the match a draw and offered his hand to the boy. "After every game we always shake the hand of our opponent," he smiled as the boy returned the gesture. "Well played old boy!" he laughed. As the words left his mouth it suddenly occurred to him that he didn't know the boy's name; it was something that he would try to put right over lunch.

Once in the 'pavilion' Deacon set to work making the sandwiches as the boy prepared the drinks. As they sat at the table Deacon produced a pen and paper and drew a picture of himself. Above the figure he wrote his name and pointed to himself. Next, he drew a picture of the boy and offered him the pen. The boy put the pen down and shrugged his shoulders. Deacon paused before he spoke again, "I can't call you nothing young man, so we shall have to find you something suitable," he said, "And I know just the place to find you a name; after lunch that is exactly what we shall do."

After lunch Deacon took the boy through to his study and booted up the computer.

"We'll find a search engine with images and we will find you a name young man," Deacon said as he tapped on the keyboard. The boy looked around the room at all the neatly placed books with a look of wonder on his face, he was completely transfixed. He reached out to touch the gold lettering on the spine of an old, ornate copy of the Bible. Deacon turned and saw the boy's hypnotic gaze. "It will be a while before you will be able to read that young man," he smiled. Then he indicated for the boy to take it down and take a look inside. He knew that the beautifully decorated illustrations would impress him. The boy took down the heavy book and began to carefully turn the pages as Deacon returned to his computer and the job in hand. Deacon's first port of call was to select pictures of famous cricketing legends. He looked at the great Donald Bradman and turned to the boy. *Hhmm, you don't look like a Donald that's for certain.* The next one up was Sir Geoffrey Boycott, *No. you are not a Geoffrey either.* He took a cursory look at a man described as possibly the greatest cricketer of all time, W G Grace and he decided that perhaps a cricketing name was not best suited after all. His next foray was into the world of art. The boy meanwhile was carefully studying the marvellous patterns of colour and shade on the garments of the characters from the good book. Suddenly the boy stopped turning the pages and carried the Bible over to Deacon. He saw that the boy had opened the book at the birth of Christ in the stable and he followed his finger as he pointed at Saint Joseph and then to himself. Deacon rocked back in his chair and roared with laughter, "Why Joey of course! You are a Joey my boy if ever I saw one. That is your name from now on young man, Joey!" The boy's eyes lit up with his wonderful smile and that was confirmation enough for Deacon and he held out his hand. Joey took his hand as Deacon laughed, "My name is Richard and I am delighted to make your acquaintance Joey."

It was not the most elaborate christening in history and certainly not in accordance with the book from which the name was chosen but it was a christening just the same and for the unlikeliest of friends it was as joyous as if it had been conducted in Westminster Abbey or in the waters of the great river Jordan.

Chapter Thirty One

The afternoon was going to be glorious of that Deacon had no doubt. "Right Joey," he said as he hoisted the football to his chest height, "Now it's time for us to take advantage of my football field out there and play some Samba football like they do in Brazil." Joey of course could not hear but he could see the general idea was to go outside and have some fun. With the ball under his arm and Joey loaded up with two pullovers as goalposts they headed off into what in Deacon's imagination had become the 'Stade Du France.' Joey placed the goalposts on the grass and stood between them as Deacon began taking shots. He was careful not to kick the ball too hard for fear hitting Joey's frail body and doing some damage but he need not have worried, from the way Joey flung himself at every shot it was obvious that he had played the game before and in no time at all they had worked out a system of three goals scored and the goalkeeper became the striker. Deacon then decided that they would have their own 'world cup finals'. He pointed to his watch and indicated that each team had to score as many goals as possible in two minutes. The tournament would start in the quarter final stages so that meant that Deacon and Joey had four teams each. The teams scoring the least goals dropped out until there were only two left. In the final Deacon was Peru and Joey was Scotland and after a scorching four minutes of shots and saves in the blistering heat in front of a capacity crowd the game went to penalties which Scotland won 5-1. After the match Deacon collapsed onto the turf in a dramatic dejected heap whilst Joey did a lap of honour with the ball above his head. Deacon looked on like a proud father as his tiny opponent danced around the perimeter of the massive lawn, *My God, Sebastian was right, how stupid and selfish was I to have missed all this?*

After his lap of honour Joey returned to Deacon and held out his hand, he had remembered how gentlemen behave after a game. "Well played again Joey," Deacon smiled, then as he took the ball from Joey's hand and let it drop onto the grass he shouted, "Come on, I'll race you to the house," and he sprinted off with

Joey laughing in hot pursuit. Back at the house it was Deacon's turn to make the drinks and they sat in the shade of the vines over the lattice covered part of the courtyard to enjoy the rest from their sporting exertions and the lovely fresh fruit drink. Joey seemed to have recovered from his fever and apart from his lack of body weight—which Deacon planned to remedy—he looked fit and well. Still, it was best not to do too much Deacon thought, so a good long break before tea would be the plan for the next couple of hours…or so he thought.

Deacon suddenly remembered how Joey had slipped out the night before with something under his arm and he thought that then would be a good time to try to find out what Joey had been up to. There was always the possibility that he had been sleep-walking and would remember nothing which presented Deacon with a very interesting dilemma. He knew that any questions posed to Joey would have to be mimed in such a way that he could work out roughly what he was saying, but how would Joey react if Deacon asked him something that he had no recollection of, that might easily frighten him and that was the last thing Deacon wanted. *Yes, I shall have to tread very carefully with this one, do I say nothing and lock the door at night to keep him in, or do I try to find out what he was up to in a way that will not be intrusive? No, I can not make a prisoner of him, I have to bite the bullet and ask him, my days of ignoring the issues of young people like my own son Sebastian are over.* Deacon put his glass on the table and waved for Joey's attention. His miming felt awkward as he signed in the air to ask if he went out last night in the dark and if so where did he go and why, but with Joey's natural intelligence and his experience at working out other people's attempts to communicate, he understood the question. The smile on his face turned into a look of sadness as he slowly put his glass onto the table. Deacon could see that Joey was embarrassed by the fact that he had seen him and he wished that he could take back the question, after all he was free to come and go as he pleased. Then, to his surprise, Joey stood up and beckoned Deacon to do the same. With a deft movement of his head Deacon understood that Joey was about to answer the question by showing him rather than miming and as he started off in the direction of the postern Deacon was obliged to follow. Joey went out into the woods and turned north along the riverbank. They walked for half a mile or so until they came to a shallow part of the river where it was obvious that in the past someone had laid partially submerged stepping stones. Joey stepped into the water to cross and Deacon followed. On the far bank Joey turned south for a couple of hundred metres before he left the path and headed out over some rough grazing land. Deacon could see a small wood up ahead and it appeared to be their destination. He wondered where and what on earth Joey could be doing but he wouldn't have to wait very long to find out. As Deacon anticipated, Joey headed straight for the wood and soon they were on a path through the cool shade of the trees at the height of their summer foliage. Joey suddenly veered off the path again and thirty metres or so into the undergrowth he stopped and turned to Deacon who was following a few metres behind. Joey had stopped at a point where the ground hollowed out like a small crater and in the centre of it there was a small man-made earth mound. As Joey walked down into the crater Deacon had the surprise of his life. A small black mutt of a dog emerged from within the earth mound with its tail wagging and as Joey dropped to his knees the dog playfully licked his face. Deacon's question had been answered in full and not only that, he could see what the bundle under Joey's arm had been. At the mouth of the mound he saw a bowl from the kitchen which Joey had filled with water. Deacon observed that the mutt was almost as skinny as Joey as he watched the two of them continue with their greeting ritual. Deacon suddenly had a potentially life-changing decision to make. He fully understood why Joey had kept the dog secret and that was because if people chased Joey away, then it didn't take a genius to work out what they would do to a flea-bitten mutt. Joey had hidden it to save its life and therein was the decision that Deacon had to make. All of his life he had fervently avoided anything that remotely looked as if it could be infested with germs of any kind, yet within the last few days of meeting Joey he had been forced to challenge his phobia and he did so without really realising it. He had disposed of Joey's old clothes and he had exposed himself to whatever fever Joey had been suffering from and he was still around to tell the tale, but this...this mangy mutt that was practically alive with all manner of seen and unseen infestation, could he find the courage to face this ultimate challenge? He looked at Joey and the mutt who by this point were looking up from the crater at Deacon, both doe-eyed and helpless, awaiting a verdict like two innocent Dickensian characters standing accused of stealing bread in an unforgiving Victorian courthouse. *Well if Joey isn't afraid to let the dog lick him, then neither am I, a man has to die of something and being licked to death is as good a way as any to shake this mortal coil.* Deacon dropped to his knees as Joey had done and he opened his arms with a smile; Joey, the mutt and all the germs in the world dashed forward and the three of them rolled on the ground laughing like a litter of playful lion cubs.

Chapter Thirty Two

Despite the initial inroads into overcoming his phobia, Deacon was intent on giving the mutt a complete makeover as he had done with Joey's old clothes. He drew the line at putting the mutt in the bath, so he set-up a makeshift showering system in the courtyard using an old tin feeding tub from out in the stable and buckets of warm water. As usual Deacon had to think things through and carefully plan the assault like a military operation with the germs, fleas, galloping bugs, imagined or real of course being the deadly enemy. When he was certain that he had wrestled his dread into submission he was ready to go. Joey was to hold the dog still in the tub as Deacon went into the kitchen to fill the first bucket for the initial onslaught. Joey burst out laughing as Deacon emerged from the kitchen carrying the bucket, because he was clad in a pair of bright pink marigold gloves and a handkerchief over his nose. He looked like a cross between a mad surgeon and a camp cowboy. Joey recovered enough to hold the dog as planned and Deacon dowsed the poor thing rather like a bomber would open its bomb bay doors. The water seemed to shoot everywhere with the splash and the dog instinctively shaking itself sent gigantic soap bubbles billowing out over the tub and into the air; once again Joey burst into fits of hysterical laughter as the dog decided to snack on the bubbles. Undeterred Deacon went back for another load, but this time he delivered it from a more reasonable height and the tub filled up as opposed to the surrounding area. The poor dog didn't know what was happening and sat there with a bemused expression on its face as Joey set to work soaping it up and giving it a good scrub. Deacon dropped to his knees and assisted in the scrubbing with his marigolds flashing all over the dog's saturated black fur. Joey cupped a handful of bubbles and clapped his hands at Deacon who responded by throwing a kind of bubble snowball back. Before long the three of them were having a monstrous water fight and all of Deacon's fears and phobias evaporated into the air with the fun and laughter. He never would have thought that washing a smelly old dog could be as much fun as playing cricket or the beautiful game of football. Finally, after several more bucket loads, some on target and some woefully amiss, the three of them collapsed onto the grass away from the washing area to allow the sun to dry them off. Deacon was satisfied that most, if not all of the dog's unwanted passengers would either be dead or swimming for their lives back in the feeding tub, either way the dog could now be accepted into his growing community of misfits. With everything squared away it was time for a bite to eat before they all settled down for the night, Deacon found a few scraps for the dog which it wolfed down in seconds and he put a pan of soup on the boil for himself and Joey. Joey sat at the table as the dog flopped down behind the kitchen door looking up at Deacon as if to say, 'I hope some of that soup is coming my way because I'm still a little peckish.' The sight of the dog looking at him set in motion a train of thought concerning where the long-term lodgings of the dog might be and the purchase of some proper dog food. It occurred to him that he didn't have the foggiest idea of how to care for an animal. However, he came to the conclusion that Joey would know so he would seek his advice. Turning to Joey he started with the basics and successfully mimed,

"What is the dog called?"

Deacon smiled and gave a sigh as Joey clearly signed, "My friend."

Immediately Deacon's mind darted back to the day in the grounds of his mansion when he brushed aside the undergrowth to read the inscription on the dog's neglected grave. It read: *Tina. A true friend and a lady to the end.* He also remembered the questions that he had asked himself back then; *Can a dog really be a friend? Can a dumb animal really invoke such feelings of loss in a grown man? How can a human being love an animal more than another human being?* He looked at Joey and his *friend* and the answer dawned on him in a glorious epiphany. Joey had been let down by his family and shunned by humans probably since the day he was born, so it was easy for Deacon to see how a human could love an animal more than other human beings. It is because an animal's love is unconditional and loyal right until the end. "I think we should call our friend Tina," Deacon announced, "What do you think of that, Joey?"

Joey beckoned Deacon to come closer so he could put his fingers to his neck. He wanted to feel the vibrations in his voice as he said the name. Deacon said the name again with the emphasis on the 'T' three or four times and he was amazed when Joey began to repeat it out loud over and over again. He looked to Deacon for approval that he had it right before he used it on the dog. He stood up and tapped his thighs and he called out: "Tina." The dog leapt up wagging it's tail and began the ritual face licking of Joey all over again. It was Joey's way of asking for the dog's approval of it's new name and by all accounts it was an emphatic 'Yes!'

"Tina it is then," Deacon declared, "Tomorrow we shall find her a basket to sleep in and some fine linen worthy of a true friend, we shall all have food in abundance and no more fleas!"

Chapter Thirty Three

The trio were up and about for an early morning walk before breakfast and a day of doggie shopping for Tina in the town. The look of the sky promised a beautiful day and luckily it was market day in the town, they would soon have everything on their shopping list and hopefully, time for game of cricket before tea if everything went according to plan. Deacon threw a ball for Tina to chase and as she darted off in pursuit the idea that she would make an excellent out-fielder at cricket occurred to both Deacon and Joey at exactly the same moment and they smiled at each other as she came running back with a look of satisfaction on her face.

After the walk and a hurried breakfast the trio moved out into the courtyard, "Tina will have to stay put," Deacon said with the appropriate signs. His first thoughts were to tie Tina to the door handle of the cave where she could lay down in the cool shade whilst he and Joey were out shopping. When he explained to Joey what was on his mind Joey shook his head and smiled, he obviously had other plans. He took Tina over to the cave and knelt down to whisper in her ear, she immediately lay down on the grass with her paws crossed in front of her face and she laid her head on them. Joey walked back to the car and nonchalantly slid into the passenger seat as Deacon looked on speechless. Tina showed not even the slightest flicker of movement, it was obvious that she was not going to move a muscle until Joey returned. *So much for my great idea of tying her up!*

Deacon opened the gates and pulled the car out onto the road outside, within minutes they were whizzing past cornfields and vineyards towards Petit Saint Jean. He knew from his last trip to town on market day that it would be wise to park in the first available place, so that is exactly what they did, they pulled in and parked the car about a five minute walk from the town centre. First on the list was dog food followed by a basket for Tina's bed. Next would be their own food and finally any other bits and bobs that might catch Deacon's eye. "Food for Tina," Deacon said as

183

Joey nodded and set off towards the pet shop. In the shop Deacon made sure that there was plenty food, biscuits and one or two other doggie treats before he and Joey selected a suitable bed for her. After pointing at one or two options and meeting with a less than favourable response from Joey, he decided that it would be best to let him take charge. Joey impressed Deacon with his choice, it was smaller than he expected but it was also made of a smooth plastic which would make it easier to keep clean and that aspect suited him just fine. Their final purchase was a snug lining for the basket and a pillow just the right size for Tina to curl up on.

"Right Joey, now for our food," Deacon said as they stepped out onto the pavement and in amongst the crowds of market shoppers. Stopping at more or less every stall to buy or to browse, they soon had enough food to last them until the next market day. Suddenly Joey gripped hold of Deacon's hand and pulled it. Deacon turned and saw that he was staring straight ahead. Following his gaze he saw the big police officer that he had seen on his first day in town up ahead standing with his back to them. It was obvious that Joey wanted to avoid any contact with him and Deacon clearly understood why, he had probably at some point in the past been clipped around the ear for trying to earn a few coins. "You will be safe with me," Deacon assured him, "No one will hurt you again; that life is in the past." Joey readjusted his grip on Deacon's hand but he didn't let go. Joey's action made immediate sense to Deacon, he was showing the townsfolk that he was more than just a shopping carrier and that no one had the right to 'shoo' him away. The pair walked calmly on past the police officer who was so engrossed in his conversation that he didn't even notice. At the far end of the main street where the stalls ended Deacon saw the clothes shop where he had bought Joey's new clothes.

"Hhhmm, whilst we are here, Joey, I think it is in order that we fix you up with some Wellingtons and some trainers for our sporting sessions and our trips to the river," Deacon said as the pair headed stealthily towards the shop. As he opened the door there was the same, almost comical figure of the buxom, middle aged saleswoman he had encountered whilst buying Joey's clothes and she looked as though she had remained in exactly the same position, only this time the look on her face was one of disdain rather than forced pleasantry. Joey entered the shop in Deacon's slipstream and it was then that the woman pounced like a wildcat. She began her tirade by flapping her hands in front of her as if she were rounding up chickens, Deacon didn't have a clue what she was saying but it was painfully clear that she did not want Joey in her establishment. Deacon immediately stepped forward and held his body side on between the demented woman and Joey. "MADAM!" he shouted, and the woman was instantly stunned into silence. She looked at him as if she had only just noticed that he was there, probably because she had been so intensely focussed on throwing Joey out. "This young man is with me!" Deacon continued in a commanding tone of voice, "And we shall not leave these premises until we have purchased what we came in for." The flustered woman backed off sheepishly having been firmly put down, but she was not happy and the look on her face was one of suppressed anger. Deacon pointed to the footwear section at the rear of the store and indicated that Joey was the customer and should be treated with respect. She tried to salvage some face by calling for her assistant to deal with things. A neatly dressed young woman appeared from a storeroom and after some agitated dialogue on the part of the older woman she ushered Joey and Deacon into the footwear section. Between them Deacon and Joey told the young woman what they wanted as the older woman watched the proceedings like an eagle from her sanctuary behind the counter. But far from carrying on with her business duties she was making mental notes to add to the notes she had made after her first encounter with this 'brutish Englishman'. It was the second time that she had seen Deacon and it was the second time that his eccentric actions had made rather less than a sparkling impression on her. As far as Deacon was concerned the matter was forgotten, he had dealt with her on both occasions in the same no-nonsense manner that he dealt with all his employees and associates. But she was not a woman to let things drop so easily, she felt insulted and ill-used and she had resolved to use all her weight around the town to teach Deacon and *the filthy little gypsy* a lesson.

Deacon paid for the goods and the young shop assistant smiled politely as she handed them wrapped and bagged to Joey. As the customers left the shop she could feel the burning anger emitting from her boss and she knew that her brewing vendetta against them would be sanctioned and implemented the moment that Deacon was out of sight. Oblivious to the trouble stirring in their wake, Deacon and Joey made their way smartly back through the town, loaded up the car and headed off back to the cottage for a bite to eat before an afternoon of fun by the river and perhaps an innings or two of cricket.

Chapter Thirty Four

Joey excitedly tried on his Wellingtons again and goose-stepped round the kitchen as Deacon made sandwiches. Tina looked on bemused and tilted her head to one side as Joey marched to and fro with his chest puffed out. She took a tentative sniff at the rubber as if she was trying to identify a potential future snack every time Joey stopped to turn, and after finally deciding that they wouldn't, she flopped to the floor.

During lunch Joey took a piece of paper and drew a fish. It had been years since Deacon had done a spot of fishing so he was ready to give it another go. Joey was obviously good at it, so Deacon had a feeling that his next foray into the world of angling was likely to be more fruitful than his last, he was also curious to know where Joey had his rod and line stashed.

With their sandwiches eaten and Tina fed and watered they headed off into the afternoon sunshine in the direction of the river. Deacon followed Joey's lead along the riverbank as Tina lagged behind to sniff butterflies and generally mooch about in the undergrowth before running to catch them up. Deacon was expecting Joey to veer off the path at any moment to retrieve his hidden rod but he skipped along happily without stopping. After a mile or so Joey pointed to a bend in the river where the water was visibly shallower and he indicated that they were at his chosen spot to fish.

"Where is your fishing rod?" Deacon asked as he flicked his arms as if casting out a line. Joey smiled and put his finger to his lips as he gently waded into the water. Tina immediately sat at the edge of the riverbank at the spot where Joey had entered and she didn't move a muscle. Deacon stood on the bank and watched as Joey made his way slowly to a line of rocks sticking out from the water just beyond the mid point in the river. Joey reached the rocks and gently slid his hand under the surface. *Surely he hasn't hidden his rod there? It is bound to have been washed away.* Deacon was suddenly wrenched from his thoughts as Joey lifted up his arm with a big fat trout flapping away furiously in his outstretched hand. *Oh my word, he's tickled it!* Deacon let out a whoop of delight as Joey made his way triumphantly back to Tina and Deacon with his catch. Tina lifted her front paw as Joey slid the trout beneath it and she put it down again trapping it, it was obviously her job to look after the fish until Joey was finished and Tina made certain that the fish was going nowhere. Joey beckoned to Deacon and he knew that it was his turn to try his hand at catching his own supper. Joey led the way back towards the rocks and as Deacon followed he began running through his mind and letting his imagination run away with itself as to how horrible the slimy fish would feel beneath his fingers. *Get a grip Deacon and stop behaving like a sissy, Joey has had to do this to stay alive in the past and who knows? One day I might just have to do the same.* With that thought chasing away his squeamish nonsense he steeled himself to do the manly thing and make Joey proud of him. Joey stopped at the chosen rock and he showed his unlikely student where to start. Slowly Deacon lowered his hand into the water and under the rock; his heart began to pound in his chest as his fingers came into contact with the soft, cold belly of his supper. He held his breath as the dozing fish allowed him to stroke along its length. He looked at Joey and indicated with his eyes that he had made contact with his prey and Joey knew that he was asking for direction as to when to spring the trap. Joey held up three fingers and touched each one in turn to say that he would give him a count of three. One…Deacon wanted to claw the fish out but managed to contain himself. Two… the tension was like playing Russian roulette with five clicks already gone. Three…Whoosh! The trout was hooked up into the air with the finesse of a seasoned poacher. Joey clapped his hands and jumped into the air in celebration, even Tina looked suitably impressed, Deacon was certain that she too would have clapped had she not been on fish restraining duty. "Joey my boy, you are a genius," Deacon laughed as they waded back to the bank with their supper. Once the pair reached dry land, Tina picked up her fish in her mouth and greeted the smiling Joey with it. "Now this is what I call team-work," Deacon said as he held out his hand to his teacher. "Thank you Joey, I haven't had as much fun as this in all my life," Joey couldn't hear a word but he knew instinctively what Deacon was saying.

They were on a massive high as they strolled along in the afternoon sunshine. This time, Tina led the way home and the fishermen lagged behind drinking in every moment of their success. Deacon couldn't remember the last time, if at all he had felt so good and he had only a poor gypsy boy to thank for it. *And thank him I shall*, Deacon thought. *I seem to remember seeing a leaflet for a theme park on the day I arrived. Well if I can find it, tomorrow Joey is going to have the time of his life.*

Back at the cottage, Joey didn't waste a minute on preparing the fish for the pot. As he did so Deacon browsed through the stack of leaflets. He soon found it amongst the distilleries and castles. He gathered from the directions that the place was not too far away, so if the weather was fine on the following day, then Joey was in for a treat. Deacon couldn't wait until the following day to give Joey the news because he wanted Joey to feel as excited as he did. After all, the excitement of what is about to happen is almost as good as the actual event. Joey stood at the cooker with his back to Deacon and that was the perfect position. Deacon unfolded the leaflet and standing behind him he lowered it down in front of his face. Joey took the leaflet and turned to look questioningly at Deacon. "You and me young man, tomorrow!" Joey let out a shriek when he realised what he was in for and Tina added to the celebrations with a howl. It was all set then, if the weather was good on Friday they would set off early and make sure that they took a ride on every single attraction.

Soon it was time for Joey to turn in; it had been an eventful day in so many ways and one they would remember for a very long time and despite his fuelled excitement he was exhausted. Deacon waited until he was sure that Joey was asleep before he settled down with a welcome glass of whisky. It had been the most enjoyable day of his life and it had cost him nothing. His new life had descended straight from paradise and he was discovering so many wonderful things in a world where he thought he had seen it all and had it all. He raised his glass to his unbelievable good fortune, what could possibly go wrong...

Chapter Thirty Five

Joey had already been up and dressed for an hour before he woke Deacon up. He was going to wait for Deacon to wake in his own good time but when he had looked at the clock approaching 7am and the brightness of the sunny morning he could contain his excitement for what lay ahead no longer.

Deacon woke up to witness the culmination of a night's pent up excitement. Joey was on one side of his bed pushing down on the mattress and Tina was on the other side bouncing up and down on the floor as is she were on springs. When Deacon realised what was going on and came fully to his senses Joey ran over to the window and opened the curtain to show that it was a glorious day. "All right you two, I am up and ready for some fun," he laughed as he threw off the duvet. "Give me five minutes to shower and we will hit the road."

Breakfast disappeared almost without touching the sides and by 7.30 the car was heading to Petit Saint Jean with Deacon at the wheel, Joey at his side acting as navigator and Tina on the backseat sitting like royalty watching the world glide by. The theme park was about forty miles west of Petit Saint Jean and the road out was on the far side of town. Deacon drove up to the main street and stopped at a red light. At first he didn't notice the pedestrian who was about to step out to cross the road in front of the car, but he couldn't help but notice her as she crossed the road from one side to the other without taking her eyes off Joey who visibly shrank down under her withering look...it was the woman from the clothes shop. Tina added to the growing tension by letting out a low suspicious growl. Deacon pulled away the moment the lights changed and as he did so he looked in his rear-view mirror, he was certain that he saw the woman still standing at the side of the road and appearing to write something in a notebook. *How very odd, I wonder what on earth she is up to?* Deacon turned to Joey and tossed his head in the direction of the woman. Joey answered by pushing his nose into the air and pulling a face. It was obvious that they had crossed swords at some time in the past. Nevertheless, they were out on a day trip to the theme park and nothing was going to stop them having the time of their lives. On the far side of town Deacon gunned the gas and off they flew.

Half an hour or so later and the great towers at the entrance to the theme park came into view and Joey's eyes widened at the awesome sight. Only when they pulled into the car-park did Joey realise just how immense and impressive the theme park was. His mouth dropped open as he saw the giant, multi-coloured, roller coaster corkscrewing through the air at what seemed like the speed of sound and the sight of all the screaming passengers took his breath away. Deacon handed Joey a twenty franc note to put in his pocket as they walked to the entrance kiosk. They had taken a chance in taking Tina along but Deacon had a plan B if she was refused entry. Luckily he didn't need it because dogs were allowed so long as they were kept firmly on a leash. Once inside the park they raced from one ride to another and as Joey whizzed around on each one Deacon and Tina shared every turn and thrill from their position firmly on the ground. At the far end of the park there was a botanical garden and a wide open grassed area where people could sit and enjoy a picnic. They hadn't had time to prepare one of their own but there was no shortage of burger bars and hot-dog stands along the way to the gardens. They bought a selection of fast food for lunch and Deacon bought a frisbee for the three of them to play with on the grass afterwards.

As with most days when people are having fun the time flies and before you know it the day is at an end. Things were no different for the three of them. The crowd thinned out towards five in the afternoon and it was time to make their way home. On the way back to the car Joey stopped at an ice-cream vendor and used some of his pocket money to pay for it. The ice-cream seller smiled cheerfully as he handed Joey his change and Deacon looked on proudly because Joey had remembered to buy them all a treat.

The journey back to Petit Saint Jean didn't seem to take as long as the trip out and before long the car was heading back through the town. Everything seemed quiet and the streets were almost deserted but it was then that things took a sinister turn. Deacon stopped at the same traffic lights as in the morning and the thought of what had happened flashed into his head and he remembered the look of suspicion, almost hatred on the woman's face. He looked in the mirror and as the lights changed he saw a police car emerge from a side street and head in their direction. At first he thought nothing of it, he had done nothing wrong, but as he weaved his way along the quiet country roads towards the cottage with the police car still behind he began to feel distinctly uncomfortable. Joey could sense the sudden change in Deacon's posture and he began to wonder what could be on his mind. He watched as Deacon's eyes flitted between the road ahead and the rear-view mirror and he quickly gathered that they were being followed. Deacon was careful not to do anything which might give the policeman reason to pull him over; the effect that would have on poor Joey was too much to contemplate. He kept well below the speed limit and he drove as though he had a driving examiner sitting next to him. His car was brand new so he knew that there would be no bulbs out. The police car remained on his tail but stayed at a reasonable distance so the tension in Deacon's mind eased a little when the immediate danger of him being stopped seemed unlikely. The relief in his stomach seemed almost tangible as the cottage came into view over the brow of the road. He pulled over at the gate but neither he nor Joey got out, instead he waited to see if the police car appeared. Moments later it loomed over the brow and slowed down. Deacon fully expected the officer to stop but he didn't, instead he sped up once he had passed them and he drove off into the distance. Deacon couldn't help but laugh as Joey put his hand to his head and pretended to wipe away the sweat. When he was happy that the coast was clear Deacon opened the heavy gates and parked the car in the courtyard for the night; all in all it had been a wonderful day, but all through their evening meal the spectre of the woman at the traffic lights and the police car hung over cottage. Perhaps it was just coincidence, but something about them was niggling at Deacon and he couldn't shake it off. There was trouble in the air and although it was left unsaid, both he and Joey could sense it.

Chapter Thirty Six

Deacon had a rough night, the kind that allows short naps in between worries that grow out of all reasonable proportion and gnaw at the mind until the head is sick. He knew that his thoughts were being illuminated by the fact that he had no waking distractions but that knowledge did not help to alleviate the problem. He slid out of bed and went downstairs to make himself a drink. At the foot of the stairs he found Tina in a similar state of unrest. "You feel it too eh Tina?" Tina looked up as if she understood and was happy that he could sympathise with her troubled mind. "Your face says it all, there is something looming isn't there? There is more to that woman and that policeman than meets the eye." Deacon turned and there in the light at the foot of the stairs he saw Joey who was fully dressed and ready to leave. That said it all; if all three of them felt the same sinister gloom hanging over them then there was definitely something brewing. Joey picked up a pen and drew a map of the river and the surrounding district to let Deacon know where to find him once the coast was clear. Deacon was loathe to allow Joey out into the night alone, but he also knew that they were all expecting a visit from the police at any moment and Joey would avoid that contact at all costs. It had been Joey's acute sense of foresight that had kept him alive for all of his short life and Deacon knew that more than anyone; he had no choice but to let him go. Deacon quickly filled a bag with food for Joey and Tina and he gave Joey a blanket. *My God, this is like a scene from some Gestapo movie.*

"I will come for you when they have been," Deacon said and Joey smiled to say that he understood. Moments later the door was opened and he and Tina had slipped out into the pitch darkness of a moonless night. There was some consolation in Deacon's mind and that was the fact that at least the night was not rainy and Joey could easily cope out there alone. *This whole damn show is ridiculous! What the hell is going on around here? Why does Joey feel that he has to run from the law, he can't have committed any crime at his age?* A shower of thoughts stung his mind like driving sleet and

195

provided the necessary distraction from his sleepless worries but his waking worries were amplified even more because he did not know what was happening and he was not in control of the situation. That was an uncomfortable position that he had rarely ever been in and he did not like it one little bit.

Sleep was as unlikely as the policeman not turning up so Deacon went through to his study and began to put his thoughts down on paper to see if looking at them would make things any easier, it helped a little and as dawn approached all traces of tiredness had evaporated and he was ready for the policeman's inevitable knock.

Dawn broke fully to a beautiful morning so at least he knew that Joey and Tina were safe and warm for the immediate future. He had once written in one of his novels that an army commander marching towards a battle felt more confident if he could choose the ground upon which he fought, the course of history had been decided many times on that simple strategy and he was determined to use it to his advantage. He would feel more comfortable if he were to face his enemy out in the courtyard so he drew up his battle lines by having breakfast at the table in the courtyard. Just after nine o'clock he heard the unmistakable sound of the well worn Peugeot engine that had followed him home on the previous day. The car stopped a few feet before it came into view and he heard the sound of at least three pairs of feet stepping onto the road. *Sounds like they have come mob-handed; I wonder if I am going to be arrested?*

The devil in him almost wished he would be arrested because even though he was in a foreign country he was only a phone call away from calling on the finest legal minds in the world to wipe the floor with any opposition. He had done nothing wrong so he had nothing to fear. He sat impassively and simply looked up at the gate as the police officer entered the courtyard quickly followed by a small balding man in a badly fitting suit who was in turn followed by a smaller man with an even worse fitting suit. They were obviously some kind of local officials. If it wasn't such a potentially serious matter Deacon would have openly laughed at

196

the odd looking posse. It seemed as though the more ill-fitting the suit, the lower the social rank in the echelons of local government. *I hope you are not expecting me to speak first gentlemen because where I come from the prosecution opens.* The policeman must have been expecting Deacon to jump to his feet but the fact that he remained seated and unruffled seemed to put him in an awkward position. He stopped in his approach to the table and started again after being prompted by the taller of the two smaller men to step closer. In Pidgin English he began to speak, "We are believe that a boy you have here, is this so?"

"I live here alone," Deacon replied coolly.

"Tomorrow, a boy in your car I saw," the policeman said.

"You mean yesterday old boy," Deacon corrected, "Is there a law against that?"

Just then the smaller of the two men said something in French to the policeman and all three of them looked at Deacon as if to scrutinise him more closely. Pointing to the smaller man the policeman said: "This man knows you, is this so?"

"I have never seen him before in my life," Deacon said, and just to antagonise his unwanted guests he sniffed the air to indicate that they were abhorrent to his senses. The taller of the two men was clearly not pleased and he raised his voice to the policeman, who immediately passed on the message. "This is a very important man and he asks if you want to stay here in France?"

"I haven't decided yet," Deacon smiled.

"Well if you play games, we will decide for you, so where is the boy?"

"The boy is free to come here and go as he pleases and at this moment he has chosen not to be here," Deacon said, "So in answer to your question, I don't know where he is, and you can tell this man, whoever he is, that I do not respond to threats. Furthermore, to behave like this as a guest in my home is the height of bad manners, so if that is all I suggest you leave."

The policeman lifted his head and looked down his nose at Deacon, "I will not pass this words on because it would not be good for you. Instead I look around your house; it will be easier that way."

"The boy is not here I tell you," Deacon said, "And you will not be looking around anywhere on my property."

"If this boy is free to come and go as you say, then why have you been buying him many clothes and other things that he could not take with him if he had left?" The policeman asked.

I might have guessed, this has all come from that poison woman in the clothes shop, she has sent these heavies here to teach Joey and I a lesson.

Deacon got to his feet and towering over the comic looking trio he walked over to the doorway. "Show me a search warrant and you can look around until you are blue in the face, but until then you will only pass over this threshold over my dead body old boy." By the look on Deacon's face the policeman could see that it was no idle threat. He turned to the two plain clothes men and an agitated conversation followed before he turned back to face Deacon. "It would be better for you if you let me take a look around; if you have nothing to hide it will be just a matter of us saying good day and leaving."

Deacon stuck to his guns, not because he was being pig-headed, but because he knew that they would not leave Joey alone, even if they didn't find him there this time they would be back. His plan was to buy himself some time so that he could fully prepare his battleground. "Show me a search warrant and I will gladly step aside," Deacon smiled, "Now if you will excuse me gentlemen, I have some *important* things to deal with."

The policeman turned and spoke to the two men who looked at Deacon with a look of pure hatred, probably because they would have to explain to the woman who appeared to be behind all this bother that they had come away empty handed and of course that they would have to raise a search warrant before they returned. The three of them filed out of the courtyard and out onto the lane like a scene from a Marx Brothers movie. Deacon followed them to the gate and watched as they made their way to the car, he was surprised to see that another police car was parked further down the lane with two officers standing beside it smoking. *The crafty old bastards they even sent someone round to watch the back door in case Joey bolted! They must want him pretty badly.*

Back in the house Deacon wasted no time in picking up the phone, *now Sebastian my boy, it's time you made your extortionately expensive education useful…*

Chapter Thirty Seven

"Hello, Morrison and Deacon's," Sebastian's secretary answered in that sweet, yet no-nonsense voice that solicitors secretaries tend to use. Deacon spoke in an equally no-nonsense tone. "Put me through to Sebastian."

"Mr Deacon is busy sir, if you would like me to give him a message he may wish to call you back," she said politely.

"Tell him this is his father on the line calling from France and I need to speak with him this minute."
Her voice changed audibly when she realised who she was speaking to and she paused to compose herself before she asked him to hold the line. The next voice Deacon heard was Sebastian's

"Father, I hope you are not drunk," he said without any emotion.

"Sebastian, I know you have every right to put the phone down, but before you do, hear me out, I am in trouble and I need your help." Sebastian was caught on the hop because he never in his wildest dreams would have thought that his father would need his help, let alone lower himself to actually ask for it. He needed to know more before he said anything else, so he used his courtroom experience and pushed back to tease more out of him. "Father, you have a battery of legal brains at your beck and call so why would you need mine?"

"Who said I needed your legal brain?" Deacon asked in a fine riposte.

"Now I really am enthralled," Sebastian said, "Why else would you need me if all I have is the education that you never stop reminding me about and the extortionate cost of it."

"I need your powers of persuasion," Deacon said matter-of-factly, seemingly ignoring the obvious sideswipe.

"Ok I give up," Sebastian sighed, "so instead of dancing around like two mating scorpions just tell me what sort of trouble you are in exactly and who I am expected to persuade to do your bidding."

"Perhaps you know me better than I thought," Deacon said, "I need you to find Maria and put her on the next available flight to Bordeaux."

"What, just like that? Why don't you do it yourself?"
Deacon took a deep breath because he sensed that Sebastian would want to know far more than he wanted to reveal before he may consider giving him his help.

"You should know the answer to that little conundrum; you know that if *I* ask her she will say no because she knows it will be one of my whims. But if she knows that I have asked you to do it then she will know that it is serious."

"I have a good mind to put the phone down right now, you scheming old bastard. I can't believe you are telling me that you are asking for my help to get you out of trouble just because Maria knows you would never ask for my help. You are using me simply so that Maria will see the depth of trouble you are in. Do you understand that what you are actually telling me is that I mean absolutely nothing to you, except perhaps as emotional collateral?"

Deacon squeezed the receiver as if to summon up the strength to say the words that were dangerously close to becoming stuck in his throat. "It is because I have recently come to realise that you mean everything to me that I need you to do this one thing for me. I want to put things right before it is too late and I have the chance to do it, but I need Maria to help me."

It was at that point that Sebastian softened and saw that his father really was trying to say something. What he couldn't work out was if it was an apology of some sort, perhaps for the last time they had crossed swords over the missed birthday, or if his father was loosing his mind. It was obvious that there was something very wrong; he had never heard his father go anywhere near an apology for any of the selfish things he had done over the years and here he was almost begging for help right out of the blue. Sebastian tried a different tack: "Let's just say I do ask Maria to come over to you and she says no to me; where will that leave you in relation to the trouble you are in?"

Deacon's voice dropped to little more than a whisper: "I guess it will leave me still stuck right in the middle of it. Son, I know I have no right to ask you to trust me, but it is a matter of life and death. I will explain everything in due course, but I need Maria here right now."

"I need my head examined," Sebastian said, "Do you have a number that I can call you on if she won't come? It sounds like you will need a plan B if that is the case."

"Sebastian, if you ask her she will come," Deacon said.

"Leave it with me," Sebastian said.

"But when will you call her?" Deacon asked raising his voice to one of urgency.

"You have asked me to trust you father, so now I am asking you to trust me." With that, Sebastian put the receiver down and left Deacon hanging on the end of a dead line alone with his thoughts.

Sebastian immediately pressed the intercom button and spoke to his secretary. "Jane, book two seats to Bordeaux on the next available flight..."

Chapter Thirty Eight

Maria and Sebastian dashed through the crowded airport departure lounge and made the flight with moments to spare. If Deacon had thought that Sebastian would simply pass on the message that Maria was needed urgently in France by her former employer he had another think coming. Sebastian had lived with his father's eccentricities all of his life as Maria had done for the past few years of her life and he knew that a drama was about to unfold that was just too good to miss. After putting the phone down on his father, Sebastian had a sudden eccentricity of his own. He told his secretary that he was going to be away from the office on life-or-death business and he would be back within the week or when the situation was resolved, whichever came first. When she asked what she should tell enquiring clients as to his whereabouts he gave a typically Deaconesque response: "Make something up which will make people sympathetic to my sudden unavailability." He then drove over to Maria's house and implored her to accompany him to France as his father had asked. Maria, for her part agreed to go without a flicker of hesitation. Deacon was the most arrogant, enigmatic, frustrating person that ever walked the planet, but he was also the most irresistible, lovable, charming character she had ever met or was ever likely to, and life with him on any level was far more exciting than life without him.

She threw a few things into a holdall and once again flung herself into the abyss of life with Deacon. Sebastian planned to surprise his father so he asked Maria to phone him just before they boarded the plane to tell him to collect her from the airport in Bordeaux in two hours time, he would never suspect that his son would also be there.

Deacon was in his study looking at the drawing Joey had done of where he could find him. The pangs in his stomach to dash out and bring Joey home were momentarily relieved by the sudden ringing of the telephone. "Mr Richard is that you?" Deacon was overjoyed to hear Maria's sonorous voice. "What time do you land?" Deacon asked without any pleasantries or the remotest trace of thanks for her answering his bizarre—third party call—under such circumstances. She was tempted to call his bluff and say that unfortunately she couldn't make it, but somehow she knew that it would be futile. He knew that she was in the departure lounge and she knew that he knew it. Instead she decided to play him at his own brusque game to see how he felt.

"Be there in two hours time…with a bouquet of flowers, or I will be on the next flight home," she said.

"Maria, I will greet you with a carpet of gold, see you in two hours." With that the phone went dead.

"What did he say?" Sebastian asked

"Do you really need to ask?" Maria said as the pair approached Passport Control.

"What I wouldn't give to know what the hell he has got himself into this time," Sebastian said, "It would save me so much mental anguish."

Maria smiled and shrugged her shoulders. "I know exactly what you mean. If I didn't catch this plane and go to him I would spend every minute of every day wondering exactly the same thing…*what is he up to*, the cruelty would be unbearable."

On board the plane Maria gently slipped her hand under Sebastian's and said: "Thank you."

"Thank you for what?" he asked in surprise.

"I'm not really sure why I need to thank you, but I think it is something to do with you being here," Maria said.

Sebastian frowned, "I don't understand."

"Well, put it this way, I had to come because I know he would not have asked for me if someone else would have done, he needs me, but why did you come after the way he treated you on your birthday?"

"I think he needs me too," Sebastian said, "I don't know exactly what it is but he said something on the phone today that had a far deeper meaning than appeared at face value, I think he was tempting me to work it out and I think I have."

"This sounds like a passage from one of your father's novels," Maria said, "You can't possibly stop now, please tell me what he said."

"I don't think it would sound the same or have quite the same impact if I said it," Sebastian said shaking his head.

"Oh no, you can't lead me this far and then let me down." Maria pleaded.

Sebastian thought for a moment. "You would have to imagine yourself in the drama of the moment when he said it to appreciate it."

"Try me," Maria said.

"Ok, but if it sounds ridiculous, you are not to laugh," Sebastian said.

"Cross my heart and hope to die," Maria smiled.
Sebastian clicked his tongue against the roof of his mouth before he spoke: "He said that he has recently come to realise that I mean everything to him and that he wants to put things right before it is too late."

Maria suddenly put her hand to her mouth, "Oh my word, do you think he is dying?"
Sebastian shook his head, "No I don't Maria, but something pretty bad is hurting him and he doesn't know how to handle it. One definite thing I have managed to work out about my father over the years it is that he never hurts people out of malice, he hurts people he thinks he can hurt with impunity. In other words people like us who he thinks should make allowances for the way he is. On reflection I believe he missed my birthday because he thought I would understand that he was busy and anyone else except me would be offended."

Maria interrupted: "Offended is not the frame of mind you were in when your car screeched to a halt in front of the house that day, I think homicidal might be more accurate."

"Exactly my point!" Sebastian said triumphantly, "If I thought my father and I were as close as he thought we were I would have forgiven him instead of wanting to kill him, so you see the fault is mine and not his."

"Sebastian, just rewind for a moment because you are not making sense, how can the fault be yours and not his?" Maria frowned.

"Because we should have made ourselves get to know him as much as he knows us. The very fact that he knew I would ask you to haul yourself over to France at the drop of a hat and the fact that he knew you would drop everything to go proves my point. Plus the fact that we are here wondering what he wants and what sort of trouble he is in just shows that we don't really know him at all," Sebastian explained.

Maria sat and thought for a moment not really knowing what to say in response. "I think we will have to come back to this conversation at some later date, I don't have your professional powers of reasoning to go along with your theory, and there is always the possibility that you are playing with me just for my reaction."

Sebastian answered with a pained expression on his face: "Maria, I respect you far too much to be kidding you over something like this. Do you think I could be right or am I way off the mark?"

"Ask me again in a few hours time when your father drops whatever bombshell he is holding right into our laps," she smiled, "and in the meantime please accept my thanks for coming along with me, I feel so much better knowing that I am not the only person prepared to put my life on hold for something so potentially ludicrous as one of your father's whims."

Sebastian agreed, "Yes of course you are right; all this speculation is pie in the sky until we find out for sure what is on his agenda, but whatever it is or how ludicrous, you can bet your bottom dollar that neither of us will have seen it coming."

The plane's engines droned a little louder as it taxied out onto the runway, moments later the engines roared into full throttle and the plane lurch forward and bumped into the air. If they lived for another thousand years, neither of the unlikely travelling companions could have guessed what surprise awaited them.

Chapter Thirty Nine

Deacon was taken completely by surprise when he saw Maria emerging from baggage with the smiling Sebastian. He didn't know whether to jump for joy or jump for joy with a "whoop" at the top of his lungs. In the end he kept his composure and did something almost normal for once. The word *almost* being the operative word, he stepped forward, kissed Maria and as Sebastian held out his hand Deacon brushed it aside and threw his arms around his neck. "So good to see you both!" he gasped in the ear of his dumbstruck son. Then, before another word was spoken he went on: "You two must think I have finally flipped my lid, well in a way I have, but before I explain let's get you to the cottage because we have a lot of work to do before morning and I have someone special that I want to introduce you to."

Sebastian was not only taken aback by the hug from his father but he was stunned by the genuine warmth that was so obviously discernable.

"Where are my flowers?" Maria asked in a playful voice.

"All in good time," Deacon smiled as he took hold of her baggage and led the way back to the car almost at a canter.

At the car Deacon opened the boot, but before he put the baggage in he took out a dazzling bouquet of beautiful fresh flowers. "There you go my dear," he smiled as he handed them to Maria, "Never let it be said that Richard Deacon is a man to renege on a deal or a promise."

Maria looked at the flowers and put two and two together only to come up with five. *He has found a woman and fallen in love and he needs me to interpret for him.* Exactly the same thought occurred to Sebastian. The warmth of his father's hug was the give away; yet neither he nor Maria mentioned what was on their mind. They had learned over the years that with Deacon, the master of double guessing, it was always better to wait and see.

The car was soon out of the airport traffic and back on quiet country roads. Sebastian turned from the futility of trying to admire the countryside as it flashed by the window and said to his father: "We have dropped everything to be here to help you with whatever is the matter, so does that entitle us to a tiny clue as to what it could be?"

"It most certainly does not Sebastian," Deacon said, "but what I will say is that the rewards of you coming will be two hundredfold."

"But you didn't know that I was going to come," Sebastian said. Deacon gave a wry smile: "Perhaps not, but I am so glad that you did. And on second thoughts I will give you a clue. Coming to France was the best day's work I ever did and it could very well prove to be yours too."

Maria sat quietly in the back seat listening to the conversation of father and son. She was convinced that Deacon had a woman waiting back at the cottage and she was the whole reason behind her recall to domestic duty. Sebastian had a second attempt to catch at least the merest glimpse of the French countryside. He had read somewhere that its forests and vineyards had inspired some of the most beautiful art treasures ever captured on canvass, but all he could see as his father sped along was a blur of green and gold against a background of cerulean blue sky. In the end he gave up and leaning his head back against the headrest he closed his eyes and tried to relax for the remainder of the journey.

It wasn't long before the village of Petit Saint Jean came into view and then disappeared again in double quick time into the rear-view mirror. Maria only had time to make a mental note of how quiet and how lovely the old place looked. It was obvious— yet unspoken by either Sebastian or Maria—that Deacon would be a whole lot happier once he was back at the cottage. They deduced that it was either a comfort thing or he really was a man on a burning mission.

The cottage appeared as Deacon slipped over the brow of the road and his first words uttered for the past half hour were simply, "Here we are then…" No sooner had the words left his mouth he had the gates open and the car parked under the trellis of the courtyard. Sebastian took in a deep breath of the mingling of fresh air and scent from the foliage as he stepped from the car. He opened the rear door for Maria as his father unloaded the baggage. "First things first," Deacon said as Maria stood in the courtyard and saw the serene beauty of it all in that very first moment. "I'll show you to your quarters so that you can freshen up," he continued before turning to Sebastian and quietly saying, "Despite being my honoured guest, you are on the sofa downstairs."

Sebastian smiled, "Now how did I manage to work that one out for myself? Still trying to toughen me up so I can meet the world head on?"

"Not at all Sebastian, the alternative is to share a bed with me, which is still an option if you would rather," Deacon laughed.

"The sofa will be just fine," was Sebastian's immediate response.

"Touché," Deacon said as he dropped Sebastian's bag on the kitchen floor and proceeded to take Maria's holdall up to her bedroom. "Follow me Maria," he called over his shoulder as he breezed through the living room towards the stairs. Maria was still taking in the sheer size of the garden and the exquisite beauty of the cottage from the spot where she stood in the courtyard; she was completely captivated by it. Instinctively she snapped out of her reverie and followed the sound of Deacon's commanding voice. Sebastian collected his bag that had been so unceremoniously dumped on the floor and took it into the living room where he put it beside the sofa which was to become his bed. When Maria came in he nodded to the foot of the stairs to direct her to where Deacon had gone. Maria headed up the stairs and she was followed by Sebastian.

"In here," Deacon called when he heard them out on the landing. Deacon had put Maria's case neatly on a trunk at the foot of the bed. "Would you like a quick tour of the place before we eat?" Deacon asked. Sebastian and Maria knew that they were going to get one whether they wanted one or not so they agreed. Deacon led them first to his bedroom, then into Joey's recently vacated bedroom. It was seeing the third bedroom that had Sebastian completely puzzled. If his father had met a woman, then she would surely share his bedroom? Maria was in one bedroom so why was he relegated to the sofa when there was a perfectly good bedroom not in use? Rather than beat about the bush he put the question directly to his father.

"If you have a bedroom that you are not using father, then why am I on the sofa?" Deacon made a face to indicate that his son had asked an awkward question, but none the less, a very good one, "I am glad you asked that question Sebastian, because the answer to it is the crux of why I need Maria's talent so badly. Let's go downstairs and I will explain everything."

Over the next hour or so Deacon gave Sebastian and Maria the full story of how he had met Joey and how the town's officials had suddenly taken a sinister interest in the burgeoning of their unlikely relationship.

Chapter Forty

Sebastian and Maria sat motionless listening intently as Deacon unfolded step-by-step the curious tale of Joey and Tina and how they had become his most welcome companions. He even showed them the note left by Mrs Bennett about the local scugnizzi.

"So let me put this in a nutshell," Sebastian said as his father drew his tale to a close. "You met Joey not long after you arrived here when he offered to carry your shopping and you gave him a few coins, then he brings you a fish, then he comes down with a fever and after you cure him you find out that he is deaf, homeless and probably an orphan. You feed him and clothe him and generally give him a place to live, then, you are suddenly visited by the local constabulary and several town officials who accuse you by implication of what? Harbouring a criminal or kidnapping a minor?"

Deacon took a deep, thoughtful breath as Maria sat in silence totally absorbed by the whole account. "Yes, your nutshell of events does sum it up vaguely I suppose, but the authorities knew of him well before I arrived in France of that I am certain. I am not certain that they accused me or suspected me of anything except knowing where he was. They seemed to be happy to let him roam about in rags scavenging for scraps until they suspected that I had taken him in. Then they came here mob-handed and demanded to know where he is, the whole thing is most peculiar. Surely if they wanted him so badly they could have rounded him up anytime, he is only a slip of a boy. Anyway, I packed the blighters off with a flea in their ear and told them to show me a search warrant if they wanted to look round my home."

"Probably not the smartest move from a legal standpoint," Sebastian mused.

"It wasn't a planned reaction Sebastian it was a spare of the moment thing. It was all I could think of to buy myself some thinking time."

"So they will be back tomorrow with a search warrant?" Sebastian asked.

"That's about the size of it," Deacon nodded.

"So what do you think they want him for?" Sebastian asked.

"That's the part I just don't know" Deacon said, "I can't imagine that he is guilty of any public offence."

"I think the first thing we need to establish is why they came round here mob-handed, it sounds a little like overkill for one small boy," Sebastian said.

"I am certain that the woman in the shop is behind it all, I think there is some history between her and Joey," Deacon said.

"What possible harm can he have done, he is deaf and dumb isn't he?" Sebastian said.

"He is deaf and dumb but he has intelligence well in advance of his years and despite being deaf, he knew when the police were on the prowl and that's why he's hiding, he has developed some kind of sixth sense," Deacon said, "Something or someone has frightened him, perhaps Tina bit the old bat's ankle when she tried to shoo Joey off the street. On second thoughts it can't be because Tina would have poisoned herself on her bitterness, she really is a dragon."

At that point Maria joined in the conversation, "Perhaps she is thinking of her livelihood. She may think that having a ragged little boy in the town is bad for business and you suddenly looking after him and feeding him will only prolong his stay, or even worse, attract others. Once you leave your holiday home he will be left behind and his new clothes will turn to rags again and the little gypsy boy will become a big gypsy boy; that could be the reason why she wants rid of him."

Sebastian looked at his father, "Maria has raised several good points; what *will* happen to Joey when you return home?"

"I hadn't even thought that far ahead," Deacon said, "I have simply been enjoying his company for what it is. I showed him how to play cricket and he showed me how to fish. I know it sounds ridiculous when I put it like that but damn it, the boy has opened my eyes to a whole new world; he offered me what was potentially his last bite of food for all he knew and I want to help him. In this world of takers it was just so good to find someone with nothing who was so willing to give me everything. You will see exactly what I mean when you see him for yourself."

"That is all very well, father, but it doesn't really answer the question. What happens to him when you leave?" Sebastian asked again. Before Deacon could answer Maria said: "Shouldn't we bring Joey in from wherever he is, especially now that you and the authorities are no longer so unevenly matched in terms of numbers? I can't bear the thought of him being alone out there; surely he would be better off either back here with us or in the hands of the authorities."

"I agree," Deacon said immediately, "I only allowed him to go so that I could give myself time to get help and as help has arrived then I should bring him in."

Sebastian held up his hand, "Just hold on a minute. Let's just say the authorities have been looking for him to re-unite him with his family. Yesterday you withheld information as to his whereabouts and demanded they attain a warrant. You could be getting yourself into serious trouble by not telling them where he was. As it is now you have done nothing wrong that they can prove, but if you bring him in now it will prove retrospectively that you knew where he was yesterday. At the very least that could be construed as wasting police time. Now on the other hand, they may just be curious to know what your relationship is with him. Much as I hate to be the one to point this out father and without putting too finer point on it, they may believe that you have some ulterior motive for befriending him."

Deacon paused briefly to reflect on Sebastian's last comment before he put his hand to his mouth. "Oh my good Lord, I hadn't thought of that."

Sebastian slowly stroked his upper lip with his thumb and forefinger, "The chances are that they will have thought of it."

"Instead of speculating about what they want with Joey, or what they want with you Mr Richard, why don't we wait until tomorrow when they return?" Maria suggested, "Then we will know for certain."

Sebastian and Deacon turned to Maria simultaneously "Now that is precisely why I wanted you to come over and help Maria, your common sense is worth its weight in gold," Deacon said, "Damn it I knew that you would know what to do."

Sebastian agreed, "That is exactly what we should do. The welfare of the boy is paramount and if that is the way the authorities are looking at it then either way the boy is going to have a better life from now on, so there is no point in doing anything silly. Let's get a good night's sleep and wait for the police and the rest of the entourage to return before we decide what to do next."

Deacon felt immediately better now that they had a short-term plan and he felt able to relax for the first time in days. "I don't like the idea of him being out there alone for another night any more than you do Maria, but if it has to be then so be it. However, I have decided that whatever happens tomorrow I am going to bring him in. Now, would either of you like a drink?" Deacon asked.

"I will have a large whisky," Sebastian said.

"Nothing for me," Maria said, "I'm hungry; why don't you two have a drink whilst I cook something,"

Deacon smiled as he filled two glasses with fine old whisky. "Now you're talking Maria, nothing like a good meal and a couple of smooth drams for loosening up the old chatter muscles. I have told you what I have been up to lately so let's hear about you two."

Maria went through into the kitchen to prepare a meal as Sebastian took a long sip and savoured the woody caramel of the whisky. "I have been building up my business."

Deacon nodded, "Yes, I have been told that you have been busy making quite a name for yourself in the big city."

"And what else have your spies been telling you?" Sebastian asked.

"They have told me that you have a driving ambition to make it to the very top of your career, that you are ruthless with your opposition, refusing to take prisoners," Deacon smiled as he raised his glass.

Sebastian raised his glass in return, "I wonder where I could possibly have inherited that from?"

Deacon suddenly said something totally unexpected: "Did I ever tell you how incredibly proud I am of you? You are definitely a chip off the old block."

Sebastian was clearly puzzled by the sudden change in the direction of the conversation. "As you haven't touched your whisky yet father I can't presume that it is the drink talking, so in answer to your question of pride the answer is no, you never have father."

Deacon took a sip and smiled again, "Then I am saying it now Sebastian. I am as proud of you as any good father is of their children."

Sebastian smiled back at his father: "You never said it father, in fact, I used to dream that my real father was somewhere else in the world, perhaps in far away Bombay or in some other exotic place. I used to think that my mother had had a secret affair and I was the fruit of their love."

"It sounds like you have inherited my romantic imagination too, Sebastian; perhaps you will make a fine novelist one day," Deacon said, "However, you are mine; your mother was far too loyal to do anything remotely untoward."

"Why didn't you ever take an interest in me when I was growing up?" Sebastian asked.

Deacon answered without hesitation. "I have Joey to thank for what I am about to say and this is why he means so much to me. When he was ill with a fever I had nothing to do but watch over him, he looked so small and frail just like you did when you were his age. I thought he was going to die and I would have given anything to save him, and I mean everything. That brought something home to me that I will be eternally grateful to Joey for. He showed me that the best things in life are free, but they still have to be worked for. If you want love or friendship from anyone, you have to earn it and I spent my whole life buying it. I have no excuses other than I wanted you to be strong and tough so that you could make it like I had to do in the world that my father brought me into. When my father died I had to learn to be tough very fast and I fought like a demon to build on what he left me. I knew that I would one day pass on my empire to you and I wanted you to be strong enough to keep it and in turn build on it. Missing out on watching you grow up was the price I paid for building my empire and Joey made me realise that the price was too high…because you were paying the price too. I remained distant from you because I thought it was the best way to unlock your full potential. I never in my wildest dreams thought that love could unlock your potential far more easily. I wanted you to learn that emotions have nothing to do with business and that success is greater than love. I wanted you to bring me success without me having to ask for it, that is why I never came to watch you play cricket or act in the school play. When Joey brought me that fish without me asking for it I realised that it was I who should have given you everything—including myself—without you asking for it. Seeing the smile on Joey's face when I gave him a simple cricket bat made me realise that I had made a terrible blunder in the way I brought you up. I was too damned wound up in the pursuit of success to see that in having you I was already the wealthiest man in the world. Thankfully Joey has come along and I have the chance to put a tiny part of the wrong I did right. I love you son, and I am immensely proud of you, can you forgive me?"

Sebastian could hardly believe his ears, nor could he believe that the man before him was the great Richard Deacon, a man renowned all over the world not only as a great writer and best-selling novelist but also as a shrewd and ruthless businessman. He searched his mind for the right words that would let his father know that it was not too late to put things right. In the courtroom he would have had no trouble at all finding an instant response to any dialogue, but try as he might he just couldn't find a single syllable. He simply stood up and held out his open arms. Deacon stepped forward and took Sebastian into his arms; neither man, despite their professional stoicism could keep from crying. Sometimes in this life words are not enough and Maria—emerging from the kitchen—being met with such an unbelievable sight knew instinctively that the wounds of time had been healed with nothing more than a hug between father and son. She slipped back into the kitchen un-noticed by the men and she rattled a few pans together to alert them. Her ruse didn't work because as she entered the room for a second time the men were still locked together like Siamese twins. She coughed gently and Deacon looked over, "Maria, please join us; this is as much to do with you as anyone."

"Are you two alright?" Maria asked.

"We are going back to the beginning and starting all over again…aren't we Father?" Sebastian smiled.

"Yes we are Maria," Deacon continued, "And I also owe you an apology for the way I have treated you over the years. You have become an important member of our family. And although I recognised that years ago, I never made it official as I should have done."

"You always treated me well Mr Richard and I was well paid," Maria said.

Deacon shook his head, "You kept my head from exploding on more than one occasion and one can not put a price on that; a lesser individual would have walked out on me and never looked back. How on earth did you put up with my nonsense?"

"I ignored you completely," Maria said without changing her facial expression.

Sebastian burst out laughing, "I'll drink to that."

"Your obsession with numbers and germs would have driven me insane if I would have taken it serious so what else could I do but ignore it?"

"You have a good point Maria, you did the sensible thing. My nonsense about germs and numbers and beating it is something else I have to thank Joey for. I was curing his fever and he didn't know it at the time and he was curing my phobia and I didn't know it at the time. I think it grew from a childhood thing I

217

had about germs which I allowed to get the better of me. I even used to keep sweet wrappers in my pockets rather than drop them into a litter bin. It must have driven my poor mother to drink— God rest her. The reason was that I believed that the wrappers had become infested with my germs once I had touched them and by throwing them away I was throwing my own germs away. I thought that if I threw away too many then I would leave myself susceptible to viruses and other riotous diseases. It was just something I never grew out of and as I got older and combined the weird obsession with things like superstition then the whole thing went out of control, rather like the behaviour of a secret alcoholic."

"Do you know how crazy and that sounds?" Sebastian asked.

"Yes I do," Deacon said. "And as I said, I only have Joey to thank for curing that particular lunacy."

"How did he do something that no one else could?" Maria asked.

"The answer to that is simple Maria, he needed me to get a grip and face reality, if I was going to be of any use to him at all when he was ill. There was no one else here, just me; so I was thrust into a situation that I had to deal with if you like. Otherwise it could have cost Joey his life. He was living rough when I first met him and living off the land. If he had allowed himself to be tormented by the same ludicrous fears and phobias that affected me then he would have not have lasted two hours out there on his own. If he was so brave about facing his very real problems, then what right did I have to be afraid of something so unreal? Joey is a genius and a jolly wee chap to boot; I can't wait for you to meet him."

All in all it had been a very strange 24 hours for each one of them and for very different reasons. Sebastian had seen his father in a new light and likewise Deacon understood for the first time that his son had turned into a man who was more than capable of holding his own in any company, social, legal or financial. As for Maria, she was completely bowled over by Deacon's astonishing revelations, but more than that, she too saw a vulnerable man who had struggled all his life behind a facade of manufactured confidence, built to hide his weakness. She suddenly understood the reason behind his outrageous eccentricities and why he behaved the way he did. Before her she saw a man who wanted to start his life all over again by allowing Joey to start his life all over again, and, as she went to bed that night she had only one thought on her mind...that she would do everything she could to help Deacon to secure a good life for his new found companion.

Chapter Forty One

Maria was awake early on the following morning and she picked up with the chores where she had left off months earlier—those of looking after Deacon. The only difference this time was that she did it, not as an employee but as a friend. Deacon had work to do and for that he would need a good breakfast, in the words of arguably France's greatest military leader 'An army marches on its stomach,' so Maria set to work feeding her troops with a burning passion. She had ghosted past Sebastian asleep on the sofa in the living room but the smell of sizzling bacon woke him up and he soon joined Maria in the kitchen.

"What do you make of all this, Maria?" Sebastian said as he poured himself a coffee. Maria gave a playful shrug of her shoulders. "I have seen your father in many different circumstances but I have never seen him quite like this. It would seem that he is the helpless little boy in this case and Joey is the adult. That young man must be quite a character; I can't wait to meet him."

"Me neither," Sebastian answered thoughtfully in a low voice, "He has certainly turned my father's life upside down."

"Well if these people are as determined to find Joey as your father seems to think they are, then we will meet him soon enough. This breakfast is ready now, do you want to wake your father or shall I?" Maria asked.

Sebastian shook his head, "You do it Maria, I don't want to go up there and find an empty bed and see that this has all be nothing more than a surreal dream."

Maria made a 'tsk' sound before she spoke: "You men are all the same when it comes to facing an awkward reality. I bet your father is lying in bed afraid to come downstairs in case he thinks *he* only dreamed that you had arrived with me to help him."

Maria went upstairs and knocked lightly on Deacon's door.

"Come in Maria, its open," came the reply from within.

Maria opened the door—*sounds like old times*—to find Deacon fully dressed and standing by the window looking out towards the woods.

"Are you alright Mr Richard?" she asked.

"Thank you Maria I am fine," he said without turning from the window, "I just hope that we can do something for Joey, not only today but for the rest of his life."

Maria stepped into the bedroom and joined him to look at the scene below. "Why don't you come down and eat a good breakfast so that we can all do our best for him. I don't have any 'brainfood' but I have the next best thing, good old bacon and eggs with hot toast."

Deacon smiled and did as he was told.

The three of them sat round the kitchen table and ate the breakfast. Sebastian could not remember the last time such an ordinary, wonderful thing such as that had happened, if at all. *I hope with all my heart that this is the setting for many more mornings like this*, he thought.

Sebastian helped Maria to clear away the dishes as Deacon went out into the courtyard to sit in the early morning sunshine. He was happy to see that the day was so bright because it meant that Joey was at least warm even though he could well be hungry, it had been almost two days since the poor boy had eaten that Deacon knew of. He looked at the gate and hoped that the posse of Joey-hunters would hurry up so that Joey could at least have a decent meal and take the first faltering steps towards his new life...wherever they might lead.

It wasn't long before Sebastian appeared out in the courtyard, but rather than sit down with his father he seemed to be preoccupied with something. First he walked to the opposite side of the courtyard which directly faced the front gate. Then he moved towards a clump of shrubs at the far end of the latticework.

"Why on earth are you sneaking around like a sniper?" Deacon asked.

221

"I am looking for the optimum wide angle for my camcorder," Sebastian said without shifting his focus on the job in hand.

"This is no time for family snapshots Sebastian; we have some serious business to attend to."

After some more adjusting Sebastian finally looked up. "Father, we are about to be visited by the police and who knows who else. And with your talk yesterday of them not getting over the threshold unless it is over your dead body, I am just setting up a little insurance cover in case things do turn nasty. A well placed surveillance camera can be as good an ally in the courtroom as a top barrister and it is a fraction of the cost."

"Well I'll be damned, who would have thought of that? You just might be a genius after all," Deacon laughed.

"Not just a pretty face father, there is something going on between these ears. Now, can you see it if I place it here amongst these shrubs?"

Deacon squinted at the shrubs, "Isn't technology a wonderful thing? You know, years ago a camera made to do that sort of work would have weighed half a ton, now they are no more than a few ounces."

"I threw it in my suitcase at the last minute hoping to catch some footage of the vineyards and medieval French architecture; I never dreamed that I would be using it to film your imminent arrest," Sebastian said dryly.

"Well, either way you will capture something to remember your stay by."

Maria appeared at the door with a tray of orange juice and the three of them sat down at the table. Neither of them spoke, it was approaching mid-morning and the heaviness in the air was tangible. They knew that at any moment the battle of the Strawberry Garden was about to begin.

At the sound of the engine that Deacon knew to be that of the policeman, he nodded to Sebastian who set the camera filming amongst the shrubs.

"Let them into the courtyard father…and be polite! Let me do the talking through Maria just so that there is no misunderstanding; and remember to let the camera have a clear shot of all the action."

"I will be polite, but they can let themselves in, like they did yesterday," Deacon sniffed indignantly as he remained unmoved in his chair. Sure enough the three men from the previous day appeared at the gate and entered without asking. They looked stony faced and businesslike as they approached the table. Sebastian stood up and moved protectively to his father's shoulder.

"Good morning gentlemen," Sebastian smiled as Maria interpreted in perfect French. The three men stopped a respectable distance from the table and their demeanour seemed to soften on hearing Maria speak. "What can we do for you?" Sebastian continued. The policeman looked at his colleagues briefly as if to confirm that he had been silently elected to act as their spokesman. Although he could speak English; he decided— probably to avoid any misunderstandings—to use Maria's interpreting services and he spoke from then on in French. "We are here to search this property," he said coldly.

"May I see the warrant?" Sebastian said.

"And who are you?" The policeman asked.

"I am Sebastian Deacon and I am my father, Richard Deacon's legal adviser. Now may I see the warrant and may I have your names please, before we go any further."

"My name is Dubois, I am the head of police in Petit Saint Jean," then pointing to the bigger of the other two men he introduced the mayor as 'Mayor Laurent' and his smaller accomplice as the town clerk 'Mr Moreau'. Dubois then asked the mayor for the warrant which was taken from the attaché case of Moreau and handed over to Maria in comical fashion via the mayor. Moreau had looked decidedly uneasy since the mentioning of the name 'Deacon,' he looked thoughtful and somewhat puzzled.

Maria opened the paper and began to read through it.

223

"Is it from the Justice Department?" Sebastian asked.

"There is no mention of it here," she said, "This headed paper is official Town Hall stationary, so I presume it originated there."

"Will you show it to the camera Maria and make a point of exaggerating your movements before you hand it back to the mayor," Sebastian said as Deacon sat impassively watching the proceedings. Maria did as she was asked and showed the warrant to the camera as the three men looked on bemused. "Now let them know that their *warrant* has been recorded on film Maria," Sebastian said, "And ask them how they think the French Justice Department will react when they learn that their representative officers are trying to gain illegal entry into private property by using bogus search warrants."

Maria relayed the message word for word and the immediate effect was to put the cat firmly amongst the pigeons. The three men began to remonstrate with each other and despite not knowing exactly what was being discussed, Deacon gathered that their ruse had been rumbled and each man was trying to wriggle out of it. Maria confirmed it when she began to relay what was being said. The mayor blamed his clerk and Dubois blamed both of the town officials for getting him to do the mayor's wife's dirty work. Through the fog of accusation and counter accusation the whole farcical scene was becoming patently clear as Sebastian explained when Deacon asked what was going on. "To obtain a warrant they would have had to prove to the local magistrate by the presentation of material evidence that they had cause to believe that a criminal was being hidden or that some other crime had been, was being or was about to be committed. They had no such evidence so they put something together on official looking paper hoping that you would not be able to read it."

"Now then Maria," Deacon said, "Would you kindly ask our friends to leave my property."

Sebastian stopped Maria as she was about to interrupt the warring trio and send them on their way. "Father just hang fire a moment here, let's just remember why we are here, we are here for

Joey and now we have a spectacular opportunity to turn this stand off around 360 degrees into our favour."

"How can we do that?" Deacon asked.

"We have them on the ropes, so now we can go for the knockout. Let them know who you really are and they will soon know that you have the clout to hang them out to dry. You have sold over five million books here in France and your international business empire employs French people in every town, so how will it look in the national press if it is leaked that the local mayor has employed the constabulary to illegally harass one of its most influential allies."

"Sebastian, you are now officially a genius," Deacon smiled, "Tell them who I am Maria and let's see what they have to say to that."

Maria took great delight in telling the three men exactly who Deacon was and what he represented. The look of bewilderment on Moreau's face turned to one of almost triumph.

"I knew you were someone I had seen before!" he cried and his face broke into a glowing smile as he moved towards Deacon with his outstretched hand. "Of course Mister Richard Deacon, I am so pleased to meet you."

In that split second Deacon also saw an opportunity to exploit the bizarre situation even further. Normally he would never have offered his hand to such an unknown source of germs, but on that occasion he thought by doing so he could gain an important ally from within the enemy ranks.

Dubois looking on could see thirty odd years service in the police force suddenly evaporating into nothing right before his eyes and he too thought it would be wise to abandon the mayor's rapidly sinking ship. He left the mayor standing speechless as he too marched towards Deacon as though they were long lost brothers. "I am so pleased to meet you too Sir, I just wish we could have made a better start to what I hope will be a lasting friendship; and may I say that I was right against this action from the very beginning."

Mayor Laurent was no fool either and he knew how to use his years of experience in local politics to back out of a sticky situation and leave his honour in tact. "Mr Deacon, this whole exercise has been carried out for your protection. I take a personal pride in looking after our valued visitors to our region and I wanted to be certain that you were not being hounded out. I have had reports that a vagabond has been making a nuisance of himself and that you were perhaps being threatened into giving him food and shelter rather than have your property damaged. For me to gain the proper court papers would have taken days if not weeks so I had this paper drawn up which enables us to move vagabonds out of our region without going through the lengthy legal channels. Moving them on quickly minimises the mess and damage they often leave behind."

Dubois and Moreau looked at each other and mentally agreed that the mayor had come up with a spectacular about turn that surpassed even his own reputation. It was at face value the most reasonable explanation which could possibly salvage the situation for everyone. Moreau's support of the mayor's story involved him staying silent but Dubois was more active. "The mayor is right, Sir, it was for your protection, but I was against it because I prefer to take the more direct approach to these matters. I am for finding these maggots and thrashing them soundly to within an inch of their life, that way you needn't be bothered by any of this at all."

Although Maria was horrified by what Dubois had said she decided to water down his response during her interpretation. She too could see that the situation was turning in Joey's favour so there would be nothing gained by igniting the volatile side of Deacon's nature. She relayed everything to Deacon and Sebastian and changed the words 'thrashing to within an inch of their life' to 'a clip around the ear.'

Deacon would have reacted very differently had she interpreted fully what Dubois said, but his reply was still pretty heated and confrontational for Sebastian's liking.

"Yesterday you threatened me, you said, 'It would be better for me not to play games.' Now who is playing games? To hell with my protection, I can look after myself in any circumstances. What exactly do you want with that boy?"

The mayor took in a deep breath and gave another political style response, "You have to put yourself in my position; I have a duty as mayor of this town to listen to the people that I represent and to act when they are not happy. A lot of their income comes from tourism and from people like you having holiday homes here. In recent years we have been plagued by teams of vagabonds appearing from nowhere. The women ply their trade selling rainwater spells and potions and other nonsense and the men browbeat home owners into having needless property repairs done. We have a zero tolerance on these people so they must not be encouraged. Yesterday I was getting a little annoyed by not being able to communicate properly with you. I was wrong and I apologise; so now you see why we must find this boy and send him on his way. If others of his kind find out that he is prospering here, then before we know it the whole town will be overrun with them. So if you tell us where he is we will make certain that you are not troubled by him again."

Maria relayed the mayor's answer and looked to Deacon for direction; the ball was back firmly in his court. After an agonising pause Deacon leaned forward in his chair and cupped his hands together across his stomach. "If you were to find him, where exactly would you send him on his way to?" he asked.

"When we find him," Dubois said confidently, "We would question him as to the whereabouts of his family and we would round them up and reunite them before escorting them beyond the limits of our department and from there to the country from which they sprang."

Deacon looked at Dubois thoughtfully and said: "There are two major faults with that line of action. Firstly the boy has no parents, in fact, no family whatsoever. Secondly, he is profoundly deaf so to question him would get you absolutely nowhere."

"How do you know this?" the mayor asked.

"Give me one minute," Deacon said as he moved towards the cottage door, "And you will see for yourself."

Deacon went into the cottage as the opposing sides wondered the same thing, namely what on earth he was up to.

Moments later he emerged with the two drawings that he and Joey had used to communicate. Deacon placed the first one on the table. It showed his drawing of the stick boy in between two parents. Deacon pointed to the crosses that Joey had scored out the parents with. "You see, he crossed out the people and drew in the trees to indicate that he lived alone in the woods. This picture proves also that he is deaf, why else would we have to communicate using pictures."

Moreau looked closely at the drawing and said: "How does this prove that he is deaf? He may be reluctant to speak because of the language barrier."

"A good point," Deacon conceded, "But I have enough software on my computer as you can imagine, to transpose any phrase into any language. If he could hear I would have been chatting, perhaps badly, I will grant you that, but speaking just the same and quite well enough to be understood."

"Yes of course, I see your point," Moreau said nodding.

The mayor took up the picture briefly and laid it back on the table. "So now that we seem to have established that the boy is deaf and has no family, it will be a simple matter of finding him and handing him over to the proper authorities, deaf or not deaf, orphan or no orphan, he is still the offspring of travellers and does not belong here."

"Now just a moment," Deacon said as he took up the picture, I have shown you evidence to support my claims. What evidence can you show the rest of us to support your claims?"

The mayor's face took on a bewildered expression, probably because he had no evidence and no clever political answer. Suddenly his face brightened and he turned immediately to Moreau and Dubois to ask with an air of supremacy. "Mr Deacon is right, what evidence do we have that the boy is indeed a gypsy?"

Moreau answered in an instant: "Dubois told me he was and I never thought to question his knowledge."

Dubois looked at his colleague with a badly disguised scowl in his eyes before he tried to shore up his crumbling defences with: "Everyone in the town says that he is a gypsy boy, I just went along with everyone else."

Sebastian saved Dubois from further embarrassment by offering them all an opportunity to save face.

"I believe I have circumstantial evidence which will prove beyond any reasonable doubt that the boy is anything but a gypsy, traveller, vagabond or whatever you wish to call him."

Dubois was quick to seize the chance to find respite from the awkward situation that Moreau had pushed him into. "I would be eager to see such evidence."

"To provide it, I would need to question my father," Sebastian said.

Deacon could feel his eyes narrowing in intrigue as to what his son was up to. Inwardly he chastised himself for allowing a flicker of emotion to slip and perhaps give away some perceptible sign of weakness that his opposition could seize upon. In an instant he regained his cool exterior and no one was the wiser. *I am putting all my trust in you now son, so please know what you are doing.*

The mayor opened his arms inviting Sebastian to continue. "Please, go ahead."

Sebastian looked into his father's eyes and instead of the cold, stoic Spartan that he had always known him to be in all of his dealings he saw the vulnerability of an ordinary man. What struck him more was the overwhelming feeling that his father's vulnerability brought him a tremendous responsibility not to fail him. His father needed him now more than at any other time in his life. Something told him that the next few minutes were going to shape not only the future of Joey but also the future relationship between him and his father.

Chapter Forty Two

An expectant silence fell on the gathering and all eyes turned to Sebastian. Under any other circumstances a young man suddenly finding himself in such a situation would have buckled under the pressure. However, Sebastian had cut his professional teeth in the courtrooms of London and as such had come up against some of the toughest, most ruthless barristers in the legal profession. He had defended an array of clients accused of anything from breaking and entering to international money laundering and attempted murder. On more than one occasion the future of his client's had rested wholly on his cross-examinations and summing up speeches and he had prevailed more often than not. This situation was perhaps not as potentially devastating if things went wrong as it could be in his courtroom dramas, but it didn't stop him applying himself as if his father's life depended on it. He believed that Joey had catapulted himself into his father's heart and that from that moment on their lives would be inextricably linked; somehow he had to pave the way to make this gathering believe it too. Through his courtroom experiences he had learned that a great barrister does not offer a conclusion to the jury, he merely leads them to the conclusion that he wants them to arrive at. That way they feel safe with their final decision because they believe it to be of their own making.

Sebastian moved in such a way that he questioned his father in full view of the three men, at no time would he turn his back to them, that would imply dishonesty.

"Father, do you remember the first time you ever had contact with the young boy?"

"Yes," Deacon replied, "It was in the town on market day."

"Can you tell us how you met him?"

Deacon could not see where the line of questioning was going but he went along with it, trusting his son to know what he was doing. "I was in a shop trying to buy bottled water and there was no one around to take my money. Suddenly the boy appeared and showed me that it was alright to take what I wanted and leave the payment in an honesty box on the counter."

Sebastian posed the next question to his father but looked briefly over at Dubois before he spoke. "So am I right in saying that you could have taken anything from the shop without paying for it?"

"Yes," Deacon replied.

"And if you wanted to you could easily have walked out with the honesty box?"

"Yes, easily," Deacon said.

"Then I must also be right when I say that the boy could also have stolen anything he wanted and walked away with the honesty box?"

Before Deacon could answer Moreau interrupted. "No one would ever dream of doing such a thing!"

Sebastian turned to Moreau, "Not even a gypsy or a vagabond?"

Moreau laughed sarcastically, "Are you kidding, they would take everything."

"That is exactly my point," Sebastian said calmly, "he could have taken anything and everything, yet he took nothing. In other words he acted like any other honest citizen and nothing like a gypsy."

Dubois looked at the stunned Moreau. "Why, he is absolutely right, why didn't I think of that?"

Before Moreau could answer Sebastian put up his hand, "I haven't finished questioning my father yet, if I may continue."

"Please do," Dubois said.

Sebastian could see that Dubois was warming towards Joey and heading to the conclusion that he wanted him to reach. All he had to do now was convince the other two.

Sebastian turned to his father. "When was the next time you saw him?"

"When I had finished shopping on the market that same day he offered to help carry my shopping."

"Did you allow him to help?"

Deacon looked at Laurent and was mindful of his policy on not encouraging gypsies, so he was careful to justify his answer. The last thing he wanted to do was undermine the good work that Sebastian had already done in building up sympathy for Joey. "I remembered thinking at the time that I should perhaps send him on his way, but he had been so helpful to me earlier and he looked in need of a good meal, so I agreed to let him help me."

"And did you offer him payment?" Sebastian asked.

"I offered him 10 francs." Deacon said. He was aware of Laurent's sudden intake of breath so he was quick to reach the point of Sebastian's questioning without being invited. "But to my amazement he wouldn't accept it, he asked instead for 2 francs."

This time it was Moreau's turn to be impressed by Joey's honesty. "A gypsy boy would have snatched your hand off!"

Two down, one to go, Sebastian thought.

Sebastian paused in his questioning just long enough for Moreau's interjection to have maximum effect and he burned its impression on the minds of the gathering with an emphatic, "Indeed."

Deacon could feel his heart swelling out to the size of a pumpkin, he was so proud of his son's performance. He wanted to leap from his chair and hug him until his arms ached, but once again he knew that anything other than steel composure could ruin everything.

Sebastian made a rolling movement with his hands to indicate the passage of time. "Now let's move on a few days to the incident with the fish and the rabbit" The three men looked at each other equally intrigued as to where this new line of questioning could possibly be taking them, *the fish and the rabbit?*

Sebastian continued, "The boy caught a fish and left it on your doorstep, did he not?"

"Yes he did," Deacon said, "I didn't know at first who had left it there or why and I was confused as to what I was supposed to do with it. I thought perhaps that it was a welcome gift from my neighbours."

"So what did you do with it?"

"I put it in the bath."

Laurent laughed at Deacon's answer and his laughter rippled through the trio. The three were pleasantly surprised that a man of his wisdom would not know what to do with the gift of a fish no matter how it had arrived. Sebastian waited until the laughter subsided because he knew that his father's ignorance and innocent actions regarding the fish would only substantiate the story should there have been any doubts.

"Then what happened?" Sebastian asked.

"Then I found a dead rabbit on the doorstep."

"I 'ope you put that in zee pan and not in zee bath," Dubois said in broken English, it was his attempt at humour.

Deacon shrugged his shoulders, "Actually I put it in the rubbish bin."

The smile dropped from Dubois's face as if some great sin had been committed. "Why did you do that?" he gasped.

"Simple my dear man," Deacon smiled, "Because a live fish can be kept fresh for a long time, whereas a dead rabbit would start smelling in this heat in no time if it wasn't cooked and I have no idea how to cook a rabbit or how long it will keep in its deceased condition."

Sebastian interrupted the tangent conversation. "Let us forget the eventual fate of the dead rabbit for a moment; I would like to concentrate on what happened next regarding the fish."

"After I found the rabbit I decided to try to find out who was leaving these things at my door. It seemed pretty obvious to me that the person wanted to remain anonymous so I hid in the cave knowing that he or she would have to pass that way to reach the doorstep. That is when I met the boy for the third time; that is also when I realised that he was deaf. After waiting for a while in the cave I saw the boy walk by with another fish. I called to him but he didn't hear me. He only knew I was there when he turned and saw me."

"What happened next?" Sebastian asked.

"Well, after I worked out that the boy was deaf, I asked him by using signs if the fish was really for me. He replied that he

233

had caught two fish and only needed one. I then said I had no idea how to cook it."

Laurent's eyes widened as if he was eager to hear how the story of the fish concluded. For some reason it seemed more important to him than the other two men.

"Carry on," Sebastian urged.

"Then I invited him into the kitchen where he made a fire in the stove and cleaned the fish before he cooked it in a bottle of white wine."

"Stop there, I have heard enough!" shouted Laurent. "That boy is no more a gypsy than I am! He has obviously been brought up to value manners and kindness, and only from a truly cultured teacher would he learn how to cook with such passion."

Sebastian had won over the mayor and successfully led all three to the conclusion that he wanted them to arrive at. His work had been done; all that was needed now was for Deacon to seize the opportunity to establish himself as the indisputable leader of Joey's rescue plan. In typical, no nonsense Deacon style—never slow to exploit a favourable business situation—he left no one in any doubt what was going to happen next.

Chapter Forty Three

"Please, sit down gentlemen," Deacon said through Maria, "I have an idea as to what should happen next if you would be so kind as to listen and perhaps give me your advice." Then, turning to Sebastian he asked him if he would be so kind as to go to the cave and select the best wine he could find and offer a glass to everyone. Deacon knew that the finer points of any deal should be outlined and settled over a glass of vintage wine. Whether he knew it or not, that simple gesture had no greater effect than right there in France because to the French way of thinking it makes any businesslike situation more civilised, more amiable and altogether more digestible. Laurent was eager to know what wine a man like Deacon would have in his cave believing that the stature of the man can be easily discerned from the contents of his cave.

It had been established so wonderfully by Sebastian that Joey was nothing more than a little boy who needed help. So now it was Deacon's turn to show why he was the man to orchestrate the help and support that Joey was going to receive rather than allow the established authorities to take control. His plan was quite simple—as with all his business deals—if things didn't appear to be going his way he would make them an offer they couldn't refuse.

In the cave Sebastian began his search for a suitable wine by brushing away the dust from the older bottles and scrutinising the labels. If Sebastian had learned anything from his father and from his socialite colleagues on the London legal scene—besides how to outwit an opponent and how to show off—it was how to tell a good bottle of wine from a great one. He was deeply impressed by the quality of wine as he unearthed one great vintage after another. *The chap who stocked this little larder certainly knew what he was doing.* The thought struck him as to why the previous owner of the cottage had left it all behind. Perhaps it was the thing to do? *Perhaps it was father's eagerness to take immediate possession of the property that made them leave it behind.* That last thought rankled with him a little because of the new leaf his father appeared to have turned and he was sorry that he allowed it into his conscious mind. *Still I can't be expected to dispel a lifetime of disappointment in just two days.* The real reason the wine was still there was of course that Mr Bennett had unfortunately become too ill to savour its delights.

At the far end of the cave Sebastian found two bottles of Chateau Troplong Mondot vintage 1945. *How very appropriate, a fine vintage from the year marking the end of hostilities in Europe, this should help my father to broker a deal that will bring young Joey the peace he deserves.* That thought made amends for the previous negative thought about his father and he felt so much better for it.

He emerged from the cave with the wine as Maria broke off from her role of interpreter to bring classes for the intruders-cum-*guests*. As he made his way to the table he knew exactly what would be on Laurent's mind regarding his father's stature and knowing what he had in his hand he was confident that it would seduce him into doing anything his father suggested from the moment the cork was popped.

He made a well concealed yet intentionally dramatic sweep of his hand with the first bottle of wine so that Laurent could see the label and hopefully indicate his acceptance. Instead of an almost imperceptible nod, as one might expect from a real connoisseur, Laurent's eyes widened and he almost fell off his chair. One bottle alone would cost him a month's wages and here he was being invited to give his approval. It was obvious from his reaction that Deacon's stature was suitably established. If he thought that was impressive then what was to follow was about to blow his mind completely.

Laurent managed to compose himself long enough to let Sebastian know that it was indeed safe to pour. Sebastian charged their glasses and took his seat at the table. With a roll of his hand Deacon invited Laurent to be the first to taste the vintage and he courteously accepted the honour. He closed his eyes dreamily as his flared nostrils hovered above the rim of the glass to savour the stunning, roasted berry bouquet. Deacon knew that Laurent was now firmly in the palm of his hand. For the promise of a wine of that calibre—perhaps even on a more regular basis—any man would defy his wife no matter how ferocious her demands. Laurent's mind floated off to paradise even before his lips touched the glass, but Deacon's mind was on the woods and the whereabouts of Joey and Tina. The sooner he could have Joey back in the safety of the cottage, the sooner his new life could begin.

"The first thing I think we need to do is give the young boy an identity, be it temporary or not. I have known him as Joey, so if we refer to him as such from now on is that agreeable to everyone?"

Laurent was still away with the wine fairies so Dubois spoke for the group. "Joey is as good a name as any…why not?"

"Good, then to start things moving my suggestion is this. I will go alone to find Joey and bring him back here. For some reason he has a deep mistrust of men in uniform so to be accompanied by you Mr Dubois or any of your officers would be counter productive." Dubois knew full well why Joey had an aversion to men in uniforms and that was because of more than one 'clip around the ear' but he didn't let on, instead he nodded sternly, "An excellent idea."

"Once he is safe we will make sure that he is fed, bathed and rested before we bring in a doctor to examine him. I will ask the doctor for a full report and bring it round to you Mr Laurent at your office. In the meantime Mr Dubois can make enquiries into how Joey could possibly have found himself in this situation and where he could have come from?"

Dubois looked over to Moreau who obviously had some say in what Dubois did with his time. However, it didn't take too long to discover exactly what that was.

"I can make a cursory enquiry of course, but because it would be of low priority that is the best I could do, in these financial times I have to be careful on how I use my limited resources."

"I think it is of the utmost importance to fully establish who Joey really is no matter how much time it takes and no matter what the cost," Deacon said.

Moreau joined the debate with, "Of course it is important to establish where he is from because that will ultimately decide where he goes from here. However, to undertake such research would cost money. It is my job here in the town to balance the books, we have a church which needs a new roof, we have a town hall that has not been renovated since the war and we have a chronic staff shortage at the hospital. Now how can I justify diverting funds away from these necessities when we are more or less certain that the boy is safe and well?"

Bingo! Deacon had just been presented with the perfect opportunity to be the major player in shaping Joey's future, he couldn't have hoped for a better opening and he wasn't slow in spectacularly exploiting it. Usually he would have teased the situation a little more rather like a fisherman playing with a particularly game fish, but with Joey out there in the woods alone it prompted him to bring in the big guns at this unexpectedly early juncture. "Of course these necessities you mention are highly important but they are easily rectified with the right kind of support and I can provide that support. Tomorrow morning you can go ahead and engage the contractors to do what needs to be done at the church and the town hall, I will also underwrite the funding of the hospital staff shortage for the next five years. Will that do for starters Mr Moreau? And as for your enquiries Mr Dubois, I will of course pay for a full and exhaustive search."

The three men sat motionless and in stunned silence for what seemed like an age. Collectively they thought, *did he just say what I think he said?* Maria and Sebastian however didn't bat an eyelid; they knew that what was on offer was nothing more than a drop in the ocean of Deacon's wealth.

Laurent was the first to respond: "You would do all this for us...why?"

Before he answered Deacon looked over to Sebastian with a knowing look in his eye that he knew only he would understand: "My dear Mr Laurent, I couldn't explain why if you gave me a thousand years and besides, you would never begin to understand; suffice it to say that I will do it because I can."

Deacon's answer was not as enlightening as Laurent perhaps would have liked but under the gift-horse circumstances he thought it was better not to push any further and once again his political savvy kicked in. "Your offer is one of enormous generosity Mr Deacon," Laurent said, "but it is beyond the authority of the three of us alone to accept it, we must convene a meeting of the town council and decide as one body."

Far from being phased by Laurent's response—as a lesser negotiator might have been—Deacon understood that Laurent was shrewd enough to need to buy some time to first of all let what was being proposed sink in and secondly to look for and at any possible negatives that might arise from accepting such an unbelievable gift. Had the roles been reversed Deacon would have done exactly the same thing. It may well have been that Laurent needed the approval of his council, but no one would have argued if under the circumstances he had made an executive decision and bitten Deacon's hand off. However, it was an option open to him that Deacon chose not to point out. Instead he used the situation to serve his own immediate needs which were to break up the gathering and bring Joey back.

"I fully understand how these things work Mr Laurent and by the time we have done our individual tasks you may be in a position to let me know what has been decided. In the meantime I will find Joey, you will call your meeting and Dubois can make his initial enquiries. I will ask Maria to exchange our telephone numbers so that we can keep each other up-to-date. Now is there anything else gentlemen?"

Laurent raised his glass: "All that remains is for me to congratulate you on your excellent choice of wine; I have never tasted anything quite so good. I have heard people say that in years to come other countries will produce wine to equal that of France, such people have never tasted the nectar of Bordeaux."

Dubois and Moreau joined Laurent in thanking Deacon, Maria and Sebastian for turning an 'odious' civic duty into a most pleasant morning.

Deacon waited until the three men were well on the road back to Petit Saint Jean before he allowed himself to smile. "Sebastian my son...you were magnificent!"

"Let's see if you still think so when I send you my bill," Sebastian laughed.

Turning to Maria Deacon said: "How can I ever thank you?"

Pointing in the direction of the woods she said: "You can thank me by finding Joey and bringing him back home in time for lunch, the poor lad must be starving."

Without saying another word Deacon set off towards the postern, he was a man on a mission, soon he would be re-united with Joey and that was worth more to him than anything money could buy.

Chapter Forty Four

Deacon thought he would head for the spot where Joey had kept Tina hidden from the world so successfully; that seemed the most likely place that Joey would be. He reached the shallow crossing in the river in no time; the spring in his step was charged by the fact that he had imagined Joey's wonderful smile that he knew was bound to greet him. Before long he reached the edge of the secret crater and looked expectantly down into it. He thought Tina would come dashing up towards him at any moment. One or two smart whistles imitating the intonation of his voice calling her would surely do the trick he thought. He was wrong. All that did was make it clear that neither she nor Joey were anywhere near the immediate vicinity. *Hhmm, what now?*

His next plan was to continue along the same bank for half an hour walking at a good pace and calling Tina every couple of hundred yards or so. If that produced no sign then he would find the next available place to safely re-cross the river and make his way back towards the cottage and further on if needs be in the opposite direction. Tina was likely to hear his calls on a calm day like that for anything up to a two mile radius.

His plan was thwarted at first by him being unable to find a shallow enough crossing so he compensated by crossing at the usual place and walking back away from the cottage to begin a search of that side of the river. He turned back when he had estimated he had covered the same length of river as on the opposite bank, but still there was nothing. He could feel the early onset of anxiety beginning to fester in the pit of his stomach as he allowed possible negative scenarios to develop as to where Joey was. *I wonder if those other two policemen who were posted down the lane to watch the back door when the posse first arrived the other day have picked him up? By God if they have harmed one hair on his head I will have them skinned alive!* The voice of reason suddenly kicked in to spare him any more self inflicted torment, Joey was far too smart to let a couple of dozy plods get the better of him.

Soon he arrived back at the point on the bank directly opposite the cottage and it crossed his mind to engage the help of Sebastian. He thought better of it when he realised that Joey may well stay hidden if he saw him approach his hideout with someone he didn't know. *No, I will press on alone as per plan.*

He paused just long enough before he resumed his search to take in the full tranquil splendour of the cottage. It was truly a dazzling jewel set in a cluster of swaying emeralds sparkling in the summer sunshine. *This place is too much for just one man; it needs to be filled with vibrant laughter with the sounds of family gatherings drifting on the breeze out to the river and beyond.* He put that beautiful thought on hold as he readied himself for the search of the only place left to look. If Joey wasn't to be found there then the search would have to be widened.

He looked at his watch and it was just turned 2pm, he would walk for forty minutes at the most and if that was no use then he would have to say that Joey was indeed missing. His mind being what it was he wanted to begin planning the next stage of the search before he had even finished the current stage and it was a struggle to pull his thoughts back to the present. *Being one step ahead of my rivals in business is one thing but in this situation a lapse in concentration could mean that I miss a vital clue.*

He pressed on pausing every now and then to call Tina and he kept his eyes whirling all about him like a submarine commander scanning the horizon through his periscope. Soon his watch told him that he was not going to be lucky, it was 2.40pm before he knew it and it was time to head back. *Where could he be?* Deacon thought for all he was worth as to where he could possibly have gone; he had only ever known him in that area, *perhaps he has other places further afield that he could hide...or take refuge?* That final thought hadn't even occurred to him until then and a sudden pang of sadness gripped his heart. *What if he does have somewhere else to go?*

There was no time to waste or to spend on idle speculation; it was time to get a grip and set his mind pondering his next move as he made his way feverishly back to the cottage. He thought of alerting Dubois to see if he could muster anything like a decent search party. Then he wondered if Dubois would indeed treat Joey as a bona-fide missing person and therefore call on all the help at his disposal. One thing was for certain and that was until the general townsfolk knew the truth about Joey they would never get involved in a community style search, to them his loss would be good riddance. If necessary Deacon would draft a search party in from back in England, all it would take was a telephone call.

He covered the forty minute outward walk in about half the time and soon the cottage came into view. Even before he crossed the river he was going through the contact database that he carried constantly in his head. One of the first people he would contact if Dubois was reluctant to set up a thorough search was Daniels—his financial adviser—who he would instruct to put a team together and arrange for their flights out to France. As he neared the postern he was surprised to hear the faint sound of laughter from within the cottage grounds, he stopped to listen closer and there was no doubt about it. He heard the distinctive voice of Sebastian as it carried on the breeze; he appeared to be shouting 'well done'. His frustration at not finding Joey and hearing Sebastian apparently having fun just deepened his anxiety. He flung open the postern and almost leapt into the grounds like an enraged bull might enter a bullfighting arena. However, the sight that met his eyes made him stop dead in his tracks. Sebastian had set up the cricket equipment and was preparing to bowl a 'Yorker' to a smiling batsman...who just happened to be Joey!

Deacon could hardly believe his eyes and his face immediately exploded into a wonderful smile of utter relief. Joey ignored the ball flying down the wicket when he caught sight of Deacon and he dropped the bat at his feet to take off towards him quickly pursued by a yapping Tina who had been resting at Maria's feet over by the table. Deacon dropped to his knees as Joey arrived with his arms outstretch to greet him, he gathered Joey up in his arms and walked triumphantly towards Sebastian.

"Can somebody tell me what on earth is going on? Where did you find him?" Deacon asked.

Sebastian shook his head, "As a matter of fact, Joey found us. Maria seems to think that he has been watching the house from a distance and worked out that we were on your side after the police and other officials had gone this morning."

"I told you this boy was a genius, didn't I tell you that?" By this time Maria was strolling towards the group gathering round Deacon. "Maria, perhaps you can explain?" he called.

"Joey turned up about twenty minutes after you left to look for him, you must have missed each other by seconds somehow."

"Well this is the best surprise I have had in a long time, this calls for a celebration!" Deacon laughed as he let Joey down on the ground. "Who is winning at cricket?" he added.

Maria smiled knowingly as she said, "If you think finding Joey was the best surprise then I might just have a better one."

"Believe me Maria, nothing could top finding this little fellow," Deacon said.

"Not even if I told you that he is not profoundly deaf?"

"How do you mean; not deaf?" Deacon said incredulously.

"Well how do you think I knew he has been watching the house and he knew when the coast was clear?"

"Are you saying that he speaks too?"

"He has a hearing problem for sure but he is not deaf and I am fairly certain that he is Spanish."

By this time Joey was tugging at Deacon's sleeve and pulling him towards the cricket stumps.

"First things first," Deacon smiled, "Joey clearly has his priorities right, let's finish this game of cricket and then you can tell me what you know in the pavilion over tea and sandwiches."

Maria gave the boys a playful shrug of her shoulders and a shake of her head, she knew it was pointless arguing. She made her way back to the 'pavilion' knowing that the most unlikely combination of cricketers the world had ever seen would grace her with their company only when they had had enough.

Sebastian watched amazed for the next hour or so as he, his father and Joey finished off the game in the afternoon sunshine; it was a sight that he never believed he would ever see. Each player had two innings each as combatants in a three cornered contest, after Deacon had announced that it was, 'every man for himself.' Deacon won by four runs with Joey a close second, Sebastian blamed his lack of practice for his poor show and Tina was voted best out-fielder.

The players walked back to the cottage with different pieces of cricketing equipment under their arms as Maria brought out the sandwiches and laid them on the table.

"Now, tell me how Joey turned up and what you know about his deafness Maria," Deacon said as he slumped into his chair.

Maria handed the boys a drink and began: "I was hanging out some washing behind the stable when I heard the postern opening. I looked over expecting to see you and in strode Joey with his dog as if he owned the place. I couldn't believe how confident he was, he was nothing like the shy little waif that I was expecting to eventually meet."

Deacon nodded and smiled, "Yes he does seem to produce that admirable straightforward approach when he needs it."

Maria continued: "He came straight over to me and made signs asking where the tall man was. I managed to let him know that you were out looking for him and his dog. I told him that you would be back soon and I said you would want him to wait."

"So what makes you think Joey is not completely deaf?" Deacon asked.

"Because I remembered what you said about the paper you used to communicate with him using drawings and I thought I would do the same. I drew a picture of myself to try to tell him my name and I heard him faintly say the word 'woman' in Spanish. So I wrote in Spanish that I was your friend and Sebastian was your son and we were here to help you both. He took the pencil and wrote that he was your friend too. I asked him if he was deaf and he said his hearing was very bad and his ears often hurt but he didn't think he was completely deaf."

"What else did you ask him?" Deacon said excitedly, "Where is he from, does he have any family?"

"I didn't want him to feel like he was being interrogated so I told him he would be safe from now on and that we would do everything we could to help him."

"That's when I suggested a game of cricket," Sebastian interjected.

"Why on earth didn't Joey speak to me?" Deacon asked.

"Probably because he knew that he couldn't hear very well and he had already guessed that you were a tourist from abroad, your car registration plate might have been a giveaway that you are English," Maria said.

"Yes, that is possible I suppose and it does make sense. We need to find out everything we can so that at least I will be able to give Dubois something to go on to try to trace his family. Ask him where he is from," Deacon said.

Maria wrote the question down for Joey and he took up the pen. No one could have imagined what he was about to reveal. He wrote that he did not know where he was from but that about a year ago he was in a car which he thinks crashed. The next thing he remembered was lying on the riverbank with a man rubbing his face. The man took him back to his family who lived in a caravan and he stayed with them for almost a year until they had to leave the area. He wanted to go with them but they said the police would not allow that to happen. They gave him Tina to be his companion on the day they left and he has been alone ever since.

"Oh my God," Deacon whispered.

"Putting two and two together," Sebastian said, "that explains virtually everything."

"What do you think happened?" Maria asked Sebastian.

"Well it sounds like something happened to the car he was travelling in and he suffered some kind of head trauma. Perhaps Joey was injured and found by gypsies who looked after him. That would explain why the locals think he is a gypsy boy."

"Why would the gypsies keep him instead of handing him over to the hospital or the police?" Maria asked incredulously.

"It could be that the gypsies were responsible for the crash and there was a fatality, they may have panicked and fled, there is definitely a connection between what happened to Joey in that car and him being taken in and held for so long by the gypsies, or whoever did hold onto him"

"But why would someone virtually kidnap him, then let him go and be so kind to him?" Maria asked.

"Well, let's draw back from these suppositions for a second; we could be way off the mark. Why don't we ask Joey what he thought of the people who took him in if that is indeed what happened?" Deacon said, "That might help us piece things together properly rather than speculating. I want to be able to tell Dubois what I know not what I think."

"I agree," Sebastian said as Maria set to writing down the question.

"Joey wrote that the family who took him in treated him well and they were his friends, they taught him how to catch fish and how to make money from tourists by carrying their shopping. He said the family were very sad when they had to leave him behind."

Deacon shook his head, "I think the people who took him in were victims of a series of extraordinary circumstance. It sounds to me like they found him injured and couldn't hand him over because it would incriminate them, perhaps because they were illegal immigrants."

"Depending on whether the family can be traced—which seems unlikely—I doubt if we will ever know what happened," Sebastian said, "What are you going to tell Dubois?"

"I will drive into town later and tell him what I know, but before that happens Maria, we will all help Joey to make himself at home and let him know that he will not have to run and hide from anyone ever again."

"Shall I run Joey a bath before I call a doctor to check him over as you told Laurent we would?" Maria asked.

"An excellent idea Maria," Deacon said before he turned to Sebastian and asking him how long he could stay in France.

Sebastian smiled, "Whether we will ever find the real truth about Joey or not, there has definitely been at least one injustice carried out against him either by accident or design and I am in the business of fighting injustice and protecting the innocent. I am in this right up to the end, I have waited all my life to feel this good about something for so many reasons, so I am not about to let this opportunity slip away, no, I am here until the final act is played out."

Deacon gave a wry smile because he knew exactly what Sebastian meant. By ensuring that Joey could lead a normal life from now on Sebastian had the chance to put right some of the perceived injustices he suffered as a child at the hands of his father who was always too busy to be a father. Over the past few days he had seen changes in his father that were of gigantic proportions and witnessing those changes had brought about equally great changes within himself. He understood his father for the first time and he knew that his father had finally learned that love—in all our human relationships—is the only key to everlasting happiness.

Chapter Forty Five

A doctor arrived within the hour; he knew the address because he had visited it on numerous occasions in the past few months to treat the weakening Mr Bennett. The doctor was a middle aged man with a look of calmness in his eyes. He raised his hat to Maria as she answered the door and a smile lit up his kind face as he introduced himself as Doctor Jones. Maria thought she had misheard his surname but when she repeated it questioningly he simply nodded. Maria showed him through into the living room where Joey was busy drawing features onto the outline of a face that Sebastian had drawn. She introduced the doctor to Deacon and Sebastian and on hearing that they were English the doctor spoke in fluent English from that point on. Deacon shook the doctor's hand and said: "We would like you to examine Joey doctor; I will be taking care of him for the immediate future and my first concern is that he is fit and healthy. He has been living rough for a while, no one knows exactly how long and he has a problem with his hearing."

"Let's take a look at the young man then," the doctor smiled.

Maria explained to Joey that the doctor wanted to take a look at him to make sure he was healthy. She laughed when Joey asked if the doctor would take a look at Tina too. The doctor smiled and turned to look at Tina who was curled up over by the door, "Tell him that I can see just by looking at her lovely shining, wet nose that she is fine."

The doctor listened to Joey's chest and after looking into his eyes and mouth he began checking his fingernails. He seemed to be spending quite a lot of time pushing them and scrutinizing every tiny detail. Deacon was eager to find out why so he asked the doctor what was so interesting about them. The doctor patted Joey's hand and nodded approvingly. "The study of the fingernails is almost a branch of medicine in itself, we can learn so much from them and even detect illnesses in the body before they have had chance to develop. For example white nails with pink at the tips could imply cirrhosis of the liver due to alcoholism."

Deacon immediately looked at his own fingernails as Maria looked on and gave an inward groan. *With the amount of alcohol you have consumed in your life I wouldn't be surprised if your nails were pickled.* Unknown to Maria, Deacon was thinking exactly the same thing and his healthy looking nails made him doubt the wisdom of the doctor's claims.

The doctor went on: "I was checking mainly for cracks or chips in his nails because that would indicate some nutritional deficiency or lack of minerals and protein."

"So what did you see?" Deacon asked.

The doctor gently lifted Joey's hand and pointed to several ridges going across the nail. "These ridges tell me that Joey has recently had an infection of some kind, possibly flu; that could also explain his ear problem." If Deacon was sceptical at first about the doctor's claims he was soon won over because he knew Joey had recently had an infection.

The doctor let go of Joey's hand a second time as he gave his medical opinion: "Joey is a little on the thin side but it is my professional opinion that he is in general good health."

"What about his deafness?" Deacon asked.

The doctor took something like a small black torch from his bag. On the end of the torch was what looked like a watchmaker's magnifying glass: "Yes, his ear condition sounds like it could be a cause for concern, so we had better take a good look at the problem." He gently cupped Joey's face and inserted the thin end of the eye piece into Joey's ear. He did the same to both ears and he took his time. Deacon was impressed by the doctor's thoroughness. After several minutes of examination the doctor looked away with a thoughtful expression on his face, it looked as though he was deliberating with himself.

"What is it Doctor?" Deacon asked.

"If I am right, I believe his condition is treatable. I think the term in English for what could be causing his deafness is Glue ear."

"I have never heard of that," Deacon said, "How has he caught it and how is it treated?"

The doctor put away the instrument: "One does not catch it, it comes as a result of infections and it is quite common in children. I would say that every child has at least one bout of glue ear in their life to differing degrees of severity. The ear is divided into three parts, the outer ear, the middle ear and the inner ear. In a healthy ear the sound waves come into the outer ear and hit the eardrum to make it vibrate. Behind the eardrum is the middle ear which has three tiny bones in it, these bones pick up the vibrations and pass them to the inner ear and on to the brain. The middle ear is where I believe Joey's problem is. In a healthy ear it should be filled with air but after infections it sometimes fills up with a glue-like fluid. In most cases the hearing is dulled, but in others it can be dramatically reduced. The treatment in Joey's case will involve a visit to an ear specialist who will probably do a small operation to insert grommets which will drain off the fluid and his hearing will hopefully return when the fluid is cleared."

"Do you know such a specialist?" Deacon asked.

"I do and I will make the arrangements for Joey to see her next week. There may be some cost involved."

"I will pay for whatever treatment he needs," Deacon said without the slightest hesitation. With that, the doctor gathered up his bag and started to move towards the door. "Is there anything else I can do for you?" he smiled.

"There certainly is Doctor," Deacon said, "Two things, could you give me a note outlining Joey's condition and his recommended treatment and can tell me how a French doctor has a name like Jones?"

"Ah," the doctor smiled, "This first request is straightforward enough but the second part needs a little explaining." As he began writing the note he gave an account of how he came by his unusual name. "My grandfather was a soldier in the South Wales Borderers during the First World War and he was wounded at the battle of Chelvult. He was taken to the nearby hospital where my grandmother worked as a nurse. She nursed

251

him back to health and they fell madly in love. My grandfather remained in France after the war and married his sweetheart. He told me in later years that the credit for that action at Chelvult went mainly to the Worcester regiment for what has gone down in history as their 'Advance to recapture Chelvult.' It was an action that some historians say saved the whole of the allied forces from being cut off from their supply ports on the northern coast of France, which would have lead to their capitulation. Yes the Worcester regiment is credited with it but my grandfather's regiment was definitely involved and I still have the shrapnel from his wounds to prove it. I think the romance of that whole story is why I chose this profession."

Deacon took an instant liking to Doctor Jones; partly because he was obviously a very capable doctor but mostly because he always favoured people who could tell an interesting tale and he made a mental note to use his services if ever they were needed in the future, either as a doctor or a teller of interesting tales.

The doctor said he would be in touch soon and he left the residents of the cottage in a much happier, more optimistic state than he found them. For the remainder of the evening Deacon— with the help of Sebastian and Maria—explained to Joey all that the doctor had said and how Deacon was going to go into town on the following day to speak to the mayor and to Dubois…they would have plenty to discuss.

Chapter Forty Six

On the following day Joey and Sebastian remained at the cottage whilst Maria and Deacon made their way into town. Deacon's first stop was the police station. The officer on the front desk wasted no time in showing them through to Dubois; he had obviously been briefed of his imminent arrival, in fact, if Deacon was any judge at all of small town life he suspected that the whole townsfolk were discussing nothing other than the eccentric billionaire and the penniless gypsy boy. Nothing spreads faster than a closely guarded secret.

With the help of Maria, Deacon explained to Dubois everything that Joey had told him about the probable car crash and the family who took Joey in at some point shortly after it. The instant reaction on Dubois's face told Deacon that the news meant something to him. Dubois stroked his moustache thoughtfully—and rather dramatically—before he said: "I can possibly throw some light on the family of travelers he speaks of because I personally moved them on." His demeanor was irritatingly boastful for Deacon's liking but he knew he would get more information out of him if he allowed him his self indulgence.

"Can you remember exactly when you moved them on?" Deacon asked. Rising to his feet and walking over to an old filing cabinet he said: "I don't need to remember, I have the preliminary eviction papers right here and they are dated."

"What are preliminary eviction papers?" Deacon asked. Dubois smiled, "They are a little invention of my own, legally they mean nothing, but the message it sends to the gypsies is that when I return with my officers with the actual eviction order we will leave their homes with just the wheels so that they can drag the sorry remains back to where they came from."

Poor Maria wanted to slap his face because she knew that he meant it, but she too had to swallow her anger in order to get what they came for which was more information about Joey's origins.

"When you served those preliminary papers on the family do you not recall seeing Joey amongst them?" Maria asked.

Turning to Maria with an air of arrogance bordering on incredulity at her naivety he said: "The business of men, no matter what their rank or social standing is conducted between men, not their women and children."

You chauvinistic pig, Maria thought, but the words, "I see," were all she could muster in response, probably because her tongue was wedged firmly between her teeth.

"Have you any idea where the family went?" Deacon asked, "Perhaps they could be traced and questioned about their involvement with Joey."

"These people have their own laws and their own secret codes, if I found them again today and beat them half to death they would never tell me anything that would be of any use. But do not give up hope just yet, what you have told me today just might lead me something which could be interesting."

"What could that be?" Deacon asked.

Again Dubois stroked his moustache and his stubbly chin with his hand to create the illusion that he was onto something which could be jeopardized if his thoughts were revealed too early.

"Leave it with me for a while Mr Deacon, it is just a policeman's hunch that I follow. I will contact you immediately if my hunch turns out to be...shall we say... profitable."

The emphasis on the word 'profitable' made Maria guess and Deacon know for certain that Dubois would be looking for more than just the cost of his enquiry if he did find anything worthwhile. Deacon was of a mind that if Dubois did find something worthwhile, whatever he wanted for his troubles would be little more than peanuts in the grand scheme of things so he took the opportunity to sweeten the purse, but he did it in his own inimitable way, "Mr Dubois, I will be most grateful...most grateful indeed if you can throw any light at all on to this whole unfortunate case that is threatening the future of an innocent young boy."

Dubois smiled as if he already had the money in his back pocket. "The moment I know something Mr Deacon I shall deliver the news to you personally."

With that Deacon and Maria left his office and headed over to see Mayor Laurent to deliver the doctor's clean bill of health for Joey.

"I could cheerfully slap that weasel!" Maria hissed once they were clear of Dubois's office. "Maria, have you ever heard the term, 'Slime runs down the wall,'?" Deacon said calmly.

Maria smiled huffily because he had made her smile when she didn't feel like smiling, "No I haven't, but it sounds like something suitable for that pig back there."

"The apt phrase was first coined for exactly that reason. The higher up the ladder some people climb the more corrupt and greedy they become no matter what their station or office to do what is right."

"You are not going to pay him extra for doing what should be his job are you?" Maria protested.

"His won't be the first grubby little mit that I have greased to get things done and it won't be the last, besides having a chap like him on the payroll until Joey is safe has its advantages. I will play ball with him if he comes up with the goods, but I will make him dance to my tune."

Maria wasn't at all happy but she knew that Deacon had a good point, Dubois had them over a barrel and until Joey's future was secure they would have to accept the situation.

Chapter Forty Seven

Maria and Deacon dropped in to their next port of call, Mayor Laurent's office. Deacon had a sneaky suspicion that Laurent would have called an emergency meeting of his council colleagues the night before and briefed them to keep a lid on things. The amounts of money being dangled in front of them would have been too much of a temptation to waste any time in deciding to accept it. Plus, he would have wanted to be one step ahead of the game in an attempt to maintain the cool exterior that he believed—mistakenly—that he was impressively showing to Deacon. Deacon had already established that Laurent liked to give the impression that he was in control of all matters to do with his town and in order to do that officially he needed the full support of his colleagues.

It was obvious that Laurent had been expecting an early call from Deacon because he was dressed in his finest clothes, something normally done for a presidential visit or some other state occasion. His secretary too had been given a crash course in protocol; her immaculate dress was not the giveaway it was the nervous curtsey she gave as she asked Deacon and Maria if they would wait until she had spoken to the mayor to see if he was free to see them. As they waited Maria looked up at the peeling paint hanging in sheets from the ceiling and walls of the once opulent building, there were cracks in several of the stained glass window panels and the wood looked tired and neglected. She could fully understand why the building was in such dire need of repair. To restore it to its former glory when France was at the height of its colonial prowess would cost a fortune and yet to try to repair it on the cheap would have been sacrilege.

The secretary knocked lightly on the heavy oak door of Laurent's office and she was dramatically invited in. Maria found the whole thing wonderfully amusing but Deacon was well used to such staged performances designed to beguile and seduce the inexperienced.

The secretary emerged from the office and asked Deacon and Maria to follow her. Deacon expected to find Laurent plowing through piles of official—blank—papers and he was not disappointed. Deacon knew that Laurent's next move would be to come from behind his desk and meet him in the middle of the floor so that he would have complete control of the negotiation area, rather like controlling the central squares on a chess board. Just out of devilment Deacon entered the room at such a pace that he occupied the centre of the room before Laurent had the chance shuffle his blank papers into a neat pile.

"Good morning Mayor Laurent," Deacon smiled.
Laurent felt both the presence of Deacon and the pressure of his positional opening gambit. He was so flustered that he forgot to dismiss the secretary in the manner that they had rehearsed and she stood awkwardly waiting for Laurent's instruction. After her second polite cough to hint at his cue went unheeded, she took matters into her own hands. "Will that be all Sir?" she asked. Laurent composed himself long enough to offer his *unexpected* guests a morning coffee and Deacon's acceptance eased the situation. The secretary left to bring the coffee as Laurent indicated towards a small table to his left. If he couldn't command the negotiation area then sitting on equal terms was better that nothing. "Shall we take a seat?" he said. The two men waited until Maria was seated before they took their seats to face each other.

"Now, what can I do for you Mr Deacon," Laurent asked.
Deacon took the letter from Doctor Jones from his pocket and handed it to Laurent. "I have brought this note regarding Joey's health and overall condition from your good Doctor Jones as I said I would. And I have delivered some information about his possible origins to Dubois which may speed up his enquiries."
Laurent took the note and examined it. "I see the boy is being referred to a medical specialist."
Deacon smiled: "Yes, it would appear that his hearing condition is not permanent, I will take him to the specialist and hope for the best."

The secretary entering with the coffee couldn't have been timed more perfectly because it gave Deacon the opportunity to have a little fun with her boss whilst she was in the room. "I don't suppose you will have had time to convene a council meeting to discuss my offer of financial aid Laurent," Deacon said as he casually stirred his coffee. He smiled inwardly as the secretary and Laurent locked eyes. She knew there had been a meeting but she also knew that Laurent would hate to admit it because it would have exposed how desperate he was to get his hands on the money. The fun part for Deacon was seeing if her boss would tell a blatant lie on a matter as crucial as that to maintain his illusion of authority.

Laurent broke away from his secretary's expectant glare. "Mister Deacon, these walls may be lacking paint, but they have no shortage of ears. We will resume our conversation when the coffee has been served." He waited until the secretary had left the room before he answered Deacon's question. "Let us just say that I have sounded out one or two of the more influential members and they have offered me their full support. I know how eager you are to help us but you must understand that not everyone is as enthusiastic as I am in accepting your help. I know that your offer is genuine and should be taken at face value but some people—the more skeptical amongst us—believe that you have designs on extending your business empire here in Petit Saint Jean. Some of them are old and set in their ways which makes them resistant to change, they will need to be persuaded to support us and it will take every ounce of my being to bring them around."

I might have known...he is on the take too just like Dubois. Here am I offering millions to prop up the infrastructure of the town and all he is interested in is an opportunity to cash in. Despite his thoughts Deacon played his hand in his usual ice-cool way. "I understand and accept that you will have a struggle on your hands to make people see that my offer is sincere and without conditions either now or in the future. But if you can do this for me I will personally see to it that your efforts are adequately rewarded."

258

Deacon could sense the nausea rising in Maria's throat and he knew that he would have to get her away from there as soon as possible. "So Mayor Laurent, the moment you have news of my offer being accepted, have your secretary give Maria a call and we can put the finishing touches to the business over a glass of wine."

Laurent could hardly contain his excitement, not only had he negotiated a deal which would completely renovate the town's once prestigious buildings, he had brokered a potentially massive kick-back for himself into the bargain. To cap it all off he was drooling at the thought of sealing the business over another bottle of Deacon's superb vintage wine. He offered his hand to Deacon as he rose to his feet and he shook it heartily. Maria felt her skin crawl as he lowered his head to kiss her hand. For possibly the only time in her association with Deacon she could understand his bizarre phobia of other people's germs, she couldn't wait to get out of his office to run her hand under the nearest tap.

The secretary curtsied again as Deacon and Maria walked stealthily out of the building. Laurent turned to the window and punched his hand in triumph. *Big talking businessman, throwing his money around, it was like taking candy from a new born baby.*

Maria sat stony faced in the car as Deacon fired up the engine. "I know that business back there was upsetting for you and if I could avoid putting you through it I would," he said apologetically.

"Just drive me home," she hissed, "I need a bath and I want to be sick and not necessarily in that order."

Deacon tried to temper Maria's disgust with a little home-grown philosophy; "I was fortunate to learn very early in life that business and sickness were brother and sister. My heart goes out to you but at the same time I find your naivety so very refreshing."

"I could understand their greed if you were chasing a business deal that would net you millions but all you want to do is help a poor boy. To do that, you are prepared to spend millions renovating their crumbling town and yet that is not enough."

Deacon shrugged his shoulders, "Maria, for some people the whole world would never be enough, but in the grand scheme of things Dubois and Laurent are insignificant, not good enough to stand in Joey's shadow and it is for him that I will play their game. Yes, I will give them their money, but mark my words; by the time this is over they will have earned every single penny..."

Chapter Forty Eight

Deacon and Maria arrived back at the cottage to find Sebastian, Joey and Tina playing football. The sight of Joey running round and having such fun served to ease Maria's vexation at what she had witnessed earlier in the offices of Dubois and Laurent. *Perhaps I am being too hard on Mr Richard; he is only doing his best for Joey.*

Deacon could feel the ice surrounding Maria melting at the sight before them and he took the opportunity to try to dispel the cloud completely. "It's been a while since I treated you Maria, why don't I take us all out to the big city tonight for the best food that France has to offer. Joey could do with fattening up and you could do with cheering up."

Maria looked at him knowing full well that she should take the olive branch but she decided to tease him a little. "You can't buy me as easily as you can buy those officials, who by the way should be doing their duty for nothing other than their wages."

"I have to admire your integrity Maria, that and your natural beauty and worldly wisdom are the reasons why you are so special to me. There is not enough money on the planet for me to even begin to compensate for having those qualities so close at hand. You are like a flower in the desert, a spring of fresh water in an ever expanding wilderness."

Maria made her now familiar tsking sound when she knew she was being cajoled.

"If that is a quote from one of your books I will never forgive you," she said half jokingly.

"Maria, what an impossible position you are forcing me into, I can not buy you with money or treats and I am not allowed to win your forgiveness with the words from my heart. Mind you, you have a jolly good point, they are rather good, I think I will find a suitable place for them rather than let them go to waste," he smiled.

She looked at the wicked twinkle in his eye and laughed aloud, "Just for that I am going to order the most expensive meal on the menu."

"Am I forgiven then?" he asked.

"I shall tell you after dessert," she called over her shoulder as she walked towards the boys playing football to join in the fun.

Deacon sat at the table beneath the shade of the latticework and watched the game like a proud father. The scene evoked feelings and emotions that previously only inhabited his imagination and of course the pages of his novels, the feelings were strange, but perhaps the strangest thing of all was that he liked them and he wanted more.

Deacon was taking a bath getting ready for his night out when the telephone rang. Maria lifted the receiver to find it was Doctor Jones. He had wasted no time in persuading the consultant to take a look at Joey and he was calling to tell Deacon to be at the consultant's clinic in Angouleme on the following afternoon. She was long since out of the habit of keeping his diary but she knew that on this occasion he would not have missed that appointment for the world. Maria thanked the doctor and told him that they would be in Angouleme at the appointed time. Deacon was doubly pleased with how the day had unfolded, he had started the day with a potential result from the town officials and he was about to end the day with a special meal with his adoptive family. The news about the appointment was a wonderful added bonus. Maria took no time in letting Joey know the good news and his smile lit up an already illuminated room.

It didn't take Sebastian and Maria long in joining forces to select the place they would most like to dine and they found it in what was obviously an exclusive shopping area of the city. In amongst the designer stores and jewelers boasting of branches in New York and London they managed to find…a McDonald's! The look on Deacon's face was an absolute picture as Maria, Joey and Sebastian raced to be the first through the door. By the time Deacon reached the door the laughing trio was already at the counter perusing the overhead menu. Maria turned and flashed an impish smile at Deacon, she had never seen him looking so utterly lost for words or a reaction; it was as though he had been stuck by lightning. He saw her smile and realised that he had been set up. The question now was would he enter the restaurant thus crossing the great divide between his world and that world that he only ever looked at through the mullioned windows of his ivory tower…the world of ordinary folk? Beneath that menu stood his whole future and he suddenly saw the poignancy of it, that trip to McDonalds was an invitation from them to make the commitment to being part of their lives in every way rather than just giving them what he thought they needed. He stood for an agonizing moment with his hand on the door handle. Maria thought she heard a choir of angels as his face broke into a smile when he pushed the door open and strode in. Sebastian motioned with his eyes to the menu,

"What's it to be father?"

"Hhmmm, four Happy Meals seems rather appropriate," he smiled.

"These are on me," Sebastian said, "Because I for one have never been happier."

The four sat down and enjoyed what was probably the happiest meal of all their lives for a very long time.

Back at the cottage Maria settled Joey down for the night ready for his big day in the morning. Sebastian and his father sat at a table on the patio at the rear of the cottage and opened a bottle of wine. "Maria tells me that Dubois and Laurent are looking for a little bonus for making things happen," Sebastian said quietly.

"Yes and she wasn't happy about it, but I see it as greasing the wheels of progress nothing else," Deacon shrugged.

Sebastian held his glass up to the light as if it held the answer to some ancient enigma. "I don't suppose they are doing anything illegal, immoral perhaps, but then again immorality has a foot in both the camps of right and wrong. We are allowed to be immoral when it is the name of doing something that we believe is fundamentally right."

Deacon nodded, "I once thought that I had discovered the source of all ethics through one of the characters I created. He would do or say nothing in life that he wouldn't do or say in front of his mother."

"Sounds pretty watertight to me," Sebastian said.

"That's exactly what he thought until he found his mother in bed with his girlfriend, then, he could quite cheerfully have strangled the bitch! Conclusion, ethics has no guidelines or boundaries except those which we set for ourselves. Dubois and Laurent will have their exotic holiday or whatever at my expense and I will have what I want at theirs, it is as simple as that."

Sebastian laughed out loud and said: "I am glad that you are my father, but it took me a long time to realise it."

"And I am grateful to Joey for making me realise that I have a wonderful son."

The two men chinked their glasses and finished off the bottle knowing that tomorrow was going to be an eventful day in the life of a very special young man.

Chapter Forty Nine

The Deacon household was up at the crack of dawn getting ready for Joey's big day at the clinic. Even Tina could sense that there was a tangible air of excitement about the cottage and what was about to take place. Maria fussed around Joey making sure he looked his best for his big day. He looked down at his highly polished shoes as Tina sniffed at them and he smiled at the novelty of seeing her reflection in the gloss. As far as Tina was concerned there was absolutely no question about her not being in on such a momentous occasion in Joey's life. Deacon would have to stop short of taking her right into the clinic but she would travel with them as far as the door where Sebastian would be put on dog-sitting duty.

They piled into the car and soon they were heading off to Angouleme. It was too early in the day for the sleepy town of Petit Saint Jean to be busy and it was just as well because Maria didn't want Dubois or Laurent to share any part of their prospective happiness.

The unlikely group arrived in the city as what looked like a gathering for the start of a carnival was setting up. Joey looked on in sheer amazement as jugglers and stilt-walkers went through their warm-up routines in their brightly coloured costumes and painted faces. Behind the warm-up area in a small square a group of musicians dressed in orange suits struck up a jazz tune reminiscent of the sounds of New Orleans. They played as they weaved in and out of the spectators and the children of the band members handed out oranges. It was obviously some ancient ritual, probably in celebration of a good harvest and it reminded Deacon of the carnivals he used to watch as a child, where the corn dolly, made from the very last ear of corn was paraded through the fields and streets like a sacred effigy; occasions now sadly missing from the town and country social calendars for one reason or another. They would have stayed longer and watched it until its conclusion but for the appointment; reluctantly they left and headed off in the direction of the clinic with the sounds of

265

Dixieland ringing in their ears. If all went well at the clinic then Joey would be able to savour such musical delights at the next carnival he ever stumbled into.

At the clinic Sebastian took over his duties looking after Tina as Joey, Maria and Deacon went to the reception. The receptionist smiled and asked them to take a seat; she told them that Doctor Morand would be with them shortly. Several minutes had elapsed when a pretty young lady in her late twenties appeared in the reception area and asked to see Mr Deacon. He looked at her neat auburn hair which was tied behind in a pony tail and expected her to show them through to the doctor's consultation rooms. He was surprised to learn that she was in fact the consultant. In her office she made sure that Joey was relaxed before she took her time to examine him. Her findings supported Doctor Jones's opinion that Joey had a severe case of Glue ear and he would need a surgical procedure to cure it. Both Deacon and Maria felt the immediate pangs of relief tinged with apprehension; his condition could be fixed, but it would need an operation and no operation is without its risks.

"What are the risks?" Maria asked as Deacon attempted to hide his anxiety by making faces at Joey. Doctor Morand spoke quietly and assuredly: "All operations can go wrong and there are no guarantees of success, but the chances of failure are very remote. Infection is the biggest problem, but, if that does happen it can be cured with antibiotics. The procedure itself is relatively small and Joey would be able to go home the same day. The thing he might find strange after the operation is that he can hear and could easily be startled if he hears loud noises. I know it sounds obvious to mention this but it is something that parents often overlook until the child suddenly screams in fright."

Maria relayed all that the doctor had said to Deacon. "When can she do the operation?" he asked.

The doctor said she could do it on the following day or the earliest after that would be on the following Wednesday. "What day should we go for?" Maria asked.

266

Without hesitation Deacon said it should be done the following day. "I agree," Maria said, "The sooner the better."

"It has nothing to do with time Maria, tomorrow is an even day and next Wednesday is an odd day which would never do!" Maria was about to give her ex boss a piece of her mind when she saw the smile on his face, she had fallen for it hook, line and sinker.

So the time was set for the following day, Joey would be brought in to the clinic in the morning and by the evening he would be taken back to the cottage with his hearing well on the way to being restored. The procedure was explained to Joey and he was happy for the plans to go ahead. All that remained was for them to find a café for Joey to drink a Hot Chocolate because up until the operation it was nil-by-mouth. Maria felt worse about not being able to feed him than she did about him having the operation. He was still desperately thin and like any woman in her situation she couldn't look at him without wanting to sit him down and make sure he cleared his plate.

Sebastian had done a grand job keeping Tina happy with a walk in the nearby garden and he had kept himself happy by spending a pleasant hour watching one sweet scented French beauty pass by after another.

Together they found a café and ordered the hot chocolate; Joey took his time to savour every last drop, not because he would have to fast for the remainder of the day, but because it was the first hot chocolate drink that he could ever remember tasting…and it tasted delicious.

In the car on the way back home Deacon and Maria told Sebastian all that had unfolded in the clinic and how Joey would have the treatment done on the following day.

"We were lucky then to have him in for treatment so soon; it sounds like a fairly straightforward procedure."

"Yes, I was a little taken aback at first by the consultant's youthful looks but she certainly knew what she was talking about. I wonder at what age a person decides to be an ear specialist." Deacon said thoughtfully.

"You will be able to ask her tomorrow," Maria said jokingly.

"I might just do that," Deacon said.

"You were expecting the consultant to be some old crone weren't you?" Maria laughed "And you were surprised for once in your life."

"I must admit I would have struggled to give a consultant character in one of my books such smoldering good looks, unless of course it was set in Miami, so yes, you could say I was surprised."

Maria gave a smile of satisfaction: "I'm really glad to hear that because it means that you and I have found something we can agree on since I arrived in France, I too was expecting a colleague of Doctor Jones to be around the same age as him."

"In a situation like this, you and I are not completely in control of our thoughts, even though we think we are. The stereotypes of consultants that we immediately imagined were embedded onto the human subconscious—sometimes known as the collective consciousness of mankind—by my fellow writers of fiction when man first began to communicate using the written word. Consultants are no different than witches on broomsticks or lions being the kings of the jungle even though they have never lived in jungles." Maria was willing to let the conversation end by not responding, she could sense one of his boring monologues brewing and she would rather tickle Joey. It was left up to Sebastian to take up the conversation which he couldn't resist because he had an ideal opportunity have some fun at his father's expense.

"I agree father, writers are at the root of the way this world conducts itself and they have a lot to answer for."

"How so, if it was not for writers the world would still be trapped in the dark ages and our glorious seats of learning would still be hunting grounds for illiterate kings. The world would be devoid of greater kings like Keats and Wordsworth," Deacon enthused.

"Yes and without the written word the world would be devoid of every conflict this world has seen since man learned to convey messages other than by mouth. People say that politics, religion and world economics are the cause of war. But every single war for the last thousand years has been started by a written declaration and ended with a signed surrender."

Deacon took his eyes off the road for a moment to give Sebastian a sideways glance of manufactured disdain; "I should know better than to argue with a solicitor even if it is my own son, who by the way is clearly pulling my leg."

Sebastian smiled: "I had you going for a minute though didn't I?"

"A truce," Maria announced assertively, "when we get home we are going to plan a party for Joey so I want no talk on subjects that have no conclusion. You would be better employed learning to bake cakes Mr Richard if Joey is going to be around for any length of time. You two can start to fill his head with nonsense when he is eighteen and not a minute before."

"A truce it is then," Deacon said, "But why eighteen before we enlighten him in the ways of the world?"

"Because before that age he will not be able to vote in support of his views no matter what they are and after that age he will be old enough and wise enough to know that he will be far better off keeping his views to himself rather than elect people like Dubois and Laurent into power to manipulate his views to suit their own ends."

Maria was still smarting from her involvement with the two officials so Deacon deduced that a truce most definitely included him not saying another word on the subject. The rest of the journey back to the cottage involved Deacon driving in silence, Sebastian finally having the chance to look at the beautiful French countryside and Joey being tickled mercilessly by a giggling Maria. Tina sat in the footwell at Sebastian's feet and snoozed the whole way home.

Back at the cottage the joint decision was that none of them would eat until Joey's imposed fast was lifted, so the only food on offer was the food that Tina was served. It was almost as though she had included herself in the decision because instead of gulping her food down in seconds as she usually did, she sniffed gingerly at the bowl and turned instead to settle down at her favourite spot over by the foot of the door. Deacon watched as she turned twice before slumping down with her head on her paws. There was no doubt in his mind that Tina knew exactly what was going on and she was aware of the shadow of anxiety over Joey's operation that had descended over the cottage. Deacon knew that the following twenty four hours were going to be the most difficult of his life. Everything that he could do to change Joey's life had been done and everything he could do to make his operation a success had been done. The future now was beyond his control and so beyond his influence; that in turn made it a situation in which he had little faith. He believed that anything that could not be bought or owned was unstable and arbitrary and liable to be either rebellious or uncompromising. *With what can I buy the favour of the Gods?* He scoffed at his thoughts, *how many men through the ages have asked such a question?* All he could do was offer a compromise to his inner self and hope that it was indeed somehow connected to the same collective consciousness of mankind that generated stereotypes. *If the collective consciousness of mankind has a direct route to God, then Joey will be safe because I have never wanted anything so badly, if not, then Laurent and Dubois and a million other men like them will indeed inherit the earth and the sum of my life from this moment on will amount to nothing. Cure his deafness Lord just like you cured the lepers and the blind and I will make sure that he knows it was you. Not only that Lord, I give you my word that Joey and I will build a haven right here for the people who looked after him when he needed help. We will do it despite Dubois and Laurent. After all Lord, where you not the original traveler?*

Chapter Fifty

The morning arrived sooner than Deacon would have liked, he had spent what seemed like the whole night tossing and turning. He was filled with apprehension but he knew that he couldn't show it, he had to act as though Joey's operation was nothing more than a walk in the park. When Sebastian was little he had his fair share of trips and falls and illnesses, several of which needed hospital treatment—like the time he scalded his had in a bowl of soup that he had reached over. But with Joey it seemed so different. Perhaps it was because Deacon had taken on the responsibility for Joey's wellbeing and he wanted everything to go to plan or he would be to blame. It was more likely however that the feeling of apprehension was because poor Joey had not had much of a life up until that point and Deacon didn't want to make a mess of what could be Joey's only chance to turn his life around.

Maria had Joey up and ready bright and early and she took him out into the garden to give Tina a run out before the drive into the city. She took the chance to ask him how he felt about having his operation not expecting to find herself having to contain a tear as he answered in only a way that Joey could. He gave her one of his wonderful glowing smiles and let her know that he was excited at the thought of being *just like everyone else.*

Sebastian was standing at the window watching Maria and Joey in the garden when Deacon came and stood alongside him.

"What are you thinking Son?" Deacon asked.

"I'm thinking how lucky you are to have found him," Sebastian smiled.

"Sebastian, you are likely to have a long and illustrious career in law, but I can promise you this, you will never say a truer thing."

Sebastian motioned with his head towards Joey: "He is deaf and doesn't speak our language, yet he has said more to you in a few short weeks than I have in my whole life, why do you think that is?"

271

"I know exactly why it is Sebastian," Deacon said without hesitation, "it is because I thought in my own tiny world that because I had given you everything I thought you needed that I didn't have to listen to you. With Joey I knew I had to find a way to communicate with him so that I could understand him which made me realise that you had so much of value to say and I missed it. Sometimes speaking the same language is a barrier to communication because it allows us to hear but not to listen."

"Do you know why I became a solicitor?" Sebastian asked.

"No, but I have often wondered, I thought perhaps that your mother was the voice on your shoulder behind that curious decision," Deacon said thoughtfully.

"It was all my own doing and I did it because I once heard you say that you hated solicitors."

"I don't follow," Deacon said in surprise.

"Don't you see that through the eyes of a child having your hatred was better than having no emotion from you at all?"

Deacon gave a heavy sigh: "I think that is why I am so afraid right now. I am afraid that I might be bringing Joey out of a world of innocent silence—a world almost of make believe—and leading him into a world which resonates with greed and gunfire and bigotry and all manner of foul abuse."

Sebastian shook his head, "Father you paint such a gloomy picture of a world that has been extremely good to you; in amongst the greed and gunfire the same world also sings with the gurgling of new born babies and the laughter of lovers on bright summer afternoons. We have to show him how to tune his senses to all that is good in this life. We can't live his life for him, but we can help him to live the life he chooses, rather than have to cope with the life trust upon him like the two of us had to."

"I know now that I made your life so unhappy, I feel ashamed and foolish, even though I brought you up the only way I knew how," Deacon said in a voice charged with emotion that was just above a whisper.

Sebastian turned from the window and looked directly into his father's eyes: "A man should never feel ashamed or foolish about what he doesn't know, only about what he should know and chooses not to learn."

The conversation fell silent; partly because neither father nor son had expected that level of honesty and partly because there was not a lot more to be said.

Maria and Joey returned with Tina and it was soon time to leave. Deacon pulled the car onto the lane outside the cottage and Joey bounded into the back seat hoping to be tickled again no doubt. The sky above was cloudless and bright, if ever there was a fine day for a miracle it was on a day like that.

Just after ten o'clock Joey was ready to be taken through to the operating theatre and Deacon was asked to return in the afternoon. Joey gave Deacon a smile and clasped his hands together to indicate that they were friends, it brought a lump to Deacon's throat and the composure he was determined to keep almost cracked under the strain. Both he and Maria waited until Joey was out of sight before they left the clinic to meet up with Sebastian; he too would be eager for news even though he knew it would be several hours before there would be any real news. They found him strolling in the park and together they spent the time looking round the shops for a suitable gift for Joey to come around from the anesthetic to. After several false starts it was Maria who found the perfect gift...a chromatic harmonica!

"That's brilliant!" Sebastian smiled, "I think it is so fitting that the first musical notes he hears are those that he creates himself."

Deacon had to agree, it was a stroke of genius to choose such a gift, but typically he had to go one better by ordering a piano to be delivered at the weekend. "I knew that beautiful cottage was missing something," he said.

Maria thought it would be wise—bearing in mind the expense—to remind Deacon that none of them could play the piano.

"We can learn!" Deacon said stuffily, "Besides a piano is a wonderful piece of furniture." So a harmonica it was…and a piano!

The hours until the allotted time for checking on Joey dragged on forever, if ever time stood still it was in those final minutes just before they were due back at the clinic. When the clock struck 3pm Deacon led the charge as the entourage galloped up to the reception desk to see if they could collect him. Sebastian of course was left at the entrance with Tina. The receptionist buzzed through to Doctor Morand to let her know of their arrival. Deacon could have kissed her when her give away smile assured him that everything had gone to plan. "Can we see him?" he asked excitedly, "Is he ready to come home?"

Doctor Morand switched easily from smiling woman to serious professional. "The operation was a complete success as far as we can see, it will be several weeks before we know for absolute certain, but there were no complications."

Impatiently Deacon nudged Maria's elbow, "Ask her again if we can take him home, I don't think she understood."

Maria looked at him as a primary teacher might look at a naughty boy. "She understood perfectly well Mr Richard, but as you can see she is trying to explain something so please let me listen."

The doctor continued, "Please remember what I said about sudden noises, you must introduce him gradually to the sounds that are commonplace to you, to him they will sound like thunder. Now, before I take you through he is still very groggy and he hasn't eaten anything yet, so go carefully."

With that she turned and led the way to the recovery room. Deacon dared not have imagined he would see the famous Joey smile, so he was overjoyed when it lit up the room the moment he and Maria entered. The good Doctor Morand was right about Joey being groggy because his tiny legs almost buckled underneath him as Deacon helped him to his feet. When Deacon was sure that Joey could hold his own weight he allowed him hold himself up with the support of one hand on the bed. The doctor had put a kind of protective helmet over Joey's head which covered the dressings on his ears. He had to keep it on at all times for at least one full week when his dressings would be changed. When Joey's dizzy head was clear, the first thing he indicated to Maria was that he wanted to see Tina. Maria let him know that she was outside and looking forward to seeing him again too. Maria was given his painkillers by the doctor and she explained the dosage; all that remained was for Deacon to thank the doctor and of course settle the bill which he did at reception as Joey was led out into the sunshine to greet Tina and Sebastian.

The ride home took longer than usual because Deacon was careful not to jar the wounded hero as the car bounced along the country roads. Maria couldn't wait to get home so that she could eventually get some food into him. The harmonica had been purposefully hidden in the boot of the car and would be presented to Joey in an appropriately fun ceremony immediately after tea.

The day had been stressful for everyone but as the cottage came into view Deacon turned his mind to God and he acknowledged inwardly that the miracle he had asked for had been gratefully received. He had no way of knowing that Sebastian and Maria were doing exactly the same thing.

Chapter Fifty One

With Joey safely asleep with his new harmonica under his pillow and an exhausted Maria in bed in the room next to him listening—even in her sleep as only a woman can—for when her charge may need her help or perhaps just a reassuring cuddle. Deacon and Sebastian sat in the easy chairs downstairs with a nightcap. Although nothing was being said between them the atmosphere around them was lighter than it had ever been, a kind of tranquility almost. Their mutual confessions earlier in the day had been absorbed into their very souls and neither man wanted to speak because to break the spirit of reflection would have ruined the surreal beauty of the moment. Finally Deacon raised his glass and broke the silence: "You know something son, in all my time as a writer I have created many characters and situations but never in my wildest imagination could I have developed a plot like this. What is it all about? Where will it lead?"

"If the situation has you at a loss, then how are the rest of us to fathom it all out? My advice is, try not to analyze everything by looking for little boxes to put things in. If my profession has taught me anything it is that everything in this world is unpredictable in how it will behave or react. Why does an 80 year old man suddenly murder his wife after 60 years of marriage? Common sense surely tells us that if he was going to kill her he would have done it sooner?"

Deacon laughed: "Perhaps the old boy wanted to avoid a long sentence?"

Sebastian nodded: "That is exactly my point, I would have predicted one outcome for a couple who wanted to kill each other and you would have predicted another. Every situation in life, no matter how outwardly similar they appear to be are as different as fingerprints. They all have a different causation and they all have a different ending. So in answer to your questions, what is it all about? It is about you and Joey and of course Tina. And where will it lead? It will lead to its conclusion, just like everything else in this universe."

Deacon sat for a moment deliberating what Sebastian had said. "If ever I need a great philosopher in one of my future novels I will base the character on you."

"Feel free, but make my nose a bit smaller, add a couple of inches to my height and make sure that the leading lady falls madly in love with me," Sebastian smiled.

"That, my son, is why you are a lawyer and I am the novelist." Sebastian slid his empty glass down on the coffee table:

"Goodnight father, I'll see you in the morning."

Deacon had one more nip for the road and turned in for the best night's sleep he had had in a long time.

Even the rising sun appeared to have caught the infectious feeling of optimism surrounding the cottage as it lifted the weight of a beautiful morning into the eastern sky. Maria stepped out into the morning freshness as the rest of the cottage slumbered. The dewfall gave off the most glorious smell as the sun gently roasted it from the grass beneath her bare feet. Had she been told that her former boss would be able to survive one single day without either writing like a demon or pouring over his vast business interests, she would never have believed it. After knowing him for so long she understood that there would never be a distraction strong enough to tear him away. After all, his wife had been missing for two years and he hadn't even noticed. However, strolling through the garden like that it was clearly evident how Deacon could so easily abandoned the habits of a lifetime. The Strawberry Garden was indeed a paradise on earth and its delights could only be fully absorbed with the passing of time. If ever there was a place anywhere with the same magical powers of seduction described in the pages of ancient Greek sagas, it was right there in the middle of the French countryside and it belonged to Richard Deacon.

Her thoughts were suddenly brought back to reality with the appearance of Tina who had come from the direction of the cottage to gingerly sniff Maria's ankles by way of saying, "Hello." Maria dropped to her haunches to return the friendly greeting and scratched Tina's ears. She looked over towards the cottage and saw the tiny frame of Joey standing in the open doorway. "Come on Tina, let's go and see how our brave boy is feeling today."

Maria gathered Joey up in her arms without breaking her stride and she sat him on the kitchen table to administer his morning dose of medication. She asked him how he was and if he was hungry. The smile on his face told her that he was feeling good and his nodding head told her that he was ready for breakfast. Maria knew that Deacon was liable to be a while before he was up and about so she decided to take breakfast with Joey. She sat opposite her patient over breakfast and as she looked at the protective helmet she wondered if the operation had been a success and to what level Joey's hearing might have been restored. It was then that the most amazing thing happened; it was nothing more than a telephone beginning to ring out in the hallway, but to Maria it was like a message from God because Joey turned to the sound having clearly heard it. "You can hear it!" Maria laughed excitedly. Joey smiled and indicated that she should pick it up.

"Oh, how clever you are, of course I should answer it," Maria said still reeling from the wonderful revelation. If she had known who was on the other end of the phone she would have let it ring forever…it was Dubois. Maria could feel the hackles rising as he asked if that was indeed Deacon's number. Despite the fact that Dubois had just interrupted one of the loveliest, most poignant, moments of her life, she remained calm and professional. "Yes it is; what can I do for you?"

"You can tell Mister Deacon that I have some good news for him which I will deliver in-person at 3pm…tell him that I will be alone." With that the phone went dead.

"Hello, hello," Maria shouted not realising at first that Dubois had brusquely put the phone down. When the penny dropped she held the receiver to her mouth and said: "Goodbye then, you ignorant pig of a man."

She went back into the kitchen and almost immediately her feeling of euphoria returned when Joey slowly repeated what he had heard her shout on the phone. "H-e-l-l-o," he said. She stopped in her tracks and laughed out loud, "Why Joey you little genius, hello right back." The sound of her laughter brought Sebastian through from his makeshift bed in the living room to see what all the commotion was about. Joey said it again to show that it wasn't a fluke. The sound of his first spoken words in heaven knows how long made her almost grateful for the interruption of Dubois and his chauvinistic attitude. Sebastian could hardly take it in and he stood shaking his head in a daze. She offered her outstretched hand to Joey, "Come on young sir, let's go and say a big hello to Mr Richard."

Maria's heart was racing as she tapped lightly on Deacon's bedroom door and waited for him to answer. "Is that you Maria?" Deacon's voice sounded from inside. Maria put her finger to her lips to let Joey know that they were about to surprise him. She turned the handle and as the door opened she gently pushed Joey into the room. Deacon sat up in bed and looked at Joey with a half smiling curious expression, he could tell that there was something going on but he had no idea what. Suddenly Joey opened his mouth and said: "Hello,"

Deacon almost fell off the bed as a laughing Maria sprang into his room. "He can hear and he can talk," she laughed, "he heard the phone ringing earlier and he copied me speaking," Maria explained. Deacon was more excited than Maria. "You know what I'm going to say now don't you? 'This calls for a celebration!' The moment that helmet comes off and we have the all-clear from the clinic, we are all off to the theme park that Joey loved so much the first time around."

The three of them sat on the bed for the following twenty minutes exchanging words and sounds, some of which even Deacon had never heard before. It was only when Sebastian appeared in the doorway eating a piece of toast that Maria remembered who was on the telephone earlier. "What did he say?" Deacon asked sensing that it could be important.

"He said he may have some good news and that he will be over at 3pm to deliver it in person," Maria said grudgingly. She didn't want a man like him to take any part in their happiness and here he was inviting himself round as if he owned the place.

Deacon thought for a moment before he spoke: "Excellent!" he smiled, "Right, not a moment to lose." Then flinging the blanket from his legs he was like the Deacon of old, barking out orders as he began dressing. "We have things to do and we have to work fast. Sebastian, you take Maria into the bank at Angouleme, show your identification and collect the equivalent of £40,000 in cash. In the meantime I will call Daniels and tell him to set up the transaction, you won't have any trouble."

"Father, even if you are thinking of giving Dubois and Laurent 20 grand apiece, isn't that taking the 'greasing of the wheels' to excess?"

"Son, in legal matters I would not question your judgement, so in money matters, leave it to the expert." Then turning to Maria he said: "I know you don't approve my dear but after the enormous progress we have seen here these past few days I would be a fool to jeopardize any part of my plans by haggling over loose change."

"This is hardly loose change," Maria said, before she quickly conceded, "But in the light of what it could buy, I suppose it is relatively small."

Deacon was happy with her response, "I want you to trust me like you have never done before and if you do that you will see that everything always turns out in my favour."

"I do trust you," Maria said, "I just don't want to let Joey down."

"That's the ticket, now off you go and don't spare the horses," Deacon smiled, "Joey and I will take Tina for a walk by the river and see if we can't locate a nice spot for a picnic this evening when Dubois has been and gone."

Sebastian and Maria headed off to the city as Deacon called Daniels to make certain the money would be waiting for them when they arrived. Daniels was well used to Deacon's unorthodox business dealings so he did as he was told without question and within minutes the international business was done.

Chapter Fifty Two

Maria hadn't really given the task in hand much thought; despite the amount of money in question she treated it as just another errand for Deacon. Sebastian however, was not used to such things and he had let his imagination run away with him on the drive to the city. He imagined being greeted at the door of the bank by a smiling bank manager before being cringingly ushered through to a private room where they would be shown the money being counted and packed into a suitable case. Then it would be handed to a burly security guard who would walk with them to their vehicle. In the event his imagination was far more fertile and exciting than reality. At the bank Maria spoke to a young woman at the reception desk. She in turn used an intercom and out from a door off the main hall of the bank walked a middle aged man carrying a briefcase; he simply handed the case to Sebastian and bade them both a good day. *Surely there should be some kind of security check, some kind of verification of identity and so forth?* Sebastian thought. What he didn't realise was that Daniels—via Deacon—had given exact details of how the money should be handed over and they were carried out to the letter. Sebastian looked at Maria, "What now?" he asked.

"Back to the car and back to the cottage…unless of course you want to stop off somewhere and pick up something glitzy with all this cash. It would make me feel so much better than handing it tamely over to those two creeps," she said in a grudging tone.

"That would make us thieves just like them," Sebastian said dryly.

Maria playfully made an idiotic looking face at him, "That is exactly my point, the only difference being that they get away with it and we never would; it just makes me sick to think how they use their positions to feather their own nests with complete immunity."

The rest of the walk back to the car was covered in silence, Sebastian though it would be best to let the matter drop rather

281

than to stoke the embers of a potentially lethal fire and ignite the wrath of an angry young woman.

At the car Sebastian sat in the driver's seat and dropped the briefcase into Maria's lap. The drive home started in the same stony silence as the walk had ended but Sebastian sensed that Maria had more to say on the subject. He waited just long enough to let her know that he was not going to begin any further conversation... so Maria took the initiative.

"I wonder at what point men like those two become corrupt?" she said thoughtfully.

"The minute they take their first kickback," Sebastian answered without hesitation.

Maria tsked, "Sometimes Sebastian you can be just as infuriating as your father, so clinical and one dimensional."

"I am being neither clinical nor cynical, nor am I being one dimensional, I was speaking from a legal perspective. It is not a crime to contemplate stealing something, it is only a crime if you actually steal it," Sebastian said defending his initial response.

Maria tapped on the briefcase as if to emphasize her points as she spoke: "What I meant was, surely as a young man Dubois joined the police force for all the right reasons, such as wanting to uphold the law and protect the innocent, that sort of thing. Laurent too must have set off in his local political career as someone who thought he could make a real difference to his town. So at what point did they depart from those honorable ethics and become dishonest? Does it happen overnight? Is it a conscious decision to suddenly sell off their beliefs and moral values to the highest bidder?"

Sebastian thought about his answer for a moment, he was deliberately running it through his mind so as not to sound too 'clinical'. "Howard Hughes—one of the world's first billionaires— is reputed to have said something like, 'Every man has a price, it is just that some men's price is higher than others.' From what I have seen of the world so far, I think he made an excellent observation."

"Is that supposed to make me feel better about Dubois and Laurent?" Maria asked.

"That's not fair," Sebastian protested, "Now who is being one dimensional? You asked me a question and I gave you a valid answer. The point at which an honest man becomes dishonest varies in relation to how much it takes to buy him; and cold as that may sound it applies to all of us."

Maria suddenly changed the direction of the conversation by saying: "Can I come and watch you the next time you are defending a criminal?"

Sebastian laughed, "I don't defend criminals Maria; I represent clients...that is *if* I believe they are innocent. But in answer to your question, yes you will be my most welcome guest. I didn't realise you were that interested in law."

Maria gave a cheeky smile, "Who said I was interested in law?"

By then the cottage was just minutes away and the conversation was at an end. They entered the courtyard to see Deacon and Joey in the middle of the garden taking turns at looking at the surrounding wildlife through a pair of binoculars. Maria called and waved at them and the birdwatchers waved back. Sebastian dropped the briefcase onto the garden table as he passed and he went through to the kitchen to pour himself a cold drink. Deacon and Joey walked over to greet Maria following the yapping Tina. "Did you have any trouble?" Deacon called when he judged he was within earshot.

"No, the chap at the bank just handed it over and we came straight back," Maria shrugged, "What have you two been up to whilst we have been away?" she added.

"Joey and I have been working on a surprise for you," Deacon smiled. Maria looked at the binoculars dwarfing Joey's hands and wondered what they and a surprise for her might remotely have in common.

"And what if I don't like surprises?" Maria teased, aiming her response at the smiling Joey.

"You will," Deacon said slowly and deliberately as Joey copied the pronunciation.

"Y-o-u w-e-el," he said.

Sebastian appeared at the kitchen door with a jug of orange juice and four glasses. Deacon looked at his watch and it was 2.30pm, Dubois was due at 3pm and Deacon still had to separate the cash into two equal amounts. He looked at Maria:

"Will you be alright to handle this meeting?" he asked.

"I will be the epitome of sweetness and light," she said, "Though I would rather scratch his eyes out."

"Either way, your input will be as invaluable as ever," Deacon replied choosing deliberately to take the last part of her answer with a pinch of salt.

Joey drank his orange juice and wiped his mouth with the back of his hand before he slid from his chair and disappeared into the rear garden with Tina. "That's just as well," Sebastian said, "The business about to take place here is really no place for a boy."

Deacon separated the banknotes as Maria went inside to change and freshen up. She was back outside when she heard Dubois's car pulling up outside in the lane and she went to take her seat. "Don't sit there," Deacon said, "That chair is for Dubois."

"What's the difference where he sits, the outcome will be the same?" Maria said.

"It would just be better for me if he sat in that chair," Deacon said.

Dubois strode through the door at exactly 3pm and Deacon took the unusual step of rising to his feet to offer him a place at the table. Dubois noticed the change in Deacon immediately and sensed that the meeting would be far more affable than the last one; especially in the light of what he was about to reveal about Joey's past life and the fact that on the table there was an exceptionally large bundle of banknotes. Dubois looked at the banknotes as he sat down opposite the smiling

Deacon. Maria placed herself where she would be best suited to interpret.

"How is the boy?" Dubois asked as he looked around the area. Like most experienced policemen he asked questions with one eye already looking for the answers.

"He is round and about somewhere," Deacon said with a sweep of his hand, "He had an operation for his deafness the other day which was good news, speaking of which I believe you have some further good news for us," Deacon added. Dubois looked at the bundle of notes already burning a hole in his pockets and he shifted uneasily in his seat.

"I would rather do our business elsewhere," he said with a nervous cough.

"Have you anywhere else in mind?" Deacon asked.

Dubois looked around the immediate area and said: "This property has a patio on the other side hasn't it? Let's do our business there." Deacon could see that Dubois was ill at ease so he gathered up the banknotes and led the way through the cottage to the patio at the rear. "Would you like me to sit in with you father?" Sebastian asked. Deacon shook his head: "This won't take long I am sure."

The three of them settled into the chairs around the table on the rear patio. "So," Deacon said, "tell me the good news."

Dubois sat back, visibly more comfortable in his new chair; he was clearly more relaxed than he had been at the front of the cottage, the rear being for more secluded. "I circulated details of Joey's sudden appearance in the area along with a rough estimate of the probable date to other police divisions within a 50 kilometre radius; I also mentioned the possible car crash. I asked if anyone could throw any light on how a young boy might suddenly appear out of nowhere. It was not long before I heard back from a colleague who tells me that about that time he was called to a car accident involving two old people—a man and wife I believe—in which their car left the road and slid into the river about 30 kilometres north of here. They were both killed, the man died at the scene and the woman died later in hospital without regaining

285

consciousness. They were from the Seville region of Spain." Dubois paused dramatically as if to build up the tension now that he had his audience intrigued. Perhaps he was amazed at the size of the bundle of notes in front of him and decided that he had better pad out his story to earn the full amount. Either way he got no response from Deacon whose expression and posture remained the same, giving nothing away. Dubois continued: "There was no one else at the scene and it was presumed that they were on a touring holiday. It was only after finding a young boy's clothing in their luggage that my colleague decided to take a closer look. An investigation began and it was discovered that they were in France to collect their grandson. Their daughter came to France a few years earlier to work as an au pair in Paris. She fell pregnant by an unknown man and brought the boy up alone. Her parents disowned her because of the disgrace it would have brought on the family who lived in a very small community. She was told never to return to her home in Spain. Two years ago she developed a particularly aggressive form of cancer. When it became apparent that she was going to die she pleaded with her parents to look after her son and they drove up from Spain to collect him. By the time all this became clear to the police a full week had elapsed since the accident so the young boy was presumed to have been drowned and his body washed away without trace. My colleague had the presence of mind to collect DNA from the couple just in case. So it can be proven one way or the other if this little boy is one and the same." Deacon asked if the old couple had any other relatives. Dubois sat back with a smug expression on his face, "I am ahead of you here; I contacted my counterpart in the old couple's village only two days ago and found that they have no other family."

Maria looked at Deacon, "So that means that apart from us, Joey is alone in the world."

"It certainly sounds like it," Deacon said thoughtfully.

Dubois leaned over and patted Maria's hand as he said: "This unique situation would make it relatively easy for a man like

Mister Deacon to arrange for custody of the boy, a kind of 'finders-keepers'," he grinned.

The touch of his hand against hers made Maria want to dash from the table to scrub the back of her hand. *Oh, my; I am turning into the old Mister Richard! This is exactly what he would have done a few months ago,* she thought.

Deacon saw the pained expression on her face but he could never have imagined what was going through her mind. "Are you alright Maria?" he asked.

Maria relayed what Dubois had said to Deacon and he immediately understood why she suddenly looked nauseous. "I am not expecting things to be easy, especially where the welfare of a child is concerned. I expect the authorities to scrutinize every aspect of the elements that have a bearing not only on his present situation but also for his future. I am willing to do whatever it takes to secure what is best for him and that includes applying for custody; time is not really an issue," Deacon said.

Dubois tilted his head to one side and taking a handkerchief from his pocket he mopped his brow. "All you have to do is look at the situation to see it would be difficult to place him under anyone's jurisdiction. He is a French boy granted, but with Spanish family who are no longer alive. He has lived all his life in France, he has no extended family and our orphanages are already overflowing, so who wants another headache in the system?"

Deacon nodded, "Put like that I suppose it would seen fairly straightforward seeing as he is in my custody already and he doesn't really belong anywhere else. Nevertheless, I will go through the proper channels to make sure that everything is above board and deemed by the courts to be what is right by everyone."

"Then in that case I have nothing else to add, all that remains is that we conclude our business and I will be on my way," Dubois said.

Deacon pushed the bundle of notes towards Dubois. Dubois put his hand into his inside pocket and produced an envelope. "This is the invoice for the cost of my official enquiries,

I have been asked by Moreau to deliver it personally because they are substantial."

"It will be settled before the day is out," Deacon said casually.

Dubois then pushed his chair away from the table and told Maria to let Deacon know that he wanted to be alone. Dubois was nobody's fool; he wanted no witnesses to him taking the money. Deacon couldn't care less because he had all that he wanted and it was worth every penny. He and Maria moved from the table and went into the cottage. Dubois waited until they were well away from the table before he leaned across and scooped up the money tucking it deep into his tunic. Rather than go through the house he made his way round the cottage and let himself out of the front gate. He fired up the noisy engine and within a matter of moments he was out of sight.

"I take it that this is mission accomplished?" Sebastian said.

"Let's just say the first part is concluded," Deacon smiled.

"Where is Joey?" Maria asked.

"He will turn up in a few minutes, no doubt," Deacon said calmly, "I have every faith him."

Sure enough, two minutes after the departure of Dubois, Joey turned up with a smile and a yapping Tina. His step was accompanied by the sound of Joey playing his harmonica which was rapidly becoming his constant companion. "Have you been teaching him how to play that harmonica?" Deacon asked Maria.

"Don't look at me; I thought you had introduced him to your Mozart collection."

"He sounds awfully tuneful," Deacon said as he looked at Joey and gave him the thumbs up. Joey returned the gesture and took hold of Sebastian's hand pulling him towards the door; besides a thirst for music he was rapidly developing a passion for sport and he clearly had his sights set on another game of cricket. Sebastian was only too eager to take up the challenge.

Chapter Fifty Three

Deacon had a strong suspicion that Dubois would have reported his findings to Laurent before he had delivered them to him. Therefore he knew that it would just be a matter of time before Laurent showed up. He would not want to miss out on the offer of so much money being pumped into the community by Deacon adopting Joey and deciding that he no longer needed any civic input. His suspicions were proved right when the phone rang just as the Deacon household was sitting down to their evening meal. Maria took the call which was from Laurent's secretary. Maria put her hand over the receiver as she asked Deacon if Laurent could call over to see him tomorrow, she added that it was urgent. Deacon asked Maria to tell him to pop over at 11 o'clock. "No surprises as to what he wants," Sebastian said.

"No, he wants to tell me that the council have agreed to accept my offer of support for the community," Deacon said assuredly.

With equal assuredness Maria added: "And to collect his little bonus."

Deacon brushed aside the business of Laurent by saying: "Let's not dwell on such mundane matters, today has been a mixture of joy and happiness for Joey and together we have to move forward very carefully. We may have found Joey's real identity, but we have also learned that his mother and grandparents have all died so tragically."

Sebastian put his hand on Joey's back as he said: "I think we should take professional advice on how to break the news to him, he is still weak from his time foraging alone in the woods and he is still sore from his operation. I think we need to takes things very slowly."

"You are quite right Sebastian, we will say nothing for the time being; getting him back to full physical health has got to be our main priority. I will conclude my business with Laurent tomorrow. Sebastian, you start putting the legal wheels in motion for securing custody of Joey, do whatever needs to be done and employ only the services of the very best; I don't want a long drawn out affair. Maria, will you resume your employment with me and look after the pair of us from now on?"

Maria's reply was instant, "Do you really need to ask?" she smiled.

"That's settled then," Deacon beamed, "I can sleep easy in my bed tonight."

Early on the following morning Deacon, Sebastian and Joey took Tina for a walk on the banks of the river. Deacon showed Sebastian where Joey had taught him how to catch a fish without a fishing rod. "I fancy doing a spot of fishing," Sebastian said, "Why don't we pop into town and buy some tackle?"

"That's an excellent idea, Maria is going into town before Laurent arrives to pick up some groceries, why don't you pop along with her and buy a couple of rods," Deacon said, "I think I would like to do a spot of fishing too, we could have a competition. Joey has taught me how to catch fish without a rod, so it seems only fair that I return the compliment"

Back at the cottage Maria and Sebastian headed off to town; there would be plenty of time to get there and back before Laurent arrived. Whilst they were gone, Deacon and Joey went to the cave to select a good bottle of wine that Laurent would no doubt be sniffing after. Deacon took the opportunity to give Joey his first lesson in identifying a fine wine.

It wasn't long before Maria and Sebastian returned from the town. Deacon and Joey were already waiting at the gate to help carry the shopping. Deacon was surprised to see that his car was immediately followed by another. As the cars drew closer he could see that Laurent was the driver of the second car. Joey could see it too and instinctively he took off with Tina to the relative sanctuary of the stable. Deacon held the gate open for Maria to drive in as Laurent parked on the grass verge opposite the cottage. Deacon looked at his watch as Laurent emerged from his car and saw that it was just after ten. Maria joined Deacon at the gate as a flustered looking Laurent made his way across the lane. "I am sorry to be so early for our meeting but my secretary tells me that she has double booked an appointment so I am trying to juggle everything," he said as he held out his hand to Deacon. Deacon knew that he was talking nonsense but he wasn't bothered by it. *Impatience is a subsidiary of greed and that is why you are here so early.*

Deacon led the way to the table in the front garden and offered Laurent a seat. Then, turning to Sebastian he asked if he would bring out the bottle of wine he had selected earlier and the bundle of notes. Laurent feasted his eyes first on the bundle of notes then on the bottle of wine. "I hope it is not too early for such a fine vintage?" Deacon smiled.

Laurent licked his lips: "It is a little early, but one would be committing sacrilege not to take at least one small glass, after all it has waited half a century to breathe again."

Sebastian poured as the two men raised their glasses: "To the future of Petit Saint Jean…a town that is about to change forever," Deacon said.

"To my future town and to your future family," Laurent added.

"Do I take it that the town meeting went as we anticipated?" Deacon asked.

"I had to use every once of my persuasive talents to convince some of my colleagues to accept your very generous offer," he said, adding, "A man like you is worth exhausting oneself for," just for good measure.

"I can't thank you enough for your using your influence so wisely," Deacon said as he tapped the bundle of notes on the table, "This is your reward and you can rest assured that this will not be the last time that I make full use of your services."

Growing in confidence—and greed—Laurent smiled, "In that case, besides my little reward I will take another bottle of this fine vintage for my darling wife, who after all is the instigator of all this good fortune that is about to descend on our town."

"Be my guest," Deacon said turning to Sebastian and asking him to furnish Laurent with a bottle for his wife.

"I shall instruct my secretary tomorrow to engage the contractors that I have selected to carry out the work on the Town Hall and at the church," Laurent said as he waited for Sebastian to return. Maria clenched her fists under the table thinking: *No doubt you will have another fat pay day coming from the contractor as part of your selection process.*

Laurent took the bottle from Sebastian as he filled his pockets with the banknotes. He was not as particular who saw him doing it as Dubois had been. Deacon walked him to the gate and watched as he drove away. *Enjoy that bottle Laurent because it will be the last of my wine to cross your lips.* He turned from the gate and looked at Maria; her face was a picture of disgust. "I know Maria…please don't say anything to make me feel worse than I do for having to put you through this ordeal. Hopefully the next time I ask you to do this, it will be for more agreeable business."

"I hope there doesn't have to be a next time," she said as she cleared away the empty glasses, "Nothing about those two could ever be agreeable." The sudden appearance of Joey and Tina from the stables lightened the atmosphere and put an end to the conversation. Deacon welcomed the timely dispersion of any awkwardness. He smiled at Joey and made a sign as though he was casting out a fishing line as he slowly said: 'Fishing'. Joey repeated the gesture and the word as he ducked happily into the cottage to pick up the fishing tackle. An afternoon by the river for everyone was the perfect antidote for the unsavoury dealings of the past two days.

Chapter Fifty Four

Sebastian had wasted no time at all in setting to work clearing the way for his father to formally adopt Joey, it would be a long legal process and would involve the input of many services and child welfare agencies, but without any formal objections it would not be too difficult. Deacon could employ a whole bank of acceptable surrogate mothers if needs be to make up for the fact that he was divorced, but in modern times a stable home is more important than a marriage license and no one could argue that Deacon could not provide a very stable home.

Sebastian awoke the following morning to the sound of his mobile phone ringing; it was a partner in the law firm in England he had employed to do the initial groundwork for the adoption proceedings to begin. The partner was calling to report that the process had been started and the French authorities had been contacted. Sebastian shared the good news with his father over breakfast. The news made it the best possible start to a day which Deacon had planned to unveil some potentially good news of his own.

"Maria, I would like you to contact the offices of Dubois and Laurent to invite them over this evening," Deacon suddenly announced, "And before you say anything or throw up all over the kitchen it is part of the surprise that Joey and I have been working on for you," he added.

"I think I would rather be scalded with molten lead than have anything to do with those two. In fact, if I never saw either of them again it would be too soon," she said.

"You don't really have to be here when they arrive, I suppose we could get by on Dubois's limited grasp of the English language, but it would be infinitely better if you were here and it would be of enormous help to Joey," Deacon said in a pleading voice.

"Tell me what it is about and I might consider it," Maria said.

"But that would ruin our little surprise completely. I will tell you what I will do though; I will make you a promise that if you are not absolutely thrilled with your surprise then I will give you anything your heart desires."

"Don't you dare include me on your list of things that can be bought; despite what Sebastian says about some billionaire I have never even heard of; I am not like every man, I do not have a price!" Maria snapped back at him.

Deacon put his hands up indicating that he realised he had overstepped the mark. "I am sorry my dear, I wasn't thinking, my eagerness to make you happy momentarily clouded my judgement."

Maria knew that she had overreacted and that Deacon's reasons for saying what he did were well meant, "I am sorry too," she said, "I am venting my anger at you rather than at the people who deserve it. Of course I will call them and I will interpret for you…but I warn you, it had better be good!"

Deacon turned to Sebastian, "You see now why Maria's services are priceless."

"I wish I knew what you are up to?" Sebastian said thoughtfully, "I used to think that the courtroom was the height of real life drama, but ten minutes living with you makes life in the courtroom seem rather tedious."

"You will see what I am up to soon enough. Now, after Maria has made arrangements for our guests to come over this evening, I vote we load up the car and hit the seaside. Can I have a seconder?"

"Now that sounds like a plan," Maria smiled, "You can buy me an ice-cream and I will forgive you."

After breakfast they would load up the car ready to head off to the coast; a day at the seaside is always the best remedy to relieve family tensions.

Chapter Fifty Five

As Deacon and the boys began loading the car with various sporting equipment for playing on the beach, Maria prepared to call the offices of Laurent and Dubois. She stopped Deacon as he walked through the garden with a frisbee and a set of wickets underneath his arm.

"What reason shall I give for the invitation?" she asked.

"Tell them that I have plans for more building work which will greatly benefit the community. Tell them that I would like to discuss it with them over a glass of wine. With the scent of more money in the air it should bring them scurrying out like rats running from the whiff of a polecat."

"And what time shall we say?"

"We must do this in a civilized manner, so tell them seven thirty for eight," Deacon said.

Sebastian knew that his father was up to something but he knew better than to ask; besides he was enjoying the intrigue.

With the car loaded up they headed west and within an hour they would be at the seaside. Tina was the first onto the beach quickly followed by an awestruck Joey, he had never seen so many people in one place and the colours all around him took his breath away. He ran towards the sea as Tina rolled in the sand discovering its feel for the very first time. Every now and then Joey stopped to push his feet into the sand and look back at his footprints. Soon Maria, Sebastian and Deacon joined him at the waters edge. Deacon rolled up his trouser legs to just below the knee and introduced Joey to that wonderful British institution known as paddling.

At lunch time they walked up the beach to a terrace café to sample the local seafood which was of course followed by Maria's choice of ice-cream. The food seemed to compliment the beauty of the day so well, mussels in a white wine sauce and French fries with a basket of bread piled so high that Joey could barely see over it. Deacon deviated from his usual tipple to join Sebastian and Maria in a bottle of ice-cold beer, he even drank it straight from the bottle—a thing he would never have done a few months earlier even with a gun to his head.

The afternoon was spent back on the beach with games of cricket and volleyball. Maria and Joey teamed up to easily beat the father and son combination, they were no match for Maria's athleticism and Joey's blinding speed around the court which was drawn in the sand. As with every trip to the seaside the time to head home arrived all too soon but the fun didn't stop there. The ride back to the cottage was accompanied by one song after another with Maria teaching Joey the words to several traditional French folk songs.

Back at the cottage Deacon asked Maria to prepare the living room for the *dishonourable guests* as she had taken to calling them. She was surprised at his request because the daylight didn't even begin to fade until after 10pm. Nevertheless, she knew better than to question him, he obviously had his reasons. Maria was surprised further still when Deacon asked that Joey should be allowed to sit in on the meeting, which meant that after his bath he was to put on clean clothes rather than his pyjamas. By 7.15 pm the room was prepared with seats for everyone. "Shall I bring some extra wine from the cave?" Maria asked. It was to be an evening full of surprises as Deacon calmly answered: "Our guests will not be in the mood for wine and pleasantries Maria, not tonight and not for many nights to come." Just as she was about to ask what he meant she heard the sound of a car pulling up in the lane outside. Joey, Sebastian and Maria remained seated in the living room as Deacon went out into the garden to see his guests through into the living room.

On seeing Maria, Laurent took up the most comical supercilious pose and said: "So my secretary tells me that you have plans for further building developments in our town. If that is the case then I might as well tell you now that there will be no new buildings at all. As Mayor I have inherited the ancient title of town guardian which includes a responsibility to preserve the pristine medieval architecture of my beloved Petit Saint Jean. I would oppose your plans vehemently with every fibre of my being. "

In other words you will need far more than 20 grand this time.
Maria thought.

Sebastian looked at his father thinking that for the first time in his life he had seen him firmly put in his place and left speechless. However, he had no idea of the astonishing events that were about to unfold. "Thank you for that," Deacon began calmly: "Now if you would be so kind as to take a seat, I will explain exactly what you are going to do. I have no plans at all to build anything; the plans will be entirely yours. You are going to submit plans to the town council for the building of a permanent campsite for travelling families. It will be complete with a school, a store, a shower block, a laundry and a workshop where they can make any necessary repairs to either their caravans or their towing vehicles and what is more, you are going to fund it from your own pockets."

Sebastian couldn't believe his ears and Maria was having equal difficulty taking in exactly what she was interpreting. They thought Deacon had finally gone completely mad. Laurent looked at Dubois for his reaction and saw that the initial look of stunned confusion on his face was beginning to crack into a knowing grin."

"I thought for one horrible moment that you were serious," Dubois laughed, "You certainly know how to keep a poker face, you really had me going."

The expression on Deacon's face remained expressionless as he said: "I have never been more serious in my life."

Laurent added his scathing reply to Deacon's opening statement, "I think you have spent a little too much time in the sun, it has turned your brains to mush. We are in the business of ridding our town of undesirables not attracting them from every corner of Europe. You are crazy if you think I would put one cent of my money into such a ridiculous scheme. I can't believe you could invite me into your home and insult my intelligence in this way."

"Is that your final word on the matter?" Deacon asked.

"It most certainly is!" Laurent sniffed in disgust.

"And you Dubois?"

"This is one occasion where your money is worthless," Dubois said dramatically, "I hate the vermin gypsies with a passion."

Deacon nodded to Joey who had observed the conversation from his position by the television. Joey turned on the television and all eyes turned to watch it as the screen burst into life. "If that is your final word then all that remains gentlemen is for you to watch this short film and say goodbye to your positions of privilege and trust. I believe you may even be spending some time behind bars. Laurent and Dubois looked on in horror as unmistakable footage of Dubois stuffing banknotes into his tunic and Laurent filling his pockets appeared on the screen in stunning clarity. Maria could hardly control her delight as Laurent stammered, "What is this?"

"What does it look like?" Deacon smiled, "Now where were we? Ah yes, you were about to tell me of your plans to build a campsite for the many travelers that pass this way, were you not?"

"This is a sick joke!" Dubois shouted, "You wouldn't be stupid enough to blackmail us with this film."

"Blackmail is a very strong word; I would never dream of doing such a thing. You both abused your positions of standing and influence in your community to take advantage of my generosity and of this young man's unfortunate situation. You helped us only to line your own pockets and the whole unsavoury business was innocently captured on film by Joey whilst he was out playing with my son's video recorder." Laurent and Dubois turned to Joey only to see his face break into that wonderful smile.

"You put him up to it!" Dubois stormed.

"I merely showed him how to use a video recorder, the idea was entirely his," Deacon smiled, "And I would ask you to keep your voice down, Joey has had a delicate operation and your shouting is liable to cause him some aural discomfort." *Though not as much aural discomfort as Laurent's wife will cause him when he tells her of his building plans,* he thought.

298

"He's bluffing," Laurent whispered to Dubois, "He's bluffing about the whole thing just to amuse himself at our expense. Who would take any notice of such a film anyway? Today's modern film technology can create any illusion at all."

"He is right; you have nothing on us that can do us any harm," Dubois said.

"Just as you were ahead of me in your office, I am ahead of you here. I have had the film verified as genuine and unedited and in precisely five minutes my telephone will ring. One of my senior financial representatives is at this moment hosting a dinner party in London and his guest list includes several prominent members of our respective governments. The dinner party is the conclusion of two days of successful investment talks which in short, will see several of my companies providing a welcome boost to the French economy. When the phone rings you Laurent will recognise the voice of one of your senior ministers. He has already been briefed of your intentions. He will invite you to his office in Paris to discuss your revolutionary plans to ease the suffering of travelers in your area. If you turn down his invitation he will be watching a copy of the film within five minutes and your careers will crumble into dust before another day breaks. However, If you accept his invitation you will be able to maintain your illusion of honesty and integrity and who knows, your generosity in conceiving and building such a noble concept may—in time— elevate you to saintly reverence. Saint Laurent of Petit Saint Jean, has a nice ring to it, don't you think?"

At that moment the telephone rang and a deathly silence fell on the gathering. Laurent looked at it like a condemned man might look into the dispassionate eyes of his executioner. Maria lifted the receiver, "Hello," she said cheerfully. The voice on the other end could be heard by everyone as Maria calmly held it out to Laurent, "It is for you," she smiled. Laurent's hand trembled as he took it from her.

"Is that you Laurent?" the voice asked in his native French.

"Yes Minister this is Laurent at your service,"

"I have heard about your revolutionary ideas to help bring stability and a sense of belonging to the traveling sub-culture that is increasing in our country with the diminishing demarcation of our international communities. Bring your plans to my office next week so that I can give the prototype my personal seal of approval. Where better than to build and monitor such a ground-breaking scheme than right in the heart of Europe and right in the heart of France, I must congratulate you on your genius and of course your bravery. Many will be opposed to your plans but with my approval you will have all the weight you need to carry it off. My personal secretary tells me that the Chief of Police is right behind you in this, I believe he is there with you?"

"Yes, Dubois is here with me as we speak," Laurent said in a voice of utter despondency.

"Put him on then, there's a good fellow, I would like to invite him along too," the Minister said.

Laurent held out the receiver, "He wants to talk to you Dubois."

Dubois stood comically to attention as he began to speak. "Hello Minister, this is the Chief of Police at your service."

"I have had word from Richard's financial team that you are a personal friend of his. I hope you are looking after him for us. I must say as I said to Laurent, it is a generous act of philanthropy and remarkable courage, the eyes of Europe will be upon you. I don't have to remind you that I don't often lend my personal support to potentially controversial schemes such as this, but the displacement of people right across Europe needs to be addressed and holding pens at our ports are not the answer. They must be offered shelter and sanitation as is the basic human right of every European citizen. If you fail in this then it reflects back onto me, as of course will its success."

"Thank you Minister, I will not let you down," Dubois said in a dutiful tone.

"I believe Richard is there with you also, Dubois," the minister said.

"Yes Minister, shall I put him on?" Dubois asked.

"No, Richard and I will speak at the end of next month when I come to open the newly refurbished town hall in Petit Saint Jean. I have to dash now, so until next week when we meet in my office to unveil your plans, au revoir."

The line fell silent and Dubois slowly replaced the receiver. Then turning to Laurent he said: "It looks like we have some plans to prepare; I think we had better leave."

"Keep me up-dated; now that your plans have ministerial backing I would hate to lose momentum, I want the building work completed before winter sets in."

Dubois and Laurent left the cottage in silence having been thoroughly routed. They were crushed with their nerves torn to shreds. Deacon turned to Maria and said: "How did you like your surprise? Was it worth waiting for?"

"I didn't like it...I loved it! How on earth did you two do it?"

"When you and Sebastian went to the bank and then again when you went to town. Joey picked up the camera technique like a natural, he even worked out the best angles to shoot from for maximum effect," Deacon said like a proud father.

"But how did you know that Dubois would want to go round the back of the cottage?" Sebastian asked.

"Joey kept his eye on proceedings using the binoculars you caught us messing with, I thought it would give the game away but you never guessed that we were up to something," Deacon said.

"What about all this with ministers and governments being involved, where did all that come from?" Maria asked, "It was like being inside one of your novels looking back out at the reader and watching as their face contorts with every twist in the plot."

"Maria, it is no big thing, my advisers deal with ministers on an almost daily basis, they know that anything I am involved with is worth putting their name to; association with success is just another name for politics."

"I feel rather foolish now for thinking that you had let them get away with treating Joey's rescuers so badly and giving them all that money," Maria said.

Deacon smiled knowingly, "The first rule of business that my dear father ever taught me was not to let the right hand know what the left hand is doing. I had to make you think they were getting away with it in order to be certain that they thought it too. They fell for the oldest sucker punch in the book."

"What might that be?" Sebastian asked curiously.

"To beat an opponent who is used to success you have to make the cheese look bigger than the trap because it makes the prospect of getting caught look less likely and the prize worth taking extra risks for. It is of course just an illusion but it works every time. Napoleon Bonaparte is reputed to have said something like: 'Men will die for riches, but they will die more readily for ribbons.' Thus he made the prospect of a medal worth taking extra risks for. Men like Dubois and Laurent like money and power, but what they prize more is respect and standing in the community; once that was put in jeopardy the roaring lions became whimpering pups. They will build the campsite and it will be a shining beacon to the rest of Europe. They will have their photographs taken proudly; posing with other guests of honour on the day it is opened and no one will know that it was all instigated by one little gypsy boy and the greed and cruelty of two pillars of society…that is of course unless someone writes a book about it," Deacon smiled.

Chapter Fifty Six

The plans were taken to Paris by Dubois and Laurent and before winter a campsite was built complete with a school, a store, a shower block, a laundry and a workshop. There were also one or two notable additions, there was a sports hall, a cinema and a library; these were insisted on by the minister in Paris, according to him sport and culture are a birthright not a luxury and should be made available to everyone dwelling within the borders of France.

Dubois and Laurent not only put the money Deacon gave them into the project, they also matched the amount with their own money. The civic photographs that Deacon had predicted were taken on a day of pomp and ceremony with the proud Mayor and Chief of Police posing in their regimental finery alongside the cream of society. They had indeed struggled to bring the townsfolk of Petit Saint Jean round to warm to their plans and it was reported that Mrs Laurent's screams of despair and desolation could be heard all the way to Angouleme. They had used the argument to win over the people that the eyes of Europe would be upon them and after the town won its place in history the tourists would flock there in droves. The town's Chamber of Commerce realised these favourable financial implications and it was their collective vote that clinched it to give a relieved Laurent and Dubois the go ahead.

The eyes of Europe did indeed look on and they witnessed a great act of philanthropy unfolding; what they didn't see of course was the sword of Damocles hanging precariously over Dubois and Laurent that had been so cunningly set up by Deacon and Joey; the greedy pair had no choice but to make the campsite a haven for weary travelers.

Sebastian and his legal teams on both sides of the channel had no opposition in securing adoption papers for Joey, and from that point on when he was officially adopted he was known as Master Joseph Deacon.

When the time was right he was told what was known of the fate of his mother and his grand parents. He was sad of course but he had no reason to grieve for a family he never really knew.

His operation was a complete success and his hearing was fully restored. With the constant help and encouragement of Maria, he soon became fluent in Spanish, French and of course English. From his early days as a harmonica player he developed into an accomplished pianist. Deacon took an active interest in every aspect of Joey's schooling and his up-bringing. In short, he learned the art of fatherhood from the mistakes he had made with Sebastian.

Sebastian pursued his career as a barrister and went on to reach the very pinnacle of his profession before he entered politics. He married and has children of his own. There was never going to be a time when he would take over the Deacon family business empire because he simply had no interest in it. That position was reserved for Joey who wanted nothing more than to take over the reins from his adoptive father. Of all the lessons he went on to learn from his father, the most important was that it is not a sin to waste money because money can always be regained. The greatest sin of all is to waste time because only a very select few ever have the chance to live two lives within one lifetime.

Maria married a young man who came to her for Spanish lessons but she remained in the loyal service of Richard Deacon and devoted most of her working life to him. As she was from the very first day in his employment she continued to be his maid, his secretary, his mother, his sister, his sounding board, his cook and…his friend. In other words Maria constantly changed her roles according to his needs. Despite his devotion to Joey he still managed to write a further seven novels with each one out-selling its predecessor.

In grounds of The Strawberry Garden at the side of the postern there is an ornate marble headstone and on it are carved the words: 'Tina, a true friend and a lady to the end.'

The End

305

Other Titles From Cauliay Publishing

Kilts, Confetti & Conspiracy *By* Bill Shackleton
Child Of The Storm *By* Douglas Davidson
Buildings In A House Of Fire *By* Graham Tiler
Tatterdemalion *By* Ray Succre
From The Holocaust To the Highlands *By* Walter Kress
To Save My father's Soul *By* Michael William Molden
Love, Cry and Wonder Why *By* Bernard Briggs
A Seal Snorts Out The Moon *By* Colin Stewart Jones
The Haunted North *By* Graeme Milne
Revolutionaries *By* Jack Blade
Michael *By* Sandra Rowell
Poets Centre Stage (*Vol One*) *By* Various poets
The Fire House *By* Michael William Molden
The Upside Down Social World *By* Jennifer Morrison
The Strawberry Garden *By* Michael William Molden
Poets Centre Stage (*Vol Two*) *By* Various Poets
Havers & Blethers *By* The Red Book Writers
Amphisbaena *By* Ray Succre
The Ark *By* Andrew Powell
The Diaries of Belfour, Ellah, Rainals Co *By* Gerald Davison

Books coming Soon

Underway, Looking Aft *By* Amy Shouse
Silence Of The Night *By* Sandra Rowell
The Bubble *By* Andrew Powell

Lightning Source UK Ltd.
Milton Keynes UK
15 April 2010

152819UK00001B/17/P